A Twist of Fate

Christa Simpson

The Twisted Trilogy
Book 3

BLACK WIDOW
Publishing

A Twist of Fate

Christa Simpson

Copyright 2013 Christa Simpson
All rights reserved.

PRINT EDITION
ISBN: 978-0-9919070-7-6

Author's Website: http://christasimpson.com
www.facebook.com/authorchristasimpson
http://plus.google.com/+christasimpson

Cover Model Image: © Konrad Bak

Print Cover Design by: Black Widow Publishing
www.blackwidowpublishing.wordpress.com

E-Cover Art and Design by: Laura Gordon
The Book Cover Machine: www.bookcovermachine.wordpress.com

Black Widow Publishing: August 2014

Printed in the U.S.A.

ACKNOWLEDGEMENTS

To the members of my Street Team, Christa Simpson's Twisted Sisters. You girls make my life a lot less difficult and a little more colourful. Jayne Wilson and Cassandra Janey, you're the best. I truly appreciate all of your feedback.

www.facebook.com/groups/635167676517108

Tanya Vought, I heart you, for your daily dose of entertainment, inspiration and enthusiasm. I will be forever grateful to you for helping me make the biggest decision in this series.

Thank you all so much! Without you The Twisted Trilogy wouldn't be what it is today!

~ Christa Simpson

NOTE TO READER

Dear Reader,

I am so happy that you decided to come along for the ride to experience Abigail's adult pleasures and misfortunes in this, The Twisted Trilogy, which is entirely fictional by the way.

Did you know I had never intended to publish this story when I first wrote it? In fact, it started out as a single title story, until Cameron walked in the door. Bits and pieces came to me in scenes and, as I started to put them together, I realized that this story wasn't going to fit into a single book. It wasn't until I finished writing the entire story that I was like, whoa! I had to share it with someone.

As a new author you never know how you're going to do until you put yourself out there. Just the fact that you're reading this now tells me that I did something right. Thank you for your support and for sticking with me. Edwin thanks you too. ;)

I hope you are able to fall in love with my characters all over again as you follow Abby on her journey toward her happy ever after.

Happy Reading!
~ Christa Simpson

http://christasimpson.com

CHAPTER ONE

With Cameron Clarke sitting next to me, it was difficult to think of anything intelligible to say. I couldn't keep my mischievous eyes off of him. His short, chaotic blonde hair and beaming baby blues had captured my attention, but it was quickly relinquished when I caught the way his thumb brushed up and down the smooth face of his mug of hot chocolate.

I chewed on my bottom lip, watching the way he caressed the handle, just the way he touched me. I had to part my lips just to allow a breath to slip between them. It was amazing how something so simple could tickle me in the most intimate of places.

When the phone rang, Cameron reached over for it and held it out to me. "It's for you." Then his hand skimmed mine and a carnal awareness rushed me with a vengeance. He winked through squinted, sunset-shaped eyes and I melted. *Would I ever get enough of this man?*

Breathless, I answered the phone. "Hey."

"Hey, girl. Are you ready for this?" Aliah asked. Aliah was by far my best friend.

"Absolutely," I replied, being seriously excited about our ski trip.

Cameron had only just told me about it days ago, but Aliah had been planning this thing for months. I had agreed to spend my Christmas holidays with Cameron and his daughter, even though my ex-beau and housemate – Edwin – was none too pleased about it. I had even agreed to go on this trip when Cameron asked me. That was before I realized Edwin would be coming along.

"Everyone's ready to hit the road. I need you here like five minutes ago," Aliah said. "Me and Hunter are driving with you. There's no way I'm letting Maddie anywhere near him this weekend."

When Hunter knocked up Maddie, it had officially ruined Aliah's life. She wasn't about to give Maddie an inch now. Especially with the knowledge that Maddie still had it bad for Hunter.

Cameron had been watching me intently. My mouth. My eyes. And I was aware of every inch of his attention. I tried to stay focused on my conversation with Aliah, but it was a challenge, with every little tingle my body absorbed from his devastatingly sexy smirk.

"Okay. We'll be there in a few," I said, promptly hanging up the phone and grinning at Cameron. "What are you trying to do to me?"

Cameron pulled me into his arms, without a care. "They can wait." His soft lips hooked onto mine, working me into a sexual frenzy.

My heart raced as I pulled his shirt over his head, exposing every inch of sculpted flesh on his core. I fumbled with the button on his jeans and then quickly pried the zipper open to free him. I supposed it wouldn't hurt to satisfy this one delicious urge before we left. And that we did. Twice.

After a long, trying drive, thanks to the snow covered roads and white out conditions, I was relieved when we all finally piled into the lobby of the mountainside hotel. Aliah and Hunter had managed to keep me entertained for a good portion of the ride, but I was grateful to stretch out my aching limbs.

Jessica and Edwin were already lounging in the lobby when we got there, and Maddie - of all people - was at the front desk checking them in. Her hands anxiously rubbed over her bulging baby bump, while the receptionist did her thing.

"I'll go check us in," Cameron said, giving my hand a squeeze before leaving my side. He joined Maddie at the registration desk, with Hunter following close behind him.

It was amusing to watch Hunter fumble over himself to make sure Maddie was okay and even funnier to watch Aliah's failed attempts to keep his attention.

While Cameron registered us for our suite, he stared at me from afar. It made my adrenaline rush, giving me a heady reminder of how it pumped through every inch of my body whenever I was with him. Then Edwin cleared his throat, snapping me back into reality.

Smiling, I moved closer to him and Jessica. "Hey, guys."

Edwin was the epitome of casual, the polar opposite of Jessica. Her face was painted to perfection, and she was wearing clothes that wrapped around her body like a glove. Out of all the men Jessica could have had, she continued to hang off of Edwin and smooth her hands all over his astounding physique like he was hers. Edwin had told me that it was over between them.

They look awfully cozy to me.

Pulling away from Jessica's hold, Edwin stepped up next to me, draped his arm across my back and briefly squeezed my shoulder. "Hey," he said, his voice a sexy growl. "I didn't think I would see you again."

His eyes were dark and dangerous, but he released my shoulder and just smiled at me. Nothing could compare to the knives tumbling around in my belly, and that response didn't go unnoticed. Cameron's protective stare wrapped right around me and I could sense the trouble that began to stir between them.

Edwin wasn't ready to give up on me just yet. He had made that plainly obvious. I wished I didn't care about Edwin's feelings anymore. But I did.

Cameron walked up next to me and swept his left hand up and down my back. His other hand grabbed onto mine possessively, as he gave me a peck on the lips. "Ready to head up?"

I locked onto his gaze and grinned. His jealousy was adorable.

"Why don't we all head up to my room before we get too comfortable?" Maddie suggested, as she joined us.

"Okay," I agreed. "What room are you in?"

"201," Maddie announced. "See you in a few?"

I nodded at her, as Cameron retrieved our bags and pointed toward the stairs. We climbed up one flight and walked down the long, narrow hall, until Cameron let me into the suite marked 225.

After checking my reflection in the bathroom mirror, I returned to the spacious room. No expense had been spared when they decorated this suite. The rich, dark colours made it feel warm and safe and romantic. The furniture was all natural wood, stained dark, and covered in luxurious fabrics. The room had a gas fireplace for ambiance. The only thing missing was a whirlpool.

I walked around the oversized bed, where Cameron was already kicked back, looking sexy as hell with his hands laced behind his head.

"We should probably get over there," I suggested, eyeing the large, sumptuous bed with my handsome man sprawled upon it.

"You'd better make your move fast then," he growled. "Because if I get my hands on you, we'll be awhile." His devious promise was tempting, but as he reached out to grab me, I leapt over the corner of the bed and shuffled for the door squealing.

Cameron chased me to the door with a growl, and he caught my hand, but I had already pulled the door open. As he moved to lure me back inside, Hunter crossed our path and cut off our heated exchange.

Hunter looked incredibly frustrated and ignored the disturbing stare he received from Cameron. "I can't find an ice machine anywhere."

"Wrong way, buddy. I saw a sign in the stairwell," Cameron said, not letting me go.

I pried myself out of Cameron's loving grip and smirked. "Why don't you show him?"

Cameron disappeared from behind me and quickly reappeared with our ice bucket. "I'll do it. But only because I need to cool off."

I grinned at Cameron and turned to Hunter. "I'm going to go see Aliah then. I take it your room's this way?"

"Yeah. We're right next door to Maddie."

Cameron's smile quickly faded, and there was no doubt in my mind that he had stumbled upon the same fact that I had. *Maddie's room equals Edwin's room.*

I gave Cameron a chaste kiss and disappeared around the corner in search of room 201. Before having to search far, I overheard my friends chatting rather loudly. Thanks to their door being left ajar, I let myself in.

Edwin's face lit up in an instant, his sharply arched eyebrows framing his pristine aqua eyes. And when his lips curled into a smile that covered his handsome face, it unnerved me to no end.

Someone was happy to see me.

I took a seat on the bed next to Maddie, while Edwin poured me a glass of wine. I had to sip from the glass before it could change hands, just so it didn't overflow.

"Drink up," Edwin growled, slapping me with that sexy smile.

Maddie rolled her eyes, obviously disappointed that she was about to be the only sober one among us. Jessica's glass was nearly as full as mine, but Aliah had already polished hers off.

"We'd better nail down what we're doing," Maddie said, slightly annoyed. "I'm getting tired already."

"What do you want to do?" Aliah asked me.

I shrugged my shoulders, being without any ideas.

"What do you ladies say we hit the hot tub?" Edwin raised his eyebrows shamelessly.

Aliah and I looked at each other at the same time, which made us start laughing.

"Yeah, I could go for that," Aliah answered.

"I could definitely go for a nice soak," Jessica agreed, eyeing up Edwin like a piece of man candy. She would say anything to get his shirt off of him.

I wasn't exactly complaining myself.

Just then, as Maddie began to pout, Cameron and Hunter entered the room. "Aww! I can't go in the hot tub. It's not good for the baby."

"You could always dip your legs in," Jessica suggested.

"You're not going anywhere near that tub with my baby," Hunter stated, exposing his protective nature.

I was caught off guard by Hunter's demand and watched his controlling stare. Aliah showed her disgust with Hunter, before taking a swig straight from the bottle of wine.

It didn't affect Maddie one bit. "You can't control me like that, Hunter," she said, scowling. "You're not my father."

He propped his hands on his masculine hips, his voice hard and cold. "No, but I am the baby's father and that means I get a say."

"Hunter, I think it would be okay for Maddie to dip her feet in, if she wants," Aliah said, hoping to get some of Hunter's attention. "Quit trying to control her. She's been taking good care of herself."

Aliah's compassion shocked everyone. I couldn't believe how much her relationship with Hunter had transformed her overactive sass in such a short time.

"Abs, are you in or what?" Edwin asked me, waiting for my response as he topped up my glass.

I turned a blank stare on Cameron. "Do you want to go for a soak in the hot tub?"

Cameron wrapped an arm around my hip. "You do realize we have our own private hot tub." He said it loud enough for everyone to hear.

"Hey, are you guys holding out on us?" Edwin chimed.

"I didn't see one in our suite."

Cameron smirked. "That's because it's on the patio. I bet it'd feel pretty awesome out there right about now. You're all welcome to join us." He paused and then directed his jab at Edwin. "That is if you can handle the walk out to the tub."

Edwin narrowed his eyes, his face turning serious. "I can handle whatever you can dish my way and then some. Whatever it is, I'm sure I can do it better than you."

"I'm sure," Cam replied, unconvinced and uncaring.

Edwin cocked an arrogant brow. "Why don't we just ask Abby?"

I pointed an unimpressed finger at Edwin, with a scowl. "You, leave me out of this."

"That's short for: I'm better in bed," Edwin announced to everyone.

They all snickered at Cameron's expense. I was not impressed.

"Why don't you shut your mouth while you're ahead? Or should I tell everyone just how good Cameron is to me?"

"Oh, burn!" Hunter hollered, laughing and pointing.

When I turned to leave the room, Cameron caught up with me and looped his arms around my waist. All eyes were on me, so I made good use of it.

"If you guys are quite finished, we're in room 225."

"We'll be there," Jessica hollered, just as the door slammed shut behind me.

Cameron didn't let me go and I couldn't help but smile in response to his seductive stare. I rustled my fingers through his short, messy hair and when he raised his eyebrows it made me laugh. He captured my smiling lips and tormented me with a soft brush of his mouth.

"Come on," he said, leading me back to our room. "Let's get you into your swimsuit before we have company."

Back in our room, I quickly stripped out of my clothes and pulled on the tiny bikini that I had chosen expecting only one man to see me in it.

"Want a glass of wine while we're waiting?" Cam asked, as I tucked my clothes away in my bag.

"That'll be my third one tonight."

Cam smirked, glancing at my glorious rear-end. "That sounds good to me."

I smirked right back and slung my arms over his shoulders. He pulled me against him, his hands groping my mostly exposed ass cheeks.

"If I didn't know any better, I would say that you're trying to get me drunk again."

"I would never," he teased, releasing one hand only to lift my wine glass to his mouth and take a sip. Then he kissed me, drizzling the fruity wine into my mouth.

I tasted it and I tasted him, and it was so hot. He handed me my glass, but wine was now the last thing on my mind, as the tip of his tongue licked across my teeth.

His hands drifted back down to my ass, barely covered by the small scrap of material I called my bikini bottoms. When he gave it a squeeze, he growled and it urged me to touch him back. I slipped my hand between us, to find him long and thick and hard, at the same moment that Aliah barged into our room ruining my fun.

"Woop," Aliah hollered, as she passed Cameron and headed for the electronics. She plugged in her I-pod and turned up the music, ignoring the state in which she found us.

Hunter picked up our half empty bottle of wine. "It looks like they got started without us."

Without releasing me, Cameron nodded toward the ice box. "Don't worry, there's more where that came from."

I took a big gulp from my glass and by the time the others had showed up, it was already going down real smooth. The wine was clearly having an effect on me. I was hyper and loud-mouthed and careless. Aliah loved it.

"Okay, enough of this! Let's test the water," I shouted over the music.

"I'll test the water for you," Cameron said to me. "I wouldn't make you do that."

As he went to lift his shirt over his head, Edwin stormed outside and removed the cover from the hot tub himself.

Cameron dropped his shirt back down and glanced at me in disbelief. "This should be a fun weekend."

Maddie walked up to the patio door in her one piece bathing suit, wrapped up in a giant bath towel. As Jessica ran outside, a freezing cold north wind gushed into the room and some flurries scattered across the floor.

"On second thought, I think I'll just hang out in here," Maddie said, then sealed the door shut. "I look like a cow anyways."

"Good, I don't want the baby getting sick," Hunter said, honestly concerned about it.

Aliah rolled her eyes and pulled Hunter outside with her.

"You look fabulous," I told Maddie. "Your baby bump is so adorable." I gulped down as much wine as I could, put my half emptied glass on the nightstand and reached for the patio door. "You're alright in here alone?"

Cameron peeled off his shirt and Maddie couldn't remove her gawking eyes from his toned flesh. He picked up my glass, smiled at Maddie's enthusiasm and returned to the other side of the room to top up my wine.

"Yup. I'm good. Definitely good," Maddie said.

Giggling, I tip-toed to the hot tub as fast as I could and sank into the bubbling water in the only empty spot available. Right next to Edwin. I looked at him hesitantly.

"Oh, come on now, I won't bite," Edwin teased, then he whispered in my ear. "I know you only like that in the bedroom."

"Ugh, Eddie! Can you shut your fat mouth for like five minutes so I can enjoy myself?" I shoved his big shoulder, but he didn't budge.

He only laughed and it was hauntingly sexy. "I can probably do five, but I can't make any promises," he drawled, then leaned into me. "You'll probably be begging me to talk in like two though."

"Don't forget whose tub you're in." I backed away to scowl at him, just as Cameron put my glass on the edge of the tub.

When Cameron squeezed in next to me, he unintentionally squished me even closer to Edwin. There was no missing the press of Edwin's bulky arms and legs against my side. They were hot and large and thick.

Cameron reached his arm around me and gave me a slow, drugging kiss. It was nice, but I could tell it was more to piss Edwin off than to show me love. Not able to continue with the awkward attachment to Edwin's hulking arm, I curled into Cameron's and slid onto his lap. I strung my arms around his neck and gave him a healthy taste of my lips, to show everyone that there was no confusion as to who my man was.

Cameron smiled, in between kisses. "I see your glass is empty again."

"Good wine, eh?" Aliah chimed.

"Yeah, a little too good," I answered. "Cameron's been feeding it to me like water. I can hardly taste it anymore."

"Maybe I should go get you some more," Cameron suggested. He kissed me again, dropped me into his spot and then leapt from the tub, every muscle tightening in the cold, winter air. Then he calmly walked to the door as if the cold didn't affect him.

"While you're in there why don't you get me one too?" Aliah hollered, as the door slid shut.

"I can get you one," Hunter decided. "I have to use the pisser anyway."

When Hunter left the tub, everyone shifted over and it felt like I could finally stretch out and relax. "Take your time," I teased, enjoying the space.

Aliah leaned over the edge of the tub and watched Hunter exchanging words with Maddie inside the toasty hotel room. I saw Cameron popping the cork to yet another bottle of wine, as Edwin reached his arm out and rested it on the tub behind me.

Edwin leaned down and whispered in my ear, the hurt evident in his tone. "What's this, you can't even stand to be around me anymore?"

"It's not like that and you know it," I answered, softly.

He locked his aqua eyes on me, holding my terrified gaze. "Oh? How is it then?"

I blew out a harsh breath. "Maybe if you weren't always trying to piss Cam off, then we could hang out more." *Not likely, though.*

"I know I've been kind of an ass lately," he admitted, softening up.

"Kind of?"

"Fine. I've been a total jerk. But what do you expect? You chose him over me and that hurts."

My eyes were frozen on him, dread filling my sharp features, as I recognized the wounded look on his face. I wanted to hug him, to make him feel better, but I knew that would only escalate the problem. I kept my lips tightly pressed together.

"Now you're living with him and I've got the whole house to myself. It's really quiet when you're not around and not in a good way," Edwin told me.

"It's only temporary," I said. "Besides you had your family over for a few days. You weren't exactly alone the whole time."

"No, but it wasn't the same without you."

I flipped my long, dry hair behind me and the tips dipped into the bubbling water. "I'm sorry. I know it was kind of last minute, but you didn't exactly tell me your plans either." Reality began to cloud my buzz-induced smile. I dipped my chin and closed my eyes, suddenly feeling incredibly emotional.

Edwin lifted my chin with his index finger and my emerald eyes grew wide in alarm. My heart pounded hard and fast, as I gasped for air, unable to steal my eyes from his. Then his hand dropped into the water, acknowledging my distress. Though his touch was gentle, it had zapped my senses. Then he slid up next to me. Close. *Too close.*

"You know I just want you to be happy, right?"

My entire body trembled. "Okay." I should have pushed him away. *Why am I not pushing him away?*

He slowly gripped his hand on my thigh, sending my heart galloping. "If you can promise me one thing," he whispered, his breath tickling my ear, "I'll leave you two alone for the rest of the weekend."

Just the rest of the weekend? How about permanently? "Don't go too overboard," I managed to blurt.

His hand squeezed on my thigh, then he loosened his grip but it remained where it didn't belong. "I'm being serious, Abs. All I ask is that you quit with the ogling and canoodling when you're around me. It just isn't right, having to see you like that." His pain-filled eyes begged me to stop tormenting him.

"Seeing me like what; happy?" I whispered, barely able to finish the sentence.

Edwin's hand began to casually caress my thigh. "Please, just promise me."

Aliah was watching us, chiding my indiscretion. Jessica was making a good effort to mind her own business. Cameron and Hunter were at the patio doors, not having a clue as to what was going on. *Did I even know what was going on?*

Aliah flashed a look at Cameron, then scowled back at me. "Just promise the man already! You owe him that much." Her words stung me, even more than they should have.

"Please take your hand off my leg," I begged, suddenly envisioning the consequences.

Cameron approached us blissfully unaware.

"Promise!" Edwin demanded, holding his position.

Holding my breath, I stuttered, unable to take another second of it. "Fine! I p-promise!" My heart skipped a beat as Edwin removed his hand from my thigh and swam to the other side of the tub.

Cameron handed me my glass and hopped back into the water next to me. I took a long sip of wine and collected all of my hair with my free hand so it sat on my right shoulder. As Cameron leaned in for a kiss, I turned away, passing it off as though I didn't see it coming. He caught my cheek, but that didn't satisfy him.

I smiled softly and took another sip of wine. He waited patiently for me to finish, then his lips found mine. But I couldn't reciprocate after giving Edwin my word. Cameron pulled back, looking very concerned. I could only stare at the water.

"Is everything okay?" he asked, his voice stark.

I looked at Edwin, who was sitting directly across from me. I could tell he was making an effort to be a good boy, but I could see a fire in his eyes that told me trouble still brewed. Then I looked back at Cam and cupped his cheek, feeling wretched for not sharing his kiss.

"I think I may have had too much to drink." And that was the truth. But that was not the only thing I was suffering from at the moment. Edwin had left me with deplorable, chaotic thoughts.

I wanted to leave with Cam so I could kiss him until his heart was content, but I also felt the need to nurse Edwin back to happiness. My face became stripped of all its colour and Cam watched me turn seriously ill before his eyes. Edwin didn't say a word, but neither would he unlock his gaze from me. It was like he was just waiting for me to break my promise.

Cam seemed to notice how my illness was in direct correlation with Edwin's attention. "Is there a problem?" he snapped, argumentatively.

"Did I say something to you?" Edwin barked back.

Aliah put both of her hands up. "Guys, cut it out."

"Can't we all just enjoy the night?" Jessica pleaded.

"Cam started it," Edwin droned. "First he steals my girlfriend, and then he tries to rub it in my face. It looks to me like he's asking for a black eye." He turned his stone-cold gaze on Cam.

Cameron stood up and I forced my arm around his waist to stop him. But if he wanted to go, he could have gone. Every muscle in his body flexed, as I clung onto him.

"Eddie, stop it!" I screeched, afraid of what might happen if I let go.

Edwin stayed relaxed, his arms stretched out over the back of the tub, his cool glare held on me. "Why don't you and your little lover boy go screw or something? Anything to get him out of my face right now."

Cameron lifted his chest, his muscles rippling, rampant with adrenaline, his teeth exposed like a rabid animal. I could feel the vomit burning up my esophagus and, when

Edwin stood up, I was sure there was going to be a blood bath.

"Don't cross me, brother, or my fist will be in your mouth," Edwin warned.

I swallowed back the vomit pooling in the back of my throat and held my freezing palm against Cam's burning chest to pull him back against me.

"Come on, Eddie. It's not worth it," Aliah said, as Hunter grabbed onto Edwin's arm. Even he could sense the pure hatred filtering between the two of them.

"Try it," was all Cameron said, but he struck a chord with Edwin.

When Edwin leaned forward, I reached a flat hand out and pressed it against his solid chest to keep him back. After scowling at him, I glanced at Cameron, then back to Edwin again.

"It's time for you to go," I said.

"I'm not going anywhere, until I'm done fixing this pretty boy's face," he threatened.

"Right now!" Cameron hollered, calling him on.

"Hunter, you've got to stop them," Aliah wailed, noting the severity of the situation.

I fought to keep them apart, but Edwin reached around me and shoved Cam's shoulder. Cam instantly responded with a counter and drove Edwin against the back of the tub. Jessica looked like she had been enjoying a good soap opera, until Edwin's arm flailed backwards and hit her square in the face.

Jessica leapt out of the tub, her hand covering her battered cheek. "Thanks for fucking with my vacation!" she screeched. Then she spun around and ran inside, near tears.

Aliah shook her head, disappointedly. "Real smooth, guys."

Edwin ignored Cameron just long enough to show his regret, then he narrowed his eyes at him again. "Yup, it's definitely worth it," he decided aloud. "Get out of my way," he warned, as he raised a determined brow and drew his elbow back to wind up for a punch.

Cameron put his fists up ready for the challenge as though I wasn't even standing in between them, freezing my ass off. I threw my hands down in manic frustration.

"I've had enough!" I screamed. "I'm leaving. You two can do whatever the fuck you want. I'm over it!"

I climbed out of the tub and stalked toward the room, hands clenched in fists, mad as hell. I could see Maddie sitting on the bed talking to Jessica as clear as day. Thinking Jessica must have left the patio door open, I made a pass for it, and my face planted firmly against the cold, clear glass.

CHAPTER TWO

I was already madder than a wet hen, but now, after smashing my face off the glass door, I was really freaking upset. I couldn't tell what I wanted to do first: scream, cry or vomit. My little episode seemed to get everyone's attention too, and now they were all chuckling behind my back.

"Yeah, real funny, assholes," I hollered, scowling harshly at them before letting myself in the room.

Maddie came running to me with a towel and I didn't realize why, until she pinched my nose with it. "Are you okay?" she asked.

"No, I'm not okay." With my eyes closed, sadness choked me and tears flooded beneath my eyelids.

Maddie tucked my hair back with one hand and pinched my nose with the other.

When I finally caught my breath, between sobs, I explained it to her. "Cam and Edwin are being dinks and Aliah wasn't exactly discouraging it. Nobody gives two shits about what I want," I cried.

"That's not true," Maddie stated softly, but it was no use.

I had to get out of there. I was sick and cold and upset. "I really can't deal with this. I'm going home," I whimpered. I started to pack up the few things I had strewn around the room, as I held the white, blood-stained towel to my nose.

Edwin was already in the room, standing there silently, water dripping from his soaking wet shorts. Maddie excused herself to the bathroom to escape from the menacing silence. Jessica had already slunk out of the room, hoping to stay out of it. Edwin held his gaze on me, willing me to look up at him.

"I'm sorry, Abs. I promised. I won't let it happen again." He stepped closer to me and reached his hand out to caress my arm.

I jerked away from him and stomped back to the other side of my bed. "That's right! You promised," I hollered, tears blurring my vision. "How can I trust you when you keep acting like this?" I fell weakly to my knees and dropped the towel onto the floor, with tears rushing down my cheeks.

Edwin made his swift approach and mirrored my crouched position on the floor. He took one of my hands in his and held it against his chest. "I mean it this time. No matter how badly I want to smash in his face, I will leave him alone and keep my comments to myself when you're around."

"And when I'm not around?"

Edwin gently brushed his thumb over my wet cheek, his other hand still softly clasping my hand against him. "I don't want to make any promises I can't keep."

"Edwin!" I chided.

"Fine. I won't knock him out, but you can't stop me from speaking my mind. He needs to know that I'm not going to let him hurt you."

I narrowed my tear-filled eyes at him. "Cameron would never hurt me, but whatever."

Edwin stared at me through dangerously sexy eyes and pursed his perfectly pink lips. "Will you stay?"

I sighed, unable to resist his pouty lip. "I'll stay. But you'd better stay true to your word this time."

He smirked. "I know, I know."

I appreciated that Cameron had given Edwin a chance to apologize, but I really needed him now. I slowly slipped my hand out of Edwin's, feeling responsible to honour my relationship with Cameron. I stood up next to the bed, checked my nose in the framed mirror on the wall and tossed the bloody towel into the garbage pail. I would survive, but I needed some moral support. Cameron's moral support.

I peered out the patio door and Cameron instantly saw me looking for him. He hopped out of the tub to come see me immediately.

"Tell me this," Edwin asked, while we were still alone. "Whose house were you going home to if you had left?"

His eyes pleaded with me, but I couldn't let him tug me back under his wing. Besides, I was too intoxicated to think clearly.

I raised a sarcastic brow and smirked. "I guess you'll never know, now will you?"

He shook his head at me. "I'm just glad that you're smiling again. See? I can do that for you," he said, with a soft smirk. He always made me smile, even when I didn't want to.

Cameron entered the room and wrapped a towel around his waist. Within seconds he was looping his arms around me, his intentions apologetic and clear. When his lips brushed across mine, I accepted the chaste smooch. But when Cameron let me go to readjust his towel, Edwin stepped in and lifted my chin with his fist.

"We good now?" he asked, looking me right in the eye.

A breath caught in my throat. "Yup," I said, terrified to learn Cameron's reaction.

Edwin released my chin and glanced at Cameron, as if he owed him an explanation. "I was just explaining to Abby that, as her *friend*, I was just looking out for her and the last thing I want is for her to get hurt." Edwin flashed a careful smile, then winked at me the second Cameron looked away.

Satisfied that I understood, Edwin headed for the door, his wet trunks clinging to his massive legs. We both knew full well that he believed a man and woman could never be *just friends.* I pressed my lips together to stifle my smirk.

"I'll check you guys later," Edwin said, rounding the corner for the door.

"Wait for me," Maddie called. She handed me a glass of water and two Advil tablets and then hustled up behind Edwin.

He waited for her to catch up, then rubbed her round baby belly with admiration. "You two crashing with me tonight?" he asked her belly, smiling.

"Yup," Maddie answered, proudly. "You're sleeping with two ladies tonight." Her smile was radiant and her skin glowed.

"Hear that?" Edwin asked, raising his eyebrows dramatically at Hunter, as he and Aliah dried off at the patio doors. Edwin reached out his elbow and Maddie grabbed onto his large bicep.

Hunter tugged Aliah across the room and scowled at them. "It could be a boy, you know."

"How's your nose, girly?" Aliah asked me, as she passed.

"I'll live," I answered, rather unconvincingly.

Hunter gave Edwin a playful shove and focused on Maddie before he left. "You should get to sleep. Boy or girl, my baby needs its beauty rest."

They all shuffled off and the door closed definitively behind them. I sipped on my water and swished it around in my mouth. After swallowing the pills, I placed the glass on the nightstand. Cameron had me pinned with his eyes.

I smiled softly at him. "Hear that?"

"What?"

I paused for a few seconds and absorbed the silence. "Absolutely nothing."

Cameron smiled, stepped closer to me, and pulled me into his arms. I rested my cheek against his smooth, naked chest, and when he tried to kiss me, I didn't fight it. As our lips connected, Cameron unsnapped my top and lifted it off of me. I heard the wet fabric drop to the floor, then my own gasp, when his hands slowly drew my bathing suit bottoms down.

After reaching for a dry towel, Cameron gently patted my legs dry, pausing between my thighs and rounding on my wet behind. He wrapped the towel around me and drew me into the warm bed with him. He tucked me into his arms and his caress tickled my senses.

I couldn't help but feel guilty, when Edwin popped into my thoughts. *Why did he have to send me that secret message before he left, and why was he so concerned with me and Cameron all of a sudden?* We had separated for a reason. He had made his decision loud and clear.

Cameron made me happy. Things were going great - amazing really - until Edwin started to stick his nose in our business. I could only hope that one day Edwin could stand to be in the same room with Cameron and me without cringing.

"I hope you're not still thinking about what a jerk I've been tonight."

"No." I brushed my fingers across Cam's chest and watched his body respond to me. "I just want things to go back to normal. Can't we just be ordinary for a change?"

Cam rested his hand on top of mine, stopping my motion. "You'll never be just ordinary." He softly kissed my temple. "I sure as hell can't predict the future, but I can say that right now I'm the happiest I've ever been. In case you haven't noticed, I've gotten used to having you all to myself and I don't like to share." The curve of his smile crept higher.

I outlined his sexy lips with my index finger and there was no need for words. He kissed my fingers, then hovered over me to find another kiss. His hands trembled as he unwrapped my towel, exposing my naked breasts and taut nipples. He sucked in a sharp breath, as he took in my naked figure, then he lost his own towel and trailed soft, wet kisses across my flesh.

I squeezed my eyes shut enjoying the sudden pleasure, as his hot mouth closed around my nipple. "Mmm. I definitely didn't do anything tonight to deserve this."

He smiled against my skin, his tongue still teasing me. "This is just for you being you. Isn't that reason enough?" Cam's lips teased downward, until his tongue circled my belly button, tensing every muscle in my body. "I want to show you exactly how much you mean to me," he growled, sprinkling wet kisses across my hips and down between my legs.

Cam worshipped my thighs, as he gently spread them apart, his tongue doing amazing things. He closed his mouth over me, sucking gently, then dipped his tongue inside. A muffled moan sounded from my throat, as I squeezed my legs around him, overwhelmed with sensitivity.

I ran my fingers through his hair and gripped onto a handful, as every muscle in my body began to vibrate internally. With the flick of his tongue, he had me screaming inside, and with a brush of his thumb, I exploded into a thousand pieces. I yelped out in pleasure and Cameron didn't stop until the tremors quit rocking my body.

He replaced my towel, protecting me like a valuable treasure, then pulled the blankets over us. With a brush of his wet, salty lips, he gave me a taste of his handiwork. "I love you, Abigail," he said, his voice turning harsh. "And I won't let anyone get in the way of that; as long as you'll have me."

There was so much emotion flaring around the room, but I was physically and emotionally exhausted. "I love you," I whispered in response, before curling into his arms and nodding off.

I awoke to the sound of the blinds opening with a heavy swoosh. My face still hurt a little from my door incident, but it was nothing compared to my headache.

"I'm never drinking ever again," I mumbled, covering my eyes from the bright, winter day.

"Forget drinking; are you up for a little skiing?" Cam asked. He was so damn chipper and at this hour I was always so cranky.

Skiing was not my thing. "I feel like hell today. I'd bet I look even worse. I think I'll hang back."

"Oh, no you don't," he insisted, dropping to his knees on the bed. He crawled over top of me and kissed me good morning. "You're coming with me, whether you like it or not."

I couldn't help but smile. "You realize I suck at skiing, right? The last time I went I did more falling than actual skiing. You'll be better off without me."

Cameron growled insistently, the reverberations urging me to reconsider. He made it very difficult to say no to him.

"Don't forget what I told you," I warned, giving in to him. "You're going to be stuck on the bunny slopes all day and I'm even gonna complain about that." I smiled at him, though it was mostly true, then snuck another kiss before slipping out from under him.

After a shower and a very light breakfast, I started to feel somewhat human again. I plopped down and lied back on the bed that Cameron had made, and stretched my arms above me.

"I just got off the phone with Maddie," Cameron said. "Turns out, Jessica is staying back with her."

"I should really stay back too," I insisted.

Cam rested his hand on my shoulder and then smoothed it down my arm. "You'll do fine."

"I'll make a total fool of myself. You must want me to have two black eyes to go with my crooked nose."

He chuckled, but I wasn't joking.

"When does the destruction start?"

"We're supposed to meet the others in the lobby in about five minutes." Cam was smiling at me, as though he was going to burst into laughter at any second.

"What are you smiling at?"

"You." He yanked on my shirt to pull me up against his chest and started to kiss me.

Our kiss grew more heated within seconds. "I have to get ready," I said, in between scalding, hot licks of his tongue.

"Just a little dip?" Cameron begged.

"If I have to suffer out there today, then so will you." I struggled to fend him off. He looked so edible. I spun away and readied myself for the day, before I could change my mind.

Before long we were down in the lobby, where Hunter and Aliah were canoodling and Edwin was listening in on another guest's horror story about the black diamond slopes.

"There'll be none of that today," I ordered, stopping next to him. "I'd like to get home after this trip; preferably in one piece."

Edwin gawked at me, like I was a delicious piece of chocolate cake. "Hah! Abby's coming? This ought to be fun," he said to the others, as though I wasn't standing right next to him.

"Zip it," I snapped. "Cam's making me go."

"He can be the one that peels you off the slopes then," Edwin teased, as he walked toward the exit.

After tromping through the snow to the nearest lodge and renting out skis for the day, Edwin snickered at me again. "This is your last chance. Are you sure you don't want to go hang out with prego and prissy pants instead?"

I scowled at him. "I'm doing this." And after locking my boots into place, we skated toward the small rolling slopes.

I demanded that everyone join me on a practice run before we took the lift up the mountain. Reluctantly, they all hopped onto the conveyor and let it drag us to the top of the small hill. I was shaking in my boots.

When we got to the top, I tried to shuffle out of the way to wait up for the others, but my skis had other plans. They started to slip and I couldn't right myself. My skis inched forward until, sure enough, they began to carry me down the hill. Straight downhill.

Faster and faster I went, terrified that I would never stop, as I headed for the roadside ditch bank filled with snow. As I neared the bottom, I saw a rather worried skier with the same trouble and she was coming right for me. I was sure our paths would collide in a matter of seconds but, to my surprise, we crisscrossed awkwardly and fell into the snow.

I avoided the crash, and had fallen backwards onto my butt, stopping mere inches from the ditch bordering the private road. My breaths were ragged and my head ached, as I rested it back in the snow. I glanced up at the sky, begging a higher power to give me strength to get through the rest of the day. Edwin was so fast that when I looked up, he was standing over me, smiling.

It was Cam, though, who untangled my skis and lifted me to my feet. "What happened?"

"I couldn't stop. Obviously." I rolled my eyes, embarrassed but not surprised.

"Maybe you should get some ski lessons," Edwin suggested, as Aliah and Hunter effortlessly glided up next to me. "Not that I think it'll work."

"Nah, I can teach her," Hunter insisted. "Piece of cake."

After a quick refresher course from Hunter, and a few successful trips down the bunny slope, Hunter figured I was ready for a bigger mountain. I had my doubts, as we climbed up the hill toward the ski lift.

Eager to hit the steeper slopes, Aliah and Hunter lined up ahead of us and the chair scooped them up and away. Next it was my turn.

Cameron cupped my cheek and gave me a quick kiss. "You ready?"

No. And yet I found myself being pulled in front of the lift anyway. The chair swung around and came up behind us. At the last minute, Edwin snuck up next to me and hitched a ride. Being squished between the two men in my life would have been awkward on a good day; put skis on me and it instantly became my worst nightmare.

"You don't think you could've waited your turn?" I squealed, clinging to Cameron. It was scary enough hanging from a chair with sticks strapped to my feet and now I didn't even have a side to hang onto.

Cam smiled, somehow amused by my horror.

"Get over it," Edwin said. "You should be thanking me. You're gonna need all the help you can get." And Edwin was the one man that knew that for a fact.

The last time we returned from a ski trip, I had landed more than a few bruises, including a really big one to my ego. I turned to Cameron with the sudden realization of what I had gotten myself into.

"I think this was a mistake. I don't think I'm ready."

"It's a little late for that," Cam said, as we were met with the top of the smallish mountain.

Mental imagery was a waste of my time, because there were so many skis dangling from the chair. When my sticks touched down, they immediately tangled with both Edwin and Cameron's. Cameron managed to break free from me, leaving only Edwin to come to my rescue. I dropped a pole and grabbed for his arm, causing us both to tumble into a pile in the worn snow.

Edwin fell hard, sending one ski sliding down the mountain. With no control over my body, I crashed on top of him. Though the weather was windy and cold, Edwin was warm and soft.

"You've gotta be kidding me," he moaned, his head flat in the snow. He lifted his body up, so we were both on our asses, then waved a hand toward his stray ski.

I rolled away from him and stuck out a pouty lip. "This is your fault, you know."

Hunter and Aliah had been watching for us and were laughing. "You are too much, Abby. I wish I would've caught that on video," Hunter teased.

Cameron lifted me to my feet, again. I scowled at Hunter, with a sore frown.

"What about me?" Edwin asked, hobbling on one foot.

"I'll get it," Hunter hollered, skillfully retrieving Edwin's other ski. How he walked back up the mountain was a mystery to me and I couldn't quit watching in awe. "And that's how it's done," he proclaimed, as he handed the ski to Edwin. His eyes quickly strayed to Aliah, who had competitively sped off down the hill. Hunter took the bait and eagerly chased after her.

Cam stole my attention and held my gaze. "Ready?"

"No," I replied, honestly. "But I don't think I'll ever be ready."

He smirked at me, not realizing how serious I was. "You go first and I'll follow behind you. Just remember to put more weight on your downward ski."

If it were as easy as that, I would have been at the bottom already. "Here goes nothing," I said, as I started to head to the left. I instantly began to pick up speed, until I was racing out of control. As I desperately tried to turned back up the mountain, I wiped out, slamming sideways and losing a ski in the process.

Cameron hurried over to me, but he was smirking. "Try to remember to angle your skis together if you want to slow down," he said, as he reached for my snow-covered mitt.

All of those tips were but a foggy token, while I tumbled head first down the mountain. I gave Cameron a cold, unwholesome eye, and yet he couldn't stop smirking at me. I decided it was time to take my next chance at death.

When I made it half way down the mountain, I actually thought I might make it out alive. That's when I fell flat on my back and slid down the remainder of the mountainside, ass-first. Cameron found it just hilarious. Needless to say, I didn't think it was quite so funny.

Determined to give it another go, up the lift we went for round two. This time, I was amazed to make it half way down the mountain in one try. I thought I was making great progress, but I must have decided that too soon. Again, out of control, I zoomed into an icy area blocked off by the resort, marked DANGER. No warning sign was enough to keep me from slamming right into the solid ice and landing flat on my ass.

Ski patrol was on me in a matter of minutes, hollering at me to come back into the safe zone. Unable to skate on my feet, I crawled my way back, one ski in my left hand, both poles in my right. When I finally made it to the fresh, powdery snow, Cameron laughed at me and that was it. I couldn't take it anymore. My anger heated my face and melted the snowflakes on my jacket.

"I'm sorry," Cameron said. "I don't want to laugh, but it's so funny."

"Screw off." I scowled even more, wishing he would leave, so I could wallow in my failure, with my sore body and hurt feelings.

"Abby, I'm not leaving you," he insisted, his smirk still firmly in place.

"Yes, you are," I stated, then shoved him down the hill. He flashed a worried look back over his shoulder and then continued down the mountain - without me.

I pouted to myself, angered by his ignorance and also in actual physical pain from my multiple falls. I decided I would sit on this mountain all day, if it meant never having to fall down it ever again. That was until I saw Edwin skiing toward me. He stopped right at my side.

"You okay," he asked.

My arms were folder tightly across my chest. "Do I look okay?"

"No."

"There you go then," I snapped.

He didn't smile. "Hey, I'm just trying to help. If you want to give this a try, I'm not gonna give up on you. You're almost at the bottom. You can do this."

"You know I can't," I pouted, knowing I couldn't very well sit there the rest of the day either. I accepted his hand when he reached it out to me, and he pulled me back to my feet. I was terrified for my life and didn't want to let go.

His eyes rested on me momentarily and he took a sharp breath when I clung onto him. A smile softly replaced the serious look on his face, as he helped me snap my boot back into the ski.

A terrified yelp escaped my throat, as Edwin set me free. I tried to traverse the mountain but, after one turn, my skis directed me straight down the slope, again at full speed.

I screamed in fear as I sped to the bottom, but managed to stay on my feet. As I headed closer to the foot of the mountain, I slowed just enough to bring myself to a complete stop, only a matter of feet from Cameron. He was smirking again, but I was feeling proud for not falling this time.

"Will you stop?" I ordered.

He fought hard to not smile, until Edwin caught up with us. Then he had no trouble keeping a straight face.

I smiled at Edwin and he gave me a wink. Cameron caught it too and growled at him, but managed to keep his words to himself.

"I'm gonna go back up. I can probably make it down twice for your single trip," Edwin teased.

"You're so funny," I retorted, as Edwin turned away and headed for the lift.

Cameron skied closer to me and took my hand, staring at me until I met his gaze. "Are you mad at me?"

"Kind of. You hurt my feelings and I really hurt my ass," I admitted, sorely.

"I'm sorry for laughing."

It was hard to believe him when he was still smirking. "Are you done yet?" I retorted, scowling.

His smile was about ready to burst. "No, just a second." He paused, and cleared his throat. He even managed to wipe the smile from his face this time. "Okay, now I'm done."

I rolled my eyes. "I think maybe I should just watch from down here." There was no way in hell anyone was going to get me to go back up there again.

Cameron looked disappointed. "Oh, come on. You got better near the end there. You're getting the hang of it."

"Really?"

"Sort of." His smile was killer. "You went through all the trouble of renting the skis and everything. You want to end the day already?"

"Ugh. Fine. One more. But that's it!" *Damn his good looks and powers of persuasion.*

"Good. Let's go." He skied off toward the lift, before I could come to my senses.

This time around, I got off the chair with little trouble.

"There you go," Cam hollered.

"Stop with that," I snapped, getting tired of being treated like a child.

If it were at all possible, my skiing actually got worse. I found myself heading for an area for more skilled skiers. I had to purposefully fall to my knees before running into some nearby trees.

Cameron made an attempt to come help me out, but when he hit the steep slope, he slid farther down the mountain and was unable to get back up.

"I got her," Edwin hollered, with his above average skill. Edwin came slicing down the mountain and hauled me to my feet. "Why is it that I have to keep coming to your rescue?"

"Will you shut up and help me already?"

"Okay, okay. Take it easy." He tried to help me stabilize myself, but when I stood up, my feet came out from under me.

Edwin caught me in his arms, but lost his balance and crashed down on top of me. I couldn't help but laugh, even after cracking the back of my head off the ice.

"You think this is funny?" he asked, his face only inches from mine.

I couldn't wipe the smile off my face, even when Edwin's features had turned deathly serious. I was helplessly pinned beneath him, when I realized he was going to kiss me. I timidly examined his eyes and I think he could sense that I was alarmed, but he didn't let it affect his decision.

"Hey! Is everything okay over there?" a ski patroller hollered, breaking the tense atmosphere.

Edwin released me and waved to the patroller. "She's okay, I think. She just bumped her head," he hollered, embarrassing the shit out of me.

"Come on out of there, it's not safe," the patroller called.

Edwin helped me to my feet and this time we managed to inch over to safety on foot.

"You shouldn't be over there," the patroller told us. "Those slopes are for experienced downhill skiers only."

"I'm sorry. I couldn't stop," I admitted.

"I see," he replied, smiling with Edwin. "You're sure you're okay?"

I nodded, utterly embarrassed.

"Alright then," he said to me, then turned to Edwin. "You take care." He pushed off and glided down the slope with such masculine grace that it sickened me.

Before I could decide on my next move, Edwin was helping me on my way. I was surprised how patient he was being with me and I couldn't help but wonder if he was only doing it to get a rise out of Cameron. I still fell another two times, battering my already bruised body, but I finished on my feet and that was a small miracle.

Cameron was waiting for me at the bottom again and he didn't look very impressed. "I thought you got lost," he said to me, then narrowed his eyes at Edwin.

"You could say that," Edwin answered, just to push Cameron's buttons.

"Could you leave us alone, please Eddie?" I begged.

"Whatever you want. See you later." He took off immediately, heading back for the lift, where I saw Hunter and Aliah waiting in line. Aliah waved at me wildly and I raised my hand to acknowledge that I saw her.

"I'm sorry, but I'm not going again. I'm afraid I might kill myself if I try hard enough. You're not mad are you?"

"I'm not mad," he replied, with pause. "A little disappointed, but not mad."

"I knew this was a bad idea." I shook my head with regret, then I plopped my sore ass into a snow bank. "I'll just hang out down here and watch you, if that's okay."

"Okay, I guess. Why don't you watch for me and tell me how good I do." He smirked. "I'm not the most experienced skier, but I think I'm getting better with every run."

I smiled at his attempt to make me feel better, as he bent over for an awkward kiss. "I'll be back before you know it," he said, before skiing off.

Determined to put the skis away for another lifetime, I snapped them off and piled them next to me. As each of my friends glided effortlessly to the base of the mountain, I felt more and more angry. *Why did everyone insist that I engage in the one and only sport that I couldn't actually do?*

Cameron had gone down the mountain two more times and I told him how great of a skier he was, even if he was only mediocre at best. The icy wind chilled me to my core, as the frigidness sunk into me, bone-deep. The falling snow was getting heavier and it got to the point where I couldn't control my trembling body.

Cold, lonely and depressed didn't even begin to describe how I felt, as Cameron pulled up to me. I stood from the snow bank and threw myself into his arms. He knew I was done.

"I'm going to head back to the hotel," I told him. "I'm freezing to death out here."

With both poker sticks in one hand, he reached for me. "I'm coming with you."

I instantly pulled back. "No. I don't want you to suffer because I suck. I want you to go and have fun. Was this not the whole point of the trip?"

He shook his head no. "Actually, spending time with you was the whole point."

I smiled, but when I saw Hunter and Aliah making another pass down the hill, I hollered out to them. "Hey guys, I'm gonna get going, but I'm trying to get Cam to stay."

"We're thinking of heading over to a bigger slope," Hunter hollered back.

"You should come with," Aliah added.

He looked at me, unsure of what to do. I could tell that he really wanted to go.

I gave him a quick kiss. "Go. You don't need me dragging you down. I'll be fine on my own."

"You're sure?" he double checked.

"Yes!" I pushed him away so he'd take the hint.

"I guess I'll see you in a bit then."

I nodded and hurried back to the lodge to lose the skis ASAP. Still bundled to the chin, I enjoyed a cup of hot chocolate by the fireplace. The flames seemed to have a pleasant effect on me, my skin tingling while I waited for my body to thaw out.

Relaxed, but insanely bored, I glanced over to the counter and watched the people returning their equipment. Edwin was standing in line to return his skis. I watched him as he unzipped his jacket, sweat glistening on his forehead. And here I was, frozen.

"Hey!" I called, trying to get his attention.

He handed his skis to the lady and carried his boots to a nearby bench. He quickly slipped them on before coming across the room to see me.

"I wondered where you guys went," he said, looking around for Cameron.

"They went to check out some better slopes. You could probably catch them if you hurry."

"Nah. I've had enough. Do you mind if I hang with you for a while?"

Bad idea. "Sure."

He nodded and smiled, then headed for the canteen to get himself a drink. When he returned, he removed his jacket and took a seat next to me on the oversized lounge chair. He draped his arm over the back of the chair and settled in next to me. I wanted to ask him to move away, but he was so incredibly warm and I was so deathly cold.

"You're freezing," he said, looking down at me.

"I know. This is helping though," I said, showing him my warm drink.

He snuggled up a little closer to me. "Are you having fun at least?"

"Well, I was, until the whole skiing thing," I answered, a smile finally gracing my lips. "I could've done without the bloody nose last night though."

He couldn't help but laugh at me and I wished that the deep rumble from his chest hadn't warmed me immeasurably. "I think maybe you should leave skiing alone and take up something else next time. Like knitting."

"Knitting?" I shook my head no. "Not gonna happen."

He smirked, still teasing me. "I give you five years."

I shoved him playfully and he shoved me back gently with his large, warm hand.

"Oww!" I howled, suddenly feeling like a walking boo boo.

Edwin raised a brow at me. "I barely even touched you."

"I know. But now that I'm warming up, I'm starting to really feel it."

Edwin chuckled at me again and the smile never left his moist, pink lips. "Maybe we should head back and get you some aspirin. You've had a rough couple of days."

"So, you've noticed," I replied, unimpressed with my incompetence. I slowly stood to my feet and groaned from the aches and pains.

We made our way back to the hotel and again Edwin was patient, even with my turtle's pace. When we got in the hotel elevator, just the two of us, the air turned stifling. I looked up at Edwin and he grinned, as the elevator slowly headed for the second level. When the door dinged, I rushed out ahead of him.

"Let me walk you to your door," Edwin insisted.

"No," I hollered. I spun around, not expecting him to be so close behind me, and he nearly knocked me to the floor. "That's not necessary." I straightened up and whirled away, with lightening in my step.

I became very suspicious of his intentions, as he followed after me. I put my key in the door and opened it on the first try, then let it slam behind me before Edwin could slip inside.

"You're not going to invite me in?" Edwin asked. His disbelief was evident, even through the closed door.

I peered out the peep hole, wishing the dreadful feeling in my chest would go away. "No."

"That's rude," he replied, raising his eyebrows at me. He delivered me a pointed look through the peep hole, as if I had hurt his feelings.

He knew I was watching him? Tough. I was not letting him in.

"What can I say, Abs? You were my best friend, who I liked to kiss and do other fun things with." His smile grew wicked, then faded out, and his arched eyebrows fell flat.

"And now I have to feel guilty for trying to steal you from him. Bastard. I had you first."

My scowl hardened, but he couldn't see it. "Eddie, you need to back off. Whatever it is that you're trying to do here, it won't work."

"What are you saying?" he asked, not budging from my doorstep.

"You should go."

I saw how quickly Edwin became agitated. It had to be the moment when he realized how much of a hold Cameron had on me.

"You deserve better," Edwin growled.

"What do you know?"

"I know that you're settling with him and you deserve more than that."

"I'm not settling. I love Cam."

"You think you do. Time will tell," he said. Then he stormed off, not leaving me a chance for rebuttal.

I was infuriated by his innuendoes and frustrated by his words. My blood boiled and I knew there was only one way I would be able to get any relaxing in now. After running myself a hot bath, I stripped naked and slipped into the steamy water, overcome with a warmth that relieved my sore muscles and eased my mind. I soaked in it for a long while, until my eyes shot open.

"Abby, you in there," Cam called from the door.

"Yeah," I replied, rubbing my eyes.

"Everything okay?"

"I'm just in the bath. I must have fallen asleep." The water was cool and my skin wrinkly, suggesting I had been soaking a lot longer than I had planned. I quickly escaped the tub and made myself presentable.

I tousled my waterlogged hair with a hand towel, as I walked out to greet Cam. "How was it?"

"It was excellent. I wish you could've been there," he said, pulling me into his cold embrace.

I locked my lips onto his and gave him a warm kiss. "I'm glad you had fun." I smiled, but was unwilling to put up a front. "You should know that Edwin walked me back."

He sighed, not knowing how to respond. "That man's incorrigible. He really needs to learn how to mind his own business."

"I promise it was totally friendly."

"I don't trust the guy," Cam admitted.

I peeled him out of his jacket and rubbed my hands over his chest, hoping to ease his tension and lighten the conversation. "It doesn't matter, Cam, because I love *you*."

He smiled at me and his anxiety seemed to brush right off his shoulder. His eyes slowly perused over my chest and when they landed on my lips, he looked ready to devour me. His thumb brushed gently over my bottom lip, before he nibbled on it.

"Hungry?" I teased.

"You seem to have that effect on me," he said, with a slanted smirk.

Unable to elude his penetrating gaze, I looped my arms over his shoulders and leapt into his arms to kiss him fervently. His hands explored my thighs, until he dropped me on the bed, and I was as good as his.

Later that night, Cameron treated me to an amazing candle-lit dinner and showered me with love for the rest of the evening. We went for a dip in the pool, and I gave him all of my solicited attention, as the others left us to our own. Later yet, we relaxed in our hot tub and gazed at the stars, our limbs wrapped around each other, skin against skin.

It was like I was falling in love with him all over again.

CHAPTER THREE

I was lucky to be spending the last day of the year with the most amazing people. After sleeping in late, I curled up on Cameron's chest and he wrapped his strong arms around me, keeping me pressed tight against his smooth, hard body. He kissed my bare shoulder and gazed at me in such a way that made me feel so special. Never had I felt so content and secure in my life.

We shared breakfast in bed and it was so delicious. I sipped on my orange juice and had a taste of Cameron, by flicking my tongue into his accepting mouth. He lifted the tray from the bed, then crawled on top of me, urgently finding my mouth again. Our lips connected, but it wasn't enough. I needed more. My body begged for it. Cameron sank his kiss even deeper yet and, with his growing erection pressed against my thigh, I couldn't resist him.

He pried himself off of me long enough to rip open a condom and slide my panties to my ankles, then he was moving inside of me, like it was his home. It was a perfectly snug fit, with every inch of him sliding in and out, creating an enchanting friction.

With a moan and a gasp, I came undone beneath him, my nails digging into his flesh, clinging to the reality that was slipping from my fingers. His mouth covered mine, as he growled with release, but he didn't stop kissing me for a long while.

When he finally rolled aside, I showered him with my smile. "That was amazing. You're amazing," I said, sweaty and satisfied. My palms smoothed over his chest, then I climbed on top of him and leaned down to kiss his sexy lips another time.

"Speaking of amazing..." Cam replied, as his eyes devoured my naked body now straddled over him.

Feeling awfully exposed, I smiled softly and reached for my robe. I thought I would give Cameron a hand and reached for his bag, intending to pass it over to him, but he tackled me before I had the chance.

"I can get it!" he shouted.

It startled me, and when he stuffed his bag quickly into the corner, it had me very concerned.

What was he hiding?

"I made arrangements for you and your girlfriends to get pampered for the day at the spa downstairs," Cam said, stealing my curiosity. "I hope you don't mind. I wanted it to be a surprise."

Damn, I hated surprises, but he was really good at them. "Mind? I mean, I would have enjoyed it more if you were there with me. But still, how could I mind?"

Cam's smile slanted lazily across his lips. "I thought you might say that. Jessica and Maddie acted the same way when I told them."

"What about Aliah?"

"She'll be there too. Go and have fun with your friends." He smiled sweetly.

"Do I dare ask how much this is costing you? The last thing I planned to do was drain your life savings."

"You dare not ask and don't act all surprised. You should know by now that I don't half-ass anything." His blue eyes glimmered at me before he checked his watch. "I love you and I want you to be happy. Go on, they're probably waiting for you now."

"What are you going to do?" I asked, my curiosity getting the better of me.

"The guys were going downstairs to work out, so I thought I'd check that out. We'll probably just shoot the shit for a while after that. So go," he insisted.

I slipped on my bikini and flip flops and topped it with my robe. I wrapped my arms around Cameron, giving him a hard, deep kiss and a soft press of my body, before I let him go. He wouldn't forget that kiss anytime soon.

When I exited the elevator on the main level, I found my ladies waiting for me.

Aliah tapped her toe. "Is this true? Maddie tells me Cam's treating us to a spa day. She can't be serious."

I shrugged my shoulders. "Yup. That's what I hear."

Aliah's eyebrows remained high on her forehead in disbelief.

"Must be nice to have a man who's made of money," Jessica said, sounding more than a little jealous.

"Not to mention his other redeeming qualities," Maddie noted, not keeping her fascination with Cameron a secret.

I smiled to myself, recalling his hard body, sharp wit and soft lips. "I certainly can't complain."

Edwin Santora watched the door swing open to the smallish exercise room. Cameron Clarke was the last dude he wanted to see walk through that door. He didn't need that extra dose of adrenaline, or the other emotions that spiked through him, but it was out of his control, just like Abby's decision was.

Edwin had come on this trip in hopes of getting Abby out of his brain, but dumb-ass Cam decided he'd bring her along. It was bad enough he had to witness Abby ogling Cam all weekend, but now he had to put up with Cam's arrogance too. Funny how just a minute ago his muscles were feeling the burn and now, suddenly, he was ready to flip a bus.

Jealousy hung thick in the air as Cameron lifted a couple of free weights from the stand. Edwin dropped back on the bench, after loading the bar with weights way heavier than his usual limits. This was one thing he had Cameron beat at and he'd make a point of showing him that.

When he finished his third rep, he knew Hunter was impressed, but it didn't stop him from coming out with his potty mouth. The other two guests in the room decidedly took their leave, obviously intimidated by all of his large, heated muscle. Edwin chuckled to himself, wondering what a beast he must look like, every muscle flaring from his extended bout of weight lifting.

Cameron pressed out a harsh breath on his last lift, then tossed the heavy weights to the floor, gravity making them clank loudly when they connected with the ground. He sat up on the bench and lazily glanced at Hunter.

"I should probably give you guys a heads up," he announced to Hunter, though it was really Edwin who he was warning.

Edwin finished the last of his dips, wiped his forehead with his t-shirt, then tossed it over his shoulder. He padded across the floor and every muscle in his body rippled as he eyed up Cameron.

"Heads up? For what?" Hunter asked, his curiosity just as vicious as Edwin's.

"It's probably just that we're next at the spa," Edwin teased, laughing at his own joke.

Hunter laughed along, but Cam's face stayed serious, his eyes locked dead on Edwin.

"Actually, this has to do with Abigail. I thought you especially would appreciate a little notice."

Edwin lifted his chest as his lungs filled with air, then dipped his chin before his fists started flying. Adrenaline flooded his senses, as he winced at his own overactive imagination. He growled. He actually growled. "She better not be knocked up already, you fucker."

He approached Cameron, looking dangerous and intimidating, but stopped a few strides away, his teeth clenched, fists balled at his sides.

Cameron laughed at Edwin's response. "That's not it, you tool."

Edwin didn't scare very easily, but that had knotted his chest in a way he never could've imagined it would. He took a deep breath, and the knot loosened ever so slightly.

"I'm popping the question tonight," Cam said, again stealing the air from Edwin's lungs, as Cameron reached for the small bulge in his pocket. "And if she says yes, she'll be my wife."

"If," Edwin snapped, his single word hanging in the air between them like a dangling noose.

Cam pulled out the dainty, black, velvet box, ignoring Edwin's uneasiness. "I couldn't leave it in the room. Abby almost stumbled on it earlier today, but I want my proposal to catch her by surprise. I don't think she has a clue." He cracked the delicate box open and examined the large, white rock in the light.

"Whoa, you mean business!" Hunter hollered, from across the room. He roved to Cam's side and admired the sheer size of the diamond. "I don't know a woman that could turn that baby down," he said, slapping Cam on the back. "You have bigger balls than me, brother."

Edwin couldn't believe his ears. Who knew Cam would step up to the plate so soon? Not him. And he certainly didn't know how to feel about it.

"What do you think she'll say?" Cam asked Hunter.

"I told you. No bitch'll say no to that rock."

Cam hardly knows her. It should be me! "How are you planning to do it?" Edwin asked, trying not to sound like he actually cared.

"I was thinking I'd wait until after the countdown, when everyone else is celebrating, and flash her the ring without saying a word." He raised a brow in question.

"Oh, yeah. The ladies are suckers for that kind of shit. She'll definitely go for it," Hunter said.

Edwin fumed. *She would love that. But it's not me.* "She'll hate it."

"Really?" Cam was confident.

"She's always dreamt of an old-fashioned, man on his knee, professing his love to her kind of event," Edwin admitted. *Shit! Why did I just tell him that? Now I'm helping the damn guy.*

"Don't listen to him. He's just jealous," Hunter said. "You do what you want to do."

Cam looked uneasy, pinned beneath Edwin's direct scrutiny. "Yeah, I think she'll say yes."

Edwin was practically foaming at the mouth. "We'll see about that." He bumped into Cam with his massive shoulder and stomped past him toward the door.

"What's your problem?" Cam snapped.

Edwin turned back for only a second, but he made his point crystal clear. "You hurt her and you're a dead man."

After a day of pampering at the spa, instead of feeling completely relaxed, as the New Year drew closer the terrible feeling in the pit of my stomach became increasingly worse. Everything seemed to be coming together in my life. If Cam were to agree to have children with me, my life would be perfect; and that was exactly what was causing my panic.

It seemed whenever life got really good for me, fate always had a way of body slamming me back into reality. *I swear if I didn't have bad luck, I'd have no luck at all.* I started to believe that I wasn't allowed to have a happy ever after; that it just wasn't in the cards for me.

Back in Maddie's room, I watched Edwin as he snuck out of the hotel room without a send-off; as if we weren't going to notice, just because we were all consuming the most delicious room service ever. Edwin insisted that he wasn't hungry. That only made me secretly suspicious.

After our feast and a few glasses of wine, me and my ladies congregated in the small bathroom, fighting for the mirror to improve our makeup. I darkened my mascara and puckered my glossy lips. *Stunning.* That was the only word that came to mind when I saw myself in the gorgeous, red dress that Cameron had bought me for Christmas. It fit like a glove, highlighting my tiny waist and curvy hips.

"Damn, I look good," I announced, knowing it would spark an interesting conversation.

Aliah gave me a once over and shrugged a shoulder. "You look alright," she mocked, then broke into a fit of laughter.

Maddie pouted her lips. "You would wear that, while I'm over here looking all fat in my dress." She flailed an arm at me dramatically. "Next to you, I'll look like a total cow for sure."

"Maddie. That's just not true. You're the most beautiful pregnant woman I've ever seen." She'd found a dress that draped delicately from her little baby bulge, showing that she was pregnant, but far from fat. *Gorgeous.* But there was torment in the poor girl's chocolate-brown eyes. She couldn't see how great she looked and she definitely didn't know how jealous I was.

"You look absolutely amazing, Maddie." I glided my hand over her baby belly. It was perfect.

Maddie smiled. "Thanks. I hope the men look at me the same way you do. This pregnancy is doing a number on my sex drive."

We all laughed, except for Maddie.

"I'm not kidding. I *have* to get laid tonight!"

Aliah pressed her lips into a firm line, not finding that statement quite so funny. "Don't even think about it."

This time it was Maddie who laughed. "Oh, Ally. I wouldn't dream of it." There was no way she would risk her relationship with her baby daddy, for one night of sex with Hunter.

"Maybe if you drop the negativity for the night, you might pick up a stud," Aliah said, her tone changing. "Beer goggles."

Maddie didn't take offence. "I certainly hope so, cuz I could definitely use a good lay."

Laughter filled the room, as Jessica opened the door and fled the small space.

"I'm with you, Maddie," Jessica stated. "We need to find ourselves some fine, young men." She high-fived Maddie, then reached for a fresh glass of wine.

"H-E-L-L-O, ladies," Hunter announced, making us all smile.

Cameron stood up, when he saw me and he didn't take his eyes off the flaming red dress as he reached out for my hands. "Look at you. You look beautiful. And the dress..." He blew out a harsh breath. "It fits."

That was an understatement. "It fits."

He drew his hands up my waist and slid them back down, until he gripped onto my wide hips. His tongue flicked sensually over his upper lip, then he pulled me in for a kiss, smudging my gloss all over his mouth. The way his chest pressed against my skin, lit my nerves on fire. He smiled at me, as he wiped the gloss from his mouth, then reached his arms around my waist.

I licked my own well-kissed lips. "This might be a miracle, but I think I'm actually ready to go."

"Imagine that," Cameron said.

"Abby ready on time for a change. What's up with that?" Aliah asked.

I felt a twinge in my stomach, a trademark signal of the stabbing pain that would ensue. I turned away from Cam so he wouldn't catch me wincing. Things were good. For now.

"What do you ladies say we make a toast before we go?" Hunter suggested. He handed me and Cameron a glass of wine. "Here's to a night of good times, good friends..."

"...and lots of drinks!" Aliah finished.

We all raised our plastic glasses and bumped them together in the centre of our circle of friends.

Maddie took a sip from her cup. "This is so exciting. I haven't been this thrilled since...well, I'd rather not say with Ally in the room."

I stifled my laugh by tucking my head into Cameron's shoulder.

"Maddie!" Aliah hollered, scowling angrily.

"It's all in good fun," Maddie replied. "I was only teasing."

But everyone knew she wasn't.

When we finally made it downstairs, there was no question where the party was. Partygoers filled the lobby and everyone was heading for the hall. It was dark in the space, but there were flashy lights and sparkly party favours lighting up the room. The music was already going strong and the dance floor was packed with people.

"Oh, yeah. I'm definitely getting laid tonight," Maddie announced, admiring the quality of men on display. She ran her hand over a handsome passer-by and then winked at him.

"You nasty dog," Jessica teased, once he was out of ear shot.

"Do me a favour and steer clear of me when you're talking about sex," Hunter warned, catching the entire incident. "Especially when you're carrying my baby. Any man who'll stick it in there when you're like that has his own issues."

Maddie lifted her chin. "Hey, I'll take what I can get."

"No, you won't," Hunter answered, definitively. "No man will be fussing around in there around my baby. You've got three more months, I think you can wait."

"Hmpf," she huffed, then realized it wasn't up to him. "I've got needs too, you know; and the doctor says I'm good to go. I'll do what I want tonight."

If not for Maddie, I wouldn't have even noticed that there was another man in the place. Cameron looked so suave and sexy himself, that it ignited a fire within me. I would've been happy to strip him from that polished, red shirt; and in time I would.

Recognizing my attraction, Cam pulled me closer and kissed me, with slow, wet lips. I moaned, involuntarily, and everyone heard me.

"Save it for midnight," Hunter hollered.

Cameron flashed him a warning glare.

"Speaking of midnight..." Jessica started. "It's late. Where's Edwin?"

Hunter glanced at Aliah, like they weren't supposed to say. *Interesting.*

"Apparently he had a dinner date," Hunter informed Jessica. "Some chick he met this afternoon. He'll meet up with us later."

A few hours passed before I found Edwin sitting at the bar, and I didn't see his lovely guest anywhere. Jessica caught me looking at him and headed right over.

"Hey, Eddie. No luck with the blonde bimbo?"

"It didn't work out," Edwin lied. He flashed a glance at the dance floor where the blonde was chatting with another random stranger, then he pounded back a shot and chased it with his beer.

Cameron cleared his throat, to catch my attention, and handed me a fresh drink. "We'll catch up with you later," he said to Jessica, stealing my empty hand and pulling me to a dark corner.

I gazed lovingly into his eyes, a soft smile playing on my lips.

Cam took a sip from his drink. "What did I do to deserve you?"

I repeatedly kissed him, his top lip, his bottom lip, the corner of his mouth. Then I slowly pulled my mouth away and my eyelashes fluttered open.

"Look at what you're doing to me," he said, as he tried to privately adjust his pants.

I smirked and sipped from my glass and then back-stepped away from him, drawing him onto the dance floor. I knew I was supposed to wait until midnight to kiss him long and hard, but I couldn't keep away from his charming lips. Lust was definitely in the air.

We danced, and teased, nibbled and canoodled, surrounded by a mixture of easygoing and vivacious partygoers. By the time midnight was upon us, we were all celebrating like raving lunatics.

"It's almost time," Jessica squealed, as she scouted out the single men in her vicinity. The crowd was young and she had a decent helping of eligible men to choose from.

"What time is it?" I hollered.

Maddie glanced at her wristwatch made of black crystals. "Eleven forty-four," she hollered back.

I hooked an arm around Cameron's neck. "I really have to pee. I'm gonna go now."

"I'll come with," Aliah hollered to me.

"Hurry back," Cameron said, seeming very anxious.

Aliah and I rushed off to the washroom and there were quite a few ladies waiting in line before us. "That'll be our luck, ringing in the New Year in the ladies room," Aliah joked.

The line moved fast and I stumbled into the washroom, exposing my degree of intoxication. Though the skiing pains had eased, the cramps in my side were still there making me want to curl up in the corner and cry. After a quick trip to the toilet, I checked my reflection in the mirror.

"You look hot. Now let's go. We don't want to miss the countdown," Aliah said.

We hurried back with everyone else now piling onto dance floor, readying themselves for the countdown. We squeezed through the crowd and shoved our way back to the others.

"You made it," Cam said, overcome with relief as he anxiously checked his wristwatch.

I pressed a chaste kiss to his lips. "I made it."

He didn't respond, physically or verbally. *Something was off with him and it didn't seem good.*

All of our friends crowded together, as others tried to squeeze into our tight formation. Maddie and Jessica were ushering the hotties in, with masks concealing their faces and other sparkling party favours in their hands.

For a nice change, everyone in our group was getting along. Edwin had even left me and Cameron alone all night, though he was now hanging close by; likely arranging his midnight mack-up.

Cameron fidgeted, as the crowd tightened up in anticipation of the New Year. There was less than one minute before the countdown and many had already began cheering excitedly. I hugged each of my friends, excluding

Edwin, happy that I could spend the last minute of the year with my best friends.

I cheered along with everyone else as the singles bustled around to situate themselves for the countdown. What a great feeling to not have to do that. I sighed and whispered in Cam's ear. "Love you."

He softened beneath my hands, but didn't respond, just swallowed and grinned.

Okay, something is really up. I pressed a fake smile onto my lips and glanced at Hunter across from me. He had been staring and smiled back, but then turned his face away to whisper to Edwin. Edwin nodded, his face expressionless.

Uneasiness caused me to twitch and Cameron rubbed my arm to soothe me, but it was a little late for that. I watched Hunter and Aliah swaying back and forth in each other's arms, and how Jessica and Maddie had managed to scam a couple of drunk studs. The room fell silent, then the countdown began and all I could think was, the sooner this was over the better.

As we counted down, "10-9-8-7," Cam looked like he was ready to pass out. People around us waved noisemakers, stared at the sparklers spinning at the head of the room and jumped up and down. "6-5-4..." I was shoved away from Cam by the bumbling crowd of excitable drunks. Before I was able push my way back to him, "...3-2-1!"

Sparks were flying, confetti dropping and some sneaky, blonde bitch beat me to the punch. She was thin, young and beautiful, everything I would imagine Cam would like in a girl. Her long hair dangled over Cameron's red shirt, as she gripped his suit jacket in both her hands, pulling him to her mouth to kiss him.

I gaped at the situation playing out before me, my feet glued to the floor. I watched her hand slide over his chest, her lips on his mouth, and he didn't even stop her. *Oh! That's what's up.*

Cheers resumed, but my heart stopped, surrounded by others still sharing tongue-filled kisses. I started to feel dizzy, my head spinning faster than my body, as I tried to find a way out of the crowd. Anger fueled me, burning through my veins with a vengeance, masking the sadness lingering just below the surface.

Someone larger than me grabbed onto my arm and spun me around. Without even glancing at the man now facing me, not caring at this point, I reacted to my emotions, closed my eyes and accepted the hot press of his lips against mine. I rested my hands on his hard chest, flanking his silky tie, only feeling in that moment, as his tongue gained access to my mouth. He curled me tighter into his steady arms and I flung mine around his hulking frame, my eyes burning with tears as my mouth covered his again and again.

His lips were soft, skilled and surprisingly gentle. *Familiar? No. Stop trying to put reason to my feelings toward this random rebound boy. Man. Definitely a man.*

His tongue swept into my mouth again and when I skimmed my hands under his jacket, I scratched my nails over his wide back and massive shoulders. He tasted very good, like cinnamon and flames. I softened against him, snugly fitting against his chiselled body. This man responded to me by sliding his large, capable hands over my curves, moulding me like putty. *Familiar. Definitely familiar.* But I wasn't ready to return to reality just yet.

When my tongue skimmed back into his warm, devouring mouth, I finally got a real good taste of him. My knees grew weak with understanding. There was no doubt left in my mind that this random mystery man wasn't random at all, and yet there I was unable to back away.

I kissed him harder, knowing that Cameron was likely watching by now, and only hoping that it would make him hurt a fraction of how much he had hurt me. Then I reluctantly broke the soul-stealing lip-lock and slowly retracted my nails from the man's back.

Another couple bumped into us, but he didn't let me go. His hands continued to firmly stroke me and, when I gazed up into his greedy, aqua eyes, I was struck with the realization of what I had done. Disgusted with myself, I tried to escape from Edwin's arms, but he gripped me tighter, delivering a silent message that only I would understand.

Trying to sort out what the hell I was doing, my chest caved. I crumbled in Edwin's arms. I had been convinced that I loved Cameron more than I had ever loved another man. But Edwin had a way of testing my resolve. My heart squeezed as Edwin watched me and recognized my regret. I loved Edwin, but there was so much more about Cameron that I still wanted to learn.

When someone tapped on my shoulder, Edwin's powerful arms loosened and I finally wiggled out of his villainous grasp. I spun away to face the man seeking my attention. Cameron. And he had a look in his eyes that I tried to decipher. Was is guilt? Torment? Reading him was too easy. He was saddened and confused and maybe even heart broken.

Well guess what, buddy, that doesn't even begin to explain how I felt when I saw your lips on that blonde bimbo. My panic rose as quickly as the bile in my throat and tears threatened from the storm in my heart.

"What the hell?" Cameron asked, his expression devastating me.

My eyes flashed back to Edwin and he cracked a smile. *Nice.* He thought my life falling to pieces in front of his very eyes was absolutely hilarious. I flashed a quick glance at my friends, to gauge their reactions. Their mouths were gaping in shock. The longer I stood there being scrutinized by them, the harder it was for me to confront the situation logically. I was mortified.

I whirled away and hiked my skirt with one hand, so I could escape the party room as fast as I could. Tears instantly streamed from my eyes, as I ran away from my problems. But I couldn't hide from them. After the hysteria passed, I dabbed my tear stained face and tried to smear away the blackened makeup from under my eyes. I tried to pull myself together, but it wasn't going to happen. Hearing everyone else still cheering and partying more joyously than ever wasn't helping.

I stared at my reflection, feeling incredibly ashamed of my behaviour. Truth: Cameron wronged me. But what I did was cruel, and I should have never dragged Edwin into it. Edwin had probably only done it to spite Cameron, knowing he would get a rise out of him. Mission accomplished.

The worst of it was, I cared very much about Cameron, but I couldn't stop worrying about Edwin either. I smeared away the fresh tears. Why did I care so damn much about Edwin?

CHAPTER FOUR

I walked back out into the chaos. Cameron was waiting outside the door for me. "Can we talk?" he asked, and reached his hand out to me.

After all that had happened, I was surprised he'd still offer me his hand. I was finding it difficult to even look at him. I ignored his hand and shrugged a careless shoulder, acting the exact opposite of what I was truly feeling.

I headed away from the party room in silence. My hurt feelings clung to my chest walls and tears glistened in my somber eyes. Cameron followed behind me, with slumped shoulders. As we neared the front lobby, Cameron took my hand and dragged me to a free bench. He wouldn't let go of my hand, even as I struggled to pull it away from him.

"Please," he begged.

I was afraid if I opened my mouth again I would cry.

Cameron looked into my watery eyes, then collected my hand into both of his. When he looked up again, his forehead all wrinkled, my heart skipped against my ribs. "Should I be worried?"

"You?"

"I didn't mean for that to happen," he insisted. "I don't even know the girl."

Yeah, I buy that. I rolled my tired eyes that now matched the colour of my dress. "You didn't seem to mind it."

He gently stroked my chin and turned my head to face him, his eyes determined, his gaze penetrating the ice wall I was trying to erect between us. "That's not true. She caught me off guard."

I rolled my eyes again. "I'm sure."

"But you. And Edwin." He dropped his hand, showing his frustration.

"Sure, I kissed him. I would've kissed any man with a pulse. It was mere coincidence that Edwin happened to be the one standing next to me."

Cameron swallowed, trying to keep his calm but failed at doing so. "You're sure of that? If you would've stopped kissing him when you realized who it was, I'd have an easier time believing you."

Ouch. That hurt. "Yeah, because trust is a real strong point in our relationship right now." I didn't know what to believe.

Cameron shook his head. "What a disaster."

I let out harsh breath, in the same moment that Edwin walked up quietly behind us. "Honestly, Cameron? It really meant nothing to me," I admitted, not knowing we had company. "Up until you kissed that girl, you were the only man in my eyes."

Cameron's gaze focused over my shoulder, his response hidden behind a mask of fury. Edwin had overheard my confession and I could see that he wasn't particularly pleased to have walked-in on it. He remained polite and composed, but I could see that disappointment had swallowed his hollow eyes. He turned to Cameron, without ever reaching my eyes.

"For what it's worth, I'm sorry. That was uncalled for." His apology was unexpected.

The fierceness in Cameron's reaction didn't even begin to describe the rage pouring from his eyes. Bad blood boiled between them and I knew if he said anything, it would result in a fist fight.

Edwin's gaze quickly turned from apologetic to mischievous. "I can see that Cameron's dealing with it."

"Please, just give us our space," I begged. I would've done anything to keep the situation from escalating any further.

Edwin snared me with his gaze. "Guess there's no need for me to check up on you anymore." His eyes flashed to Cameron. "I'll stay out of your way." Edwin turned and walked away, his regret penetrating my heart.

Cameron and I were surrounded by joyful party goers and yet I was utterly depressed, my thoughts doing a loop de loop. Neither of us spoke, with me lost in my own head and Cameron doing his best to cool off. He was sitting so close, but he didn't touch me. He was only inches away and yet I couldn't console him. A tear tripped and fell out of the corner of my eye. Before it trickled past my cheek, Cameron scooped it up with his finger.

"You should save those for something more important," he said, his lips turning out a breath-taking smile just for me.

I managed to return the smile. "I don't know. I think this is pretty important."

He nodded in agreement. "An honest misunderstanding, right?"

"I hope so."

He cupped his hands over mine and locked them down to his lap. "I have no idea who that girl is and I really don't care," Cam stated. His words sounded genuine and heartfelt.

If what he was saying was true, then that bitch had snagged my man and ruined my night. "I might have a few words for her."

Cameron chuckled at my ferocity and looked into my eyes, pleading for my forgiveness. "I never did get that New Year's kiss from you," he hinted, leaning forward slowly.

It felt a bit awkward to me, having just tied tongues with someone else, but I was relieved that Cameron wasn't making the situation any more challenging by being difficult.

I pressed my mouth softly against his and kissed him with all my heart, losing myself in his warm, comforting arms. When we resurfaced from our life-altering peck, Cameron rummaged frantically inside his jacket and pulled out a black, velvet box. My heart throbbed in my throat and he monitored every twitch of my eyelashes.

"I can't stay mad," he said. "Hell, I can't even stand not hearing your voice. I love you, Abby, and I'm just so damn scared that I've lost you already."

It was like he took a lighter to my heart, melting away the ice that had blocked him out only moments earlier. "I love you too."

Cam smiled and glanced at the soft, velvet box, squeezed tight in his trembling hand. "I was hoping you would say that." He dropped to one knee and glanced up at me. "I thought I knew exactly what to say and do, to make you say yes, but things don't always work out as planned."

I was unable to remove my wide eyes from his glimmering baby blues, as my hand covered my mouth.

"I love you, Abby. And I want to give you this as a token of my love, so you and everyone else knows how crazy I am about you." Suddenly Cam cracked open the box and presented me with the most beautiful ring.

"Don't say it," I sputtered, pushing the box away, before I could let the sparkling diamond tempt my heart more than it already had. It was everything I ever wanted, but I couldn't let myself go through the motions just then.

Saddened and surprised, Cameron rose from his knee and reseated himself next to me. He hung his head low and squeezed his eyes shut. "You don't love me like that," he said, explaining it to himself.

"No, Cam. I do, but..."

"It's too soon. I knew it," he interrupted.

I rested my hand on his leg, to comfort him. I hated seeing him like that. I wanted to make him better. "That's not it either," I replied, squeezing his thigh.

He scrunched his brows together, confused. "Then why?" He snapped the box shut, his heart lain out on the table before me.

"Don't you think this weekend has been a bit crazy? I mean, if you had asked me before we came on this trip, I'm sure it would have gone a little differently. But I don't want to look back and remember this night as *that night*. Do you understand what I mean?"

He raised an arched brow with hope. "So, you're not saying no?"

"I'm just saying later."

He looked down at the little box in his hands and cracked it back open. "You didn't even see the ring," he said, holding the box up to me.

It broke my heart. "I'll see it when the time is right," I replied, gently closing it inside his hand.

"No, " he commanded, as he cracked the box back open. "You'll see it now." The massive solitaire diamond sparkled in his eyes, as he plucked it from the box and held it between his finger and thumb.

"It's beautiful," I whispered, near tears.

He presented the ring to me again. "I love you, Abby. I bought this ring for you. And I'd like very much for you to have it now, as a symbol of our commitment to each other. Will you wear my ring?" He gazed at me, hesitant but hopeful.

My heart fluttered. "Oh, Cam. If it means that much to you."

Happy to take any answer other than no, Cam covered my mouth with his. He pulled me onto his lap and his joy radiated through me like lightning strikes. I felt so secure in that moment, my arms clung tightly around his neck, as I kissed him again and again.

"Aren't you going to see if it fits?" he asked, examining me.

I chewed on my smiling bottom lip and reached out my right hand. He gazed into my eyes, kissed my knuckles, then lowered my right hand to my lap. He gently collected my left hand and slid the golden band onto my ring finger.

"Oh!" My hands trembled as I splayed my fingers out and displayed the sparkling beauty. Breathless, and unable to take my eyes from my new addition, I smiled, acknowledging all that it stood for.

"Are you okay with this?" Cam asked, trying to read my teary eyes.

I let out a nervous laugh. "Absolutely. I love it and everything it represents."

He smiled, his confidence returning as fast as the glimmer in his eyes. *My Cameron was back.* "Now everyone will know that you're mine."

The sunlight attacked my ring the next morning and woke me from my peaceful slumber. The diamond sparkled and glimmered unreservedly, making me smile as I held it out to examine it.

"Morning," Cameron said, as he rolled toward me.

"Good morning," I replied, unable to wipe the elated smile from my sleepy face.

He had caught me admiring the ring. "I take it you like it." With a scorching smile playing on his lips, he stretched out and then yawned loudly.

"It's stunning. I love it."

"Just like you. I knew it was the one the second I saw it."

I kissed him softly and he kissed me back, allowing his passion to expose his possessive nature. I looked into his gorgeous eyes and gently twirled his short, spiky hair around my fingers. "I'm lucky to have you," I whispered.

Before long, Cameron was loading our bags into his car, as the ladies loaded me into Maddie's. Cameron came up to my window and I eased it down to give him a kiss. "You okay?"

"I'm good. I'll see you back at home," I said.

"Home. I like that." He kissed me again and then strolled back to his car with a smile on his face. *That could be dangerous. Especially with Edwin in his back seat.*

Jessica hopped into the front seat with Maddie and snapped on her seatbelt. "Let's hit the road."

Aliah adjusted the strap across her chest, pulled out her cell phone and scanned through the emails that she had ignored over the weekend. Maddie eased her car into drive and followed Cameron out of the icy parking lot.

I stared out my window at the dull, grey sky, noting the contours of the thick clouds in the distance, just waiting for the snow to drop again. The heat was cranked on high, but it felt like I was sitting in an ice cube. Aliah rubbed her hands together and glanced at me. She hadn't even acknowledged the massive rock on my finger and there was no way she had missed it.

"So, spill it!" Jessica broadcasted, from the front seat.

"What?" I asked, dramatically. "Oh, you mean this?" My smile beamed when I flipped my hand up to flash my diamond at her.

She grabbed onto my hand to gawk and appreciate the amazing quality of the sizeable stone. "I bet it cost a fortune." She clutched onto my hand, displaying her awe on her face.

Aliah glanced at it, trying to act casual. "Holy shitballs. That's huge!" She yanked my hand away from Jessica to take a closer look herself.

"What can I say? He loves me."

"I'd say," Maddie replied, as she tried to keep her eyes on the road.

"When are you getting hitched?" Aliah asked, suddenly interested.

I yanked my hand away from her. "We're not."

"What?" Jessica looked stunned. "A man doesn't just give you ring like that. It's got to be in exchange for something."

Aliah nodded. "Hunter told me that Cam had planned to ask you to marry him at midnight. But it looked like Edwin put a kink in that plan."

"He tried to ask me when we were making up. I wouldn't let him. Not last night. Not like that."

"Like when then?" Aliah pried, dying to know.

I shrugged my shoulders. "I told him later."

"And he just up and gave you the ring anyway?" Jessica squealed.

"We're treating it as a promise ring. He said it symbolizes our commitment to each other."

"Hah! He'd say anything to get that ring on your finger," Aliah stammered.

I scowled at Aliah, angered by her outburst. "What's your point?"

"You shouldn't have taken the ring. It's not fair to Cam," Aliah said.

Yeah, cuz she was such a model citizen. "What do you know?" Pissed, I stared out the window and gave Aliah the silent treatment.

"Cam's a great guy. He deserves more. Don't act like *later* you'll accept his proposal."

Unable to outright ignore her, I scowled at her again. "I will."

"Mmm hmm. I saw you with Eddie last night; and in the hot tub the night before. I don't doubt that you love Cam, but there's obviously something still there with Eddie. You need to figure that out first. Just face it: you had your chance at happiness with Cam and you blew it by kissing Edwin."

"I blew it?" I screeched. "Cam was the one making out with that blonde chick! Edwin just happened to be the one I took my frustrations out on."

"How convenient for you," Aliah said, rolling her eyes.

"Screw you! I love Cam and there's no question about that."

"You're right, there's not. But he's not the only one."

I stared out the window again, folded my arms across my chest and tucked my hands in, so I didn't accidentally pummel my fists into Aliah's face. My heart was racing wickedly. I was outwardly appalled that she would sink so low, though in my heart I knew that there was still something there with Edwin, whether I liked it or not.

I tried to explain it to myself, replaying those same words over and over again. "Eddie doesn't want kids now. He made that very clear. That means *we* are never going to work out. What more do you want from me?"

Aliah wasn't having it. "Whatever."

Maddie stayed silent, until I urged her to give me her advice. "Sorry, Abby. But you're going to have to figure this one out on your own."

"What am I supposed to do? I love Cam, more than anything."

"Do you?" Aliah asked, pointedly.

I narrowed my eyes at her, until they were but irritated slits cut from my face. She was being so mean. "I love him a lot. He loves me. He makes me happy and his daughter's a total sweetheart. He can give me the babies I've always wanted."

"You seem so sure," Aliah announced, knowing I wasn't.

"Well, we haven't exactly talked about it yet," I admitted. "I was just hoping that he'd agree to what I wanted."

"Yeah, I see how that worked out for you last time." Aliah's words were as sharp as her wit and as harsh as the colourful streaks in her dark brown hair.

"Ugh! I can't take it anymore!" I hollered.

"Leave the poor girl alone," Maddie urged. "She's been through enough this weekend."

"She's delusional," Aliah blurted.

I slammed my hand onto the seat beside me and leaned forward, until my face dipped into the front seat. "That's it! Stop the car."

"I promise I'll stop in one minute," Maddie swore. "But I don't want to get stuck in a snow bank."

Jessica looked up from her cell phone. "Edwin says Cam will stop at a place they saw up ahead. It's less than a kilometre from here."

I bit my tongue, silently fuming to myself, planning my escape from the car the second it rolled to a stop. Ignoring the others, I watched as Maddie pulled the car into the parking lot, then I jumped the second she had her foot on the brake, dove out my door and headed straight for the building.

Cam came running in after me, seeing that something was wrong. "Hey, what's up?" He looked so concerned.

I sighed and stared at the floor. I couldn't very well tell him what we were arguing about. It would crush him. "Aliah's being a total bitch. I can't stand her right now."

"I see," he said, with a smirk.

It was so heartfelt that I nearly burst into laughter.

"So, I've been thinking. I know maybe now's not the best time," he said, "but I've learned that waiting isn't necessarily the right way to go either."

"Spit it out, Cameron." I let a smile slip from my mouth, as I yanked on his jacket collar and pulled him closer to me.

"I know I only asked you to stay at my place for the holidays, but I have to admit that I was hoping you wouldn't want to leave."

My smile grew wider. "What are you saying?" I wanted to hear the words come from his lips and see the satisfaction when he heard my answer.

"Will you move in with me?"

I flung my arms over his shoulders, while a joyous smile erupted from my lips. "I'd love that."

Cam kissed me, exhilaration spilling from him as he lifted me into his arms. I was so happy to see his smile and feel his body pressed against mine.

Hunter approached us, having waited for us to finish. I could tell from the look on his face that he had overheard our conversation. "Do you mind if Aliah rides with us the rest of the way?" he asked Cam.

Cam gazed at me in question and I nodded. "Sure."

"Cool." Hunter instantly turned away and disappeared out of the building.

I kissed Cam again and squeezed him a little closer. I was glad Hunter had asked, because I couldn't stand another minute with Aliah. Cam smirked, reading my thoughts, then bound our hands together and led me outside into the blustery weather. When I walked toward the car, Cam didn't want to let go. He extended his arm out, clutching onto my hand as long as possible until our fingers pulled apart.

I smiled back at him. "I'll see you at home?"

"Home," he repeated. "I like the sound of that." Cameron turned away and got into his car.

As I gripped the cold, passenger handle on Maddie's car door, Edwin startled me.

"Hey," he said.

I pulled on the door and Edwin held it open. I didn't want to allow him to be all chivalrous toward me but, when he leaned closer, I had no other option but to drop down onto the seat.

Edwin stuck his head inside the car. "Do you mind if I ride with you guys?"

Maddie glanced over her shoulder. "That's up to Abby."

I brought my left hand to my chin, as though I was thinking about it, my only intention to flash him my ring. It didn't seem to scare him off. "I don't care," I said. Then I slid my butt to the far end of the bench seat, while my heart screamed: Nooooo!

I flashed my eyes out the windshield, worried to see Cameron's reaction. His eyes were locked on Edwin as he got into the seat next to me. I rested my left hand on the arm rest and spread my fingers to display my ring, as Edwin snapped on his seatbelt.

"Abby?" Edwin asked.

I brought my hand back to my chin, so he couldn't look at me without seeing it and turned toward him. "Yes?"

Edwin winced at the sight, and it took him a minute to right himself after having been electrocuted, but it gave me the peace of mind I was so desperately clinging to. "I guess it can wait," he said, then glanced out his window as we sped away.

The ride wasn't nearly as uncomfortable for me as I expected it would be. My ring seemed to barricade the gap between us, until Edwin started to fidget.

"Abs, you really need to rethink what your priorities are in life," he blurted.

I looked at him, with anger swelling in my eyes, wondering where the hell that had come from. I quickly realized that he wasn't looking for a response. I wanted to scream at him, but instead I took a deep breath and cleared my head. *My priorities are in order.*

Edwin was staring out the window again, but that wasn't going to stop me from standing my ground.

"I'm sorry my priorities aren't what you want, Eddie. But that isn't my problem, is it?"

His eyes scanned over me then dropped to the floor. "Nope, I suppose that would make it my problem."

Great. Sitting with Aliah was bad enough. Now, I was sure to self-combust if I had to spend another hour next to Edwin. I clenched my fists and closed my eyes, hoping I could garner enough control to last the entire ride. Not a half hour later, I could feel Edwin's eyes reaching me again.

I didn't want to start another argument, but I couldn't take it anymore. "What?"

"I can't look at you?"

"No, Edwin. You can't. Not like that." My heart began to race.

"You're too good for me now that you're dropping anchor with Cam; is that it?"

"It's not like they're getting married," Jessica said, then slapped her hand over her big mouth.

"I knew it."

I shook my head. He didn't know. "Don't even. You don't get it."

"No, I think I do," he retorted, evidently convinced of his own smug delusions.

I nearly lost it. "Maddie. Pull over please." I narrowed blame-filled eyes at Edwin. "I need some air."

"What are you doing?" Edwin asked.

"You deaf? I need some air." I didn't want him to see me cry.

Maddie brought the car to slow stop and I stormed out into the snow, slamming the door shut on Edwin as he tried to follow me, nearly taking off his leg. I tromped down the desolate, snow-covered road and the silence swallowed me whole.

I stopped and zipped my jacket up to my chin to shake the chill that instantly overcame me; then I stuffed my trembling hands into my coat pockets to hide them from the frigid air. I took a deep breath and it misted before me on an exhale.

The crisp air helped to clear my head, to the point where I started to feel guilty for being so inconsiderate to Edwin. He was entitled to his opinion. I tugged my hood over my head and buried my tear-stained cheeks into the neck of my coat.

Edwin fled the car and followed the trail of small, boot prints, demolishing them with his own. I heard the snow crunching behind me. *I would recognize that casual, masculine approach anywhere.*

My cheeks were already frozen, and the north wind wasn't letting up. For that reason alone, I hoped Edwin would be short with me.

"I take it you got the nastiness off your chest. You didn't run away from me," Edwin harassed, stopping just behind my cold shoulder.

I peeked over at him, but kept my feet planted firmly in the snow bank. *Damn. Why did he have to look so attractive?* I stole my eyes back and stared down at the sparkling snow, his body language charming the boots off of me. "I'm sorry for being so mean," I said, with a whisper. "It's not entirely your fault."

The brisk wind whistled and I wondered if he had even heard me. That was until I realized that he was now standing at my heels.

"Not entirely?" he said. "Can't you just..."

"The answer is no," I snapped, afraid to hear what he had to say.

"You don't mean that," he said, resting his large, warm hand on my shoulder.

I spun around, knocking his hand off of me. My lashes fluttered and my eyes were met with his warm, flowing gaze. "All you have to say is: I accept your apology."

"Oh, is that it?" Edwin said. He smirked, loving the way I wriggled beneath his gaze. "That easy, huh? You don't want to hear how I set up this whole master plan to ruin your relationship with Cam, so I could swoop in and steal you up for myself?"

My jaw dropped and my eyes filled with panic. It couldn't be true.

"Yep. I helped that blonde girl with her boyfriend troubles and she was going to help me with mine. I guess I didn't work my angle hard enough."

I became disoriented from the rate of speed the conversation had turned on me. "The blonde girl was in on it? *You* did that?"

"It doesn't matter now. You're wearing his ring." His words were woeful, as he stared at the rock plastered to my forehead.

I shook my head, trying to put the pieces together. "You tricked me."

"Oh, come on; it was just some harmless fun." When he smiled and ran his tongue over his full, bottom lip, I knew he was recalling our long, drawn out kiss. "You didn't seem to mind it at the time." His pale lips curved into a deviously sexy smirk.

"Harmless fun? Where do you draw the line? This is my life you're toying with, Eddie."

His smile didn't budge. "How was I supposed to know you were going to plant one on me? The plan was ingenious and that part actually couldn't have worked out any better."

My lips parted, frustration feeding my anger. "I cannot believe you made a game of this, planting all these ridiculous feelings in my heart and ideas in my head. You've had it out for Cam since day one. And for what?" I looked to Edwin, demanding an explanation.

He just stood there, smiling.

Is he even listening to me? "You're just letting me harp, aren't you?"

"Yeah, you really need to get it out of your system. That's not healthy at all."

"Ugh!" I screamed.

"You can be frustrated with me all you want, but I can see there's more to it than that."

I felt like my world was being stomped on and I needed a distraction before I fell to pieces. I squeezed my eyes shut, but I couldn't close out the world. My head was on fire, though the rest of my body was numb from the cold. I wished I could numb the warm feelings I had for Edwin.

Out of nowhere, Edwin spoke; and it was as if he had plucked the thought straight from my brain. "You liked it."

"I don't know what you're talking about," I stammered.

"The kiss. You enjoyed it as much as I did."

I glared at him, vowing never to admit it.

He smirked, his confidence annoying me. "I knew it."

Maddie blasted on her horn, as her car slowly crept up next to us. I yanked the door open and slipped inside.

"Get over yourself," I snapped, as I squished as close to my door as humanly possible.

The rest of the ride passed rather quickly without any more arguments. Maddie dropped me off at Cam's house first and Edwin didn't ask any questions. He'd figure it out when I didn't come home tonight.

I pulled my bags to the front door and stood outside of it anxiously. *Do I knock?* It just didn't feel right letting myself in. Embarrassed that my friends got to witness my indecision, I knocked three times, turned the knob and pushed inside.

Cam rushed to the door, his bags already cleared from the entrance. "I didn't hear you pull up." He reached his arms out for a hug. "Everything okay?" he asked, noticing how I held on to him extra long.

I smiled and kissed him. "It is now."

CHAPTER FIVE

The first day back to work came and went without any natural disasters, but it was only a matter of time. I could sense it. Most of the staff had already gone home, when I finished talking to Maddie.

"Don't worry about Edwin. He's resilient. He'll bounce back," she told me. "He always does."

It surprisingly relieved some of my worry. "Thanks, Maddie. Have a good night."

"I will, once this little stinker stops kicking the crap out of me." She rubbed her round, baby belly and walked away smiling. "Night, Abby."

The rest of the office was dark, except for the light beaming from Cameron's office. I crept over to his room and peered around the corner to see if he was still busy. I watched him for a minute or so, admiring his unconditional effort and handsome features as he concentrated on whatever it was he was doing.

He had already done away with his constricting suit jacket and had rolled up his crisp white sleeves. I loved the way they bunched just above his elbows, slightly exposing his incredible arms. He continued to squint at the page, his forehead wrinkled in thought, his thumb pressed against those full lips. I debated stealing him from his work, because I had other less productive things in mind.

Then his chair squeaked. "Abby? Is that you?"

I froze in place, hoping that he hadn't actually seen me, but he swiftly dashed to his door and caught me in the act of spying.

"Hey. I was hoping it was you. Do you have a minute?"

"Sure," I muttered, worried that he was ready for that talk I'd been avoiding.

I pulled the door partly closed and followed him inside. He stood behind one of the arm chairs and held the back of it, hinting for me to sit. After I did, he returned behind his desk and leaned back in his chair. Despite seeing him sitting behind his thick, wooden desk, in a position of power, I suddenly felt like the one in control. *Why was I so turned on by that?*

He knew exactly what I was thinking and I held his restless stare as I stood up and rounded his desk. He didn't even flinch when I eased myself on top of him and straddled his lap, full mount. His baby blues electrified me, as he devoured my body with his devious gaze and erotic grin. I settled against his lap and could feel him launching beneath me.

He wove his fingers into my hair, goose bumps spreading across his arms, as I provocatively leaned into him. I drew my parted lips across his neck, my tongue wetting his heated skin until my teeth found his ear lobe and he let out a growl of masculine arousal.

My eyes flashed to the door, still held a crack open. I clutched on top of the hand that he had gripping his chair and lifted myself to my feet. "I'll be right back," I said, with a breath of seduction.

I swaggered toward the door to close it and gave it a little kick with my heeled shoe for visual effect. When the door slammed shut, I let out a devious giggle and then spun around to face him. I locked the door behind me, all the while flashing him a devilish smirk.

When I approached him, my heels clicked across his hard floor, until I was standing right in front of him. He watched with fascinated interest, as I wiggled out of my panties and kicked them aside. His gaze never left mine. I then gave him *the look*, his invitation to touch, but he didn't move. I spread my legs farther apart, as far as my skirt would allow, and I knew then that Cameron wouldn't be able to resist me for long.

When he raised his eyebrows, an electrifying shock surged through my body. Then he stood up from behind his desk and tossed his phone on top of it. I couldn't contain the sensations swirling around me. Before he could straighten himself, I was already pouncing on him like a wild animal.

I crashed against him, my mouth hot and heavy on his. The heat raging from his body was outrageous, so I ripped open his shirt to free the flames and yanked it over his shoulders and down his arms, pinning them to his sides.

He groaned, as I smoothed my hands up and down his chest and licked my tongue across it. While I devoured his rock-hard body, Cam managed to slip free of his shirt and lifted mine up and off me. I deftly unbuttoned his black slacks, ripped the zipper open and dropped them to his ankles together with his boxers.

I looked up at him with a ravenous need, as great as the sight right before my eyes. He answered to my urgency by hiking my long pencil skirt high on my thighs, lifting me into his strong arms and dropping me on top of him. My feminine gasp encouraged him, as he forced his pelvis forward, slamming into me. When I wrapped my legs around his waist, he sank deeper yet and growled as he moved inside of me.

Cameron's muscles were held taut and glimmered with perspiration, him being the only thing keeping us grounded in the middle of the room. With every flex of his hips, a jolt of pleasure streamed through me, until he had me bouncing on top of him with his hands on my hips, driving himself into me with a monstrous force.

Unable to stave off the mounting wave, Cam plowed on until he was stifling my squeals with an open mouth covering mine. Far from finished, still planted deep within me, he carried me to his firm, leather couch, as my insides continued to clench around his hardness. Cameron gently dropped me onto the smooth, leather seat and hovered mere inches over me, assessing my desire.

Still clutched to his shoulders, my eyes pleaded with him to come back, but I wasn't expecting him to rush deep inside of me the second he had covered himself with a condom. He drove so hard and deep that it jump started my senses and sent me into a flurry of awakened arousal. I couldn't restrain my pleasure, as rainbows meandered around us and fireworks splashed across my eyelids.

The louder I moaned, the harder he worked to please me, more and again. My next orgasm launched me into full-on dreamland and my eyes rolled into the back of my head as he found his release and exploded inside of me. His mouth found mine, his sweat-streaked chest pressed against me as he took what was his.

Watching him exhale so deeply, exhausted from our brisk lovemaking, only made me love him more. He made me feel so special. Wanted. Needed.

Cameron chuckled, breaking me out of my fantasy. "So much for that talk."

He dropped a wet, consuming kiss on my lips, then stood up from me. A cold breeze tingled across my moist, exposed skin. Not wasting any time, I pulled my skirt down, refastened my bra and slipped on my blouse. As I did up the top button, Cam pulled me back into his arms.

"We work well together."

"You call this work?" I teased, though he looked like he had just finished a very intense workout.

His hair was all sweaty and sexy. "I mean us, Abby. *We* work. I thought I had been in love before, but it felt nothing like this."

All I could do was sit there smiling and I couldn't knock the feeling of how fortunate I was to have this amazing man professing his love to me. I felt tears welling up in my eyes, as Cam lifted my hand and straightened my ring. In that moment, when my heart twitched with guilt, I knew that there were unresolved feelings for another man that I would have to unravel before we could spend the rest of our lives together.

Cam glanced at his watch, instantly breaking the intimacy of the moment. He dashed to his jacket, yanked it off the hanger and shrugged it on. Cam looked at his watch again. "Shit!"

"What's wrong?"

"My six o'clock is probably waiting in the lobby. I didn't realize the time." Cam straightened his tie and delivered a chaste peck to my lips. "We'll have to finish this later."

As I slipped out of his office discreetly, my legs trembled. The trembling would only get worse. I knew what the night had in store for me. I had to tell Edwin I was moving out.

Cameron stopped me before I made it to the lobby. "Hey," he called, from the boardroom door. "You'll need a key." He dangled one out to me. "I had it made this morning."

I smiled, softly. "I was just going to head over to my place to get some things and maybe grab a bite to eat."

"I can come with you," he said. "I shouldn't be too much longer here."

I peered over his shoulder, where the clients were waiting patiently for him to resume their meeting. "Take your time," I said. "I'll be fine. I can handle Edwin."

"I'd really like to come with you." He wasn't asking.

"Cam, we've discussed this before. Nothing's going to happen between me and Edwin. You have to trust me on this one."

Hesitant, he sighed. "I do trust you. It's him I don't trust." After a second of reluctance, he nodded at me. "Okay, but I'm only a phone call away if you need me."

I smirked as he struggled with his internal battle to order me to wait. "Thank you." After a chaste kiss, I rushed outside into the blizzard.

My emotions hooked me, just like the wind, and an unexpected gasp escaped my mouth as the first tear dripped from my eye. *What is wrong with me?* As I backed out of my parking spot, my tears streamed harder and I couldn't control the outrageous sobbing. Cam had let me go. So why was I such a blubbering mess? *He trusts me.*

But could I trust myself?

The icy road had a fresh coat of wet snow on top of it and I had to clasp both hands on the wheel just to keep it on the road. As I pulled down my street, I thought I was in the clear, but when I pressed on my brake to slow down for my driveway, the tires skidded against the slick road and my car slid out of control.

I slammed the brakes and jerked the wheel to avoid the oncoming hydro pole. After missing it by mere inches, the car stalled and skidded to a stop on the edge of road a few houses past mine. Unable to contain the agony bearing down on me, just thinking about asking for Edwin's approval of my new sleeping situation, I broke down. I hugged the steering wheel and rested my head against it. The cool leather felt nice against the boiling heat radiating from my forehead.

The tears came and I tried to wipe them away, but more took their place. I was in no shape to face Edwin right now. I flipped open my mirror and glared at my reflection. With red cheeks and black rimmed eyes, I scowled into the mirror, then slapped it shut and slammed the visor up. When I tossed down my tissue in the seat next to me, something out the window caught my eye. I froze in place when I spotted a black figure standing outside my passenger door.

Immobilized with fear, my eyes darted to the side. I watched the large man as he tried to peer through the tinted glass, with big hands cupped around his eyes like binoculars. I prayed that if I sat still enough the person might just leave. Then I questioned whether my doors were even locked. I was too scared to move, let alone hit the lock button. My breaths were short and raspy, as my mind ran through all the possible outcomes from this situation.

The man pressed his forehead to the window. "You gonna let me in or do I have to freeze out here some more?" the man yelped.

I turned my head and squinted through blurry eyes, then let out a foggy breath. "Eddie?" I hurriedly unlocked the door and he hopped in, the interior lights quickly fading out.

"I thought I saw you in here."

The car was dark, with only one street lamp nearby, but I couldn't hide my condition from Edwin. He knew me better than that. A state of unease was thick in the air. Edwin squinted at me and rested his hand on my arm.

"Are you okay?"

He always knew when something was wrong and, if I wasn't careful, he'd have me spilling my guts in no time. Instead of digging myself into a deeper hole, I opted for keeping my mouth shut.

He didn't take the hint. "You weren't answering your phone at work and you didn't leave a note at home. I was afraid you were hurt." His cold hand cupped my warm, wet cheek. "Are you?"

I shook my head no, with my lips pressed together to hold in a sob.

He studied my face, scrutinizing my every breath, then tucked a stray hair behind my ear. "I saw your car spinning out and I only thought the worst. You were sitting so still."

"I'm fine; just a little shaken."

"Glad to hear it," he said, sarcastically. "Too bad now I'm a fucking mess."

My heart flooded with relief as Edwin laid it on thick, with the what ifs and don't you dares, all while keeping his hands to himself. Instead of answering his ridiculous accusations, l just attacked him with a great big, bear hug. He was only wearing a long sleeve shirt and a toque, so I expected him to be absolutely freezing, but instead his arms were warm and affectionate.

As Edwin began to rub my back, I became more and more aware of how awkward it was becoming. I instantly released him from the death lock and he wasted no time getting out of the car. I watched him round the hood in mere seconds and open my driver side door.

"Move over. I'm driving."

I didn't have the energy to fight with him, as he scooped me out of the chair and placed me in the passenger seat. He quickly spun my car around and pulled it into our driveway.

"Why are you so upset?" he asked, as if it weren't eating away at him.

"I told you, Eddie. I'm fine."

He cast an assessing gaze over my muddled appearance. "You don't look fine."

How was I supposed to convince him, when I was actually so far from fine right now? In fact I was about as far away from fine as it got.

We walked to the house and he unlocked the door, letting me enter first. He followed me to the closet where we hung our coats in silence. He was being so reserved that it made me very nervous.

"I have to tell you something," I stuttered, hoping to pass it off as a response from the cold.

"Let me guess. You haven't eaten yet," he answered.

My stomach growled on cue, loud enough for him to hear, but I wouldn't let him control me that easily. "It's not that. It's important," I insisted, slamming my purse on the chair.

Edwin waved me off and walked away. "It can wait. I'm starving." He entered the kitchen and left me standing at the door.

I stomped after him and stopped abruptly, with my hands on my hips, keeping my distance. "I'm really not up for this right now, Eddie. Look at me. In case you haven't noticed, I'm a natural disaster."

He raised a sexy, arched brow. "Who said you needed to get all done up? We're not going anywhere. It's cuisine à la Edwin tonight, baby!"

That was enough to make me smile and, even though I tried so hard not to, my mouth puckered against my will.

"I'll take that as a yes." He pulled open the pantry door, searching for something to throw together. "Hmm. What's on the menu for tonight?" His hand scrubbed his soft, stubbly chin; the same chin that had scrubbed all over mine a few short nights ago.

As I walked away, I could hear the clatter and clanging of pots and pans and started to wonder how long his little stunt would take. It was late and I hadn't yet told him the point of my visit. Edwin just seemed happy to see me back home.

I raced up the stairs and hurriedly pulled together my favourite outfits from my closet. While Edwin cooked, I packed, knowing that the longer I took the more worried and suspicious Cameron would become. I had to do my best to hold onto his trust while I still had it.

After dinner, Edwin stared at me for a long while with a half-smile on his face. "You're beautiful," he said at last, breaking the long silence.

How can this man make me feel guilty for moving in with a man that I love? "I'm a mess. You don't have to try and sugar coat it. I'm not blind and you certainly aren't making this any easier on me."

He flashed a devilish smile. "I'll make it easy for you. Choose me."

"Hah!" And if I hadn't laughed, I surely would have cried. I had dreaded this day ever since the day I signed the deed to our house. My smile faded as I dropped my dishes into the sink.

I left the room and dove onto the couch, face down, wishing that I could bury myself from this existence. I heard Edwin's heavy footsteps approaching, then nothing. I peered over my folded arms to see where he had gone, only to realize that he was kneeling right next to me. I jolted back, startled by his closeness.

He rested his hand on my back and gently rubbed me. "I'm here for you when you're ready to talk."

I sighed and buried my face again. *Why does he have to be so good to me?* Knowing that pouting wasn't going to fix anything, I clambered to my feet and sat back down. Edwin slid up beside me and carefully placed his hand on my thigh.

"Eddie," I warned, taking his hand off my leg and placing it on his own.

"Oh, come on," he replied, playfully pushing me back down onto the sofa.

Before I could pull myself back up, I found him over me, with a very serious look on his face. Then he leaned in and kissed me before I even realized what was happening. My eyes had never closed, but that didn't stop him. It also didn't stop the tingle in my lips that lasted long after his mouth had left them.

I pried myself from his vice grip and pushed him off of me. "What do you think you're doing?"

He let me have the ounce of space I had placed between us. Then, the look I dreaded appeared on Edwin's face.

"This game of cat and mouse; it's not fair to Cam and it's not fair to you, Eddie. I'm so sorry..." I swallowed, but my voice still sounded hoarse. "... but I'm moving in with Cam."

A look of horror and disbelief formed instantly on his face, but Edwin quickly covered it up with anger. "No, you're not." He leapt to his feet and opened his mouth twice to say something, then just didn't. After burning me with a fiery glare he stomped angrily to the bottom of the staircase.

I knew the very moment when he found my packed bags, because he mumbled some obscenities then heatedly punched a hole through the drywall. Edwin stormed outside, into the blustery weather, without grabbing a jacket. His truck engine roared alive and he stepped on the gas, shooting out of the driveway sideways before speeding off.

I raced to my room to grab a few last minute things. The more I took now, the less of a chance I would find myself in this kind of predicament again. I dropped my last bag into my trunk and slammed it shut, relieved to be on my way. It was getting late and I was sure Cam would be getting worried by now, so I drove straight there.

Not feeling quite at home yet, I knocked on Cam's door before letting myself in. Hands full, I nudged the door open and dropped a pile of things into the entryway. To my surprise, I heard little footsteps galloping toward me and then Pheobe appeared, hobbling at full speed for a hug.

I went down to one knee and opened my arms for her. "You're back!"

"Abby!" Pheobe cheered, wrapping her arms around my neck.

I pulled her back to check her over. "Look at you. You must have grown two inches since I last saw you."

Pheobe shook her head no and giggled, with the biggest, most happiest smile on her face. I couldn't help but smile back.

"Cute pj's," I said, winking at her. She was wearing the adorable nightgown Cam and I had gotten her for Christmas.

"I love these ones. They're so fuzzy and warm," she said, hugging herself.

When I looked up at Cam, I didn't receive the same warm welcome I had been looking forward to. "Pheebs, can you please go brush your teeth and get ready for bed?" Cam asked.

"Oh, Dad. I want to stay up with Abby. Can I please?"

"Pheobe. Now. You have school tomorrow." Cam had made it clear that he was angry, but I found it hard to believe he could be mad at her. She had seemed so happy when I arrived.

Pheobe huffed and puffed, then grumpily made her way to the bathroom. With her out of the room Cameron's gaze fell to me. I felt more than a little uneasy, with the tension between us being at an all-time high.

"Is there something you need to tell me?"

"No," I answered; his heated stare causing me to speak more vulgarly than I intended.

Cam stroked his bristly jaw. "I just got off the phone with Ashley. She tells me she was driving past your house tonight and saw you making out with some guy in your car." Cam paced so close it hurt. "Please tell me she's lying, Abigail."

I could tell his pride had been wounded and he was furious with me. *He actually believed his back-stabbing sister, Ashley?* I scowled at him, aggravated with the thought. "You know what? I think we'd better have that talk now," I said. I had planned to tell him everything anyway. I only figured I could get through the god-damned door first.

He stormed away from me and sat down on the couch. The last thing I wanted right now was to be fighting, but I couldn't help the ache in my heart itching me to face the situation head on. Suddenly the phone rang. Cam slammed his fist on the coffee table, nearly breaking it in two, as Pheobe returned to the room.

"Daddy?" She looked so concerned that it broke my heart.

Cam narrowed his eyes at me. "I'm going to put Pheobe to bed. Why don't you get the phone? Then we'll talk." His voice had softened a bit, but I had to believe it was only for Pheobe's sake.

Not wanting any further confrontation, I hurried to the phone and answered quickly. "Hello?"

"Hey, it's me."

"Edwin?" I said, my voice scratchy and low.

"No, the milkman. Yeah, it's me."

"I can't believe you're calling me here; especially tonight." I flashed an anxious glance down the hall. Cameron didn't materialize.

"Just let me say my part and then I'll leave you to do whatever it is that you do over there." He sounded calm; too calm for the little time that had passed since he had taken off.

The words had left my lips before I could think them through. "Make it quick."

"I think you're taking things too fast with Cam. You need to slow it down a bit. You don't really want to move in with him. If you want me to tone it down, I will. But you're making a huge mistake."

"If you're worried about how this will affect our arrangement with the house, don't. I'll still pay for half of the mortgage and taxes. You'll just have to pick up the utilities."

"That's not it and you know it. Don't do it, Abs." His voice was strong and thick with emotion.

I hung up the phone, stunned by his orders. My hand clung to the receiver with a death grip and I stared at its base, waiting for it to ring again. It didn't.

Cameron walked into the room observing me in my frozen state. "Who was that?"

I swallowed the lump from the back of my throat. "Edwin."

"What did he want?" he asked, his voice cool and assessing.

"To tell me what a big mistake I'm making moving in with you."

Cameron nodded, like he wasn't surprised. "And what did you tell him?"

"Nothing. I hung up on him."

Cam's face didn't hint as to what he was thinking, but he swiftly approached me and wrapped his arms snugly around my waist. He tucked my head gently on his shoulder and I nuzzled into him.

"I'm sorry for taking Ashley's word," he whispered, next to my ear. "I should have given you the benefit of the doubt. Can you forgive me?" He pulled back and pressed his forehead against mine, our noses touching, his breath warm on my lips. "Please?"

My heart fluttered at his passionate pleading. I couldn't resist him another second. I tilted my head and softly brushed my lips against his. Once. Twice. Electricity passed through every soft touch, reigniting my desire for him.

Cameron exhaled a deep breath, dousing the flames running across my body. "Now that we have that out of the way, what is it you needed to tell me?"

CHAPTER SIX

I took a seat on the edge of the bed and twiddled my thumbs, procrastinating. "Why don't you go first?"

"Alright. It's about Pheobe," Cameron said.

My heart squeezed, worried that it was a bad thing. My hand rested over my heart, as I placed my other trembling hand on his knee.

"I had a talk with her about you moving in." He paused and my heart stopped. "Of course she's ecstatic about it."

Relief settled into my bones, making my limbs feel like noodles, my heart pattering at a terrifying pace. Then he spoke again and it terrified me.

"I've done a lot of thinking lately. When I ask you to marry me, and trust me I will ask you again, I would love for you agree to adopt Pheobe as your own."

My eyes grew wide and I held my breath, every emotion crashing together as I considered what he had just proposed.

"I know it may be premature and maybe a little sudden," he said, "but I think that Pheobe would love nothing more than to have a mother figure in her life. If that's something you'd be willing to consider, then I think it would make both her, and me, very happy."

"Wow. What can I say? I'm shocked; honoured, but shocked."

His thumb brushed softly over my knuckles. "I don't need your answer now. We can take it one step at a time. But I just wanted you to know where I see things going. If you ever think you're getting in too deep, you need to tell me." He rested his hand on top of mine and stared me in the eyes, his expression turning more serious. "You said you weren't kissing Edwin in your car and I believe you."

I swallowed, wanting to make myself clear, so there was no confusion later. "Edwin was in my car, and he did try to make a move on me after dinner."

Cameron winced, but squeezed my hand to stop me from explaining further. "Did you kiss him?"

"No."

"Then I don't want to hear another word about it."

"But you need to know he did kiss me," I blurted. "I stopped him though, and I told him how it was going to be from now on."

"And how is that?" Cam asked, an angled smile lighting his handsome face.

"I told him I'm moving in with you and that I need some space. He's pretty hard headed, but I think he finally got the point when I hung up on him tonight."

Cam smiled, and the twinkle returned to his eyes, just in time for my turn.

"I guess what I have to say is similar in nature. It's about blended families," I stated, drumming up some courage.

"You're going to have to elaborate on that one," Cam said, smirking.

"Babies," I blurted.

Cameron's eyes popped open and his mouth rounded out, his stunned expression rather disturbing. "Oh!"

"I've always wanted kids of my own and, while I would love to be that mother figure for Pheobe, it's just not the same. As long as I'm physically able, I'd like to make a baby of my own. Or two."

Cameron's mouth held that puckered O and his eyes drove through me like a dagger to my heart.

"Do you think Pheobe would be okay with having a little brother or sister?" More pressing, how do *you* feel about it? I was too petrified to ask.

"I can't," he said, releasing my knee, breaking all physical contact with me. "I'm sorry. I should have said something sooner."

My heart skipped a beat then began to pound hard and fast. "What?" I couldn't even form a sentence, my tears clouding my thoughts.

"I can't have any more children, Abigail," he said, spelling it out for me.

"You're impotent?" I blurted, my disappointment obvious.

"No. I have no problem getting it up. But after Tessa died, I couldn't imagine ever bringing another child into this cruel world."

"And now?" I breathed, ready to shed my tears.

"I've been fixed. Problem solved. Now I can never do to another child what I've done to Pheobe."

I gasped for a breath, unsure how I was supposed to take the news. "You haven't done anything but love her, Cam. And if you truly feel guilty, don't you think leaving her as an only child is equally as wrong?"

He closed his eyes and shook his head, placing a difficult distance between us emotionally. "You don't understand."

He was right. I didn't understand. I didn't understand why he didn't tell me this before asking me to marry him. I didn't understand why he thought I wouldn't want a child of my own. And I didn't understand why he was still so grief-stricken, that he couldn't bear to bring another child into this existence.

I had fallen for Cameron hard and fast and his daughter was wrapped right up in that ball of mistakes. The happiness and pride that I had felt when Cam suggested I adopt Pheobe had swelled my heart to an immeasurable size, but I still couldn't imagine a life without bearing my own child.

I was too exhausted to think about it anymore, so I dropped it. I literally zipped my lips shut, plunked my head down onto the pillow and let the tears stream, complete with unattractive sobs. My heart stung with the painful knowledge that I would never have a child of my own blood.

Cam swathed his arms around me and whispered his apologies in my ear. He truly did sound sorry, but I was more sorry; sorry I had made the same mistake twice. Edwin had only said *not now*. An icky feeling rummaged through my innards with the realization that Cam was saying *not ever*.

That night I fell asleep sobbing in Cameron's arms, mourning the child that I would never have.

A heavy depression had settled over me and even after all the time that had passed, it hadn't changed a thing. Day after day I tried to stave off the loneliness I felt, but nothing could take my mind from it. I pushed away all of my friends and it wasn't long before Aliah grew tired of my moaning and stopped calling altogether.

It was too difficult to see Maddie with her growing belly and Hunter with his glee about the gymnastics his child was performing before his very eyes. My jealousy raged silently and I felt myself pulling away from any and all sources of socialization.

I stared out the car window at the dreary, winter sky, as Cam drove us to a local video store one night. "This is just what we need," Cam said, certain it would brighten my rotten mood.

I didn't respond. Instead I turned my gaze to the mirror on the side of the car. Pheobe stared out the window too, equally as lifeless. She looked miserable. I was bringing everyone down.

Cam had tried to explain to her why I was feeling the way I was, but she was much too young to understand. Nobody could understand.

As we strode toward the new releases Pheobe ran ahead to check out the video games. We stopped in front of the tall wall of blu-rays and Cam read the backs, likely in search of a movie that wouldn't set me off. I was uninterested in choosing a movie. Instead, the young kids nosing around the bottom shelves for their own show claimed my attention.

A little boy, with shaggy brown hair, who couldn't have been more than two years old, had his finger in his nose. He came out with a huge booger, much too big for a boy his size, and looked around for a place to wipe it. I zipped open my purse looking for a tissue, but it was too late.

Cam was standing closest to the toddler, and the boy grabbed onto his leg, wiping his snotty little finger all over Cam's pants. Cam smiled at me and patted the cutie pie on the head, but the boy didn't budge from Cam's leg. I hadn't laughed in weeks, but the fact that Cam hadn't even noticed what had happened, just made me hysterical.

A few bystanders flashed me a curious glance, together with Cameron, but he seemed the most surprised to see me smiling. I couldn't stop laughing and when the little girl next to me realized what I was laughing about, she started to giggle too. She pointed at Cam's pants and covered her mouth as she squealed about it

"Ewww! Look at his pants!" she chirped.

An older boy, with a healthy round belly, laughed next to her. Then he started slapping his knee. "Ha, ha, ha!"

When Cameron finally realized what the hoopla was all about, he didn't seem very impressed. "Aww, that's just great!" he said, looking at me sternly.

Cam looked so adorable, with the cute, little boy still clung to his leg. I imagined what my little boy would look like attached to his thigh and his anger couldn't even phase the fantasy that I had created for myself. I tried to stop snickering, but I couldn't.

"It's really not a big deal," I said, with a huge smile on my face.

The mother of the children came running up to Cam to pry her little guy off of him. "I am so sorry. He just snuck away. You look a lot like his father," she explained, scooping the the boy into her arms.

Her daughter pointed out the booger and she blushed, biting her lip, as she wrestled a tissue out of her purse. "Here's a Kleenex."

Cam didn't accept it, and so I did for him, wiping the sizable nugget from his pants.

"Again, I do apologize. Kids," she stated.

I nodded, smiling. "Thank you. Really, it's nothing."

Cam continued brooding silently.

The mom smiled at me. "You must have kids."

I pressed my lips together in disappointment. "I don't, actually. But I've always dreamed of having them."

Cameron flashed an annoyed glance at me and my misery returned with a vengeance. He was being a total jerk. I would have thought that, being a single father, he would have been a little more forgiving.

The woman rested her free hand on my shoulder. "Well *I think* you'll make a good mother someday," she said, before flashing a sharp eye at Cameron.

The fact that this woman could read into our situation so easily gave me a horrible feeling in the pit of my stomach. The woman hiked her son up higher on her hip, then turned on her heel to head back to the children's section.

After the lady walked off, Cam whispered in my ear. "That's exactly why I don't want to have any more kids."

He had to know that would hurt me on so many levels. And if it weren't for Pheobe coming back to my side, I would have shared a few choice words with him.

Later that night, after suffering through most of the movie, Cam carried Pheobe to bed. When he returned, he could tell that I was done with it. I felt like a useless shell of a person and couldn't stop thinking about it. I was put on this earth for a reason: to reproduce. I struggled with defining the point to life, if I didn't make babies.

Cam watched my eyes as he turned off the TV. "What's the problem now?"

I turned my glare on him. "As if you don't know."

"Please tell me this isn't about the baby thing again. It's all you ever talk about and it's really starting to test my patience."

"Why? I'm not entitled to have feelings too?" I tried to stay hushed, but it was difficult in my angered state.

Cam seemed very distant, but he was sitting right next to me. "I didn't say that."

"You might as well have." I forced him to look at me, to see just how serious I was. "I've dreamt my whole life about having babies and raising a little person that I can say is a part of me. I want that, Cameron. Don't you see?"

"Yeah, well, forget it. Been there, done that. It's not gonna happen. Not as long as you're with me," he added, with such ease that it hurt.

"See, there's the problem! You've already experienced all that and you refuse to look at it from my perspective. This is really important to me, Cam. I'm trying, I mean really trying, to get over it. I don't know if it's something I can give up."

"You don't mean that," he said, understanding the consequences of what I was saying.

A tear fell down my cheek. "I do." I started to wonder if he truly loved me. If he did, wouldn't he at least consider having his surgery reversed to try to make a family with me?

"It's late," he said. "Why don't we go to bed and talk about this in the morning with clear heads."

As if another night would change anything. "My head is clear, Cameron. But I'll do it. For you." I let out a long, slow breath. "I'm telling you now, though, it's not going to change how I feel."

I decided to go along with Cam as he drove Pheobe to her school. It was rather sunny for a cold, February day and it gave me hope that my mood might follow suit. I waited in the car, as Cam brought Pheobe inside. It was then, watching him holding Pheobe's hand, with her smiling up into his eyes, that I admitted: I *have to* have my own baby.

When Cameron rounded the hood of the car, he watched me intently. After sliding into his seat, he cupped my cheek and gave me a brief kiss. His eyes begged me to tell him what was wrong. *He didn't want to hear what I had to say.*

Even I was getting tired of rehashing over it, but I had to tell him the truth. "I'm having a hard time getting over what happened last night. How you treated that little boy."

He searched my eyes, then dropped his hand to put the car in gear. "Didn't you see what he did? And his mother, she was no better." He glared out the windshield.

"What is your problem, all of a sudden? You're so great with Pheobe and I thought you loved kids." I raised my voice and I couldn't believe the emotions it evoked.

"I love Pheobe and I do like kids, but that doesn't mean I want another one. I know that's what this is all about," he said, waving his hand over the steering wheel.

I didn't reduce my volume. "Even if it means losing me?"

Cam turned his head and shot me a fathomless, blue glare. "Are you breaking up with me? I thought we made a promise."

That look stabbed through my heart. "The whole point to my existence is to bear children, Cameron, and you want to take that opportunity away from me." My voice softened, as I lost my fuel.

He tried to soothe me with his mesmeric voice. "You won't be without a child. We'll have Pheobe."

My anger stewed, as we pulled into the parking lot at work. "It's not the same." As soon as the car stopped, I got out, slammed the door shut and stomped into the office, scowling. I couldn't face him. Right now, I only wanted to shake some sense into him.

"Abby, wait!"

I had a good head start and, though he jogged after me, there was no way I would let him catch up. I thrust open the lobby doors and dashed inside. Taylor greeted me when I stormed in, but I was too preoccupied with myself to respond.

Cameron followed behind me. "Sorry about that," he said to her. "She's having a rough morning."

I was out of sight, but not far enough off to be deaf to his remark. "Speak for yourself!" I shouted, putting the entire office on notice not to mess with me this morning.

Cam came up behind me and gently grabbed my arm. "Can we please leave this conversation for home?" he asked, with harsh, accusatory eyes.

I yanked my arm from his grasp and lowered my voice. "Don't worry. I'll be professional. It'll be as though that conversation never happened," I said, bitterly.

He let out a breath of exhaustion. "Please don't do this, Abby. I don't want to fight."

"Give me a family and the fight is off. It's as easy as that." I had made my point loud and clear to all that listened.

"We'll talk about this tonight," Cam said, warning me that our argument was far from over. He spun on his heel and disappeared around the corner.

After glowering at the wall for a few more seconds, I turned to find Owen standing there.

"Everything alright out here?" he asked.

"It is what it is," I said. *None of his damn business*. I walked straight to my desk, leaving him standing there, confounded by my behaviour.

After a silent dinner, Pheobe went to her room to play. Even she didn't want to be around me. I couldn't stomach the thought of suffering through another week like this, and it was devastatingly clear that none of us would be able to tolerate it much longer.

Cameron was a handsome, caring man and an amazing father. There were plenty of women who threw themselves at him every day and they wouldn't give a second thought about giving up having children to be with him. But I wasn't one of those women. I could see it in his eyes, when he decided it was time to get back into it.

"This isn't over, Abigail. Not even a little bit." He sighed. "Don't think I'm going to quit on you like that, because I'm not. I don't give up that easily." He grabbed onto my hand and pulled me into a hug that was so tight my lungs became starved for air.

"Are you saying you'll give me a baby, after we marry?" I whispered.

He replied, softly. "I didn't say that."

I swallowed back my disbelief and looked up into his tired eyes. "Cam, I love you so much, and I've found the more I learn about you, the more there is to love. But this? This really hurts. And I can't get over it."

"You took my ring," he reminded me, but pointing fingers wasn't going to fix anything.

I couldn't help but return the jab. "That's because you promised me endless happiness, and at that time I actually believed it could be true. I want to know what it feels like to have a baby growing inside me, Cam." I rested my hand on my flat belly.

Cameron stole my hand and held it in his. "I know you. I could still make you happy."

I shook my head to disagree. "You don't know a thing about me. Because if you did, you would realize how important this is to me."

"I know that I love you, Pheobe loves you, and you love us back. Isn't that enough?"

I fought the tight feeling in my chest as a tear streaked down the side of my face. "No. No, Cam. It's not enough." I cried, softly, unable to bring myself to make eye contact with him.

It felt like my swollen heart was slowly oozing toward my throat, making it difficult to breathe. There was no stopping the imminent doom that was closing in around me. I gasped for air, but sucked in a mouthful of fear instead, not knowing what to do next. "I should go." I wanted to tear out of the room, but my legs were so wobbly.

Cameron didn't move. "You said you would never leave me."

I stopped at the door, unlocked it and turned back to him, tears falling steadily down my face. He approached me slowly and held my blurry gaze.

"It's not the end until I say it is." He reached by me and relocked the door, blocking my only exit. Then someone knocked at it. He reluctantly opened the door and found his mother waited patiently on the other side of it.

"Is Pheobe ready?" she asked, ignoring the nature of our dispute. "I told her yesterday I would take her to the store for a special treat tonight."

"I'm sorry, Mom. I totally forgot. Come on in." Cam started to walk down the hall and hollered out to Phoebe.

"I hope I'm not interrupting anything," Sadie said to me, acknowledging my fragile state.

"It's okay. We're just trying to work some things out."

Distracted by the glimmering rock dangling from my finger, she picked up my trembling hand, inspected it and smiled at me like only a mother could. "I'm sure you'll be able to work it out."

Pheobe came speeding down the hall. "Grandma!" After a squeeze around her thighs, Pheobe happily slipped on her hat and mitts with her grandmother's assistance and together they stepped out into the darkness.

"Be careful," Cam hollered after them, then closed the door.

The house fell quiet; so quiet, it was suffocating me.

"Where were we?" Cam asked, pinning me with his sardonic gaze.

I was just leaving. "I believe you were just telling me that it's not over."

His stormy eyes confirmed that story.

Damn him. Cam had a way of making me feel however he wanted me to feel. There was no refuting that I was incredibly attracted to this man. Of all the things I could think of in a moment like this, there was only one factor that hung in the forefront of my mind: *he is damn good in bed.* And in the shower. And on the table. And wherever he wanted me at this very moment.

With all of the barriers dividing us lately, I couldn't turn away his silent invitation to reconnect. I pounced on him, full of emotion, and he was more than willing to accept my desperate mouth, drinking from his lips and breathing from his lungs.

Cam eased me to the floor where he urgently showed me just how good we fit together. Then he stopped, as he nearly gave me a gift I would have loved to accept from him before the surgery that stole his lively essence.

Reigning in his emotion-filled desire, he lifted me from the floor and into his arms. He carried me to the bedroom, laid me out on his bed, and showed me all the other reasons why I should stay. While my every sexual desire had been fulfilled, that was not and had never been the problem. Yes, it was the best I'd ever had; but it was hardly enough to make our relationship work as is.

Lying there, curled up on his bare chest, I considered how much he loved his daughter. If anyone could convince him to have another baby it was her.

Yes. There are ways I can change his mind.

CHAPTER SEVEN

Deciding to tone it down for a few days, to let things settle and give us all a break, was having a positive effect on everyone. Everyone but me. While I appeared to be calm and collected on the outside, it was only because inside I was secretly crafting my master plan to convince Cam to give me a family.

Throughout the work day he continually, nonchalantly, brought up things to show why having another child is not such a good idea. Every time he made a stupid comment, I just grinned and nodded, totally ignoring it. My mind had not changed. It would never change. I would have my baby, with him or with another man who understood how important it was to me.

Another late work night just added to my stress. While sitting in the boardroom with Cam and Owen, I acted busy though wholly distracted with my thoughts. When Cam's cell started to ring, it gave me reason to take my eyes off the useless scribbles on my page. Then concern spread across his face, and I thought the worst.

"Has there been an accident?" Owen asked him, feeding off of my anxiety.

Cam shuffled his papers together. "It's the babysitter. She says Pheobe needs me." He picked up his things, rounded the table and kissed my temple. "I'll see you at home."

Cam blasted out of the room before I could even say goodbye. You could cut the atmosphere with a knife. Getting anymore work done was unlikely. Owen turned to me, as if he had something important to say.

"That was odd. At least now I've got you all to myself."

Stunned, eyes wide with horror, I watched Owen slide his chair closer to me. When he rested his hand on mine, it should have been creepy, but instead I felt cherished.

"I know it's best to keep our relationship professional, but, but..." He paused; not hesitant, just choosing his words carefully. "I can't imagine a world without your babies in it."

I suddenly found the energy to pull my hand away when my mouth dropped open. *Did he just ask me to make babies with him?*

"Cam told me that you want to have kids and he doesn't. He's really struggling with it because he doesn't want to lose you. But I've known Cam for a long time and he's not going to change his mind on this one, Abby." Owen watched me and repeated it, as if reading my mind. "Trust me. He won't change his mind."

"You can't know that," I snapped, not wanting to believe what I already knew to be true.

"I do. And I know what I have to do." The brief silence did nothing for me to prepare for Owen's honest eyes. "I can give you the babies you've always wanted. You can have as many as you want." He was being very serious and somehow sweet, but it didn't stop me from responding with a full body shudder.

"Let me get this straight. You want to make babies with me?"

"Yes. Exactly," he replied, matter-of-factly. "For you."

"Owen," I said, with pause. "You are very sweet - a good friend - but you must know that I'm not *in love* with you. I love you more like a brother and I am deeply in love with Cameron."

"Forget about Cam. You could learn to love me like that. It could work."

I giggled out of anxiety, though I knew it was inappropriate. "Owen..."

He pressed his fingers to my lips. "Not another word." Before I could realize what was going down, he attacked me with an awkward kiss.

Though he tried so hard to make it meaningful, I felt nothing. Looking into his desperate, hazel eyes, I wondered if what he was proposing was so terribly wrong. Edwin wouldn't give me what I wanted. Cameron couldn't. We'd both get a loving family out of the deal. Could I learn to love him?

No! What was I saying? I shook my head and closed my eyes. I couldn't live without Cameron, could I?

The room was soundless for a long minute and my mind went blank. Black. Empty. Soon the silence ambushed me with emotion. When I opened my eyes, Owen was staring at me, analysing my every expression. Overcome with nothing but guilt, I pushed my chair back, rolling myself a few feet away from him. I could tell from his expression that he understood my new behaviour.

"Please don't do that ever again," I said, with pain soaking every word. "This never happened."

Owen – my boss - nodded with understanding and wiped all emotion from his face. "I'm sorry. It won't happen again. I just," he paused and sighed. "I had to try. We could be great together, you know? I want children too and I had planned to have a couple of them by now. There would be lots of love. You would love me for giving you children, Abigail. I know it."

I lowered my head and pressed my fingers across my forehead. "I seriously appreciate your sincerity, but it's just not going to happen."

Emotional pain was etched in Owen's expression, wrinkling his typically smooth forehead. "Maybe now's a good time to call it a night."

"Yeah, I think we've had enough craziness for one day."

When I got home, I let myself in and found Pheobe and Cam sleeping snuggly in her bed. I headed back to Cam's room and shut the door behind me. I ran a bath in the ensuite and pulled out the phone, deciding it was time to make things right with Aliah. I dialed her up and she answered on the first ring.

"Hey. You up for a bitch-fest?"

"Absolutely," she answered. "I thought you'd never ask."

"Just so you know, I plan to do most of the bitching. But you can add in your two cents whenever you want."

"Bring it."

"Let me start by saying I think I'd rather fall on a knife than lose this debate with Cameron. No, I refuse to lose. It's the very reason for my existence."

"Okay, what about a knife?" Aliah asked, confused. "You aren't going all suicidal on me are you?"

I ignored her ridiculous question, feeling more sure of myself now than ever. "I really believed that Cameron was the one, but he's being super difficult about the baby thing. I'm finding it hard to justify staying with him if he refuses to have a family with me, when I rejected Edwin last summer for the very same reason. I have to convince him."

"He's really that sure he doesn't want another kid?" Her disbelief startled me.

"Let's just say a doctor's taken care of that decision for him. I swear life would be so much easier if I had never met Cam at all."

"Yeah, but if he came to you right now and said *let's make babies*, you'd be all over him and then live happily ever after."

"I wish."

Hunter was in the background. "Who are you talking to?" he asked Aliah.

"Abby. She's going to break up with Cam."

"Aliah! I never said that," I corrected, but Hunter couldn't hear me.

"You didn't have to. But at the end of the day, you're the one who has to live with yourself."

I glanced at the closed bathroom door. "I don't want to leave, but he's making it hard to stay. He has to change his mind."

"You can tell yourself whatever you need to, but I can't see it happening."

"Thanks for the encouragement," I moaned. "I'm sure Edwin will have some *encouraging words* for me too."

"Don't you dare," Aliah warned. "You steer clear of Edwin. That's the last thing you need right now. If you want to discover yourself again, then do it. But do it yourself. If you want Cam, then keep Cam."

"You're right."

"I'm always right."

"Don't listen to her," Hunter hollered. "She lies."

"Hunter! You stop that right now," Aliah yelped, in my ear.

"It sounds like you've got your hands full," I said, smiling. "I'll let you go."

"Hope you figure things out. Now I'm gonna go beat up Hunter for being such an ass. Laters."

I hung up the phone feeling a lot better about things. No matter how mad I was at Cameron for not wanting children, I hadn't stopped loving him, and he wouldn't be the man I fell in love with if he didn't stand his ground.

It was difficult, but I managed to get through the next morning; even with Cameron's hackles raised the entire time. I stared at the clock on my computer, waiting for lunchtime to arrive. I planned on doing lunch somewhere. Anywhere but there.

As the clock flashed twelve, I reached for my bag and when I spun around to leave, Edwin was standing there with his jacket on. "Hey!"

My breath hitched. "Oh! Hey, Eddie."

"Do you have plans for lunch?" he asked, all bundled up in preparation for the winter wonderland outside.

"Umm," I mumbled, as I tried to think of a good excuse to stay out of trouble. "Uhh," I said as I struggled to come up with anything worth saying. "Nope. I guess I don't." I yanked on my jacket and did up the buttons, steadying my trembling hands.

"I'm heading out to Jaci's and wanted to see if I could bring you something back. But since you don't have any plans, you might as well come with me."

"I don't know." I really, *really* shouldn't.

"Come on," he coaxed. "I promise, no trouble."

Leaving with Edwin would spell trouble, and yet I couldn't stop the words from exiting my lips. "I'm starving and I haven't had Jaci's Almond Soo Guy in months." My brain must have been starving too, because I clearly hadn't thought of the consequences of our *friendly* lunch date.

"Let's do it then," Edwin said, showing way too much enthusiasm, as he led the way to his truck.

He played nice for a change and with a full belly, all seemed right in the world. When I returned to work after lunch, Cam didn't show the same enthusiasm. Now, even though I hadn't yet shared Owen's proposition with Cam, I had to deal with his concerns about sharing me with Edwin too.

The drive home was silent, but I was getting used to that these days. There was always something, and it always stemmed from the same things: Edwin and babies.

To add to the trouble, I told Cam about the past twenty-four hours. The last thing I needed was him to believe I couldn't be trusted. To my surprise, he dropped the Edwin thing relatively quickly, totally overcome with irritation from Owen's actions. His annoyance began to swallow his features, his face turning dark and mean.

After dropping Pheobe off to her art class, I kicked my boots off and settled down for a fight. I patted Cam's arm to calm him, but he was seeing red and started to pace the living room.

"Please calm down," I pleaded. "It was only a friendly gesture."

His face looked hard and cold. "Why should I calm down? I knew that bastard was going to make a move on you. I warned him. I fucking warned him!"

Everything started spiralling out of control. Cam took off toward the door.

"Stop! What are you doing?" I squealed, making my fear known.

"What's it look like I'm doing? I'm going over to Owen's house to kick the shit out of him."

"Cam, you don't want to do that."

"Uh, yeah. I definitely do."

"Please don't," I begged.

"Why? Do you love *him too* now?" He swung his sarcasm at me and I took the blow straight to my heart.

I was crushed and it was like my chest had caved in and punctured my lungs. I stormed past him and slammed one foot into my boot. "That's it! I'm leaving. For real this time!"

Tears flooded my eyes before I could jam my other foot into my boot. It had felt as though Cam had ripped my life out from under me and left me dangling by the ankle. I couldn't bear to hang around and assess the damage. I whirled away from him and stepped toward the door, but suddenly he was just there.

"Wait. This is not how it ends," he said softly, turning on the charm. "I'm sorry. That was uncalled for."

I swiped the back of my hand across my damp cheek and snuffed unattractively, squinting at him through weary eyes.

Cam wrapped his hands firmly around my upper arms and pleaded with a mesmeric voice. "I love you. I'm just so afraid of losing you."

I blinked away another tear and shook my head, trying to clear my mind. Maybe if he didn't smell so incredibly good it would have been easier to break away and move one foot after the other.

"I love you too, Cam. But we can't keep on like this. This tension between us is killing me, and it's no good for Pheobe either."

"I want you to be happy. It's just..." he broke off, then took a deep breath. "We're good," he said, as if he were trying to convince himself.

Neither of us were convinced.

I managed to press out a smile, but the edges of my lips trembled and it almost hurt to keep it up. "Goodnight, Cam. I will see you tomorrow." With that I pulled away from his hold and he let me go.

When he spoke next, it was as quiet as a whisper. "Don't give up on us."

I slipped on my jacket, slung my purse over my shoulder and turned the icy doorknob. "I never did," I breathed, then walked out the door into the lonely chill of the night.

I felt his desperate gaze scorching my path, but I started my car and left without turning back. I made it half way home before I relived the sting from when Cam made the less than gentle suggestion that I might have a thing for Owen. I knew in my heart that his warning had nothing to do with Owen. *He thinks I'm still in love with Edwin. How could he think that?*

My tears froze to my cheeks, as I zoomed into my driveway and parked my car. I squinted my eyes, in no shape to face my nightmare, but Jenny magically appeared in the seat next to me and made no move to leave me alone.

"You are not here right now," I said, not expecting a reply.

"Oh, I'm here alright, sister. So listen up, and listen good. Stay away from Edwin."

"This isn't happening," I told myself, but I knew it truly was. "You died when you were six."

"And I've been with you ever since. I know that if it were me that had survived the crash, Edwin would have been mine. You don't love him the way I do. It should be me."

"Leave Edwin out of this," I ordered, trying to steer her away from him.

"Oh, but he is involved, whether you like it or not. And you will listen to me."

"And if I don't?"

She shrugged her dainty shoulder, as though she could actually be considered meek or mild. "Tessa's a good example of what will happen if you try to mess with me."

She glanced out the passenger window, without displaying an ounce of emotion."

"No," I cried, softly.

"I had to take care of her. How else was I going to get Cameron to come back to his home town? Pheobe's lucky I was in a good mood that night. I would've liked to take care of her too."

"No," I whispered again, distraught by the entire notion. *Pheobe's mother had died because of me.*

"It had worked like a charm though, didn't it?" she asked, pleased with herself. "It took a little longer than I expected, but I lured him here; to you. I thought it was in the bag."

"What does Cameron have to do with this?"

"You seriously haven't figured that out already. Oh, Abby. I've given you too much credit. Let's just say, you didn't meet by chance. When I discovered him some six years ago, I knew he was just the man for you. I may have had to take care of his wife, but they were on the outs anyway."

I choked on a breath, suddenly feeling very ill. The vomit reached the back of my throat, but I swallowed it down.

"What's the odds that I would find him on our eighteenth birthday? It was so perfect. I took it as a sign. He was the one," Jenny said.

Tears flooded steadily down my face, but I was unable to vocalize my emotion, only listening as the puzzle put itself together.

"That Pheobe, she's a fighter. I thought for sure I would've taken her by now, with all of her *accidents*. You would've thought after the river accident, her fall over the balcony would've done her in."

"Stop!" I screamed, my desperation echoing through the car.

"Oh, you don't want to hear about the others?"

I sobbed, unsure whether I could handle anymore, but she didn't wait for my approval.

"I knew Tanner Bradshaw was a long shot, but he did look totally hot on the beach. I couldn't believe you nixed him so fast. You really are a picky one. I had to bring Wes in, just in case Cam wasn't going to work out for the long haul."

I began to wonder if my entire life had been all planned out by Jenny. "And Spencer?" I asked, desperate for answers.

"No. You found that one on your own. I knew he was all wrong for you, but at least it killed some time for Cameron to breakdown and move back here."

I glared at Jenny, as she stormed me with her secrets. "Why are you doing this?"

"I already told you. Edwin's mine. Leave him alone and I'll leave you alone. Don't, and you'll be putting *everything* you know and love at risk. Your choice," she stated, then vanished in a pool of black, swirling fog.

At the rate my head was spinning, I figured it must have been all in my head. I buried my face in my hands in an attempt to comprehend what I had just learned, but I was so incredibly dizzy. With a deep breath, I tried to grasp reality, only to catch Jenny disappearing into the shadows of my yard, her eyes flashing red.

Feeling at a loss for security, I hurried into my dark, empty house. I took my stairs with a running leap and closed my bedroom door behind me.

Relying on the confines of my own room, to stave off the horrid feelings looming over me, I crawled into my bed and hugged my pillow. It was so quiet that I couldn't fend off my loneliness, and it only got worse by the time I heard a door close downstairs. I buried my face in my soft, fragrant pillow and hoped that it had muffled my sobs enough so Edwin couldn't hear me.

If he *had* heard me, he didn't do anything about it. He probably didn't even care. I vowed I would get it out of my system tonight, so I could have a fresh start in the morning. I fell asleep with tears still pooling in my eyes.

I awakened from a deep slumber, unsure about how much time had passed. I tried to stretch out my arms to let out a yawn, but quickly realized that I couldn't move a muscle. There was a stifling weight pinning my body and it made me feel paralyzed. I began to panic, as I tried to move my lifeless limbs. Nothing happened.

I gasped for a breath but my mouth refused to open and I couldn't escape the pressure now bearing down heavily on my chest. Sweat poured from my forehead and my eyes scattered over the space above my bed, as darkness encircled me, slowly swallowing me into the shiny black vortex.

Suddenly, a loud squeal rang in my ears. It sounded like a screaming child. I felt like I was being suffocated by an invisible force with strength much greater than my own. I tried screaming to Edwin, and used every ounce of energy I had to try to move, but was unable to lift a finger. I struggled helplessly, fighting for my self-control, but I couldn't save myself.

My eyes grew wide with madness and tears blurred my already untrusting vision. I tried to reign in my horror, but I was struggling to stave off the hysteria. Minutes ticked on like hours, as the blackness continued to swirl around me like a dark, stormy night. A hazy, colourless ring of death enveloped me and transported me down a deep, dark tunnel, away from life as I knew it.

A malicious presence continued to haunt me, just out of my range of sight. My mind shuddered, but my body remained limp, when I realized that the abrupt pressure that had just thrust the air from my lungs was that from a body. My eyes strained from their sockets to look at the being pinning me to my death bed.

I was relieved to find a beautiful, little girl, with pale skin and golden-brown hair. She was sitting very still on top of me and seemed to be looking me right in the eye. I wondered if it could have been Pheobe, but I wasn't able to get a good look at her.

I blinked and squinted, trying to make out her face when suddenly her eyes began to glow red with anger. The fog lifted and my eyes froze open with fright. I tried to scream and punch, but my efforts went unrewarded. The red

glowing eyes slowly moved closer, until the familiar face
was only inches from mine. *Jenny.*

Her long, soft hair, tickled my face and sent vicious
shivers down my spine. It was like I was looking at myself
as a child. She glared at me even harder, looking deep into
my soul. I forced a blink and squeezed my eyes closed,
hoping to shrink away and shut her out of my lost mind.

Instead, too many memories came racing back to me. I
screamed in horror, as I was forced to relive the night of the
accident that claimed my twin sister's life.

It was my birthday. Jenny and I had just turned six. We
were so happy, all smiles and giggles. Our parents had
planned an elaborate surprise party for us, so my aunt took
me and my sisters out for the afternoon. We didn't suspect
a thing. When our aunt was returning to our house, that's
when everything turned all wrong.

The accident happened so fast that I didn't even know
what had hit us. But I would never forget the blood
splattered all over the car interior and the devastating
shatter of glass when my aunt was ejected through the
windshield.

Jenny and I were in shock, just staring at the carnage
around us, hands clutched so tight that it was like we had
been sewn together. Aubrey's cry quickly turned to a
wailing scream, when no one came to her aid. That was
probably what made the man decide to retrieve her first.

Aubrey's baby carrier had been forced upward and
twisted metal from her door separated us in the back seat.
A man appeared in the side window, and the second he saw
us, he diligently set out to rescue our screaming baby sister.
Frantic and fumbling, he got the door open and retrieved
her from the seat.

Jenny pried at her door hysterically, but it wouldn't
open, and there was no other visible way out of the car. I
noticed a metal object piercing through Jenny's leg,
attaching her to the wreckage, and I wondered if she even
knew that she was trapped. Recognizing the reality of the
situation, we both began to cry, holding each other's

terrified stare, waiting for someone to save us. The man cleared Aubrey from the mangled car, then came back to us just in time.

"My leg," Jenny cried, frozen in horror, when she finally realized her damage.

The man caught her attention. "Duck your heads," he hollered.

We both did, without question, but we never stopped crying. The man smashed out the window and climbed on the back of the car, reaching in for me. I slipped out of my seat, with nothing more than a scratch, but didn't let go of Jenny until the man pried our fingers apart. He lowered me to the ground and my boots crunched the broken glass beneath my feet.

"Run," he yelled.

"No! My sister!" I wailed, terrified for Jenny's life.

He leapt from the trunk of the car and rushed me, kicking and screaming, to where my baby sister was wiggling in the wet, snowy grass. What the man didn't know at the time was that he only had time to save one of us. He chose me.

He knelt next to me, and ordered me to stay. "It's not safe near the car. I'm going to save your sister," he reassured me, "but I need you to stay here. Understand?"

I had nodded my head out of fear, and lost my eyes to the wreck that was once my aunt's car. My aunt was lying unconscious on the ground in front of it, my sister pinned inside, and all I could think to do was hush Aubrey, my voice trembling between whimpers, as I stared at the man ripping at the car, trying desperately to free Jenny from it.

The man kicked the car and howled. "Where the hell's the fire department." He stomped quickly to where my aunt was thrown on the ground and dragged her closer to us. "She'll be okay. She's breathing," he assured me, though her arm was mangled and her face was covered in a dark smear of blood.

He swiped his bloody hand over his forehead. "I can't get her out. She's stuck pretty good," he told me. "We'll have to wait for help."

I could hear the faint sounds of sirens calling far in the distance. "Please, mister. Help my sister," I begged. I was afraid for Jenny, and didn't like her being left there all by herself. She was scared and injured and all alone.

The man shook his head, showing his defeat and helplessness, but dutifully spun around to return to the demolished heap for his final attempt to save my sister. As he reached the car, there was a horrendous explosion and the hood surged in flames. The man stumbled backward, blocking himself from the fire, unable to get anywhere near the car without injuring himself.

I screamed for what seemed like forever, as the sirens grew nearer by the second. "No! No! Jenny!" I hitched Aubrey higher into my arms and rocked her more aggressively, crying to myself, while Jenny's own cries turned into a blood curdling scream. I had sensed her death then, tasted the blackness in my throat, but I could never prepare myself for that very scream to haunt me for the rest of my life.

There was nothing I could do but watch the powerless man pacing around the burning car, as Jenny - my other half - burned helplessly inside it. Her hysterical scream rattled my very existence. I could see the man struggling with his conscience, his face twisted in an agonizing frown, while we waited for the fire department only a minute away.

What I would never forget was Jenny's horrific shriek, and then the awful moment when the screaming stopped. That sound continued to haunt me to this day and had consumed what was left of my childhood. My own parents were unable to look at me, without being overcome with sadness, and no amount of therapy could ever repair the gaping, black hole inside of me.

I cried and cried. And, though the force threatened to keep me at that dark place deep in my mind, I decided I didn't care. Then suddenly, the bedroom door flew open and my eyes opened against my will. Edwin stormed into the room, half asleep, with darkness swirling behind him like a fog of energy.

I instantly regained control of my limbs, sprang from the bed and spun recklessly around the dimly lit room. "Where is she? Where did she go? Where did Jenny go?" I repeated, hollering at the top of my lungs.

Within seconds, I was crushed in Edwin's arms, crying uncontrolledly, and any remnant of darkness had disappeared from the room. Through tear-filled eyes I could see that we were alone, and though my heart still raced with fear and horror, I could no longer sense Jenny's presence. She was gone.

"It's okay, Abs. There's no one here," Edwin said, hushing me. "It was just a bad dream." His voice was but a soothing whisper.

"No," I cried, my sobbing mouth pressed against Edwin's smooth chest, my left hand pounding on him. "She was here. And she was trying to kill me."

CHAPTER EIGHT

I could feel the one sunray that had snuck its way through the edge of the blinds, before I even opened my eyes, bringing with it a feeling of warmth and peace. It was a new day. That one ray of sunshine had escaped the cold, but I wouldn't be so lucky. I scooped up my phone and slipped back into my bed. After rubbing my sore eyes, I checked my messages. The first text was from Edwin.

If you need a shoulder to cry on, you know I'm here for you, Abs.

I think I re-read that message a good one hundred times before gaining the nerve to check the next one that was from Cameron.

Abby, I am really sorry. Please let me make things right. Will you meet with me today? A public place is fine with me, if that's what you want. I know we can work through this.

A tear choked my stone-dry throat. What I wanted was a baby. If by *make things right* he meant giving me that, then I was game.

I replied to his message and agreed, knowing I wanted it to work out as bad as he did. Then I messaged Edwin to tell him that his shoulder wouldn't suffice. I would need a gigantic bucket to collect all of my tears.

Satisfied that I was doing the right thing, I tossed my blankets aside, swung my legs off the bed and dropped my phone into my purse. I stood up, stretched for the sky and yanked open my blinds, letting the sunlight flood my room of shadows. I walked past my dresser, stopped in front of the mirror and poked at the dark circles under my eyes.

I frowned at my reflection. "Oh, that's attractive." I considered covering it up before leaving my room, but decided against it.

Edwin knew I was ruined. He had seen me at my worst before and this would be nothing new for him. I dragged my ass down the stairs, clanked a bowl onto the table and snooped through the cupboards, not surprised by how little food I found stocked there.

After one bite of my cereal, Edwin walked into the kitchen. "I thought that was you," he said, before asking me countless questions that all went unanswered.

I slurped up what was left of my milk, rinsed out my bowl in the sink and spun around to face him. One sentence would give him the answer to all of his hidden suggestions.

"We did not break up. I just needed a night to think."

"If you say so." He gulped back the rest of his breakfast, then bumped past me. "If you ask me though, you're in for trouble if you need a break this early in the relationship."

I carefully shrugged my aching shoulders, then twirled around to explain myself. "We're having a difference of opinion, but it's nothing we can't get past."

Edwin chuckled to himself and it kind of hurt my feelings, but I wouldn't admit that to him. "I'm sorry, Abs. But if anyone knows how stubborn you can be, it's me." He turned to face me, and I wished he hadn't set those aqua eyes on me.

"Thanks a lot. You're really helping." My sarcasm effectively blocked the trembling in my voice, but I couldn't stop the tears from coming. Then, like a fragile child, I began to cry. "I can't believe I'm doing this in front of you," I blubbered. "It's so embarrassing."

"The last thing I want to do right now is upset you more. I was just afraid he hurt you," Edwin said, stepping toward me and taking my hand.

He did. Emotionally. "Cam would never lay a finger on me. He respects the woman that I am."

Edwin pulled me into his arms and nudged my head onto his shoulder. Those arms had always brought me so much relief in my times of need and now was no exception. I tightened my grip around him, but he broke my hold to look at me.

"I've been known to lend a good ear, if you need one," he said, not letting me get too close.

Yeah, I'm sure his good ear would love to hear what I have to say. "I don't doubt you have a strong shoulder to cry on, but you're probably not the right person for the job."

"I've already let you wipe your snot nose all over my shirt; tell me I'm not the right one."

Those words hung between us and I couldn't balance the meaning, so I let out a snort, in an attempt to laugh, and it seemed to make him happy.

"I have to get ready. I promised Cam I would meet with him today."

"Good luck with that." His sarcasm was far from thoughtful. "At the risk of giving you good advice, maybe you should consider not lying to yourself. It doesn't make the truth go away, it only delays the inevitable."

"In English?" I asked, snidely.

"You have a bad habit of holding on and trying to make it work, when your stubborn ass never intends on giving anything up. If it's over, just admit that it's over."

I didn't want it to be over. "If *I* hold on too long, then *you* let go too easily," I snapped, without thinking. This had nothing to do with him. I should have saved my words for where they were needed; with Cameron.

"I'm not trying to get you all worked up," Edwin said. "Just trying to help. You do what you feel in your heart is right and I'm sure it will all work out for you."

I rolled my eyes, officially aggravated, and stomped away. *Shit doesn't just magically work itself out.*

I walked into the local coffee shop looking fresh and fine; though inside, I was a crumbling mess. I anxiously paused inside the door, combed my fingers through my winded hair, and lifted my eyes anxiously to see if Cameron was there yet.

Looking straight to the back of the long, narrow shop, I found him. He was seated alone, at a small, shiny round table. As our eyes connected, he stood from his chair and his gaze was like an impenetrable force field. I couldn't have stolen my eyes away from him if I wanted to, but I didn't want to.

In fact, I had a desperate urge to run down the aisle and jump into his arms, to show him how much I still loved him. I managed to stop myself and instead remained completely composed. This wasn't some joyous fairy tale, where he'd tell me he wanted to give me babies and we'd live happily after. No, this was real life. I had to be realistic.

I walked slowly and reservedly toward his table. His sharp eyes dissected me and I found it difficult to walk under his scrutiny. My feet stumbled but my heart was filled with fascination. He was so stunning. Anxiety suffocated me, as I finished my awkward approach. How was I supposed to greet him?

Without a question, Cam opened his arms to me, his eyes coaxing me to accept his offer. I obeyed, collapsing in his arms from weakened knees. He held me so tight and swaddled me with love, as I inhaled his unforgettable aroma. I lifted my head from his embrace and looked up expectantly at him.

"Thank you for coming," he said, taking my left hand into his and intertwining our fingers.

A playful smirk crept onto my face. "You knew I would."

"Actually, I was afraid that you wouldn't." He sighed and lifted my hand to inspect the gorgeous ring that remained on my finger. "You're still wearing it."

"That's because I still love you," I said, finding my strength.

Cameron smiled for the first time in what seemed like weeks, and it was amazing to witness that all-encompassing smile again. He brought those masterful lips to my hand and pressed a kiss to my trembling fingers, while those squinted eyes stole all my resolve.

"I love you, Abigail. I can't lose you."

"You haven't lost me. I'm right here," I breathed.

I closed my eyes as his mouth brushed mine, and his hand smoothed tenderly over my cheek. I trembled from the electricity that unified our irrefutable bond and relished that gentle touch. Cameron tilted his head to deepen the kiss, expressing all of his unspoken feelings with his mouth. When Cam stopped, he pressed his lips tight together, squeezing his eyes shut. I tucked my chin in, hiding close to his chest, as my cheeks turned multiple shades of pink.

Cam ignored the gawkers and cupped my warm cheek to bring my emerald eyes up to his. "What do you say we go for a walk? It looks like a pretty nice day outside."

The sun had taken the chill out of the day, even with the gusty wind blowing the snow around. I nodded, not sure what else to say. Cam clasped my hand tighter and pulled me outside. I snuggled beneath my baby pink scarf to block the snow that sprinkled over us when we left the overhang of the building. We stood on the edge of the curb, then darted through traffic to cross the road.

Cam's pace slowed as he led me toward the river. "I miss you," he said, with a sigh.

Those words felt like molten lava warming my body all over. "Me too."

Urgency clawed at me, as Cam's fingers tightened around mine. He scoped out a private place, devoid of wind, and swiftly tugged me out of the public eye. He tucked me against an old brick building, the low overhang providing a ledge of protection from the weather, and bundled me in close, his nose nuzzled against mine.

He brushed his hand down my cheek, sending pleasant shivers down my spine, then kissed me softly. "I missed this," he told me, as he kissed me again.

The cold wind blasted around us, blowing my brown tangled hair in my face. Cam gently swept it away with his fingers, so he could resume kissing me. He devoured my loneliness and delivered me to a dream state. It was all flowers and sunshine all of a sudden.

Cam drew my eyes open, his forehead wrinkled, and a crooked smile spread across his face. "Turns out it's a little too cold for a walk today," he said.

Knowing what he was insinuating, I embraced my cunning self. "I haven't warmed you up enough?" I caught when his eyes zeroed in on my mouth. Using the tip of my tongue, I traced the length of my upper lip, then bit my bottom lip to swallow my desire.

"Maybe a little too much," he replied, pressing himself against me. He kissed me again, harder this time, provoking a need that went far deeper than I wished to admit.

"Will you come home with me?" he begged.

"Yes," I rasped, as if he had just popped the question.

With a slanted smile, he locked onto my fingers and we hauled ass to his car.

Was it so bad for me to engage in a moment of inexplicable ecstasy with this handsome man that I still called mine? Forgetting about our problems hardly helped the situation, but we had decidedly torn each other's clothes off, skipping foreplay, and got right down to it. I took all of him and my life shattered in his hands, until I was replete, complete and sore in all the right places.

Still wanting to feel the weight of him against me, I rolled over, lifted the thin sheets over our naked bodies and pulled him close. I snuggled back against him, closed my eyes on a tear and passed out from exhaustion.

My brain was still foggy after my sex-induced nap, but reality slowly crept back in with a vengeance. I had taken what was mine, but I knew it was of no use. No seed had been planted. I had to remind myself that there was no seed. Cameron could never give me my dream.

If it's over, just admit that it's over.

Cameron walked through the doorway and crawled back into bed, facing me. "You're awake," he said.

"Mmm, hmm," I mumbled, softly.

His fingers teased over my cheek. "Will you stay with me tonight?" He expected me to say yes, even though we both knew it was wrong on so many levels. "Just one more night?"

As in, after that there would be no other nights? I didn't like the sound of that, nor could I say no. I nodded and slid my hands over Cam's chest. "How long have you been up for?"

"I never fell asleep. I was just thinking." He paused, with a sigh. "I saw you talking to Edwin yesterday." Cameron pulled away from me and dressed very quickly. "What did he want?"

I fumbled out of bed and slipped into my clothes, taking the hint, and replied hesitantly. "Nothing really. He was going out for lunch and asked if I'd come along."

"It looked like something to Taylor," Cam accused, as he walked across the room, putting more distance between us.

I chased after him, stunned by his sudden rudeness again. "You have no reason to act jealous like that. It was nothing."

"Nothing," he repeated. "Just like what happened between you and Owen." When he glared at me, it was like he stuck me in the chest with an ice pick.

"Are you suggesting I'm cheating on you?"

"I don't want to believe it, but it sure doesn't look good from where I'm standing."

He obviously doesn't trust me anymore, so why did he take me home with him? I waved at the rumpled sheets. "All this today, for what then?"

Cameron had already thrown in the towel. "I would never deny that you're a nice fuck."

I couldn't believe the words coming from his mouth. I refused to. I dug my fingers into my forehead to dull the sharp pain now striking my skull. When it didn't work, I sighed, hoping it would air dry the tears in my eyes. "If you didn't want me around Edwin, all you had to do is say so. You coming at me like this, though... it isn't even right."

"You hanging around Edwin is not right. Anyone with half a brain wouldn't need to be told."

Oh, so now he's calling me stupid? "What is this even about?" And what was the point of arguing, when I didn't even know what kind of defence to mount. The sensation in my gut warned me that he was just going to kick me to the curb anyway.

"You were talking in your sleep," he stated, like it was a crime.

"What did I say?"

"I'm sorry, Abby. But I can't get you pregnant." He blocked his eyes with his hand, but through his tense fingers I was able to see that he was still more angry than sorry.

I could just imagine what I had said. "You're mad because of a dream?"

When he chuckled, it rolled over my ribs and stole my air supply. "My love can only stretch so far. You really need to figure out who's most important to you, before *someone else* gets hurt."

"So, now this is about Pheobe too? Do you really think I'd do anything intentionally to hurt her?"

"Don't you worry about *my* daughter. I can take care of her myself. I've been doing just fine all this time without you. I don't know why I thought you'd make it any different."

His clipped tone hacked off a piece of my heart. My anger had faded and was quickly being replaced by a hollow gloom. *Where was this coming from?*

I hesitantly stepped toward him. "I think we can work through this, if you're willing to give me a chance. But Cameron, you have to trust that it's over between me and Edwin. And there was never anything with Owen."

"You might be blinded by your friendship, but I can tell Edwin sees it a little differently. Open your eyes, Abby."

My eyes *were* open, and they were focused on the crevices in Cam's forehead as they deepened. "You know what," he said, coming to a decision. "I think it's over. This thing that we have going on, it's obviously not working anymore."

"Please don't do this, Cameron," I begged. "I love you. We can fix this."

"I'm far too broken to be fixed, I'm afraid."

I shook my head no, hating the way he shut down our communication channels.

Cameron turned his weary gaze on me, tired yet wrathful. "You should go." His words were cold and sharp, and cut me like a scalding knife. It wasn't up for debate. Cameron was over it. Over me.

I couldn't hide that having him talk to me that way hurt, but I tucked that away and pulled out some sarcasm. "I guess now would be a bad time to bring up the baby thing then."

"Get out," he ordered.

I was too choked up to argue and too upset to fight. My voice was shaky and desolate. "Fine." I strode past Cam and retrieved my purse, only to find that Cam had already packed my bags.

I shoved my arms through the sleeves of my heavy jacket, pulled open his front door, then violently pitched my bags out into the snowy yard. Cam stood sideways, a mere four paces away from me, his gaze burning a hole in the wall across from him. He wasn't changing his mind. He wasn't stopping me. My heart split into pieces.

"We're done," he said, marking the end of our relationship.

As if my bags sitting at the door hadn't gotten his point across already. But we couldn't be done. I wasn't done. He had to come around. But he just continued to stare into space, unwilling to let me in, barricaded inside his own hard, hollow shell of a body.

An exaggerated intake of breath left my mouth dry and tight. He wanted me gone. Now. Forever. As in never again. I knew that wasn't him talking.

"I'm still going to love you," I said, my voice quiet, scratchy and profound.

He didn't flinch - didn't do a damn thing - just kept on staring. Saddened and frustrated, I hurried out the door, slamming it behind me. I took one step off his porch and my knees gave out, dropping me onto my hands and knees into a snow bank. I couldn't seem to catch my breath, being panic-stricken, shaken and distraught. I gasped for air as my tears spilled onto the drifting snow.

The winter chill began to eat away at me. I forced myself to regain my footing and lugged my snow covered bags to my car. I had to get out of there before Pheobe came home. Pheobe. God. This would break her little heart.

I drove straight home, my eyes cold as ice, my heart sharp as glass. There *would* have to be a small, red sports car parked in my spot when I got there. *Just my luck.* I let myself into the house with the key Edwin insisted that I keep, fully expecting unwanted company, but not expecting to find Edwin lying on the couch with a woman.

Sure, they were only watching a movie, but I was intruding. A date? Sure looked like it. The look of shock on Edwin's face when he realized I was back, was enough to make me shudder. Feeling pale and numb, I dropped my bags, spun on my heel and rushed back to my car.

"No, wait!" Edwin hollered to me, but there was no way I would turn back.

I sped off, before Edwin could chase me down barefoot in the snow. I turned the corner, feeling lost and light headed, so I pulled my car over to the side of the road. No tears came and that only frustrated me more.

My phone started buzzing, so I dug through my purse and stared blankly at the gorgeous face plastered on the screen. *Cameron Clarke calling.*

What could he possibly want? To remind me how disappointed he is in me? How much I annoy him? How unreasonable I can be sometimes? I wanted to answer it, but I couldn't handle more of his resentment. I slid my finger across the screen. *Ignore.*

The call ended and I dropped my phone back in my purse, as thunder literally rolled. Such wicked weather for this time of year, but we were having an actual thunderstorm in the dead of winter. Then my phone buzzed again. A flash of lightening brightened the sky. I dove into my purse, expecting it to be Edwin this time.

Cameron Clarke calling. Again? Must be important. *Ignore.*

I threw my phone onto the seat next to me. It bounced off the seat and smashed into the passenger door. "Oh, shit!" I said to myself, as I tried to retrieve it from the dark floor.

Once I located it, I placed it a little more carefully into my purse and then focused on the dark, roiling clouds. I had no one. Edwin had a girlfriend. Cam had Pheobe. And I was all alone.

As if the strange weather wasn't any indication of how my life was going, I glared at the stop light up the street as it flashed red. Somehow it felt like a sign. My life had come to an abrupt stop, and I was no better off now than I was over a year ago with Edwin.

Swiping away the tears, I told myself I couldn't keep hiding from reality. Enough blubbering like a fool; it was time to get back to reality. *Edwin has a girlfriend?* So what. It's my house too. I needed to feel the comfort that only my own bed could offer me.

Settling my mind, I slammed my car back into drive and hit the gas with a heavy foot. My tires spun around until they finally made contact with the wet pavement and took me as fast as they could back to my house. *My* house.

I was surprised to find no cherry red car in my driveway when I pulled in. It was bad enough I would have to face Edwin and his pity party, I certainly didn't want to hear it in front of his new girlfriend. Finding my nerve, I decided to deal with all of my problems at once.

I pulled out my smart phone and set it to voice dial. "Call Cameron Clarke," I said, then cleared my scratchy voice. *I can do this.*

I pressed the speaker button and stared at the photo that would haunt my dreams this night and every night for the next lifetime. I tried to find comfort in the ring. One. Two. Three. *What the hell was taking him so long?* It didn't help that scary shadows flickered around the yard with every flash of freak lightening. My eyes darted around the car, then I clicked the lock button on my door.

When Cam finally answered the phone, a loud crack of thunder startled me and I watched the hydro flash out in my house. "Hello?" he repeated.

Still choking on my lack of air, I struggled to find the right words. The lights in the house flickered back on and gave me the courage to speak. "Cam, it's me."

"Abby? Oh, thank God. I was worried about you."

I ignored his bogus concern. Like I'd believe that after he ripped me a new one. "What did you want, Cam?"

He cleared his own throat. "I meant to tell you this earlier, but we got a little sidetracked."

"What is it?" I asked, without inflection. *That you're a total ass for breaking my heart and then stomping on it?*

"I've been thinking about opening my own practice. It was a long-term goal of mine, but after what Owen did, I've decided to put my plan into action sooner. Like now."

The storm forged on, while one brewed itself in my mind. "Hmm," I responded, indifferently. *How can he care about that at a time like this?*

Cam continued. "I've always wanted to be my own boss. What better time than now?"

Really? "You're definitely assertive enough to go it alone," I said, keeping all emotion at bay. This had nothing to do with me after all.

"I can definitely handle it on my own, but I think you would prove to be a valuable asset to me."

Is he kidding? I could barely stand to talk to him through the phone. He broke my heart. Oh, but I still loved him, no matter how hard I tried not to. "You know I can't do that to Owen. He's been good to me all these years." And I didn't care what he thought about that.

"A little too good, if you ask me," Cam mumbled.

I knew exactly what to say to make this conversation end and I had to say it, even if it was rude at best. "What is your policy going to be for maternity leave?"

His sharp intake of breath was enough to stab me in the gut. *He did care.*

"You're still on that?" he asked, when he knew damn well that I was.

"Cam, I will always be on that." I watched the lights in the house flash off, one after the other. Edwin must have been heading upstairs. What a relief that was.

"You don't love me anymore?" Cam asked, snapping me back into the here and now.

Yes, I love you, dammit! Why can't you get that into your thick skull? "It's not about that, Cam. Children are my reason for living."

His sigh of disappointment was heart wrenching and the gaping hole in my heart seemed to ooze a cold, petrifying liquid into my chest cavity.

"You need to hear it? I'll tell you again. There is no doubt in my mind that I am utterly and completely in love with you, Cam. But..."

"But?" he snapped. "I delivered up my heart to you on a silver platter and you can't just give it to me straight? You're either in love with me or you're not. There's nothing in between. So, what's it going to be?"

Another crack of thunder boomed, and it sounded as intense as Cam's voice. "Don't misunderstand me. I do love you. More than you can imagine..." I admitted.

"But," he inserted, rudely.

"But I don't see how we can move forward together when we can't agree on the same future. I want a family."

"And I have a family," he replied.

"This is one matter I can't budge on, Cam. I'm sorry."

"It doesn't have to be this way," he said, making my heart shatter into a million pieces. "We could have such an amazing life together."

"We *could*, if you would give me a family." I was holding my breath to stop the onslaught of sobbing, knowing what his answer to that would be.

"Not happening."

I swallowed back my emotion. "Please tell Pheobe I love her." I sniffled on an intake of breath.

"Don't think this isn't hurting me too," Cam said, acknowledging my emotion. "You took my heart with you when you left tonight."

I was glad I didn't have to respond because the call ended. Cam either hung up or the hydro killed his line. I would never know. Either way it was over.

I wiped my nose with my sleeve, slipped my keys out of the ignition and prepared myself for a fast entry. I ran up to my dark house and the wind whipped my hair in my face. I couldn't tell whether we had hydro or not, but I didn't care. I quietly opened the door and snuck inside. When I kicked my shoes off, they hit the closet door in the entrance making a loud clunking noise.

"Shit!" I whispered to myself, desperate not to attract Edwin's attention.

The house creaked from the storm as I tiptoed upstairs. Only two more steps and I was home free. But the dangling lights flickered on and a bright, white light blinded me. I crouched on the stairs, feeling like a substandard criminal.

Edwin cleared his throat, but his voice stayed low. "I'm sorry, but I have to ask. Why are you sneaking around your own house?"

I straightened myself up and spun around to find Edwin standing at the base of the stairs, his finger still on the light switch. "I didn't want to bother you," I whispered.

He started up the stairs, then paused. "Why are you whispering?" he whispered back. "We're the only ones here."

I wasn't at all creeped out by the fact that Edwin had been sitting in the dark, stalking me as I entered the door, and I certainly shouldn't have felt relieved. But I did. I cleared the rasp from my throat, but my voice was still scratchy. "I thought you might have had company."

"I sent her home. It looks like your night went about as good as mine."

I tried to hide my depression, but I was a mess and not capable of concealing my mental anguish. I inhaled a shaky, exaggerated breath. "Could my night get any worse? Not likely," I admitted. "What happened to your date?" Not that I cared. I just had to say something to take the conversation off of me.

I should have been bolting to my room to be alone, but my feet didn't move. And that was because I didn't tell them to.

"It was hardly a date. It was more like a favour," Edwin said. "Hunter suggested I have her over for a movie night and, since I owed him one, like a chump, I agreed. Turns out she only wanted me for my pimp juice, so I sent her packing."

While I knew Edwin was only trying to be funny, it only upset me more. That was the very reason why Cam and I couldn't be together. My brain shut down and I broke down from the pain in my heart. I fell to my knees in the stairwell, and tears spilled down my face.

Edwin raced up the stairs and looped his arms around me, to keep me from falling. I closed my eyes and hung my head low, unable to lift it back up. Any reserves that I had been running on were depleted and I was even having difficulty breathing. Edwin lifted me into his arms and heroically carried me to my bedroom. He lowered me to my bed, but didn't let me go.

I gasped for air and it finally reached my scorching lungs. As my breathing steadied I opened my eyes and found Edwin staring back at me.

"You'll be okay," he said, contradicting his own facial expressions.

"Eventually," I whispered, feeling completely spent. I closed my eyes again, glad that Edwin never let me go.

He leaned against the headboard and gathered me into his strong arms, hushing me after a long stretch of hitched breaths.

"If you ask me, you're crying for the wrong reasons."

I lifted my head and narrowed my red eyes at him. "I didn't ask you."

Edwin smirked. "I'm going to tell you anyway." He paused, until he had my attention. "If you want to cry, then it should be for wasting your time with Cam in the first place."

I covered my head with my arms and rolled out of Edwin's grip. "You don't think I already came up with that one myself?" I stared at the wall and the tears started to settle down, the fog slowly lifting from my head, but not budging from my heart.

Edwin didn't say a word, but neither did he move. *Why must he hang around for this?*

I rolled to face him and squinted my tear-ridden eyes. "Please tell me why you're being so nice to me."

Edwin smiled. "I can't be mean to you, Abs. Especially not when you're like this."

"Like what: a royal disaster? Go on, you can say it."

His mouth widened, and it was the beginning of a warm, handsome smile. "I won't say that, but I will tell you something you taught me last year. Sometimes following your own heart means breaking someone else's."

My eyes trailed to the ceiling, but my brain wasn't working. "Are you going to tell me what that's supposed to mean?"

Edwin chuckled. "I just mean that what's best for you now, doesn't seem to be best for Cam. Neither of you like it, but that's not to say that you won't admit later that it was for the best."

"Lately I feel like I'm waiting for something that'll never happen."

Edwin cupped my chin, sending a frisson of awareness through my frazzled senses. "You did what you had to do. You stayed true to yourself." He pulled his hand away and sighed, but it didn't stop him from talking. "If he truly wants you, nothing will keep him away."

"I wasn't thinking only about Cam," I whispered, and fluttered my lashes shut to hide from his thoughtful gaze.

Edwin spoke softly now and gently pressed his hand over my heart. "Then maybe you should stop thinking so much and start following what's in here."

I held my eyes firmly shut, and I didn't know what was happening when Edwin gently lifted my chin, until his soft, careful lips brushed across mine.

My eyes popped open, from confusion and shock. I squinted at Edwin to assess his angle and found that all humour had left his expression.

"I know. I'm a bad person," Edwin admitted. "It's wrong to take advantage of you like that."

Heat crept up my cheeks and I turned away, my lips still tingling from his soft touch. There was a light knock at the door and Edwin rolled of the bed to answer it, leaving me wondering why there were a whole crew of butterflies mingling in my stomach.

Edwin left the room, just as our impatient guest started pounding on our front door. "Apparently they don't know how to use a doorbell," Edwin called back to me, as he shuffled down the stairs. The doorbell sounded, as if summoned by him. Repeatedly.

As Edwin leapt off of the last stair, the person jiggled the door knob. "I'm coming," Edwin hollered.

Curious to see who it was, I quickly got up from my bed. I felt a little dizzy, but I stumbled out of my room before steadying myself on the hall railing.

Edwin peered out the sidelight briefly and looked back to me with apprehension. "Go back to your room," he ordered, softly. His face was so stern, that I dared not disobey him, and he waited for me to disappear before opening the door.

My curiosity getting the best of me, I stood at the edge of the wall, just out of his line of sight. Edwin opened the door, but said nothing. I peered around the corner to check who it was. All I saw was Edwin disappear outside into the cold, closing the door behind him.

Someone had clearly wanted to come in, so why did Edwin step out? Was he expecting someone? *A girl?* A shot of jealously rushed through my veins.

Then I realized who else it could be. *No. It couldn't be. Could it?* When I heard his voice, my stomach flipped with excitement and worry. I could hear light banter, just outside the door, and things seemed to be heating up. Knees weak, I snuck down the stairs in an attempt to eavesdrop. I crept behind the door and leaned against the wall.

"What do you really want?" Edwin asked, with annoyance evident in his query.

"That's none of your business," Cam snapped. "This is between me and Abby."

"Well, she's in bed. Leave her alone. She'll call you if she wants to."

"I have to talk to her. Now. We didn't leave things right."

I could sense the pain in his words. He didn't even sugar coat them for Edwin. Sadness bloomed in my belly and tears regrouped in my eyes.

"Cool story, bro. Where's the part where you back the fuck off?"

I covered my mouth to silence my gasp.

"That's it." Cam lost his patience and forced his way past Edwin, who had been protecting the door like a royal guard. But Cam had taken him by surprise and managed to get one foot into the foyer. "Abigail," he shouted, not knowing I was only a matter of steps away from him.

I held my breath and pressed myself flat against the wall, now only an arms-length away from the door. Only a millisecond passed before Edwin propelled himself back in the power position, territorially defending his castle. They bumped chests and then Edwin forcefully removed Cameron from the house. Neither of them seemed to notice me.

Edwin shoved Cameron away from the door and he stumbled into my front yard. "Give her some time, Cam. You did this to her. At least give her that."

I nearly choked on Edwin's words as they burned into my memory. The door clicked shut and, outside, Edwin continued to lay it on thick. It hurt to hear the man I loved getting hounded for loving me, but I wasn't ready to do anything about it. He didn't want me anymore.

I dashed up the stairs and down the hall to Edwin's room, as far away from the situation as possible. I had to get away. I heard the front door reopen and then abruptly slam shut. The dead bolt turned over and after a minute or two of quiet shuffling through the house, I heard Edwin start up the stairs.

Just now realizing the consequences of my retreat to his room, my mind started to flounder. I was lying on Edwin's bed, propped up by my elbow, waiting for his return. What if he got the wrong idea?

Edwin paused at my bedroom. The door creaked open. "Abby?"

"In here," I called.

He stepped toward his room and hesitated in the doorway. "Damn, I'm good," he said, praising himself. "I've already got you right I where I wanted you." His smile was big and lighthearted, but my eyes were wide and alarmed.

Edwin chuckled and casually approached the bed. "Relax. I'm only teasing. You really need to lighten up." He plopped right beside me, as if he'd already forgotten about what had just transpired between him and Cameron.

I relieved my dry eyes with a blink. "What did he want?"

"Who?"

"Don't play dumb, Eddie. I heard him. What did he say?"

"You should know. You were standing right there."

"Tell me," I threatened, but it was an empty one.

"I told you I would take care of it and I did. Cam's gone. Period. So, where were we when we were so rudely interrupted?" He stroked a playful hand down the length of my arm.

I shivered and yanked my arm away. "Eddie!"

Edwin was being fun and frisky. "What? We were all good until he showed up."

Ignoring his boyish stunts, I flopped back onto his bed with a sigh. "Thank you for getting rid of him for me. I'm not ready to face him yet."

Edwin slid up next to me and leaned in close again.

"Cut it out!" I ordered, pushing his shoulders back.

He barely budged, so I backed myself against his headboard to get some breathing room. I was feeling lonely and sad and confused, and was finding it difficult to resist his positive energy. I pressed my eyes tightly shut, hoping he would back off, but sensing again that he had moved closer.

My heart started to race. It was beating loudly in my ears, making it difficult for me to be rational. *What did he see in me anyway?* "I'm damaged goods," I whispered, knowing exactly what Edwin was thinking.

Ignoring my warnings, Edwin tucked his hand in my hair and kissed me again. He sandwiched me against the headboard, his hand cupping my head, making me feel wanted. I didn't kiss him back, but I didn't stop him either. He lingered near my lips, his breath warm on my lips.

"Sorry. I couldn't help myself," he growled, then gave a more friendly peck to the corner of my mouth. "You look really kissable tonight, tear stains and all." He brushed his thumb over my cheek and leaned in for another kiss.

I rolled away from him and curled into a ball with my eyes clenched shut. "You know I can't do this, Eddie. I'm in love with Cam."

He pushed off of the bed, his anger mounting immediately. "I thought you broke it off with him. The way he was talking, it was like you told him to go screw himself. I thought for sure it was over between you."

"It is. But feelings don't just go away like that." I snapped my fingers to make a point.

"Fine. I can respect that."

It was late and I was tired. I sighed, and it turned into an overdramatic yawn. I stretched my arms over my head, then laid back, snuggling in. I didn't want to be alone. "Can

I sleep with you tonight?" I asked, without thinking any more on the subject.

Edwin raised his eyebrows playfully and smiled a wicked smile. "Absolutely!"

I scowled at him. "Don't push your luck. I'm tired and I want to go to bed. I'd rather not be alone right now. But if you're going to be like that..."

Without another word, Edwin peeled off his long sleeved shirt and tossed it on the floor. He walked toward the door, every muscle in his wide back flexing as he reached for the light switch. When he flicked it, the room plummeted into darkness. Lightening flickered as Edwin dropped his pants to the floor, exposing a stunning body in fitted briefs.

The room was dark, but my eyes adjusted quickly. Tearing my eyes from him, I slipped under the covers and tucked them up under my chin. A cold rush of air on my backside told me that Edwin had joined me. I curled up in a ball and let out a sniffle.

Edwin wasn't shy about snuggling up behind me and, in a weak moment, I accepted his hand. I tucked our intertwined fingers under my chin and closed my eyes, wiggling my bottom to get closer, so I could soak up all his body heat. I didn't think I would actually be able to sleep, but I was surprised how much Edwin had softened my misery.

I focused on the rise and fall of Edwin's chest, concentrated on the differences between our breathing patterns, his soft and steady, mine irregular and raspy. Anything had to be better than remembering how Cam had brushed me off earlier. But even with my fingers linked with Edwin's, my loneliness seemed to swallow me whole, leaving Cameron at the front of my mind.

Edwin must have sensed it and abruptly replaced that concern with another. "You know I still love you, Abs," he whispered. "That will never change as long as I live."

I loosened my grip on his hand and he squeezed my fingers tight, so I couldn't detach from him.

"That said, I understand how you feel," he admitted. "I know what it's like to have a piece of your heart that you can never get back. I'll respect your feelings, but know this: He'll never love you the way I do."

CHAPTER NINE

"I don't know why you torture yourself with these sad songs," Aliah said, immediately exchanging my I-pod for a local radio station. She found an upbeat song, turned up the volume and started to bop her head, while I drove us to work.

"I'm fine," I answered, wishing it were true. I thought I'd be better by now.

"Yeah, you look fine," she said, sarcastically. "You need to get out more."

I rolled my eyes. "Yeah, cuz that will really help with my sleep deprivation."

"Maybe not, but maybe if you got laid you wouldn't be so uptight."

Irritated, I glared at Aliah. "It's been all of two weeks, Aliah. Give me a break!"

"Actually, it's been three. Three weeks, three years? It's all the same. Life goes on."

"You think you're my shrink now?" I asked, with a smirk.

"I wish. Then I could charge you for my advice."

Not long after hanging up my winter jacket, I had to pull it back out, along with my scarf and mittens. After Taylor went home sick, I was left to pick up the slack. As I armed myself for the frigid weather, Edwin stepped out of the copier room. His grin was contagious.

It was such a relief that Edwin didn't turn my life into a bigger mess than it already was. Ever since the night I had slept in his bed, he hadn't brought up his confession and neither had I. In fact, all of my friends were stepping up and making it difficult for me to sink deeper into the hole I wanted to hide in.

The walk past Cameron's office was getting easier every day, but I still fretted each time I had to. His support system didn't seem to be as strong as mine and I hated to see how he struggled to get through each day. It was clear to anyone who cared that he was miserable.

Deciding I could use the fresh air, even though it was absolutely freezing outside, I started my short walk down the salt-covered sidewalk with the leather mailbag slung over my shoulder. The streets were bustling with mid-day traffic and I hurried to get the mail into the big red box before the postal workers emptied it for the day.

After scooping our mail out of the oversized box, I readjusted my gloves and set off again. The streetlight flashed yellow, but I was too impatient to wait. I hurried across the street and a car zoomed in front of me, nearly running over my toes. The car maneuvered in between two parked cars across the street, pulling into a no parking zone.

I continued to the curb and turned for the clear stretch of sidewalk, as the driver in the irritating car honked their horn. I flashed a glance at the car, but I didn't know who the hell it was. The horn honked again and again, and I started to think the driver was deliberately trying to piss me off.

"Hooonnnnnnkk!"

I stopped in my tracks and stared at the ignoramus, as the driver's blackened window eased down. A woman called out to me and leaned toward the window, but my eyes were too watery from the wind to see who it was. I squinted at the young lady who was now waving frantically for me to come see her.

"Abbbbbbbyy!" she called. "Get your ass over here!"

It finally clicked. I hadn't seen my cousin, Calyfa, in months. Or had it been years? She had kind of fallen of the map for a while, which was not at all unusual for her. I started to think maybe she had run off with some young, rich stud to live in a tropical paradise.

I ran to the passenger door and hopped inside the car, escaping from the elements.

"Stunned, or what?" she asked me, her smile bursting from her perfect little face. She looked so cute, her long, fair hair tucked in a stylish cap. "Bet you didn't expect to see me." She flung her arms over my shoulders and pulled me in for a hug.

I pulled away and checked out her new look. I was always so envious of her beautiful, almond-shaped blue eyes and natural beauty. And now, rather than looking like the girl next door, with her pin straight, blonde hair and long, angled bangs, she looked edgy and stylish.

"I didn't even know it was you. You look great. And where'd you get this car from?"

"My new man," she said, unable to hide her smirk. "He bought it for me. The bastard was just charged with fraud. He'd better make that go away before I do."

"Cally, you crack me up." It was like our relationship hadn't skipped a beat and I loved it.

"What? He said it's not true, but I'm not getting involved with that shit. He knows it too. If he wants me to stick around, then he'd better fix it and fast. He's not going to drag me down with him."

I laughed and she stared at me, waiting for my all wise opinion, like the good old times. "Don't look at me. I'm not getting involved," I said, smirking.

"Don't you want to give me some legal advice?"

"I've got some advice for you," I answered, with a sarcastic giggle.

"Screw you!" she snapped back. All the money in the world couldn't get that girl to drop her potty mouth.

"So, where have you been?" I asked, stoked to hear about her life.

"I'm living in Toronto again. Just moved back to *my* condo. You know, the one I got as part of my settlement when I left Jase?" She smirked. "Poor bastard, should have signed a cohab agreement."

"You're such a whore," I teased.

"Shut up! I put up with him for two years. I earned it."

I laughed at her blunt honestly. It was refreshing. Listening to her life made my mine seem boring in comparison. The drama in hers was on a different scale altogether.

"What are you up to these days?" she asked. "You and Edwin still banging?"

I cleared my throat. "No. I found a new guy. He's a lawyer at my firm. Cameron is his name." Realization flooded me. "Well, we were dating, up until a few weeks ago." I folded my leg under my butt and Cally noticed my discomfort.

"What happened?"

"I really don't want to get into it now, but it's definitely over between us." I paused and looked out the window at the fresh dusting of snow being blown around in gusts. "I should probably get back to work," I said, avoiding her calculating gaze.

She nudged on my leg. "Before you go. Gabe owns a house in Haledon and I'm going to be there over the March break. Why don't you come out? There's a guest house and everything. You can even bring some friends, if you want."

"I don't know." I really didn't feel up to taking a vacation.

"Come on. It sounds like you could use a break. If not now, you could definitely use one by then."

"I suppose." I smiled at her and she knew it was a done deal.

Within days of telling Aliah about my plans, she had invited herself along, and Hunter too. Rumours started flying when Hunter decided to ask Edwin to tag along. *What happened to this being my vacation?*

Weeks later, when I least expected it, Cameron stalked up next to me in the lunch room. I didn't look at him, but I could sense he was staring, and he wasn't making it a secret.

"Is it true?" he asked, without waiting for my attention.

After refilling my water bottle, I turned to face him. "Is what true?"

"You're taking a vacation with Edwin?"

"I didn't invite him. Besides, Hunter and Aliah will be there." I wasn't crazy about the idea either, but what did he care?

"Sure sounds like a couple's thing to me," Cam replied. "It didn't take him long to replace me."

I sighed and stared at the ceiling. "Cam, we're not having this conversation right now. Why do you even care? We're over. You made that pretty clear. Just let me live my life." I hated being so short with him, but he left me no other option.

"That's actually what I came to talk to you about. It's official, I'm leaving the firm. I signed a lease for the building I was telling you about downtown and it's nearly ready."

"Good for you," I said, saddened that Cameron was actually leaving my life.

"The paint is dry and I've already started to move some furniture in. It's looking pretty damn good. Contemporary. You'd like it."

I continued to ignore how he related every statement to me.

"Yep. I've already given notice to Owen and he said he'd give me some leeway, considering the circumstances. March thirtieth is my last day, then I'm out of here."

I choked on my own saliva and coughed like crazy. At least I had a temporary excuse for the tears. Cameron smoothed his hand over my back as though he cared. Knowing he didn't, I fumbled through my purse and found the box I had been carrying with me ever since the day I took his ring off my finger.

"I should give you this," I said, holding the box out to him, my hand trembling. It was so symbolic of the end.

He pushed my hand away. "You keep it. I bought it for you."

I sighed, near tears, my voice but a whisper. "I didn't keep the promise. I don't deserve it. Maybe you can get your money back."

I knew it was worth a small fortune and I couldn't rob Pheobe of that money. I placed the velvet box on the counter next to him. He stared at it for a minute, then cracked the box open. He picked up the ring and held it between his thumb and index finger. He smiled, but there was no amusement there.

"I thought it was in the bag." He chuckled, again without humour. "I was a fool."

I lowered my gaze to the floor, unable to watch the sour events unfolding between us. A tear snuck from my eye, and I quickly wiped it away before he noticed. Cam returned the ring to its box and snapped it shut.

"You definitely have to come check out my new space," he said, trying to leave our conversation on a more positive note.

I smiled and nodded my head in agreement, knowing I would never follow through with it.

"My offer still stands too, if you ever change your mind."

"I won't." I could never work with Cam again. It still hurt just to think about him, and being with him now, having a casual conversation, felt so foreign to me.

He nodded, showing his disappointment. "It won't be the same without you." He took me by surprise and scooped my hand into his. My heart rate immediately went through the roof. He slowly lifted my hand to his lips and brushed a soft kiss on the back of my hand, just like he had when we first met. "I will always love you, Abby."

He squeezed my hand, but it didn't stop the violent tremor from shaking through me. I swallowed back my tears as Owen walked into the room. Reluctantly, Cameron dropped my hand, then briskly left me.

Owen didn't come near me. He only asked if I was okay. I was too choked up to answer, so I just gave a questionable nod. He left it at that.

Owen must have had Wesley Carver's number on speed dial, because he had wasted no time finding Cam's replacement. He even had the gall to invite him to start weeks before Cam was done, making Cam have to clear out some of his stuff early to share his office. I realized someone had to be hired in Cam's place, but I didn't think it would happen quite so fast. And Wesley Carver? Could Owen have chosen anyone more problematic?

On Wesley's first day in the office, instead of Owen doing the usual introductions, he made Cam pick up his duties. After making the usual rounds, Cam and Wesley showed up outside my door. Cam knocked on the wall to get my attention.

"I suppose you two already met," Cam said, recalling our first run in at the staff Christmas party.

Wesley chuckled. "She definitely met my ass. Can't blame her for grabbing it. It's a nice ass."

This man had no shame. Too bad he was also funny.

"Hi," I said, nodding. I couldn't help but smirk, covering my mouth to try and hide it, but that just encouraged him to wink at me.

Cam wasn't amused in the slightest. "You're going to leave this one alone," he stated. *And yes, it was definitely a threat.*

"Are you going to be here to stop me?" Wes argued, confident with his aggression.

"I don't want any trouble," I pleaded, hoping it would be enough to diffuse the situation.

Both men watched me for a timeless moment and it bothered me how striking their similarities were. Their dark-blonde hair was a near match, both being short, wild and unruly. I concentrated on Cam's eyes, the crystal blue softly intense. Wesley's eyes were blue too, but his were dark and mischievous. The most challenging feature to compare was their plump lower lips, both of them hanging that sexy thing out there like it was a chew toy.

I glanced away from them, as Wesley turned to Cameron. "Are we done here, boss?" He sure knew how to press Cam's buttons.

"I know I am," Cam answered, turning away and stomping off to his office.

Wesley continued to linger outside my doorway. I spun around on my chair.

"Can I help you?" I snapped.

"Now that depends. Are you single now?" He raised his hands to defend himself before I even opened my mouth. "I just want to clear up the conflicting signals you're sending me."

"Are you kidding me? You're seriously starting with me already?"

"You're a pretty girl. I'm a single man. Do you really blame me? I'm just testing the waters. Don't want to step on anyone's toes," he said, gently pinning my ballet flat beneath his large, shiny shoe.

"You want me to be clear? I'm not emotionally available right now. As you might have noticed, my last relationship is a little fresh." Fresh didn't even begin to explain how much it still hurt to think about it.

"Alright, you're not ready to see other men. Yet. I heard you've been done with him for months now, I just assumed you were free."

I couldn't help but compare him once again to Cameron. Any woman with two eyes would have done the same. But there was one difference between them that would never add up.

Wesley wasn't Cameron.

Wesley lifted his hands, accepting that it wasn't going to happen, and then backed away. I smiled, surprised by how easily I had gotten rid of him, until he promptly reappeared in my doorway.

"How about now?" he asked.

What a tease. "Get out of here!"

He smirked and trotted off toward his desk, though he hadn't removed his eyes from my face until he caught a glimpse of my smile. I was hardly in the right frame of mind to consider dating again and Wes' carefree, bad boy act wasn't even moderately appealing to me at this point in my life. Even if he would make beautiful babies.

After my trip to the hair salon, and a visit with the most talented hairdresser ever, I was feeling totally fabulous. When I got home, Edwin was standing in the living room staring at the TV.

"Hello!" I called, as I kicked off my shoes.

Edwin, being totally into the game, didn't respond.

"I said, hello!" I repeated, louder.

Edwin spun around to face me and smiled. "Look at you."

After I waggled my eyebrows at him, he chased me into the kitchen. I grabbed a water bottle from the fridge and cracked it open. As I closed the door, it wafted my fragrant hair, zinging my senses. I pulled a chunk of my long, silky hair across my nose and took a big sniff.

"Mmm. Smell my hair!" I said, motioning for Edwin's immediate attention.

Edwin casually strolled up next to me and stared with reserve, as I took a deep whiff, then flipped my hair over my shoulder.

"You're sure you want me to do that?" His tone was low and growly, as though he wouldn't be faulted for what might happen if he did.

"Um, yeah? It smells so good. You have got to smell it." I held out a lock of hair expectantly.

He watched me with intense, brooding eyes, and it was as though he were trying to mesmerize me with his stare. He approached slowly, and leaned in close, but he didn't stop at my lock of hair. The dark lock slipped from my fingers, as I tilted my head to grant him access to my neck. When he nuzzled his nose there, I closed my eyes.

It was incredibly sensual, on the brink of electric, as his touch whispered across my skin. He took a deep, exaggerated breath, then brushed his parted lips over my throat, setting fire to my blood. It coursed through my veins, flooding my body with endorphins, my body tingling with desire.

"Abby?" Edwin said.

My long, dark lashes flew open. Edwin was no longer touching me but his manly scent was still hanging over me, clouding my thoughts and feeding my arousal. "Hmm?" I said, trapped beneath his heated stare and his confident, angled smile.

"You're right. You do smell good," he said, raising one dark brow. "Edible."

I nearly creamed in my panties. What the hell was wrong with me? This is Edwin. You know, Edwin? And I thought we were talking about my hair here.

The harsh storm cloud that had been following me around for the past few months since my breakup with Cameron seemed to have lifted ever so slightly and my heart was finally feeling like it belonged to its lonely self again.

"Keep dreaming."

Edwin grinned. "Are you ready to head to Haledon tomorrow?"

"Don't jinx it," I answered, relieved that he dropped the hair thing. "Tomorrow isn't here yet."

"Hunter was saying we'll have the guest house all to ourselves. That's pretty cool of Cally."

"Yeah, it should be a good time, as long as you leave the drama at home. Do you think you can be a good boy for one week?"

Edwin's grin had returned full force. "That depends. If I'm a bad boy, are you going to punish me?"

I began to scowl at him, but it wasn't entirely believable. I couldn't even fight the allure of Edwin's mockery. "This is my vacation. I want to be able to relax. You'll be good, or else," I warned.

"Oh, I love when you threaten me."

I rolled my eyes and shook my head. There was no winning with him. "Anyways," I exaggerated. "Cally said she's only going to be there for a few days, then she's leaving with Gabe." I pulled out my cell phone and showed Edwin a photo. "See, that's him." Gabe was a professional athlete, but from the photo she had messaged me on Facebook you would have thought he was a professional model.

"She sends you photos of her boyfriend?"

"Yeah. What's the big deal?"

"Have you ever sent her photos of me?" he asked, waggling his eyebrows.

"Yeah. Naked ones. Dumb ass. No. I've never sent her photos of you. She had to look at your annoying face her entire childhood, I think she'd thank me for saving her the misfortune."

He shoved me playfully, then walked away. "You both love me."

At least I do. I had to cover my mouth when I realized I had even thought it.

When I walked out of the kitchen, Edwin was already making his way back down the stairs, with a single, black bag clutched in his hand. "I'm going to go throw my stuff in the back of the truck. Can I take this too?" he asked, pointing at the pile of bags I had stacked at the door.

"They'll get all cold out there. Can't you wait until morning?"

"I guess so." He dropped his bag down next to mine, then wandered over to the loveseat across from me. "Have you heard from Aliah yet?"

"Nope. And I didn't get a chance to talk to her today at work. I was so busy trying to get all my work done for the week, and by the time I went to see her she was already gone."

Edwin nodded. "Hunter was saying that he wanted to drive up separately anyways, in case Maddie had any baby issues."

I smiled, softly. "Did you see Maddie today? Those twins want out of there. It looked like they were trying to kick and punch their way out of her belly."

"Twins?" Edwin said, his eyes bugging from his head.

"Didn't Hunter tell you? Maddie found out at her last ultrasound, and I'm told the babies will come any day now."

"Now I get why Hunter was so nervous about leaving the City."

I picked up my phone and dialed Aliah's number. It rang three times before Hunter picked it up.

"Hey, Hunter. Is Aliah there?"

"Oh, Abigail. Sorry, but Aliah's not feeling that well."

"You're still going to Haledon with us though, right?" I flashed a look of concern at Edwin.

"I don't think we're going to be able to make it. Between her and Maddie, I think it's best if we stay back." He paused, sensing my disappointment. "I hope we aren't ruining your plans."

I was disappointed, but I couldn't be mad at him for it. I sighed. "Do you guys need anything?"

"No, no. I've got it. I have been waiting on Aliah hand and foot all night. I think she may be taking advantage of me."

I smiled and let out a hollow laugh. "Okay, well I guess I'll let you go then. If you need anything just call."

"No way," he chided. "You guys go ahead and have a good time. Don't worry about us. We'll still be here when you get back."

I looked at the phone, sorting my tangled thoughts, and Edwin watched me intently. I put the phone back to my ear. "Okay, take care then." With another sigh, I ended the call and just stared at Edwin for a long while.

"Aliah's not feeling well and Hunter wants to stick around so he can keep his eye on Maddie. Should we stay back?" I finally asked.

"You're joking, right?"

"I mean, I guess we can still go. But it'll be just the two of us." I battled with the concept, but my desperate need to get away was winning the inner struggle.

Edwin showed no resistance. "Good then, we're still on. You ready to go?"

I flipped my freshly styled hair over my shoulder. "I thought we were going tomorrow."

"Why bother waiting if we're all packed now? You really think Cally will care if we show up a few hours early? I say let's get out of here and get this vacation started."

"You're sure you're okay with this?" I certainly wasn't.

Edwin brought his fist to his chin, thoughtfully. "Let's see. I have the week off and a vacant guest house waiting for me, at no charge. If you ask me, it doesn't get any better than that."

"I mean the fact that it will be just the two of us. Smart ass."

Edwin dropped his hand. "Cally will be there. Besides, how's that any different from right now? Or are you afraid that you won't be able to resist my fetching good looks for that long?"

"Ha, ha. You're so funny," I said. "Fine. Let's go."

Edwin jumped to his feet and urgently filled his truck with our bags. He wasn't going to give me a spare minute to rethink the consequences of my decision. Lucky for him I wasn't in the thinking mood anyway. If my holiday had officially begun, then I was done thinking for the rest of the week.

I had stared at the lights of the City as they passed in a stream of colour and slowly faded into the distance. The dark of night had seemed much darker in the country, especially in the hillside, and I had no trouble finding sleep. When I awoke from my nap, Edwin had already found our destination.

"This is it," Edwin said. His headlights shone on the driveway, but it looked more like a walking path than a road for a vehicle to travel on. Edwin slowly weaved through the wilderness, and headed up the steep, winding driveway.

We passed a cute, wood cabin on the way and then disappeared back into the heavily-wooded, forest that was covered in snow. A spectacular glow hovered above the trees and a spectacular house of glass was suddenly exposed. The gravel turned to stamped concrete and led the rest of the way to the massive house. It must have been heated, too, since it was spotless.

A snow-covered patio wrapped around the second level of the house, with floor to ceiling windows. It was a good thing the house was nestled deep in the woods, because you could see straight through it to the backyard. It looked like every light in the house was on, making the fresh snow sparkle.

Edwin parked the truck and pulled on the parking brake. "Wow, you weren't kidding. This place is something else."

A moment of silence passed between us. I had texted Cally to tell her we were on our way, but a quick check of my phone revealed that she hadn't gotten back to me.

"Shall we?" Edwin asked.

"Right." I pulled myself out of my strange mood, and stumbled out of his oversized truck.

The path was cleared, but it was slippery. Edwin reached out his hand to help me up the hill. It beat tumbling on my ass, so I couldn't refuse his thoughtful offer.

As soon as I stood flat on the doorstep, in need of my independence back, I slipped my hand out of his to press the doorbell. A beautiful melody chimed through the house and, after a few seconds, I saw Cally prancing to the door. A man, who had to be Gabe, followed behind her.

She tugged the heavy door open and flung herself into my arms. "Abby!" she squealed.

After pulling herself off of me, she checked out Edwin. "Edwin. Handsome as always," she said, winking at him.

"You must be Gabe. I'm Abby."

"Yes, of course. I've heard so much about you." He ran his hand through his longish, brown hair and extended his other hand for a friendly shake. He smiled at me, his supermodel smile, before I took his hand. His face was elegantly masculine, with a sharpened narrow nose and soft stubble trimming his thin lips and square chin.

Edwin cut my handshake short, extending his hand out to Gabe. "Edwin. Nice to meet you. This is a beautiful house you have here." His shake was firm and short, and despite Edwin's nice words, his squared shoulders showed that he felt threatened by him.

Cally stood there impatiently, waiting for the formalities to be over with. "I'm glad we got that out of the way. What are you doing here so soon, and where's Aliah?"

"I tried to text you. Ally and Hunter couldn't make it. They send their regrets."

"Right, the whole baby thing," Cally said, waving an inconsiderate hand. She hooked her arm in mine and pulled me deeper into the house, away from Edwin and Gabe.

"So, you and Edwin, eh?" she suggested, quietly in my ear.

"It's not like that."

"I'm sure." Her giggle was effortless and carefree.

"I realize it's pretty late."

Cally patted my arm and gave me a devious wink. "You two should get settled in the guesthouse for tonight. I bet you had a long day. We have all the time in the world for a tour."

"Didn't you say we could stay here? In the main house. With you," I stuttered, stunned by the change of plans.

"Yeah," she said. "But that was only because there's only one bed in the guest house and I thought you were expecting company. It'll fit the two of you just fine."

Edwin yawned loudly, making it known that he was still in the room. "That sounds like a good idea to me. I'm exhausted."

Like hell. Edwin rarely went to bed before midnight, especially on a Friday night. Gabe dangled out a set of keys and dropped them into Edwin's hand.

"It's down the drive on the right. Make yourself at home, and help yourself to anything that's there. I had it restocked for you."

"There are fresh linens in the bathroom closet," Cally added, as she gave me another squeeze around my neck. "See you in the morning. We'll have breakfast together. Well... let's make it brunch."

Cunning, beotch. I knew exactly what she was doing. She was acting like she was doing me a favour, when she knew damn well that I didn't need more time alone with Edwin.

"We'll be here," Edwin answered, as he stole my hand and pulled me back toward the door. "It's been fun, but I'm ready to hit the hay. We can get better acquainted in the morning," he told me.

I turned back to Cally, feeling exasperated, but I still smiled when I waved goodbye. I couldn't stay mad at her. When she winked at me though, I intentionally ignored it.

Edwin drove super slow down the slippery driveway and relief washed over me when he pulled up tight to the quaint wood cabin. A motion sensor caught our approach and flashed a light on at the front door, highlighting the rich wood and elaborate trimmings. The rumbling engine cut out as I leapt out of the truck. I walked toward the front door, carefully gripping my feet to the ground with each awkward step.

Edwin went into the back of the truck to get our bags and slung them all over his shoulders. He didn't even ask for help, though I had brought enough clothes to effectively dress an army. I expected him to complain - waited for him to demand my help. *Nothing.* I watched him fumble with the keys until he finally got it in the hole.

"Persistence pays off, yet again," he mumbled, as the door swung open.

I reached in and flipped the light switch, not knowing what to expect. We both glanced in without moving and stood there mute, stunned by the romantic sophistication and natural charm of the cabin. I looked to Edwin and smiled.

"Ladies first," he said, raising his eyebrows.

Unable to deny him that, I stepped out of the cold and into the cozy, open space. I placed my snow-covered shoes on the small mat at the door and opened the closet to find hangers for our coats.

Edwin dropped the bags to the floor and scanned over the immaculate country kitchen, that had state of the art appliances. Then he slipped his feet from his boots. I lined them up next to mine, then hung my jacket in the closet before closing it up. Edwin hung his coat over one of the tall stools at the breakfast bar and glanced at the cozy dining space and beyond through the patio doors.

His big, shadowed silhouette did strange things to me, evoking old feelings I had long forgotten about. I turned away, in an attempt to brush off those thoughts and shake that picture of his profound stance from my memory.

I steered myself to the focal point in the room, a natural stone fireplace, perfectly centered in the living space. It was flanked with an abundance of comfy, contemporary furnishings. It was perfect. The sky light was dark, partially covered in snow, resting snugly in the high vaulted ceiling. Everything was amazing, but I found my eyes tracing their steps back to Edwin.

When my heart skipped a beat, I knew it was time to seek out some privacy. I opened the one and only solid door in the place, which I expected had to lead to the bathroom. Hiding wasn't much help at rerouting my thoughts though, when the bathroom was home to the most luxurious glass shower I had ever seen. It had twin, ceiling-mounted rainfall showerheads. It was what dreams were made of. Naughty ones. I had to escape back to reality immediately.

I turned on my heel to bolt from the spacious bathroom, but before I could take a step, my legs turned into noodles.

Edwin was leaning against the door frame, his lean hips cocked to the side, his muscular arms tugging tight on his shirtsleeves, straining the soft fabric. "Pretty amazing, huh?" He stretched a thick arm across the doorway, officially blocking my path.

"I'm definitely amazed," I breathed. I meant the house, but he could sense my desire.

Neither of us could deny that it felt like a romantic getaway for two. I only hoped that Edwin couldn't see right through me, the way his gaze said he could.

I pushed through his arm with both of my hands. "Excuse me," I said, hustling ass to the living room and plopping in the middle of a plush, brown sofa.

Thankfully, he had let me out. Because if he had stopped me, I was a goner. I could sense Edwin was behind me, even before he spoke. My sensual awareness of him became incredibly hard to understand and even more difficult to ignore. I glanced over my shoulder and found Edwin peering over the half wall to the sleeping quarters. As if I hadn't already noticed.

The bedroom was the only room in the place with three full walls, settled in the corner next to the bathroom. An oversized fan hung above the large bed, giving it the feel of a tropical oasis. The four-poster bed filled the room, with its white dressings, leaving only enough room surrounding it to get in and out of the bed.

The king sized mattress was so high, you needed a trampoline to get onto it, unless you planned on taking a running leap. One glance at the room told me it served one purpose very well, and it wasn't restful sleep. Edwin's expression proved that he got the same impression.

"You can hardly call this a cabin, eh?" I said. My voice was raw and desirous. I hadn't realized how few words we had spoken since we discovered the space so many minutes earlier.

"It's more like a grand suite. Good thing Aliah and Hunter didn't come. There would've been no privacy for the whole week. That could've gotten awkward."

I nodded. It was only just perfectly spacious for two, but the contemporary finishes turned it into a modern day fantasy. And I would have to be here alone with Edwin.

"I call the bed," he teased, provoking me. He smirked, then dropped backward onto the fluffy blankets.

"The bed is mine!" I chased after him and bounded onto the bed. With another leap, I landed on top of him, my hands flat on his chest, pinning him against the totally dreamy bed.

Edwin bumped my crotch with his thigh, drawing me up higher, forcing me to firmly plant my hands on either side of his head. My body pressed his into the bed, our faces drawn close together. It shouldn't have affected me like that, in a way that I wasn't ready to admit.

I forced a painful reminder into my head. *Babies. Edwin doesn't want any.* Feeling like I had already made a big mistake, I rolled off of him and lounged there facing the large window; away from him. I realized on a deep breath that I had been holding mine.

He turned to face me, but stayed a safe distance away, chuckling at me. "It's a big bed. I'm sure we can share it." He stretched his arms over his head and growled. "That is if you can keep your hands off me."

When I turned to face him, I saw the way his shirt wrinkled around each flexed abdominal muscle and it made me wonder whether I could. But after a deep breath, I also decided I couldn't let my sour mood ruin our holiday. It would be much more fun to play his game.

I leaned into him, flaunting my newfound confidence, and fluttered my long, dark lashes at him. "I think I can handle it. But maybe you'd better wear your shirt to bed, just to be safe." I slowly dusted my fingers across his wide chest, teasing, and tugging on his shirt.

Why do I insist on tantalizing myself?

Edwin was clearly amused, but he still took a sharp intake of breath to reign in his arousal. "I'm impressed with your self-restraint." His grin burst from his handsome face.

I patted his chest, releasing him from my grip, then flung myself back onto the pillows. "Oh yeah, this is the life."

"We're gonna have a good time this week. I'm sure of it," Edwin said, equally as relaxed now.

I smiled, because I knew he was right. We always had a good time together.

Feeling ready for bed, I whipped open the blankets and crawled underneath them. I stripped off my clothes, until I was wearing nothing but panties and a fitted undershirt. It would have been just plain cruel to send Edwin off to the sofa now, so I didn't.

"Night, night," I said, as I rolled away, to the far edge of the bed. There, I felt cozy and safe. *Safe from his advances.*

Edwin slid out of bed and turned off the light, then peeled off his jeans and sweater, being sure to keep on his undershirt to appease me. That night, curled up on my respective side of the bed, I relaxed for the first time in what felt like ages, and Edwin left me to usher in some surprisingly naughty dreams.

CHAPTER TEN

I opened my eyes and stretched my arms over my head, drawing in a long breath to relieve myself from my alarming dream, which I faintly recalled but desperately wanted to remember. I could hear running water and figured Edwin was in the shower. For that I was grateful. He had been the object of my dream that had left me breathless and overwhelmed with a fresh lack of clarity.

I squeezed my eyes shut and strained to remember the dream that had felt so real only moments earlier. Bits and pieces started to come back to me in vivid colour.

Tropical waves crashed the white sand shore, the bright sunshine warming my skin while the fresh morning air teased through my hair. There were endless views of tree-covered mountains, ridiculously grand rocks and crystal blue waters. All that was fine and great, but what tripped me up was that Edwin was there with me. We were isolated on this secluded island and I was completely happy.

I wore nothing but flowered bikini bottoms. Edwin wore fitted, white swim trunks that contrasted against his dark, tanned flesh. He pulled me into his arms and so tenderly kissed my exposed neck and chest. His hands gently cupped and caressed my breasts, leaving me aching with a need so deep I could feel it in my bones.

Every touch scorched my senses and I wasn't hiding my attraction to him, running my fingers through his hair and digging my nails into his back as our kiss became more heated and necessary. Edwin lowered me onto a large, white lounger with an overhang that blocked our half-naked bodies from the harsh morning sunrays.

Edwin caressed my eyelids with kisses and slowly, thoroughly made his way down my body. His hand traced down and around my curves and when it dipped between my legs, my entire body shuddered. My eyes were still closed and I had parted my lips to draw in a breath, just begging Edwin to carry on. Through half-closed lids I devoured him. But then he stopped.

"What is it?" I breathed.

He smirked and I felt that smile everywhere. "Those aren't going to get you knocked up," he said, pointing at the moist scrap of fabric between my legs.

I smiled back. "Then maybe you'd better do something about that."

Edwin obeyed, slipping off my bikini bottoms and stripping off his own shorts, leaving us wonderfully naked in each other's arms. Edwin had every intention of giving me the child I had always dreamed of and he wouldn't stop trying until I was impregnated. He hovered over me, his eyes gazing intently into mine as I directed him to where he needed to be.

He slowly eased inside me with a purpose. Needing more pressure, I arched my back and bucked against him, until he filled me with his hardness. His kiss softened my moan as he repeatedly worked himself deeper. He sucked on my neck and I moaned unreservedly, dazzled by the intense sensations racing through my body.

I tensed beneath him and began to climax, every muscle in my body twitching around Edwin as he prepared himself to detonate inside of me. With a final grunt of ecstasy, Edwin gave me what I wanted and I screamed out in outrageous pleasure.

Suddenly, I opened my eyes, panting this time. And there I was, in bed, caught in a whirlwind of sexual anguish and mental torment. I sat up, my taut nipples brushing against my fitted shirt, only to find Edwin walking up to me wearing nothing but a small towel draped across his hips.

"Oh, you woke up." His bright aqua eyes sparkled and I knew it was because he had noticed my arousal.

I tugged the blanket to my chin to cover my chest, but it couldn't mask my flushed face. A few stray water droplets glistened on Edwin's perfectly sculpted body and it drew my eyes to his hairless chest, looking just as good as it had in my fantasy. I couldn't contain my residual attraction to

Edwin. Especially with his own arousal now tenting from his towel.

In need of a pinch, I squeezed my eyes shut, laid back on the bed and exhaled harshly. It was a shoddy attempt to collect my bearings and, when I reopened my eyes and turned them on Edwin, it only confirmed that I was no longer dreaming.

"Do we have a problem?" Edwin asked me.

I flashed my hungry eyes away from his delicious body, terrified of what I might agree to in this moment. Edwin lifted his bag onto the bed and squinted at me, seemingly confused by my awkward awareness of his nakedness.

I put my hand over my eyes and sighed, hoping that if I didn't look at the sex-god, then maybe the attraction would fade. "I just had the craziest dream and I'm having a hard time waking up."

I heard his towel hit the floor and wished that I was back in dreamland. I kept my eyes covered, though I wanted so badly to watch. To touch. I waited for the zip of his jeans before I resumed breathing. Edwin wasted no time coming to me. I removed my hand from my forehead and looked up at him. He was still shirtless. *Dammit.*

Edwin rested his hand on my arm. Even through the blanket it seared my senses. "It's about Cameron isn't it?"

My healing heart winced. The thought of Cameron knowing about my dream involving Edwin, drilled holes through my chest and filled me with guilt. Even more disgusting was the fact that the sexual tension plaguing me now had far surpassed the relatively distant pain in my heart.

It was just a dream. Not to be confused with reality.

Edwin misconstrued my silence and dipped his hand under the blanket to grasp mine. I gasped, not realizing he was only trying to comfort me, while I fought the temptation to pull him onto me and swallow his tongue.

"Whenever you're ready to talk about it - whatever it is - I can handle it now," Edwin insisted. He let go of my hand and brushed my cheek, his touch so gentle and sensual.

Then he returned to his bag and dragged it to the foot of the bed, where he tucked his clothes into the tall, wood chest.

He glanced back up at me, catching that I was still staring. "Whatever it is," he repeated, "I hope you can set it aside for now. You really need to get ready."

I nodded, acknowledging that I did indeed have to set it aside now and forever, though I knew Cally would love to help me decipher my dream. We used to do that all the time as kids, sitting on the front porch of her parents' house in the country. Concentrating on that, I slipped out of the blankets and sunk my feet onto the thick carpet skirting the bed.

First, I had to get past Edwin. But after I rounded the end of the bed, instead of moving he stood up tall. I tucked my chin down, as my heart began to race, and Edwin turned his large frame to let me squeeze past him. I turned sideways myself to slip by and rested a hand on his shoulder, to make sure I didn't bump the dresser with my shapely behind, which I then realized was on display thanks to my lack of pants.

Edwin tilted his chin down and I could feel his warm breath on my eyelids. I knew if I only looked up our lips could meet. They would meet. A breath hitched in my throat as I brushed across him, my stiff nipples skimming along his smooth, solid chest. I deliberately stole my hand from his shoulder for my arm to cover my tender nipples and hide my arousal.

I quickly tip-toed across the cold floor, hoping Edwin would ignore me, but I heard his feet padding on the floor behind me and felt his heated stare when he stopped and trained them on my backside. Terrified to visualize his awareness of my condition, I rushed into the bathroom and locked the door behind me.

I was in need of privacy, while I took my unpleasantly cold shower. Luckily Edwin had left his toiletries behind, because I had forgotten mine in the other room and I certainly wasn't heading back out there to get them. When I scrubbed Edwin's shampoo into my hair, I inhaled his memorable scent, reminded of my intense fascination with him in my dream.

As the cool water flowed over my aroused body, I touched myself, immersed instantly into my colourful imagination. Edwin and I were back on the warm, sandy beach, this time fully clothed, but Edwin's white shirt was open. It distracted me, as the front panels dangled on either side of his body, the gentle wind parting it to expose his hulking chest and amazing core.

Edwin came to me and knelt in the sand. He nuzzled his cheek against my flat belly, then pulled me down to my bare knees. I pulled him to me and he responded with a kiss so intimate that I had to touch him to stop the tears from flowing. I freed his arms from his shirt and smoothed my fingers across his chest and down his rock hard abdominals.

I tugged at his waistband and flashed him a look of desire. With a slanted smile, he took my mouth and laid me out beneath him. He lifted my flowing skirt and pulled down my panties, his glorious eyes locked on mine, reflecting the crashing waves both in colour and intensity.

He unzipped his pants, freed his arousal and with a gentle push he was inside of me. I quickly reopened my eyes, the sound of my moan still echoing through the bathroom, while I waited to hear whether Edwin had heard me. *Great. Now I was daydreaming about him too. But damn, did I have a good imagination.*

Had my feelings truly returned for Edwin or was I just creating something from nothing? That damn dream had shaken me to my core and every inch of my body ached with a need for Edwin.

I managed to shake the dream from my mind, but it only brought me back to my reality. Only minutes earlier Edwin had approached *our* bed looking naked and delicious. I couldn't help but imagine what could have happened if I had yanked that towel off of him and pulled him into bed with me. Would he have satisfied all of my fickle fantasies, if only for the fun of it?

Irritated by my own suggestions, I cranked the water to full on cold. As the water turned icy, it sprinkled over my heated body like hail, sending a chill across my skin that only intensified the heat between my thighs. Realizing it was a lost cause, I turned the water off, quickly dried my body and tiptoed to the sink, internally scorning myself for leaving my bag in the other room.

With my ear to the door, I listened for an indication of what Edwin was doing. There was only silence. I tried to open the door, but it was locked. *Why had I done that?* When I finally got the door opened a crack, I found Edwin looking out the patio doors at the snow-covered forest and my bags resting on the floor at my feet. *Great. Edwin must have tried to bring them to me. I never lock him out.* But I *had* locked him out.

After readying myself for the day, I burst into the living room where Edwin was still sitting a little too quietly. "I'm ready!" I announced.

Edwin didn't budge and he didn't snap back with a smart-assed comment either. That worried me. Having regained control over my urges, I sat next to him on the couch, hoping to fix the problem I had caused.

I squeezed his knee, in as friendly a gesture as possible, and yet my arousal reignited full force. "You okay?"

He seemed to blink out of the zombie-like trance he had been in. "Just daydreaming, I guess." His voice was plain and hopeless.

"Happy dreams, I hope."

"Not exactly. I might as well get it out of the way now, or there's no way we'll be able to spend the rest of this week together." He paused and I gulped back a whimper.

Shit! He's caught on to my weirdness.

"I realize I kind of invited myself along," he said. "I just hope I'm not the root cause of all your unhappiness."

"I'm not unhappy," I admitted, without thinking, to my own surprise.

"You seemed fine last night, but this morning..." He trailed off, and then found the words. "Let's just say, when you woke up, you looked less than happy to see me. Then you locked me out of the bathroom. If that's supposed to be some kind of warning, I get it."

I laughed nervously and spoke again, without thinking. "That's not it at all." I hoped he couldn't read into that, since he was usually pretty good at getting me. I sighed. "The last thing I want to do is turn you against me too. It's not you. Well, it kind of is, but it's more me." I had already said too much.

"Oh, right: *It's not you, it's me.* This is the most pitiful friendship ever. Why is this so difficult when we're *just friends*?"

We were never very good at being *just friends*. Hell, he didn't even believe that a man and woman could be *just friends*.

"I'm sorry this has to be about you, but it is," I admitted. "I'm the one with the problem. I told you I'm messed up." My eyes glazed over as I stared off into space. "Just give me a chance to sort it out in my own head first, and you'll be next on my list to know what's going on. I promise."

One thing Edwin could always rely on was my promise. My only problem now was that the facts were pretty clear to me. *I want Edwin.* Even after all the love I had shared with Cam, *I want him.* Sitting right at his side, his electrifying touch sizzling against my leg, *I wanted him.* Even in light of the fact that he didn't want kids now: *I still wanted him.* That terrified me the most.

It surprised me how much relief I found, having just admitted that to myself, even if only in my own mind. When the foggy haze cleared, I realized that Edwin had watched me reach that epiphany. He could sense my uneasiness and I recognized the understanding in his eyes. Then a knowing smile spread across his lips.

"I knew you couldn't resist me. I'm just that damn irresistible."

I couldn't even defend myself, because he was one hundred percent correct this time, but seeing that smile was enough to lighten my shattered nerves. I teased him back with a fake scowl, since I knew he couldn't possibly read my mind, then shoved him playfully. He fell back on the couch as though I had delivered a life threatening blow and laughed even harder.

I rolled my eyes, though I loved how dangerously dark his own eyes had turned. "Enough about you. Cally's waiting and I'm hungry," I bellowed.

He hopped to his feet. "Then what are we waiting for?"

It was Edwin's brilliant idea to hike up the driveway, though it was fifty below and snowing like mad. Heavy snowflakes coated my hair and the wind tangled it even further. I flipped my hood on with both my chilled hands and carefully treaded up the ridiculous incline in my heeled boots.

Edwin didn't seem to be having any apparent issues and actually appeared to be enjoying our stroll. He noticed I was having difficulty and extended his elbow with a dramatic raise of his eyebrows. Regardless of his goofy behaviour, I took his arm because I desperately needed the help. Edwin linked his fingers through mine and tucked me up close to his side.

"It'll keep you warm," he insisted, making excuses.

I was cold and exhausted, so I let him keep my hand, to haul me up the slippery driveway. The land sloped steadily, until we reached the house. I stole a glance at Edwin and I noticed that he was watching me again. *What is he thinking now?*

I rang the doorbell as soon as we reached it and waited for an answer. The door swung open and Cally pulled me inside, tugging me away from Edwin.

"You made it!" Cally held onto my arm and led us through to the middle of the house, babbling incoherently about one thing or another.

A wide winding staircase led us to the second level. I caught a brief glimpse of each room as we passed them, while Cally towed me to the dining area. Edwin followed us and then rounded the end of the long, dining table. Not waiting for an invitation, he walked all the way to the other end of it, taking a seat in front of one of the place settings.

Gabe was in the kitchen, hidden behind a fabulous island of granite, in chef mode.   Cally watched him, with appreciation evident in her eyes, as I faded back into the confines of my own mind.

"Keep dreaming," Edwin said to me, knocking me back into reality.

If he only knew what I had been dreaming about. It was a gorgeous kitchen and I could easily imagine Edwin in it.

"He's just finishing up," Cally said. "Why don't you have a seat too? I'll be right back." She hurried off to help Gabe and I watched them share a chaste kiss.

I pulled out the chair next to Edwin and my skin tingled with the awareness of how close he was. Then he turned on his charming smile and flashed me his teeth. I tried to fight it, but I had to smile back at him. We stayed like that for what had to be minutes, staring curiously into each other's eyes. It should have been awkward, but it wasn't. And it wasn't until Cally clapped her hands together, that I realized she and Gabe had already joined us at the table.

Cally's smile was so easy to read, her eyes darting deviously between us. I flashed her a warning stare and she indulged me. Gabe wasn't quite so understanding and, after a few mouthfuls of food, he started to ask questions.

"How long have you two been together?"

I choked on my orange juice and a small amount squirted out of my mouth onto Edwin's plate. Edwin rubbed my back, but it didn't help. It only made it worse. Cally straightened in her chair.

"I'm so sorry!" I said, between breathy attempts to talk and raspy coughs.

Edwin turned to Gabe. "I think what she means to say is, we aren't a couple. We've done that thing before – a few times actually - but it didn't work out." He sounded so let down.

Where did that come from?

Gabe pressed a finger to his lips, his thumb hooked under his chin, while he thought more on that subject. Edwin's hand stopped rubbing, but he left it resting on my back, searing my senses, and reaching me intimately.

How could I possibly think about him touching me now, when I was gasping for my life?

Unable to regain my calm, Gabe opened his mouth again. "It's just that I saw you holding hands when you walked up to the house. Then there's the way you look at each other. Owww!" Gabe barked.

Cally had kicked him under the table, hard enough that his chair scraped backward a bit. She smiled at us sideways with her eyes nearly bugging out of her head, expressing her embarrassment.

"What?" he asked, looking at her. He clearly didn't think he had done anything wrong.

Then why were my cheeks so red? I blamed the choking.

Cally shook her head sideways. "Men. I think it's time for that tour."

After leading us around Gabe's remarkable house, we congregated back in the large living room next to the dining area. It had three walls of floor to ceiling windows. I gawked at the marvelous view, in awe of the heated in-ground pool. It was perched on the hill, overlooking the expansive rolling hillside that led into a forest of snow-covered evergreen trees.

"You have a beautiful house," I said, for lack of better words.

"Thank you," Gabe replied.

Cally cut right to the chase. "So, Gabe is actually leaving at two o'clock today. I have to take him to the airport very soon actually, but I'd love if you would come out for dinner with me tonight. We really need to catch up."

"Absolutely. I'd love that," I said.

"Yeah *we* definitely would," Edwin added.

I glanced over at Edwin and his charming smile hooked onto me. Gabe noticed the exchange and smiled. Then he turned his eyes to his feet to act like he hadn't caught it.

"Well, Abs. We should get going. I imagine they'd like to have some time together before Gabe has to leave."

Cally snickered, as Edwin pulled me away. "Oh, Eddie. How very sweet of you," she teased. "I'll call you guys later this afternoon."

"Thank you for everything," I said to Gabe, as Edwin tugged me down the stairs.

Edwin zipped up his heavy, leather jacket and gave them a wave. "Thanks again."

After slipping on my boots, I stepped out into the wild weather again. Edwin closed the door behind us and pushed his elbow into my side demanding that I take his arm. After taking it, he linked his fingers back in mine and we slowly wandered down the driveway. The hike downhill seemed a lot easier and in a matter of minutes we were back at the guest house, and I was stretched out over the loveseat.

Edwin knelt down in front of the fireplace and rubbed his hands together. "Let's get this baby going!" He started to look around. *For firewood?*

I started to laugh and pointed at the switch on the wall.

"Hey, what d'ya expect from a city boy?" Edwin drawled, then flipped the switch. He was good enough to laugh at his own stupidity.

I had taken the opportunity to admire his tight round ass, which was a mistake. Flames began to gently flicker in the fireplace and it illuminated the room with a soft, warm glow, much like the sensation that had washed over my entire body.

Edwin took a seat on the couch across from me. "It looks like we have some time to kill. What are we going to do today?"

"Absolutely nothing."

"I like that plan," Edwin said, smiling. "It looks like you're feeling better now. Do you still need that time to think; or are you going to tell me what's really going on?"

It felt like a rock went rolling down my windpipe. I couldn't manage a breath let alone a word.

"I can take a hint. I'll leave it alone for now," Edwin said, with a smirk. "But I'm setting a deadline of tomorrow. I'm not letting you worry away your entire vacation. If you don't tell me before supper tomorrow night, I'll tickle it out of you."

Edwin jumped on top of me and gave me a taste of his tickle torcher.

"Okay, okay. Please stop. Edwin!"

I could see it in his eyes that he enjoyed listening to my pleas, but he stopped after one last tickle. Then he growled and his darkened eyes hooked onto mine.

"I love when you scream my name."

CHAPTER ELEVEN

My lungs jumped back to life as Edwin backed away, chuckling. *Is he playing with me right now? That made me so hot!* He rummaged around in the fridge, as if nothing out of the ordinary had just been said. Edwin loved to toy around. *There's no way he knows how I feel.*

Knowing that before long we'd be doing dinner with Cally, I dropped it. I would have plenty of time to hash everything out with her then. Cally had called by four to suggest we dress up a bit. I spent the next hour getting ready.

"Damn, I look good," Edwin announced, as he checked himself out in the mirror.

He did look good in his white collared shirt, with a dark grey sweater vest layered over it. Not all men could pull that look off, but he did it. Very well. So well, in fact, that I had to fight myself to quit staring.

I watched him reach over his shoulder in an attempt to fix his collar, but his bulky muscles didn't grant him graceful access to his neck. Edwin stopped trying and turned to me. I just kept staring, like a love-struck fool.

"Would you get my collar for me?" he asked, looking a little helpless.

I hurried behind him. "Sure," I said, shamelessly excited by the thought of touching him.

When I moved around to face him, he stood very still, his eyes closing. That made me anxious. I held my breath as I reached my arms over his shoulders to properly adjust his collar. My fingers casually brushed across his skin and I heard him take a sharp intake of breath. He must have felt the same electricity zinging through his body as was passing through mine.

'Honk, Hooonnnk!' Cally's car came racing down the hill and stopped right outside our door. *'Hooonnnk!'*

I was relieved that Cally was there to save me from myself. "We should go."

A second later, Cally pressed her horn three more times.

"Okay, okay. We're coming," Edwin hollered, as if she could hear him.

I laughed at her impatience, as Edwin opened the door for me. I flashed him a thoughtful smile. "You'd better stop with that, because a girl could get used to it you know."

His eyes had never left mine. He had remembered the last time we had used that line. *What was I doing flipping those words around now?*

"Maybe I want you to," he growled, his voice sending delicious shivers across my skin.

Was he only teasing? He sure looked serious to me. I quickly masked my unrestrained smile because Cally was watching me. I got in the passenger seat, while Edwin locked the cabin door.

"Gabe's pretty hot, eh?" Cally said, skipping the usual pleasantries. "I told you he was gorgeous."

"Yes, Cally. He's very good looking," I said, watching Edwin through the side mirror as he opened the back door.

Edwin heard what I was saying when he got in the back seat. "Please tell me I'm not going to have to hear this all night."

"We'll keep it light for you, Eddie," Cally teased.

I didn't believe her for one second and, when our eyes connected briefly, I couldn't avoid the onslaught of giggles, and neither could she.

Edwin slapped his forehead. "Tonight is going to be a long night."

The snow had lightened up, so the drive wasn't too terrible, but the restaurant was a fair distance away and there was a gathering of people knocking knees in the cold, waiting to get inside.

"Are you sure you really want to eat here?" I asked. "It looks like it could be an hour before we even get a table."

Cally hooked her arm in mine, then clicked her lock button over her shoulder until her car beeped. "No worries. I've got connections. Oh, and reservations." She giggled.

We walked past the crowd, through the front doors and squeezed past the people waiting to get to the receptionist. Cally didn't even need to say a word.

"Oh, good evening, Ms. Jenkins."

"Sorry, we're a little early," she said, flashing the dapper young fellow her most charming smile.

"Table for three?" he asked, noting her company.

"Yes, please," she replied.

The attendant immediately whispered into a waiter's ear and we were being directed to a private table within minutes.

The waiter pulled out the first chair for Cally and Edwin offered the next one to me.

"Thank you," I said, then took my seat.

Edwin pulled out the chair across from me and settled down into it. "How do you rate that?" he asked Cally, glancing toward the front door where a crowd continued to wait for the next table.

"Gabe is a celebrity of the sort. He called in a favour, to make sure we were treated right."

"Nice guy," Edwin said.

"Money will do that for you," she answered, smiling. "This night is on him, by the way."

I flashed a look at Edwin and he waggled his eyebrows before smiling. I promptly looked away from him, but the butterflies mingled in my belly for a while longer. To distract myself, I went to ask Cally how she had met Gabe, but she held up her finger and waved down a waitress, insisting that we try the margaritas first.

When the food began to arrive, so did my third margarita. "Seriously, Cally. This is my last one."

Edwin laughed as I slurped up the bottom of my drink. He was still working on his first one.

"Fine, fine. You're no fun," Cally teased. She hadn't even finished her first one and was already sipping at her water.

The liquor caused me to talk way more over dinner than I would have ordinarily and, for a change, I was keeping up with Cally's steady chatter. When Edwin excused himself to use the restroom, I knew I would have to take immediate advantage of that, but Cally beat me to the punch.

"What's with you two anyway? Are you an item?" she asked, watching Edwin's ass as he turned down the hall toward the washrooms.

"That's the thing, Cally, we aren't. But I swear the other night our flame reignited or something."

"Ooh, you ignited an old flame. I love it."

"I felt it, at least. I don't know how he feels."

"Oh, he feels it," she muttered. "He did come on this trip with you and he knew you would be alone. That has to mean something."

"Yeah, but we've been friends forever. It doesn't mean he wants anything more than that."

"Honey, you know as well as I do: if the man is still hanging around you, he wants more. They always want more."

Edwin was already making his way back to the table and it made us both turn suspiciously quiet.

"Did I miss anything?" he asked, knowing he walked in on something.

"If you did, we wouldn't tell you," Cally said, as she shuffled her chair away from the table. "Excuse us for a minute? We need to use the ladies' room."

I tried to act like I actually had to go, but the truth was written all over my face.

"Now he knows something's up for sure," I whispered to Cally, as we turned down the private hall heading for the washrooms. "He already thinks I'm being weird lately. Did I tell you he gave me an ultimatum?"

"Oh, this is good." She tugged me into the washroom. "What kind of ultimatum?"

"He just said I'd better figure out what my problem is, because I'm telling him all about it before dinner tomorrow night or he's going to force it out of me."

Cally laughed. "He's obviously trying to pressure you, so you'll spit it out already!"

"Spit what out?"

"That you want to be with him; obviously." She rolled her eyes at my ignorance.

"No, that's not it. He thinks it has to do with Cameron." Saying his name stung a bit, but much less than it used to.

"Does it have anything to do with Cameron?"

"No."

"Then just tell him already. Don't worry, I can see it in his eyes. He has it bad for you. Just give in. It's inevitable. You two are made for each other."

"It's more complicated than that."

"You like him, right?"

"Well, yeah. We've become close again; as *friends*," I reiterated.

Cally rolled her eyes again. "Yeah, but you like him more than a friend, right?"

"I don't know." I felt guilty admitting it out loud, when I still had so much love for Cameron.

"Oh, come on now. You can't lie to me," she said. "You want him. What's the problem?"

"That I want him. I didn't even know I felt this way until a few nights ago. Then last night I had this dream about him. Let's just say, I've been seeing him in a whole new light since then."

"I have got to hear this. I love it," she cheered. "It's just like old times."

I giggled anxiously; just like old times. "I'm not telling you everything, but I will tell you that Edwin was there and it was pretty steamy. Then I woke up, and the feelings didn't go away."

"Tell me more," she demanded.

"No way!"

"It's your subconscious telling you it's time to face it now that you have no other distractions."

"Oh, Cally. I wish it were that easy. But I don't know if I can do this again. We called it quits for a reason. He's not ready for kids yet. As far as I know, nothing's changed there."

"He's single, right?"

"Yeah, I think so."

"You're good then."

"Shouldn't I just move on to new things?" I asked, like I had told myself so many times before.

"No. You should get over yourself. You have to stop being afraid of what could go wrong and start looking forward to what could go right. Look at him. The man's hot. And he's hot for you."

"You're right."

"He's hot?" she asked, both confused and surprised that I agreed with her.

"No. I mean, yes; he's hot. But he's also still hanging around even though he knows my issues."

"There you go. If he's still sticking around, then it's for a reason. He knows about your whirlwind romance with Cameron. I'd bet that's why he hasn't been too pushy in the romance department. He's probably just waiting for you to come around."

"You make a good point. But what if you're wrong?"

"At least you'll get some hot sex out of the deal. No man can pass up hot sex."

We both laughed and with hooked arms we pushed through the door.

"I think I know what I have to do," I admitted. "But it'll have to be tomorrow now, since you've got me all sloshed right now." A cheesy grin covered my face, as we walked down the long hall. "I can usually hold my liquor better. It's really hitting me hard tonight."

Cally covered her smirking mouth with her hand. "That's because I had them putting double shots in yours."

"Cally, I am going to kill you."

"You looked like you needed it. It did the trick too. Look at the striking realization you had."

"I'll strike you one," I replied, swatting at her rear playfully.

Edwin stared me down as we both took our seats, giggling. "Did you girls fall in?"

Cally turned her eyes on Edwin, stealing his warm gaze away from my rosy cheeks. "So, Eddie. What do you think about hitting a club before calling it a night?"

She was testing him. Already. And I was sure, if he said yes, that Cally's tests would only get more difficult as the night went on.

"For sure. I mean, if Abigail wants to," Edwin answered.

I slammed a hand on the table. "I don't know how many more drinks I can handle, thanks to Cally's special mix." I squinted at Cally, animatedly.

"I'm sure you can handle one more," she pressured, the way Cally did best.

I agreed, holding up one finger, and Edwin's smile grew three sizes. My desire burned strong with impatience, as I fought to keep any indication of that from my face. The two of them stood from the table and started toward the door. I followed behind, but stumbled a little before catching myself embarrassedly on a chair. They both stopped to stare at me, along with the rest of the patrons in the fine establishment.

"I can't even walk," I whispered, annoyed by my own incompetence.

Cally giggled as she nodded at the waiter to bring her the bill. "Edwin's a strong man. He can carry you if he has to."

The waiter interrupted. "Mr. Wilde has already taken care of your bill, but I wonder if I could get your signature."

"Sure," Cally answered, then scribbled her name on the white slip. When she lifted her eyes, she acted as though she recognized someone at the bar. She was so transparent sometimes. "Oh, I see someone over there I have to say hello to. You don't mind, do you? I'll only be a minute." She ran off before we could say no and left Edwin and I standing in the middle of the bustling restaurant.

"Why don't we wait for Cally at the door," Edwin suggested, dropping his hand casually around my waist to help me to the front entrance.

I glanced over to Cally at the bar, where she had made some new friends. She gave me a wink, giving up her wicked trickery. I plodded toward the door and had to pull away from Edwin to get out of someone's way. He quickly recovered by resting his hand on the small of my back.

A pleasant chill skipped up my spine and my stomach twisted with guilt. It was only a few short months ago that I was blindly in love with Cameron. My love for him had not simply evaporated, and that made things difficult.

Standing among a few scattered couples lingering by the door, we waited silently for Cally to rejoin us. As a few patrons left the restaurant, a nasty wind blasted in, chilling me to the bone. I wrapped my hands around my arms to fight off the chill. My jacket wasn't nearly as warm as it needed to be to get the job done.

Edwin thoughtfully wrapped his arm around me, and tucked me against his side, without a word. It warmed me instantly, and not just from the heat flooding from his core. A new heat bloomed in my belly and flames burst through my body like it was covered in gasoline. Edwin rubbed his large hand up and down my arm to comfort me, but it only fueled the fire.

When my eyes slowly met his, he smiled. I wanted to kiss him.

"Is that better?" he asked.

If by better he meant melting in his arms, then yes. I was much, much better. I just wanted to curl up against his naked chest and absorb all of him. Thankfully, Cally walked up just then.

"Look at you two. You make such a cute couple."

I pulled away from Edwin, naturally, and shoved Cally.

"What?" she asked. "I'm just saying."

Edwin was clearly amused, but I wasn't. I headed for her car ahead of them and when Cally unlocked the doors, I let myself into the passenger door. As I clicked my seat belt, I noticed it was Edwin getting in the driver seat next to me.

"What are you doing?"

"Cally says her margarita was a little on the strong side and I know I can hold my liquor better than the two of you put together. You just relax and have a good time."

"You don't worry about me. I'll have a good time, if I want to," I argued, wanting control of my own feelings back.

"I don't doubt it," he said, laughing, as the back door slammed shut.

I stared out the window, as Cally directed Edwin to the nightclub. Before long, we were entering the packed dance club, dropping right in on the fun. A hoard of people clogged the perimeter of the dance floor, bumping around and having a good old time. Bass was exploding out of the speakers in heavenly thuds, filling every crevice of the building. Edwin was nodding, showing that he liked it, but that could have had something to do with the loads of nearly naked women prancing around him.

"I'm gonna go get us some drinks," Cally hollered in my ear.

"Okay. Take it easy on me this time," I shouted back.

She smiled, drew a cross over her heart with her finger, and took off toward the bar. I grabbed Edwin's hand and pulled him in the opposite direction.

"We're dancing," I hollered, as a racy song hit the speakers. The combination of the beat and the bouncy beauties made it impossible for me to stand still.

Edwin started fist pumping and, though it cracked me up, the other ladies seemed to think it was pretty hot. I closed my eyes to quit worrying about everyone else and rotated my hips like a belly-dancer. With my hands over my head, I felt the music flow through me. When I opened my eyes, I learned that Edwin was enjoying the show, his face covered again with that dead sexy smile.

My mouth watered, as Edwin reminded me what those hips could do. Then the DJ blended the song into another, and Cally showed up with our drinks lifted high above the crowd.

"Thanks, babe!" I said, then took a sip from my glass. It tasted just right.

Cally danced with me and I hoped to make Edwin jealous. My plan backfired brilliantly, only giving the other spicy ladies the space they needed to move in on Edwin. And they didn't even know how much better it got underneath those clothes. That was until he lifted his bulky arms and pulled his sweater over his head, his t-shirt lifting just enough to show anyone who was watching what they were missing out on.

Even after he fixed his t-shirt, there was no missing the tight pull of fabric across his gorgeous chest. A whole crew of ladies wrapped right around him, blocking him from my view.

Why was I so upset about that?

Glancing over Cally's shoulder, I saw a petite brunette make a move on Edwin, wearing nothing more than a scrap of fabric over her womanly parts. My heart plummeted when she reached her arms around his neck. I felt utterly reckless and couldn't control the burst of madness rushing through my veins.

As though Cally's mind had a direct link to mine, she brought her lips to my ear. "It's fine, Abby. He doesn't want her."

How could she be so sure?

Cally dangled her hands over my shoulders and stared me right in the eye. "Relax. I'm telling you, he's as good as yours."

Another casual glance in his direction was all it took for me to catch Edwin removing the attractive girl's hands off of him, but then he smiled and whispered something in her ear.

What did he just say to her?

"Will you stop!" Cally squealed, breaking my glare.

I immediately checked back. I had to know what was happening. My eyes, heavy with concern, saw Edwin point in my direction. Then our eyes met. His dazzling stare clutched at my heart, holding me in a breathless trance. Edwin looked down at the girl, who appeared to be devastated by whatever he had told her. She spun away from him and stalked off, while I smiled at the fact that he had passed yet another one of Cally's tests.

Edwin approached me like a predator, wearing a sexy, slanted smile. Without asking, he wrapped his arms around my waist, twirled me around and danced with me. It wasn't anything we hadn't done as friends, but I couldn't ignore the extra spark attracting me to him tonight.

When the song finished, empty drink in hand, I headed for the nearest trash can. I quickly returned only to find Edwin alone, Cally having disappeared in two seconds flat.

Here we go again.

"She went to the ladies room," Edwin hollered, reading my facial expression.

I didn't believe it, but a really good song was on, so we continued to dance together. Forgetting about Cally, I let loose and bounced around like a crazy, wild woman. I was having so much fun. Then the song had to go and slow down on us.

Edwin secured his hands on my hips, unexpectedly, and pulled me in close. I swayed back and forth in front of him, resting my head back against his chest, glancing up at him over my shoulder. I let my guard down, just as I was met with a dizzy spell.

Edwin lifted me into his arms and immediately transported me to the bar. A bottle of water was in my hand in a matter of seconds. "I'm told there's a second level to this place. I hear the music's a bit slower paced. Want to check it out?" he asked, noticing that my light-headedness had passed.

My heart skipped a beat and I swallowed a gulp of water before agreeing. "Just let me text Cally, to let her know what we're doing."

I did as I said, and took another sip from my water bottle. With my first step toward the stairs, I started to see doubles. Edwin hooked an arm around my waist, probably only out of fear that I would fall down if he didn't hold on tight.

I may have to act this drunk for the rest of the night, if only to keep Edwin's arms around me.

There were significantly less people upstairs and the music was toned down so you could actually talk without having to scream over the music. The floor was sprinkled with a mellow crowd. Most of the people were hanging out on bar stools, with their friends hovering around them. There was still a large group of people dancing, but you could actually breathe and move around without bumping into the person next to you.

Edwin tossed his sweater over a stool and slipped his jacket back on, then we stood at the edge of the crowd for a moment, watching. "You good?" he asked me, softly running his hand up and down my side.

I took a deep breath, as a sharp pulse throbbed in my throat and thudded in my chest. "Mmm hmm," I answered, as his touch lit my senses and heightened my arousal. I squeezed my eyes shut, trying to figure out what had changed between us so suddenly that made me fall accidentally in love with him. It really didn't matter, since my feelings were obviously displayed on my sleeve.

I had to protect him from my suddenly loose lips. "Why don't you get a drink?"

"I'm good," he replied, with a chuckle. "I think you've had enough for the two of us."

One song flowed gently into the next until one of my favourite songs spilled from the speakers. "I love the way you lie," the singer crooned, as the other dancers paired off. They began to twirl around us, until we were mixed into the group.

Edwin took my hand, looked me in the eyes and smiled. "I thought you'd never ask," he growled, close to my ear. *But I hadn't said a thing.*

That didn't stop me from giving in to him, and there was no fight when he pulled me up close. I slipped my hands inside his leather jacket and clung to his back. His cologne swirled around me, teasing my senses and sharpening my desire. I didn't want to let go of this moment. I rested my head on his firm chest and closed my eyes, letting him guide me through the night. It felt so good to be free again.

When the song changed, I curled my arms around his neck, so he would know I wasn't done with him yet. He reacted to my arrangement by wrapping me completely in his arms. I felt so warm and protected. *Loved.*

I tucked my head on his shoulder again and gripped onto him tighter. His jacket was soft and cool beneath my cheek and I couldn't escape the small bit of exposed skin only inches from my mouth. Not considering what Edwin might think about it, I slowly pressed my lips against his neck and inhaled his manly scent. There was just something about this man. I was hooked.

Edwin put his lips to my ear. "This time, I'm not leaving without you."

CHAPTER TWELVE

Edwin had stunned me with his declaration. The song had ended and a brief silence hushed over the room. Edwin's aqua eyes poured over me. The flirtatious bantering had long since ceased, and we were left with nothing but raw emotion. The way he held me was possessive and I wasn't complaining.

My lips parted, as I lifted my head and turned my gaze to his mouth. His soft, pink lips were calling my name. Seemingly hesitant and insecure, Edwin lowered his head toward mine until we were cheek to cheek.

"Edwin," I breathed, with closed eyes.

He tilted his head in slow motion and sealed my lips with a kiss that set my heart on fire. It lasted but a second, but it sent fireworks zapping through my body. My heavy eyelids remained shut, a smile tight on my lips. Short of jumping his bones, which was exactly what I wanted to do, I was lost. I rested my head securely on his shoulder, unsure of what to do or say next.

"Hey guys!" Cally verbalized, as she tapped me on my back.

I jumped up instantly and pushed off of Edwin like he was a launch pad, feeling like I had just been caught doing something terribly wrong. The music was more upbeat now, but Edwin and I had still been glued together in the middle of the dance floor.

Cally had seen the kiss. I was sure of it.

"You guys ready to go? I was buzzing you, but you didn't answer."

I was a little preoccupied. "I didn't notice." I pulled my phone from my pocket and checked the crazy hoard of messages from Cally. She had sent all kinds spicy remarks, not for Edwin's eyes. I shot her a narrowed glare.

Oh, the brat had seen, and she had the photos to prove it.

Edwin remained silent, as I stuffed my phone deep in my pocket.

"I'm ready," I said, through gritted teeth, with my hands gripped on my hips.

Cally laughed, not taken aback by my fury. "You're such a sour puss." She hooked her arm around mine, then locked Edwin onto the other side of her.

As we walked through the snowy parking lot, Edwin spoke to Cally, all but ignoring me. "Do you want me to drive?" he asked her, as we reached her car.

"No, I'm good," she chimed. "I haven't had anything in hours."

Edwin watched patiently, as I got in the backseat without a fight, then he walked around to the other side of the car. I was starting to feel a little ill from the change of scenery, so I rested my hot forehead on the cold window and it surprised me how much relief it delivered. That's when the door next to me shut softly and a man filled the seat at my side. I glared at Edwin in disbelief.

"What?" he asked, his voice a low growl.

"I didn't say anything." I returned my forehead to the window and closed my eyes. Intoxication had gotten the better of me.

Cally didn't say anything but her 'Hmpf' sound made it clear that she disapproved of my behaviour. Then she turned on some music and cranked the volume much too loud. She even acted as though she was actually enjoying the loudness. *I may be drunk, but I'm not stupid.*

Edwin took advantage and shuffled over to my side of the car. With his arm lifted over the back of my seat, it left me nowhere to go. He leaned in close, his scent arousing me, making me revisit my foggy stupor. "I'm sorry. I obviously upset you." He paused, his steady breaths tickling my neck. "We can just pretend nothing ever happened."

A bone-deep chill rocked through my body as he slid away from me, leaving a void of warmth at my side. My heart ached and it took all I had to hold in the tears. My stomach was already roiling, but the flood of emotions superseded even that. Cally looked at me in the rear-view mirror as Edwin turned to look out his window. *I had done it now.*

When we reached the guest house, I went straight for the bathroom. I brushed my teeth vigorously, my entire body trembling violently from the cold. A few tears dropped down my rosy cheeks, but I wiped them away, determined not to let another drop out.

As soon as I tiptoed across the cold floor, I could sense the gloominess lurking around the room. The bed was empty. Edwin was slumped on the couch, like he had been banished there. I dropped my hands to my sides, feeling utterly exhausted, but incredibly guilty.

"Eddie, you don't have to do that," I said, softly.

"It's probably for the best."

"There's plenty of room in the bed." I held onto the half wall to stop by body from shaking, but it hardly helped.

While Edwin watched my hopeless attempts, I raised my eyebrows to show I wasn't going to move until he did as I said.

"Fine. I'll sleep in the damn bed." He tossed the blanket to the floor and bumped past me. He tossed a few pillows to the foot of the bed and pulled down the covers.

I slowly made my way around to the other side of the bed, lifted the blanket and snuggled in, but it didn't take off the chill. Edwin had lied down on the very edge of the mattress, making it feel like he was in an entirely separate universe from me. I had seriously blown any progress that I had made. *How did this night turn so terribly wrong?*

On a sigh, I clicked the remote and the lights dimmed, until they faded out entirely. I stared blankly at the shadowed, white ceiling for what seemed like hours, until it became apparent that neither of us were going to get a wink of sleep until we dealt with the situation at hand.

In the dead of night, finally, he spoke. "I have never felt so alone, as I do right now." His words were stark, spoken straight from his heart, cutting off my circulation.

It startled my nerves with a jerk. *I did that to him.* My chest heaved, trying to accommodate my rapid breaths. I turned to face Edwin and shifted in the bed, sliding a little closer, but careful not to interrupt his personal space.

"The last thing I wanted to do was hurt you," I said, with emotions spilling from my words.

He stayed cold. "You're getting good at it though."

"Hey, that's not fair." My snappy words hung in the air between us and another lash of guilt struck my heart when I realized that he was right. I was always hurting him. I had to try another angle. "Eddie, you can't possibly feel alone when I'm in the same bed as you."

"You'd might as well be in a different hemisphere, then maybe you'd be a little warmer."

It was true. I had been a cold hearted bitch tonight, but I had to protect my heart. Somewhere along the line I forgot that Edwin had his own heart to worry about.

"I'd like to join you in your hemisphere, if that's okay."

I sounded sarcastic and demanding, but I didn't wait for a response. I shimmied up against him, so we were both lying on one quarter of the massive bed. Under the blankets, I rested my hand on his solid thigh, then gently ran my fingers up and down it. I wanted to comfort him. I wanted him to know he wasn't alone, though I was suddenly feeling awfully lonely myself.

"I won't let you be alone, but we can feel lonely together," I whispered.

He nudged me aside and I backed up to the middle of the bed. Edwin turned to lay on his back and our skin touched again, but there was no electricity anymore. I felt ruined.

"I don't want to fight with you, Abby. You're drunk. Why don't we get some sleep? We can talk about this tomorrow."

I swallowed back my emotion. "Okay."

He can't possibly think I don't care about him, because I do so much.

Desperately wanting to feel our connection again, I snuggled up against him. I nudged his arm around me, nestled my head on his warm chest and smoothed my hand over it. *That did it.* I felt the very moment when the flame reignited again.

"You don't have to do this, Abs."

"I want to." I wrapped my leg around him, for good measure.

I was worried that he might try to remove me from him, but he didn't. Only moments later, the heavy shadows tried to close in on me, but I was safe in Edwin's arms drifting off to sleep. My eyes fluttered back to a happy place and I was out. In my dreams, Edwin kissed my hair and whispered to me. "I love you, Abs."

I awoke to the growl of an engine. A car was passing the guest house. I peeled my drooling mouth off of Edwin's chest and stretched an arm out with a yawn. Edwin was still pinned beneath my leg, not having moved the entire night. I slowly retrieved my leg and snuck to the bathroom. He stirred, but never opened his eyes.

When I slipped back into the bed, I was a little chilled from running around the house, so I curled up behind him again. He warmed my skin, but my feet were frozen. Desperate for his warmth, I slowly drew my foot close to his, then dragged it up his leg.

He awakened immediately. "Whoa! Cold toes," he said, but he didn't make me move my feet and so I didn't.

Clutched onto Edwin in reality, still clinging to my dream, I realized that he wasn't really mine for the squeezing. My eyes burst open on that stark realization and I tumbled back into reality, loosening up on him.

Edwin stretched out with a growl. "Well," he said. "I'm up." He certainly was. His morning wood was terrifying, but tempting.

I cleared my throat. "How are you feeling?"

"I'm fine, but I'm not the one who drank the house down last night. The question is: how are you?"

"I feel like hell," I admitted, with pause. "But better, if you know what I mean."

He groaned and it tickled my entire body. "Not really, but I'm sure you'll get around to telling me later."

Eek! I wasn't ready to talk about *that* yet. Without thinking, I squeezed him again, hating the way I worried about our relationship.

"You seem happy this morning," Edwin said, quirking up an eyebrow.

I released his stiff body, not trusting myself being that close to him. "I slept surprisingly well. You make a good pillow," I teased.

Edwin's face lit up and a smile curled on the edge of his lips. "You know some men might take offence to that."

I swirled my finger across his smooth, rock hard chest. "But you're not some men, now are you?" I struggled with putting distance between us, when I wanted to straddle him and lick every sculpted inch of his body. After that dream I had, I really wanted to shake his tree, and his morning trunk was making it difficult for me to pry myself off of him.

For my own sanity, I gave him a smooch on his nose, crawled out from under the blankets and pranced around the bed toward the bathroom. I peeked around the corner at him, flirtatiously. "I'm going to get ready now, since I know I'll be a little longer than you."

He laughed at me. "A little?"

I didn't reply, before skipping to the bathroom, and I didn't lock the door this time. I secretly hoped he would come join me in the shower, but how could he possibly know that?

After a refreshing shower, that did wonders for my state of being, I heard a knock at the door. Yeah?" I called out, standing under the warm, steady rainstorm.

Edwin cracked the door open. "You've been in there forever and I have to use the facilities."

"Go nuts," I answered.

Like an old married couple, he talked to me while he peed. After that, Edwin let on like he had left the room and, after a few minutes of silence, any other person would have expected that he had. I knew better.

As I finished rinsing my hair, I thrust out my chest and arched my back, knowing that Edwin was likely watching my naked silhouette through the foggy glass doors. After turning off the water, I squeezed out my hair then peeked my head out the shower door.

Edwin was fully dressed and leaning back against the vanity, a good ten feet away. He was watching me. He was also holding my towel.

"Edwin," I said, sternly. "May I please have my towel?"

Edwin lifted his arm and draped the towel over it, like he was my own personal towel boy. "You're going to have to come and get it." His slanted smile touched me from across the room.

"No. You're going to give it to me, or *you're* gonna get it," I threatened.

"Which one is it?" His voice was low, his words wet with sexual innuendo. "Am I gonna get it or am I going to give it to you? Either way I win."

I spoke through gritted teeth in an attempt not to laugh, but Eddie had a way of making me smile. "Edwin. Give me the damn towel."

He started to inch toward me. "Oh, come on. Just a little peek."

I pressed my lips together to stop the smiling and kept my body hidden behind the shower door. "There's nothing here you haven't seen before."

"Then why don't you prove it," he insisted, raising an arched brow.

Ah, what the hell. I had just finished shaving and was sure it would stun him if I were to be that bold. I whipped open the shower door, exposing my naked, hairless body. He gaped at me as I approached him and yanked the towel out of his hand.

"Thank you," I said, smartly, and then wrapped the fluffy towel under my arms.

He stumbled backward and caught himself on the vanity, still stunned that I actually had done that. Continuing with my shameless act, I brushed against him to reach for a fresh hand towel. Then I bent over, flipping my hair upside down to dry it. Edwin cocked his head sideways, but I was sure he couldn't see anything. And *oh well* if he did.

I flipped upright, with a towel wrapped around my head and joked with Edwin, who was still speechless. "How do I look?"

His jaw was still glued to the floor, so I closed his mouth with two fingers and brushed past him to get my clothes from the bedroom. He didn't follow me right away and it gave me enough time to pick out and slip on a matching bra and panties. As I pulled on some jeans and slipped on a wool sweater over my tank top, Edwin watched me in a daze, mystified by my vanity.

"Cally leaves tonight," I said. "What are we going to do until then?"

"We won't have access to the main house after today. I thought we could spend the day up there with Cally, if you want."

"Kay. Let's have something to eat first, then we can go see what she's up to."

Edwin went to the kitchen, turned on some music and rummaged through the cupboards, while I blow-dried my hair. He whipped up some fried egg sandwiches and didn't even ask for a hand.

When I returned from the bathroom, the table was set and the sandwiches were coming hot off the pan. "Wow, Eddie. What's up with you? You going all Molly Maid on me?"

"You shut your mouth and enjoy it while it lasts."

I dramatized my silence and took a seat at the small, but tall, table. Then I picked up one half of my crustless sandwich and admired how he had cut it into two perfect triangles. He remembered just how I liked it.

"There are other things I'm good at too," he said, trying to get me flustered. "But you already know that."

For some reason, this morning had become all about sex. Worse yet, Edwin's goofy come-ons were actually turning me on something fierce. Cleaning up the table turned into a touchy-feely job, laced with flirtations.

After I stacked the dishes in the dishwasher, I pulled on my jacket and some hiking boots, expecting to have to walk back up the hill. When I walked out the door, I saw that Edwin had already warmed up his truck. I smirked at him and gave him a little shove while he locked up the door.

"I thought my princess would appreciate the ride," he said, smirking.

I really did appreciate the gesture, even if he was only teasing. The drive was very short, but the walk would have been frosty and tedious. When he parked his truck, I leapt out of it and moseyed toward the door of the eerily quiet house. I instantly noticed a note tacked there.

I waved Edwin off and he slipped back into the warm truck, as I feverishly snatched the letter off the door. Ignoring the chill in the air, I deftly unfolded the note and read every inky word.

Hey Guys,

So sorry I couldn't say goodbye, but I caught an early flight. The pool house is unlocked just for you. I hope you two have a good time! ☺

Love ya,

~ Cally

Just another part of her plan. I would choke her for it later. For now, I had to return to the truck before suffering from frost bite. I reluctantly held up the paper to Edwin. He pried the note from my fingers. I watched him read it, but he gave no hint as to what he was thinking. His face was blank until the last word, then a smile crept onto his lips.

"'That Cally. She's a piece of work."

I felt like it was my fault. "I'm sorry."

"What are you sorry for?" He smiled at me warmly, when I shrugged my shoulders, and the last of the ice on my heart melted away. "What do you say we go check out the pool house?"

I nodded and left the truck again, anxious to discover another paradise. Edwin met me around the front of his truck and followed me down the recently cleared path. We walked past the massive house of glass to the log-built pool house, nestled along the tree lined forest on the far side of the yard.

Steam escaped from the doorway when we hurried inside. The room felt like a sauna. I watched Edwin slide his jacket off. Then it was off with his sweater and t-shirt, in another swift motion. *Damn.* I nibbled on my bottom lip, with a new heat affecting me from the inside out.

Edwin tossed his clothes over a pretty, white wicker chair. "Hey. Check this out," he said, lifting a pair spa robes out of the open faced lockers. "What do you say?"

"I didn't bring a bathing suit."

"You don't need one," he informed me, then paused to smirk. His eyes slipped over my body, reminding me of the way he gawked at my nakedness earlier this morning. "Nothing I haven't seen before." Edwin stripped out of his pants and stood there looking like an underwear model, while I was still bundled up in my winter wear.

Attempting to be as brazen as I claimed to be, I stripped down to my hottest panties and caught the thick, white terry robe when Edwin tossed it to me. Suddenly, while I wrapped it around my mostly naked body, Edwin dropped his drawers and flashed his amazing ass before my eyes. My eyes greedily consumed him, until he covered himself with the robe.

"What are you doing?" I asked.

"Oh. You didn't get a good enough look?" He flapped open the robe, flashing me his solid thigh.

I knew what was hiding just behind that panel of fluff and it made my mouth grow dry. "That's not what I meant." I pointed at his shorts on the floor, to take my eyes from that delicious handout. "Those."

"I don't want my underwear to get cold," he said, completely serious.

Skinny dipping? Shit! I am so naïve.

Edwin was definitely upping the ante and I greedily followed after him. It was absolutely frosty outside and I was instantly second guessing the idea of swimming in the middle of a winter wonderland. Edwin forged on, wasting no time. He hung his robe on a nearby hook and stood there buck naked in the dead of winter.

Standing next to the pool in all his naked glory, he looked like a gorgeous gladiator; a work of art. Shattering my dreamy thoughts, he leapt in the pool, hugging his knee. *A can-opener. Real mature.* Half of the water splashed outside the pool, a few drops spraying me in the face, making me shiver.

"Oh, yeah. This is nice," he said, with a wolfish grin.

I dipped my toe in to test the water, even though he claimed it was perfect. The steam constantly escaping off the surface was another good indicator of the temperature. Edwin reached up for me and I scurried to back away from him.

"Are you going to join me? It's downright hot in here."

I checked out Edwin's wet, nude muscles, and then turned away to work up some courage. I hooked my robe up, swathed my sharp nipples with an arm and looked to the main house.

"No one's here, Abs. What are you afraid of? It's just you and me."

That's exactly what I'm afraid of. I scowled at him over my shoulder and then slipped off my panties. Embracing my daring self, I dove right in. Pins and needles tickled every inch of my frozen body as I resurfaced.

Edwin stayed at the far edge of the pool, with his arms casually stretched out at his sides. Besides his head, his hands were the only skin above the surface, attaching him to the pool ledge. I could see the full width of his chest just beneath the clear water. After slicking my wet hair back under water, I treaded in the middle of the pool, considering my next move.

There was no turning back now. *I am going to make a move.*

I swam closer to him, the splash of the water growing more intense with every risky stroke. His eyes dipped below the surface and I let him have his look. But I kept my distance, careful not to touch him, leaving a smooth blanket of water between us.

Edwin locked his frosty, aqua eyes on mine and I watched his features harden before me. "I won't bite," he growled. His eyes darkened and he immersed his sexy stubble in the water, so his lips were partially submersed. "Unless you want me to."

Under Edwin's brooding spell I daringly swam closer, my lips now skimming the surface, mirroring his. When he released the wall, my razor-sharp nipples grazed his arm and I had to grip onto the edge of the pool to catch my breath. My fingers tingled from the cold, as my feet found a ledge to secure me to the wall. My fingers weren't the only things tingling.

Edwin kept his back pressed against the pool wall, waiting for me to make the first move. My heart skipped erratically, as I considered telling him how badly I wanted him. My emotions flared as fiery as my lust, in sharp contrast to the cold air and the velvet water. A fire burned in my heart, as every thump dared me to lay it all out on the table.

With a quick breath, I scooped the water behind me, and drove myself around Edwin, until my naked legs were spread on either side of him. My skin skimmed his, sending delightful bumps skipping down my arms and up my spine. My lashes fluttered shut and the atmosphere grew thick with desire. *His. Mine.*

I lifted my eyes to meet his and held his gaze through dark, wet lashes. "I have something to tell you," I said, my voice soft and shaky.

I flattened my palms on his chest to distract his dark stare, but he didn't remove that fathomless gaze from my face. My cheeks turned pink, but I forced myself to continue.

"Last night you kissed me."   My teeth grazed over my bottom lip, as I remembered his chaste kiss. "I haven't been able to think about anything else since."

A devious smile slanted across Edwin's sexy lips, but he didn't speak.

"I feel like I'm under your spell and I can't lie to you."

I felt his body stiffen, his confidence waning. "What are you saying then?"

"I'm saying I'm still in love with you, Eddie."

CHAPTER THIRTEEN

I couldn't believe that the words had actually left my lips and I became too terrified to cover his mouth with mine. *What if that's the last thing he wanted to hear?* I held my last breath in my lungs, waiting for his response, feeling unpredictable, unprotected and free.

Edwin didn't remark smartly or do anything to validate my feelings, and it only made me feel foolish to think that he might have felt the same way. I dipped my chin, humiliated by his lack of response. Then Edwin slipped deeper into the water and gently guided my chin upwards, forcing me to see him eye to eye. I knew that look. I recognized it well.

When Edwin slowly leaned into me, my eyes fluttered shut, my body painfully aware of his nakedness. Then he kissed me. It was gentle at first, a reproduction of our innocent kiss from the club. Then his warm tongue trimmed my mouth and dipped inside. His large hand massaged over my breasts, as he swallowed my soft whimper.

He tasted me, drank from my lips, then covered them entirely with a soul deep kiss that I felt right down to my trembling toes. When he gripped onto my bottom with both of his hands, the water swished away, leaving nothing between us. I whimpered again from the delightful friction, unable to ignore the rigidness pressed against my middle.

I slipped my hand between us, his silent praise mounting my desire at a ravenous pace. I was becoming borderline obsessive and, unable to restrain myself, I wrapped my legs around his waist, ignoring the faint unease that had settled in the back of my mind. *It was more than sex.* At least it was for me.

When Edwin finally edged himself inside of me, I panted, swept into a mindless climax. He nuzzled my face and held me close, my body quivering around him, as I surrendered to my desire. With a soft breath, he inched a little deeper.

"Are you okay?"

I lowered my head to his shoulder to regain my voice, but only giggled erotically. I ran my fingers through his sexy, wet hair and pressed my lips against his, selfishly wanting more of him. My entire body trembled as he dipped deeper yet. Then he spun me around and plugged me in to the pool wall.

When his body collided against mine, it sent repetitive earth-shattering vibrations through me. I moaned with each pleasure-filled thrust and it echoed over the snowy hillside. The deeper he plunged, the stronger my yearning grew, but the water posed a great barrier. Edwin pulled back, and stopped our vigorous kiss. *He can't stop now!*

"What do you say we take this inside?"

I glanced back at my robe, but couldn't fathom the thought of leaving his arms for the cold. My body was already shaking. Was it from the cold or everything else? I didn't know.

Edwin recognized my concern and chuckled softly, as he withdrew our connection and lifted that glorious body out of the pool, with one foot. "I want you inside," he ordered.

I was mesmerized by the sight of his wet, rigid muscles, and the promise in his deep voice. Suffering from withdrawal already, I swam straight for my robe and wrapped myself up, making a dash for the pool house. Edwin was already lounged back on his elbows on a wooden-slat bench when I got inside. His stare instantly seared my frozen nerves, his own excitement deceiving his cool composure as it tried to escape from his parted robe.

Regaining my own composure, I let my robe slip down my arms, until it dropped to the floor. I stood motionless for a moment, giving Edwin time to get his fill. Then I approached him and sprawled over his lap, my knees resting on either side of him. My hands edged inside the front of his robe, my lips touching his smooth, flat chest.

Edwin closed his eyes and smirked. "You only want me for my body."

My smile was even more devious. "Is that a problem?" I pressed myself against him and he returned the gesture with a kiss that sent shivers all over me.

Edwin was boiling inside his robe, so I yanked it open exposing the rest of that sculpted muscle. He groaned when my soft, cold skin touched him and I whimpered as he lifted me off of him. He swiftly removed his robe and laid it over the warm, wooden bench. Then I crawled onto it and glanced at him over my shoulder. He backed away to have another look.

His naked body never failed to mollify my resistance, as his desirous smile shattered my insecurities. Edwin stood over me with an impenetrable stare until his body collided with mine, and he entered me, fully erect. I rolled my head back, taking all of him, as he held onto my hips and repetitively stoked my desire.

Reaching a hand around me, his fingers slipped between my legs and he circled my pleasure zone with the perfect amount of pressure. It felt too good, so fast.

"I'm not on birth control right now," I blurted, with my hands still clamped onto the bench beneath me. "Please tell me you have a condom."

Edwin increased his pace, causing my desire to overwhelm me. I couldn't hold on any longer.

"Tell me I'm the only one," Edwin grunted, with his pelvis violently slapping against me.

"You're the one," I breathed, as tears sprang from my eyes. And before I could win against the urge to stop him, mind-blowing tremors sensually ripped through my entire body disconnecting me from reality.

Edwin groaned as my body convulsed around him, pulling him over the edge with a final pump. Seismic waves of pleasure filled me, as Edwin held on and gave me all of him. Then he dropped his spent body over mine and I flattened beneath the weight of his large frame, feeling completely satisfied.

When I turned my head sideways and rested it on my hands, Edwin lifted his heavy chest and stared into my eyes, breathless and vacant. Then he dropped a soft peck on my lips and peeled himself off of me, heading straight for the shower. After drying my sweaty, love soaked body with a towel, I pulled on my robe and walked over to the window for a distraction.

Edwin's naked body in the open shower did nothing to help wind down my sex drive, so I focused on the hills of glistening snow and heavy evergreen braches. Everything seemed so peaceful and wonderful, like the emotions crowding my heart.

Edwin wants me and he wants to give me babies. I was so joyful I wanted to cry.

When the water stopped running, I turned back to Edwin. He had already wrapped a towel around his waist and was running a small towel through his spiky hair. As he steadily approached me, my heart skipped a beat and then another. He dipped his head and kissed me.

"It's all yours, babe."

Reluctantly, I left him and hustled over to the shower. While I rinsed my hair, I noticed how he too had set up shop in front of the window. My eyes continued to drift back to him, while he stared out into the distant forest. It was like he was miles away, lost in his own mind. A violent chill struck me. *Please tell me he isn't having second thoughts already.*

I cranked off the hot water, dried myself and scurried to my pile of clothes. After pulling them on in a rush, I finger combed my hair and scrubbed it as dry as possible. Edwin hadn't moved a muscle for minutes. I was scared stiff. I slowly approached his chair and placed my hands on his shoulders. I glanced out the window, trying to find what he was looking at. Nothing had changed.

"It's beautiful out there, huh?" I asked.

There was a deafening silence. "Huh? Oh. Right. Yeah, it is."

I had just poured my heart out and made love to him, but he didn't seem too interested to share his feelings. In fact, he hadn't reciprocated anything but sexual desire. When my conscience caught up with me, I had to escape. The silence became irritating.

"I'm going to head back to the guesthouse." I turned away and grabbed my jacket, expecting to go alone.

Edwin stood up instantly and it caught me off guard. "I'll come with you," he said, acting baffled by the suggestion but sharing little else.

I slipped on my boots and we left the pool house together. The wind was now brutally cold and, in the short time it took to round the house, my hair had already turned to ice. Snow was being viciously whipped around like a cloud of dust in a storm. I couldn't lose the shivers and my teeth started to chatter.

Not only did Edwin not acknowledge the cold, but he didn't seem to notice that I was shaking like a leaf either. I stared into the forest as we slowly crept down the hill and full, heavy flakes of snow began to plummet from the sky. Frustration gnawed at my insides as I silently scooped up the keys off the dash.

When Edwin pressed the brake, I swung my door open and went straight inside. After tossing the keys on the kitchen counter, I hung up my coat and shivered from the eerie chill in the room. The fireplace had been turned off and the heat was turned much too low, but instead of kicking it back on, I ran to the bed and wrapped up in the blankets.

Moments later, I heard the rumble of Edwin's engine as he pulled away from the cabin. If it were time or space that he needed, I would give it to him. Not that I had much choice in the matter. Despite telling myself that it would be okay, that didn't stop the onset of my heartache and the debilitating mental anguish that hounded me.

I surrounded myself with pillows and soft, fluffy blankets, but it didn't shake the void emerging in my chest. I felt like I had flattened out on the bed and let Edwin cut open my chest with a knife. Then, after slicing open my heart, he sewed me back up like that. I lied in the bed, immobilized, feeling destroyed. My blood oozed internally, trapping all of my love for Edwin inside of me.

The bed was unable to offer me the warmth I so desperately sought. I inwardly cried, near hysteria, but outwardly I denied myself the release. *Crying wouldn't change anything.*

I forced my eyes shut and demanded that my brain shut down for a nap, but reminders of my plans for marriage first, baby later, ran rampant in my thoughts. *Tell me I'm the only one*, Edwin whispered in my thoughts. *You're the one.*

Why had I believed something really special had happened in that moment? If our relationship was truly over, I needed know that so I could redirect my feelings toward something more sensible and relevant. I groaned out loud, feeling like a failure, my body and mind battling it out.

With a glance out the tall window next to the bed, I noticed that the snow had picked up significantly, darkening the afternoon sky. A tremor rocked through me just thinking about the cold. I needed to think of warm thoughts. I needed to feel Edwin's big, warm arms wrapped around me. I needed to hear him growling sweet nothings in my ear. His smile could mend my throbbing heart. *I need that. I need him.*

Any hope of returning to a happy place was shattered when a disturbing memory crept ahead of those thoughts. The memory reeled before my eyelids, giving me another stab of guilt. Edwin had just realized that I was going to Cameron's for the Christmas holidays and despite his disappointment, I was so very happy. Cameron made me feel that kind of happy.

I don't want you to go, Edwin had said. *Are you sure this is what you want?*

I was so sure that Cameron was *the one*. I even told Edwin so. I still remembered how Edwin shuddered when I said the L word. But I loved Cameron.

My memories fast forwarded through every moment when Edwin had put me on the spot and I went against every chance he offered me. How could I expect him to take me back now? It was times like this that I wished I didn't have such a crisp, photographic memory.

Another hour of reminiscing came and went. Still, Edwin was gone. I hated myself for acting out on my silly fantasies, when I should have stayed true to myself. Giving in to my sexual urges, I had forced myself on Edwin, knowing that I had quit taking birth control over a month ago. Edwin knew he could have gotten me pregnant too, but that didn't stop him.

I could be pregnant now!

I opened my eyes to pitch blackness. I couldn't see a thing and I started to feel paralyzed with fright. I heard a rap on the window next to me. When I turned my head, I remembered being in the guesthouse. *Alone.* It was dark outside, but an even darker silhouette slowly passed by the window in the direction of the front door. *Had I remembered to lock it?*

Fear swallowed me whole when I remembered leaving it open for Edwin. My heart beat so loud, I couldn't hear anything over it except for the terrifying tapping sound on the skylight. Dark shadows cascaded across the ceiling of the living room. *It was only tree branches*, I told myself, to stop from having a mental breakdown.

When the floor creaked near the door, a chill attacked my body and I was sure I would lose my mind from the endless charade of unexplainable noises. Then a sudden loud thump sounded around the corner. Startled, I let out a scream. Crouched in the corner of the bed in terror, I reached for my cell phone and texted Edwin. I stared at the screen, silently pleading for help, but there was no reply.

In need of protection, I yanked a cord from the wall and pulled the large, decorative lamp from the nightstand.

There was nowhere to hide. I urgently dialed Edwin's number.

"Come on, Eddie. Pick up your phone," I begged. It rang once and went straight to voicemail.

When I heard his voice, even if it was only a message, it returned me from the brink of delirium. I slid my back up the pile of pillows until I was propped against the headboard. I lifted myself up so I could see if there was anyone or anything in the other room, still clutching the rounded lamp. My eyes scattered over the room, but I couldn't see anything. Then I heard the door creak shut.

If I hadn't been holding my breath, I wouldn't have even heard the soft footsteps approaching, sounding like that of a small child pattering across the floor. But then a heavy thud broadcast only inches from my feet. I quickly pulled my knees to my chest and hugged onto the lamp like it was my lifeline.

An unsettling energy roiled through the room and it felt like it was sinking into my skin. My anxiety devoured me, as I anticipated who or what was at the foot of my bed. I squeezed my eyes shut, foolishly believing that the danger couldn't see me if I couldn't see it. After an extended silence, my fright-filled eyes flashed open to see what was clawing at the blanket.

I shuffled higher on the bed, just as the blanket jerked away and landed on the floor with a soft thump. I held onto the lamp preparing myself to strike. I stared at the foot of the bed, waiting for the threat to show itself. *Nothing.*

"Show yourself!" I hollered, my voice but a quivering rasp. My eyes deceived me as they darted to the end of the bed. There she was.

Jenny's red, shining eyes peered over the edge of the bed, demanding my attention like I was being hexed. My own eyes watered and burned as I stared at her without blinking. She slowly crawled onto the bed and inched toward me like she was preparing to slaughter me alive. I dared her to move another inch. I would smash that lamp so hard off her head that she would die for real this time.

My lips trembled, as I wound up for the strike. "Don't move," I whispered.

She froze at my feet and then there was a clunk in the other room.

"EDWIN!" I screamed.

By the time my voice stopped ringing, Edwin called back to me. "I'm here!" He leapt to his feet and hit a switch. The light flashed on and relief washed over me, as Edwin territorially scanned over the room. But there was no one there.

Edwin swiftly came to my side. I tugged the blanket close to my chin and stared at the foot of the bed. *I thought that blanket had fallen on the floor.* Unnerved, I tossed the blanket away from me like it was on fire. My breaths were fast and irregular as I stared at the emptiness at the end of the bed, feeling very confused.

Edwin grabbed both of my shoulders and gently shook my traumatized body. "What's wrong, Abs? Talk to me."

I didn't answer.

He wrapped his arms around mine and crushed me against his hard chest. He held me for a long time, until my breathing began to regulate and the rapid thud of my heart matched his. My mind was a bit slower to return to reality.

When Edwin finally released me, I stared into his eyes, hoping to find my answers. It was like I was lost somewhere between dream and reality, and I was having a hard time differentiating between the two. *Since Edwin is fully clothed, I'm going to guess that this is reality.*

"Where were you just now?" My voice was shaky and low.

"I was sitting on the couch."

"In the dark?"

"There was light from the fire. I didn't want to wake you."

I turned my head and saw that the fireplace made light flicker across the ceiling. I spun around to look for the lamp. It was nestled on the table as if it were never touched. My head started spinning. Edwin gently pressed me back against the pillow.

"You should lie down. I don't want you passing out on me again."

Huh? I dug my fingers into my forehead, trying to flatten the deep lines of confusion. "It was so real."

"It was just a nightmare."

"How long was I out for?" I asked softly, not believing it entirely.

"It's been hours. I let you sleep. I figured you must have been really tired, what with last night and everything." Edwin shuffled to the edge of the bed. "You must be starved. Let me get you something to eat."

When he went to stand up, I frantically yanked him back down. "Take me with you," I begged.

"I was only going to the kitchen." He didn't understand.

"Please?" I could see the worry when it crept back into his eyes, then it quickly vanished.

"That must have been some nightmare."

I hooked myself around Edwin's torso and held onto his arm. He walked me to the kitchen, where I reluctantly released him to take a seat at the spacious island. Edwin stepped around me to retrieve a takeout container from the fridge. While he emptied the food onto a plate, I slowly peered toward the bed, then feverishly examined the floor to beat the fear that someone or something was still lurking there.

"There's nothing there," Edwin insisted.

"I know." But my words were so weak, they spoke for themselves.

The microwave dinged and Edwin pulled out my steaming meal. He gave it a stir, then rested the dish in front of me. "Here. You can eat first and explain later."

I took a bite of my pasta and it burned my lip. I not-so-attractively spit a mouthful back into the bowl. "Where did you go this afternoon? I waited for what seemed like forever."

Edwin's eyes crinkled at the sides, but he remained totally serious. "I have no idea what you're talking about."

I rolled my eyes and, after blowing on my linguine, I scarfed it down. Edwin remained standing the entire time, his hip cocked to the side, resting against the counter. His arms were folded across his broad chest, his shirt straining against his flexed biceps, making it difficult for me to concentrate on anything but those rippling muscles.

Trying to avoid the fact that I was losing my mind, I dumped the leftovers into the garbage. Edwin rushed over to me and helped me to the couch like I was an elderly lady. I peeked out the corner of my eye as we passed the bedroom, but there was still nothing there. Edwin even let me believe that he hadn't caught me checking this time.

I took a seat across from the toasty fireplace, where I could feel the warmth fanning over me. Edwin sat next to me, his rigid muscles toying with my mind. Any closer and he would have been sitting on my lap. But I had to protect my heart. I shimmied away from him, to the far corner of the couch, then raised my arm over the back of it and turned my attention to him.

His solid frame was slumped in the most casual position, his long, thick legs stretched out to show their magnitude. He kept his attention on the fire, ignoring my standoffishness.

"What are we doing here?" I asked.

He acted like he was confused by the question. "Taking a much needed vacation?"

"Edwin, be serious. Don't act like nothing happened today. We need to talk about this."

"What's there to talk about?" He was seriously oblivious.

"Eddie. We made love to each other today. Not just that, but I told you I'm not on birth control anymore. We didn't use protection. I told you I loved you."

"Yeah." He was still not following.

"Ugh!" I squealed, then paced to the kitchen out of frustration. I was a little wobbly at first, but quickly steadied myself, then spun around to face Edwin again.

"You've said all of two words to me since I told you I love you. You took off right after sex, without telling me where you were going, and now you have nothing to say to me? Forgive me if I'm a little off balance."

"I never took off, Abs. You must have fallen asleep the second you laid down." Edwin got up and walked toward me with his arms extended out to me.

"Don't," I snapped, stepping away from him. I didn't know what to believe.

Unexpectedly, Edwin dropped his arms down, as though he were the innocent victim in this episode. "Fine," he said. "Be upset with me. But I won't let you push me away. I thought you already knew how I felt. It hasn't exactly been a secret all this time."

I stood there motionless for a moment, replaying the events in my mind. Now I was the one not following. Edwin briskly stepped toward me and swung me around to face him. Before I knew what was happening, his lips were brushing over mine, and I was dipped backwards.

He had my full attention now.

"I love you, Abs. You must know that." He nuzzled near my ear and my heart leapt from my chest as his tongue drew my earlobe into his mouth. His soft lips trailed kisses down my neck and, when his warm breath reached my lips, our eyes met again. "You may be crazy like a fox, but I'm still crazy about you."

A trickle of excitement rushed through my veins as he stroked me with one of his big hands and held me with the other. I turned my eyes away, with a blush on my cheeks. Now I felt guilty for being so distrustful.

"Hey!" Edwin warned. "No more doom and gloom. I just told you I love you too. Shouldn't you be swinging from the ceiling beams or something?"

I smiled really big, teeth and all, and Edwin couldn't resist dipping down for an intimate, smiling kiss. He returned me to my feet and linked his fingers with mine.

"I thought for sure you knew that I wanted to be with you," he stated, like it was a crime that I didn't know.

"I knew you wanted to have sex with me. But how could I be sure you wanted anything more?"

"Abs, I would never do that to you. You know better than that. You know me."

He was right. I did know him. He was my best friend.

"It just felt like you were really quiet after we did what we did, and I worried that it didn't mean anything to you. I worried that we had made a huge mistake."

"That was a big decision for me to make," Edwin admitted. "But I wanted to prove to you that I'm all in."

The fear that had been overpowering me all day, morphed into extreme giddiness. I threw myself into his arms and he wrapped me into them again while we kissed. Saying I had overreacted was an understatement, and the fact that Edwin hadn't brought up my crazy nightmare again was such a relief.

"I'm sorry. I can't believe how I twisted this."

"It's all good," he said, with a teasing grin. "I still love you."

I nudged him playfully and he tossed me down on the couch to kiss me some more. Edwin pressed his nose into my hair and I felt so incredibly close to him. When I reached for his hand, I accidentally pulled up his shirt, exposing his rock hard abs. We both froze in place, absorbing the energy shimmering in the air. I brushed my cool fingers across his warm, rigid abs and then pulled his shirt back down.

"You want more of my sex pistol?" Edwin growled.

"What the hell did you just call it?" I couldn't stop giggling.

"You heard me," he said, stabbing me with his erection. "Want to play Russian roulette?"

"You're shooting blanks now, are you?" I teased.

"No way, baby. I'm high test all day."

I giggled some more before turning more serious. "As much as I'd like to get pregnant, Eddie, you know as well as I do that first comes love, then comes marriage, then comes the baby in the baby carriage." I smirked. "One step at a time. I don't want to rush it."

He covered my mouth with his smiling lips. "You could've fooled me."

CHAPTER FOURTEEN

Night was falling upon us quickly, as we passed our neighbours' houses. It was messy and cold outside, but to me it felt as though I was returning from my honeymoon. I looked to Edwin and smiled sweetly. "Isn't it kind of weird returning back to reality together?"

Edwin smiled at me. "I honestly didn't think my plan was going to work out quite this brilliantly. But look at us now. It's like you never broke my heart last year."

I took extreme offence to that, but I snapped at him, playfully. "All I wanted was for you to tell me you'd be my baby daddy."

Edwin chuckled. "You caught me off guard. Real romantic, by the way."

I slapped at him, as he turned his truck into our driveway.

"I have to admit, Abs. It wasn't a great feeling when you gave me that ultimatum. It was like you ripped my heart out of my chest and ran off with it."

"Eddie, I'm so sorry." And I meant it. But he just kept talking.

"I said I needed time and you left me. I didn't cry at my grandmother's funeral. I don't cry. When you left me that night, I almost cried," he admitted. "I wanted to. Because it hurt that much." He pulled his keys from the ignition and cupped his warm hand over mine.

My voice was raspy when I answered him. "You could've saved both of us the grief and just said yes in the first place."

Edwin's smirk sliced through the seriousness of the conversation. "I knew you couldn't resist me forever." Edwin leaned into me for a comforting smooch, then pushed open his door and jumped down from his truck.

While he pulled our bags out of the back of the truck, I walked up the dark driveway and paused at door to dig out my keys. Something was amiss and, despite the fear rushing into my hollow lungs, I unlocked the house and let myself in. One step in the door and the eerie feeling only intensified. I froze, waiting for the uneasiness to go away, but the inexplicable dread did not fade.

I looked back at Edwin. He was still lugging our bags out of his truck. I considered waiting for him, but knew I was just letting my nerves get the best of me. I ran my hand along the wall, blindly searching for the light switch. Before I could find it, my eyes zeroed in on the two red orbs staring back at me from the living room.

"Ahhh!" I screamed, the horrifying screech belting from the top of my lungs.

Edwin dropped all of our bags in the snow and sprinted to my rescue. He instantly crowded over me and hit the light switch.

"What is it?" he asked, his eyes scanning over the empty living room. He looked like he was ready to strike, his blood pumping to every agile muscle.

I pointed a trembling finger in the direction of the demon that had set out to ruin my life, but I couldn't look.

Edwin spoke firmly, cautious and alert. "Is there someone in the house?"

"She was right there." I pointed hard, animated with terror.

"There's no one there, Abs. Who did you see? Is she still in the house?"

Edwin seemed so confused. *So was I.*

"Jenny," I shrieked, as my knees grew weak. I crumbled, my body collapsing into itself.

Edwin managed to catch my elbow before I crashed completely onto the floor. Then he pulled me into his arms and rocked me, the cold wind blasting through the open door. Edwin kissed my forehead and cupped my face in his hands.

"I'm here, baby. It's okay." The growing concern in his glistening eyes slammed through me.

I had to pull myself together, if not for my own sake, for his. "I'm okay," I croaked, my eyes darting to the living room.

"You think you saw Jenny again?"

"What do you mean again?" *There's no way he knew I'd been seeing Jenny lately.*

"I've seen your reactions enough to know when it's happening. First she comes to you in your nightmares and then you start to see her. It's happening again isn't it."

I nodded, apprehensively. Edwin helped me to my feet and I glanced to where she had been standing, only inches from the mantle in my living room. I squinted as I noted the two red lights glowing on the flat-screen television mounted on the wall. *It couldn't be.* But it was.

A humourless giggle erupted from my chest. "I'm seriously losing it. I was so sure it was her. It was only the TV."

"I thought that you had found a dead body or something from your blood-curdling scream. I wouldn't be surprised if the neighbours called the police."

Still not letting go of me, Edwin tugged me outside with him to grab our bags, then dropped them inside the doorway. I closed the door behind us to keep some of the heat in.

"You're okay then?" Edwin asked, searching my eyes. He would think I was mental if I told him about the delusions I'd been having lately.

My lashes fluttered away. "It was nothing," I insisted. But it was *not* nothing. I could've sworn Jenny came to me. *But why was I being haunted by my dead sister?*

"If you say so." Edwin flicked another light switch, flooding golden light into our living room.

Even in the fully lit house I could sense Jenny lingering nearby, but Edwin was determined to debunk my fears. He took my hand and led me to the living room. I sank down onto the sofa next to him.

"What did Cam think about the red-eyed monster?" Edwin asked, out of nowhere.

I really don't want to talk about the red-eyed monster right now, and I never want to talk to Edwin about Cameron. "I never told him," I answered, bluntly.

"You were with him for all those months and it never came up? He didn't figure it out for himself? Some litigator he is."

"Honestly, it didn't come up. Now that I think about it, most of my episodes seem to happen the closer I get to you."

Edwin puckered his lips and grabbed onto his chin. "That's strange. I must stir up some old memories; arouse something deep inside you." He smirked. *He was only joking. But I think he might be onto something.*

Edwin dropped me off at the front doors of our office building, only minutes from nine, so I ran inside. I gave Taylor her greetings and bustled to my desk, rushing past Cam's office without a glance. The pain of missing Cameron hadn't vanished. It was just waiting there for me.

"Oh, you're back," Owen said to me, as I shuffled through the papers on my desk. "I take it you had a good time," he added, suggestively.

"Not you too," I whined. Not five minutes in the office and the whole place had already learned that Edwin and I were an item again.

"You should know by now, you can't get anything past these critics."

"Ugh. Who told you?" I knew the first day back at work was going to be incredibly trying, but right when I thought things couldn't get worse, Wesley Carver walked around the corner.

Owen smiled up at him. "Good morning."

"Is it?" Wesley asked, flashing me a sideways glance.

"You're still here?" I asked, snarling.

"Good morning to you too, buttercup," he answered, with a smile.

Owen looked at me with concern in his eyes. "Now Abby, Cam agreed to turn over the reins to Wes this week. I trust you'll help him do the same."

Wesley chuckled, amused by my distress.

"You must be kidding," I said, feeling more than a little flustered. I stared up to the ceiling. "This is going to be the longest week of my life."

"Play nice, Abby," Owen said, then stalked off to his desk.

Wesley lingered by the door.

Not again. "What do you want?"

"Ooh, if this is you playing nice, I can't wait to see you being nasty."

At that very moment, Cameron and Edwin approached my door from different directions. All three men stood in a line blocking my exit. Cameron and Edwin were both fixated angrily at Wes, and he couldn't seem to decide who was more of a threat to him.

Wesley smirked. "Hey, I'm just the new guy."

Cam was the first to nudge him aside. "Is this guy bothering you?"

Edwin shoved Wes out of the picture entirely and glared at Cameron. "That's really not your concern anymore," he said, through gritted teeth.

"I'm not looking for trouble," Cameron said, like I wasn't worth his time. "Let's go." Cam turned away and left without making any eye contact with me. Wesley followed after him, not daring to provoke Edwin further.

"You'd better watch your back," Edwin threatened.

I hoped that comment was meant for Wes, but the rage burning in Edwin's eyes told me it wasn't. When Edwin finally looked back to me, he seemed to have regained some composure.

"Are you alright?" he asked.

"I can handle myself. I'm a big girl."

"Yeah, well, you shouldn't have to handle yourself here and you won't have to once I'm done with them."

"Please leave Cam out of this. He didn't do anything."

"Don't defend him like that. He's still protective of you and that's dangerous."

I stood from my chair and tried to keep professional, but I had to show Edwin that I cared. "Calm down." I flattened my hand on his chest and patted one over his shoulder and down his arm. He was sweltering through his suit jacket.

"If you want to have a talk with Wesley, that's fine, but I prefer that he leave that meeting with all of his teeth."

Edwin's smile rendered him speechless, so I took took the opportunity to take his right hand into both of mine and shake it firmly.

"It's a deal now. You shook on it," I teased, as I pushed him out of my cubicle.

Before long, noon hour rolled around and Aliah took me to the café down the road to get the goods. I took the seat across from her and she instantly leaned in for the gossip.

"Cut the crap. Tell me. Are the rumours true?"

I picked up my mug and blew on it slowly. "Rumours? What rumours?"

Her eyes turned mean and green as she glowered at me. "Don't be dense. It's written all over your face. That smile didn't get there by itself."

I shrugged my shoulders to tease her.

"You could've called. Why didn't you call me?"

"I was busy doing other things," I said, smirking.

"I knew it!" she cut in. "You're totally doing him again. I can hear it in your voice."

"Ally, you cannot."

"Are you sleeping with him again?"

"Well, yeah."

"How did it happen this time?"

"It started with an incident in the pool. Then we took things to the pool house. Then-."

"No, horn dog, how did you fall back into Edwin's love trap?"

"Well, there is the attraction factor, and he is very persistent," I explained.

"I'd bet that's why you caved. I can't believe you! Well I sort of can." Aliah snickered. "You certainly didn't waste any time."

"I do feel guilty for moving on so quickly. Am I a bad person?" I needed her moral support.

"If Cameron didn't make you happy, then you have to find someone who will."

"That's the thing, Cam did make me happy, until I started laying down the rules."

"Stop worrying about it. Cam came into your life for a reason. He's served his purpose already."

"Ally, I really don't want to leave this one up to the stars."

"Whatevs. I take it Edwin's plan worked. He swept you off your feet and you fell madly in love with him?" she said, her voice filled with drama.

I smirked and took a sip from my piping hot drink. "Something like that."

"Don't sound so excited."

"I've been here before. I hate to run on a high, because the fall is that much harder when it does happen." I let out the sigh that I had been holding in since I had walked in the front door of the office this morning.

"Forget about the fall. Enjoy it while it lasts. Moving right along. Did you hear Miller finally found a girl to cover Maddie's maternity leave?"

"Who is she?"

"Remember Maddie's friend, Samantha?"

"Um, yeah. She has the hots for Edwin. As if having Wesley Carver in the office isn't hell enough for me." I rested my elbows on the table and settled my chin into my hands.

"I know. I still can't believe Owen hired your ex-lover's look alike."

"Aliah!" I screeched, mostly because I couldn't believe she saw it too. "Wesley Carver is a loose cannon. I don't think anyone in their right mind would bring this guy on."

"He's not that bad. I've actually heard that he's a really good litigator. Give the guy a chance. You might like him."

"Oh, no. He's all bad. I just have that feeling. He's trouble."

CHAPTER FIFTEEN

I stared at my computer screen, wondering how I was going to get through the next few weeks unscathed. Rumours about Edwin and I were running rampant around the office and it made it difficult to concentrate on work. *Hell. They weren't rumours. It was all true.*

I had already had the *it's not what you think* talk with Cameron before the March break, and I didn't have it in me to lie to him now. If he asked, I would have to come clean.

"Abby, could you come here for a minute?" Maddie called, when she heard me just outside the copier room.

I headed inside, only to find that Maddie had a sidekick with her. Samantha Harper. Maddie was looking seriously pregnant, and though she had a beautiful glow to her skin, she only made Samantha look that much more tiny standing next to her. Samantha's fashion sense complimented her long, suspiciously thin frame and flawless, pale skin.

"Can you believe Sam got the job?" Maddie chimed. "I'll be training her over the next few days. At least, I'm going to try. I hope to hang on that long, but by the feel of things I might be out of here sooner than I thought. That's not to mention that my doctor put me on bed rest and Hunter's on my case about it."

I smiled and nodded, taking notice of her overgrown baby belly.

Maddie looked back to Samantha. "Abigail works with Owen Wallace and Wesley Carver," she said. "You've already met Cam, but he'll be gone any day now. They used to date, eh?"

Samantha flashed her trademark bitch smile, straight from the fiery depths of the earth. Her bright green eyes glowed with envy. "Lucky you," Samantha said, pure evil flowing from her smooth voice.

I smiled, but it felt forced. I turned my eyes back to Maddie, my cool, green eyes warming ten degrees. "I still can't believe you're having twins." I rubbed her large, round belly.

"I can," she stated, undoubtedly. "These babies are ready to come out. They'd better soon too or I think I might burst. Hunter says they're coming tomorrow."

"You're lucky to have someone who cares so much about you," I gushed.

"Yeah, he has been a total sweetheart lately. Too bad he's got that evil succubus clinging to him every day," Maddie added, making a sour face.

Helping dig me out of that hole, Samantha changed the subject. "Didn't you say you dated Wesley Carver?"

Maddie smirked, taking the bait. "Yeah. Been there, done that. He couldn't keep up with me."

Samantha chuckled at her confidence. I was amused too, until I caught her gawking at Edwin when he passed by the doorway.

"I can't believe I'll be working with Eddie too," Samantha chimed.

Did she just call my man Eddie?

"You'll be working closely with him," Maddie admitted. "Edwin works for Miller too."

"Looking forward to that," she mumbled, under her breath.

I cleared my throat, anger warming my cheeks. "Actually that one's off limits. He's mine." I tried to keep my irritation at a minimum, but she really knew how to get to me.

"It's all good," she replied, coolly. "There doesn't seem to be a shortage of suitable men around here for me." Samantha's eyes grew wide with mischief, a seductive smile playing on her lips.

I spun around to find Cameron making his way up behind me. "Excuse me, ladies," he said, as he reached for his papers. He made a grab for them and briskly walked off, avoiding an awkward exchange.

"Mmm. He must be fair game. I didn't see any ring on that finger," Samantha announced.

"He's definitely not available," Maddie explained. "He's still hung up on Abby and he'll be out of here in a matter of days anyways."

"What?" I asked, stunned by the change of dates.

"That's what I hear," Maddie said, shrugging her shoulders.

"Then I'd better get started now," Samantha purred.

I refused to admit why, but I didn't want that bloodsucker latching onto Cameron. Maddie recognized my reaction and I couldn't even hide my annoyance as Samantha chased after Cam. Maddie followed her and I hoped it was to keep Samantha on a leash.

I caught myself scowling into thin air minutes later. I pulled myself together and hurried back to my desk, only to hear Samantha putting the moves on Cameron one room over. Then I overheard Cam inviting her to his going away party this weekend. *That was news to me.*

I stood there stewing for a moment, wishing I didn't have to listen to her annoying voice anymore. I gritted my teeth the entire time that she gushed about how great it would be to hear more about him. Cameron didn't seem to share her enthusiasm, but it still irked me worse than I cared to admit. *If that evil whore is going to his party, then I will be there.*

Two days later, when I was least expecting an attack, I found the floosy – Samantha - with Edwin in his office, and she was leaning over his shoulder, giggling. I froze in the hall, folded my arms across my chest, and cast an evil eye at her. She knew the stakes; and if I had one right now, I'd be stabbing it into her menacing heart.

She glanced up at me unbeknownst to Edwin and returned a bright green glare. She knew exactly what she was doing. And, though I trusted Edwin with all my heart, I couldn't trust her as far as I could throw her. Still, I didn't want my possessiveness to encourage her, so I dropped the glare and flashed her a false smile, as I passed the door. I ducked my head into Aliah's cubicle and found her staring into space. She jumped when she saw me.

"Oh shit. You scared me. I thought you were Bailey," Aliah said.

I was unable to get past my own troubles. "Can you believe that slut? She's already making it her full time job to mess with my life."

"Yeah, I saw her flirting with Edwin this morning... then Cameron this afternoon."

"If she's trying to piss me off, then it's working."

Aliah's responding smile was surprisingly soft. "You really have nothing to worry about though. Edwin is in love with you."

"It's not him that I'm worried about." I narrowed my eyes, when I recalled the image of Samantha hovering over Edwin at his desk, her fangs descending, warding me off.

"Relax," Aliah said, and leaned back in her chair. "I saw Edwin around her. He doesn't even give her the time of day. You have to hand it to him. I mean, she is a looker."

"Exactly. And she's throwing herself at him. I'm not about to let her sick herself on Edwin and hope he doesn't have an unsuspecting *moment of weakness*. I'm trying to keep it together here, but it's tough when you just want to strangle the girl."

"How do you think I feel? I had to watch Hunter grovelling on his knees the other night, just to get Maddie to take her maternity leave a few days early. She'd better pop those kids out soon, because she's driving me nuts."

"It's only going to get worse, you realize. Once she has the babies, she'll have two wondrous tools to control Hunter with."

"I hope you're wrong. I don't know how much more of this I can take," Aliah admitted.

"It looks like we're both in for a bumpy ride."

Edwin insisted that we meet up with the rest of the staff to kiss Cameron off from the firm. While I wasn't looking forward to our official goodbye, I had to go to make sure Sam kept her paws off of Cameron. As Edwin guided me inside the club, it was apparent that he was eager to send Cameron packing.

On the other side of the room, a crowd of our coworkers had formed next to the bar. I let go of Edwin's arm the second I saw Maddie sitting on a stool there.

"Oh my gosh! Maddie! What are you doing here?" I squealed.

She squeezed Cam's shoulder and gave him a friendly kiss on his cheek. "I couldn't miss this. Besides, I hear labour could use a little kick-start sometimes."

"I don't think this is what they meant," I answered, my lips parting on a smile.

She shrugged her shoulders and looked around the room until her eyes locked onto her target. In an instant, I realized exactly what she was doing. She smiled and winked at me and I turned around to find Aliah and Hunter making their way toward us. As I suspected, the moment Hunter found his baby momma sitting there, all hell broke loose.

"What in the world are you doing here?" Hunter hollered.

"Relax, I'm not drinking. Cam deserves a proper goodbye," Maddie insisted.

Hunter lifted her from the bar stool, careful to protect his babies. "You're not staying here. I'm taking you home right now." He tried to gently guide her away, his other hand bracing her back.

"You're crazy! Lighten up," she said, smiling. She had him right where she wanted him.

"Lighten up? You're eight and a half months pregnant, with twins. You could go into labour any minute!" He growled, with wolfish frustration. "Sometimes you can be downright stupid."

Hunter looked to Aliah to apologize. "I'm sorry, but I have to do this."

Aliah flailed her hand uncaringly, but I knew it had to hurt.

"I'm going to pull the car up and you'd better be at the curb when I get there," Hunter threatened. He stormed off angrily, as Maddie tried to hide her giddiness. Her plan had worked like a charm.

Maddie gave Cameron a hug and he gently cupped her huge belly with both of his hands before he let her go. That small exchange sent an arrow through my heart and gave me the urge to scream out in frustration. I was short on breath, when Maddie came to give me a squeeze goodbye.

Aliah stomped to our side. "I'll walk you to the car. Wouldn't want you to get lost on the way." *Oh, she was mad.*

"You be careful, girly," I said to her discreetly, before letting her go. "Take care of yourself."

Maddie spun around with the grace of a cow and walked out the door to the waiting car. Aliah followed behind her like a shadow.

When I turned back to the guys, I was surprised to find Edwin patting Cameron on the back. I had to force myself not to watch, even as Samantha slithered her way in between them. Edwin kept talking, and I could hear Samantha laughing at everything he said. I couldn't get my wits about me, when I saw how Edwin continued to pat Cameron on the back like they were buddies.

It was all too weird for me to watch, so I tried to focus on Aliah, who was already knee deep into a bottle of vodka. "Do you see Samantha eyeing up my man like he's dessert or something? I want to slap that slutty smile right off her face."

Aliah nodded, having noticed it herself. "She is so blissfully unaware of your wrath," she slurred, already three sheets to the wind. She raised her drink to me. "May she suffer from dealing with other selfish bichez like herself."

Already roused, I clinked my plastic cup off of hers. "I'll drink to that."

After downing the rest of my drink, I straightened up, feeling a little better prepared to deal with Cameron. I ducked under Edwin's arm and squeezed my way between him and Samantha. She tossed herself purposefully into Cameron's arms and he caught her cooperatively. I smiled up at Edwin, to dodge Cameron's reaction.

Though I may have driven Samantha into Cameron's arms, I had to be happy that I had saved Edwin. That had to be enough for me. *So why wasn't it?*

I sipped from my drink, annoyed by Samantha's mischievous behaviour. She was still all over Cameron, nuzzling her nose close to his ear and hanging off of him like a cheap air freshener. He wasn't exactly knocking her off of him. *A taste of my own medicine.*

Edwin gave me a swift peck on my lips, and then told me he'd be back in a bit. I was glad. I wanted him as far away from that scandalous hoe as possible. Cameron caught my glaring green stare and instantly realized that Edwin was gone. He peeled Samantha off of his side and smiled at her, then casually wandered next to me. Samantha slunk away and dragged Taylor along with her.

"I didn't think you'd come," Cameron admitted. "But I'm glad you did." His tone was soft, reminding me just how gentle he used to be with me.

Edwin watched me from a distance and I smiled to show him that he had nothing to worry about.

"I hope everything works out for you. And for Pheobe," I said, emotion choking my words.

"Thanks. That means a lot," he replied, leaning in sideways for a hug. He sensed my hesitation and stopped, mirroring my frozen stance. Then he wrinkled that adorable forehead. "One friendly hug won't kill you, Abby. Edwin's right there. Do you really think I would try anything?"

Though his smile was tense, I wanted nothing more than to ease into his arms and give in to the wayward effect he was having on me. I gulped back my nerve and reached an arm around him for a friendly squeeze. Cameron held on a little too long and a little too tight. His cologne made me feel dizzy and confused, triggering painful recollections of our happiness together.

I pulled away from his tempting embrace, and gazed into his resolute eyes. One of his hands lingered on the curve of my hip. He was aware of my discomfort, but wouldn't allow me to detach from him. He leaned forward. He was going to kiss me and I couldn't move.

His lips slipped right past my mouth and landed on my cheek.

Duh. Why would he kiss me on the lips? I gasped for air, as his mouth continued to my ear.

"I hope you're happy," he said, softly. He wasn't being mean. It actually sounded like he truly wanted me to be happy.

He hovered near my ear, with his eyes closed, and inhaled me before dropping his hand. When I didn't answer him, he turned and walked away.

I thought I was happy. He could likely see that I was happy. But now, after resurfacing from his arms, I wasn't sure that I knew what happy was.

Could my life truly be happy without Pheobe and Cameron in it?

CHAPTER SIXTEEN

Watching Samantha tug Wesley and Edwin out onto the dance floor was like a splash of cold water to the face. The seductive smile she flashed directly at Edwin was no secret. She was taunting me. I flew over to them and tore Edwin's arm from her grimy little paws, stealing away his body and his attention.

"Oh, there you are," Edwin said to me, brushing my hair away from my face.

I wrapped my arms around his neck and kissed him passionately, to remind him why he loved me so much. He gladly reciprocated the love. After a few songs, I lightened my grip on Edwin. The crisis seemed to have been averted and the rest of our group, with the exception of Aliah drowning herself in free shots with random strangers at the bar, had made their way to the dance floor.

Catching me off guard, Samantha caught my arm and proceeded to pull me away from Edwin. "I'll only steal her for a minute," she chimed, over her shoulder.

After we were completely separated from our party, I yanked my arm from her grip. She came to a full stop and spun around, wearing her other face.

"You want to do this here?" she wailed. "Fine! Quit moving in on my game. You can't have them all."

"I don't know what you're talking about. I have a man. You keep your hands off of him and do what you want with the others."

She tilted her head to the high ceilings and laughed. "You couldn't keep your eyes away when Cameron had his hands on me."

"Puh-lease. You were stuck on him like a pesky mosquito."

"If you weren't sending him your secret signals, he'd be mine already," Samantha snapped, clasping onto my wrist.

My faint view of Edwin was obstructed by the other dancers. "You're delusional."

"Oh, I think not. Can't settle on just one? I'll help make that decision easier for you."

Done with her shit, I freed my wrist from her grip, dashed back into the crowd and convinced Edwin to take me home.

As Edwin pulled me away, he raised a hand to Cameron, who was lounging against the bar with Aliah. I couldn't escape the agony in Cameron's longing gaze. The tightness in my chest only squeezed tighter when I noticed a steady red glow reflecting in the mirror behind him. *Reflections. That's all they are.*

Edwin's pace slowed as we got caught in a foot traffic jam near the coat check. An icy finger trickled up my spine, despite the overheated room. I turned back to check on Cameron and froze in terror as her glowing eyes burned black holes right through my heart. Jenny was here, and she was standing only a few feet away from Cameron, in the flesh.

I blinked harshly, hoping it was only a figment of my imagination. *No. It was definitely her and she was a spitting image of me.*

Jenny turned away, releasing me from her horrifying glare, only for me to realize that Cameron was still watching me, worry wrinkling his adorable forehead. I looked away, my only hope being that Cameron would forget about it, and Jenny would go back to where she came from. *Maybe she could take Samantha with her too.*

I promised myself, just one last glance. Jenny was gone, making me wonder if she were ever there at all. Cameron insisted we make eye contact and I gave it to him. *Big mistake.* His fingers were slanted, his fingertips touching, and his brow was furrowed, toying with my very sanity. When a flicker of misconstrued understanding arched through him, it tugged at every last one of my heart strings.

Why couldn't he just hate me? It would be so much easier if he did.

I finally managed to pry my eyes from his, as Edwin helped me into my jacket. Trying to act ignorant to the connection that had just occurred, I clung to Edwin's core and held on tight as he moved us closer to the door. Edwin lifted his arm around me and tucked me against his warm body as I cringed, recalling that Cameron's official goodbye was now over.

On Monday morning, I fretted over the eerie quiet that had settled over the office now that Cameron was gone. That's when I heard Aliah's screech. I dizzily hurried past the curious onlookers, who had their noses sticking out of their offices to hear what was going on.

"No! Really?" Aliah squeaked, staring into space. She hung up the phone, clearly in shock. When she turned to me, it was evident that she had gotten as much sleep as I had this weekend.

"What is it?" I asked.

"Maddie was having cramps this morning and Hunter rushed over to her place to be with her. She's in labour, Abby. Hunter's taking her to the hospital as we speak." Aliah's eyes were wide with fright and started to water. "Should I go?"

"Didn't you and Hunter talk about this before now?"

"Not really. Maddie's pregnancy has been pretty taboo for me. It's gotten increasingly worse. Hunter didn't even come home last night. He just stopped in for a change of clothes and took off again when Maddie called him." Aliah's words were laced with jealousy.

"You should probably go. Hunter is going to have two babies handed to him in a matter of hours. He's going to need some emotional support."

"You know I don't do emotions," Aliah insisted.

"I suggest you fake it then."

Flustered, she shutdown her computer. "Fine. But only because you're making me." She reached for her purse and rushed toward the front lobby.

I followed after her and stopped at the reception area to get my daily dose of office gossip from Taylor. There was a couple of clients waiting in the lobby, so we had to keep quiet.

"Saturday night must have been pretty wild for Samantha to not make it in this morning," I said.

Taylor rested her elbows on her desk and dropped her chin onto her hands. "I guess Cam turned Samantha away when we were all leaving, so she moved onto Owen instead."

My mouth dropped to the floor and curled into a startled smile. *I did not see that coming.* "She certainly didn't waste any time."

"Tell me about it. And with Owen? That's not like him at all." She shrugged a heavy shoulder. "I have yet to get Sam's side of the story. Have you talked to Sam today?"

I shook my head no. "I thought maybe you had, since she didn't show this morning. I can't say I'm terribly surprised."

"True. But she's not answering her phone. I called her yesterday to check on her. I'm honestly getting a little worried."

One of the clients stood from their chair and approached the desk, so I knew I had to keep it short. "She probably just slept through her alarm. I'm sure she's fine."

I dialed Aliah's cell, eager to hear some news. Before I could even breathe, Aliah snapped at me. "Why did you make me do this? This was the worst idea ever," she squawked, as a woman's muffled scream sounded from her end of the line. "I was already pretty sure, but now I definitely know, I will never have kids!"

"Is everything okay?"

"No. Everything is so far from okay right now," she cried. "I saw one of the babies heads coming out, Abby. Hunter's all, *Oh, it's such a beautiful, natural thing*. Screw that. It's the most disgusting thing I have ever seen in my life. There's nothing natural about it. I will *never* get that image out of my mind. I'm seriously scarred and it's all your fault."

I smirked after hearing her horrified version of events.

"Then there's the blood. It's everywhere. And all the nurses are all smiling at Maddie, cooing to her, *You're doing great, Maddie. Keep up the good work,*" she mocked. "Trust me when I say that she does not look great. After what I saw, I can guarantee you she will never be great ever again."

I giggled with excitement, happy to hear the progress. "You left before the babies were delivered? You have to find out what she had! I just have to know."

"Why don't you get your ass down here and see for yourself?" she demanded. "Hunter might be doing just fine, but I could use your support."

"We're already short staffed, with you and Sam off. I'll swing by after work."

"Ugh. I swear to you, I am not stepping foot into that labour room again until they're out. No bloody babies for me, thank you very much."

When she ended the call, I couldn't help but chuckle at her lack of enthusiasm. But she was missing out on one of the most amazing experiences of Hunter's life; the birth of his first child. I was sure it marked the beginning of the end for them.

Maddie breathed through gritted teeth, staring at the white wall with sheer determination. "Ahhh," she screamed, as she gave another push.

Hunter stood hunched at her side. He brushed a sweaty lock of hair from her eyes, his other had fisted beneath her back to ease the pain.

"Just one more push, honey," the nurse instructed. "You're almost there."

"Come on, Maddie. Just one more push. You can do it, baby," Hunter cheered.

Maddie pushed with all her might, screaming at the top of her lungs. "He wants out now. Please take him out!"

With that final push, out came a shoulder and a baby boy was born. Before long, Maddie felt the urge to push again. Hunter's facial expressions suggested he could feel her pain.

"Slow down little one. Just one more minute," the doctor cooed, as he flipped the second baby with the forceps.

After a little bit of coaxing, baby number two came out to meet her new parents. "It's a girl," the doctor announced, promptly handing the baby to a nurse standing by.

"A girl?" Hunter asked, stunned.

"A boy and a girl," Maddie chimed, with tear-filled eyes.

Baby number one had already been tested and was swaddled warmly in a blanket. The nurse handed the baby to his emotional father.

"Hey, buddy," he said, staring at his healthy baby boy. "I'm your daddy."

Words weren't sufficient to describe the joy Maddie was feeling in that moment, as Hunter approached her with her brand new baby.

"Come and meet your mommy," Hunter said, as he reached the little bundle to Maddie and helped her position his hungry little mouth. Moments later, Hunter held his little girl, wrapped snugly in his arms, eagerly awaiting her mother's milk.

Maddie watched on with a whole heart, as Darien fed from her and their precious baby girl wiggled in Hunter's arms. After the labour mess was cleaned up, the hospital staff all filed out of the room.

"We'll give you some time alone," a nurse said. "I think you two seem to have things under control. Just make sure that both little ones get some more of mommy's milk. If you have any trouble or need anything, just hit this button here." The nurse wrapped an emergency button around the side of Maddie's bed. After scribbling her name on the marker board, the nurse left the room.

Maddie started to hum, filling the silence with a sweet tune to relax the squirmy, little guy while he continued to suckle at his mother's breast.

"So much for calling this little one Raymond." Hunter gawked at his baby girl, choked up with emotion. "You're just a bundle of surprises aren't you?" he cooed.

"I wasn't crazy about that name anyway," Maddie admitted. "What would you like to call her?"

"You're honestly asking me?"

"If you're going to play an equal role in our babies' lives then it's only fair that you have a say," Maddie answered, softly.

Darien started to fidget again and so Maddie resumed humming. It calmed him instantly.

Hunter watched her, not understanding the emotions running through him. This moment was so intimate. "I've got it," he said. "It's perfect for our little angel."

"What is it?" Maddie asked, curiosity fueling her excitement.

"Do you trust me?"

"Yes," she answered, without a doubt. "You know I do."

"Melody," Hunter said. "Darien and Melody Wight."

Her face warmed and she smiled at him with all her teeth. "Oh, Hunter. I love it! I love you..." Her eyes grew wide and she shuddered with embarrassment. "I mean..."

"It's okay. You're emotional. I know the feeling," Hunter said, appreciating everything she had been through to birth his children.

Maddie softened and smiled again. "Why don't we call her Melody Rae?"

"It's perfect," Hunter replied, then looked into his beautiful baby's eyes. "What do you think, Melody Rae? Do you like it?"

Maddie smiled, consumed with happiness and overwhelmed with love for her new family. "How did you come up with that name anyway?" she asked Hunter. "Just curious."

Hunter smiled. "You were humming to Darien and I was just thinking about how beautiful your singing voice is. Then it came to me," Hunter admitted, without realizing the implications of what he had just said. He brought Melody Rae to her mother and lifted Darien back into his arms.

Maddie watched Hunter, as he took a seat in the padded chair and leaned back in it, to rock Darien to sleep.

"I think I could use a nap myself," Hunter said to Darien softly, closing his eyes for a rest. Hunter slowly rocked the chair, while Melody Rae re-acclimated herself with her mother's breast.

Maddie stared at her child with admiration, as a tear of joy dropped down her cheek. "Melody Rae," she whispered. "A perfect name for a perfect baby."

After arguing with the nurse for fifteen minutes in the maternity ward, Edwin and I finally caught Aliah pacing at the end of the hall. She hustled down the long corridor the second she noticed us.

"It's about time!" she hollered. Her voice echoed through the quiet halls and a baby started crying in a nearby room.

The nurse let us pass. "We came as soon as we could," I said, softly. "How are they?"

"They're fine. Maddie's exhausted, but she's totally elated. Hunter's no different. It's actually pretty nauseating to be around it. I can only handle them in short spurts."

"Are you going to come in with us?" I asked Aliah, when I noticed her hesitation.

"I'll walk you there, but I think maybe it's time for me to run."

I flashed a serious glance at Edwin and he lifted his eyebrows in recognition of my concerns. Aliah led us to the last room on the right. Edwin knocked lightly on the door and then peeked inside.

"Hey, guys. Come on in," Hunter called, softly.

Aliah waited in the hall.

"Congrats," Edwin said, reaching his hand out for a shake.

Hunter seemed rattled as he struggled to free a hand with Darien in his arms.

"It's all good, brother," Edwin said, withdrawing his hand. "I'll get you later."

Hunter smiled with appreciation. "Thanks."

I walked right up to Maddie's bedside. "How are you feeling?"

"A lot better than I look," she admitted, with a soft smile.

"Stop," Hunter said, catching everyone's attention. "You look absolutely radiant. Tell her she looks beautiful, Edwin."

"You look beautiful," Edwin conceded, smirking.

I leaned over the bed to take a peek at the tiny bundle of sweetness in her arms. "And who do we have here?"

"This is Melody Rae. Isn't she an angel?"

I took the baby's little hand in between my finger and thumb. "Oh, is she ever. I thought you were having boys."

"What can I say? Things change," Hunter confessed.

"These two definitely change everything," Maddie added, sharing a gentle glance with Hunter.

Aliah stomped into the room in misery. "Okay, I've had enough of this.   Will you two stop with the whole everything's changed bull shit? I don't care if you spit out a couple of kids, it doesn't make Hunter yours."

Darien started to cry from Aliah's harsh tone and Hunter's reaction made everyone step back from him. He turned on his smile for his baby, as he gently bounced with Darien to soothe him.

"It's okay, buddy. Please don't cry. She didn't mean to upset you," Hunter cooed, then planted a kiss on the baby's forehead.

"Oh, *I* upset him?" Aliah squealed, dramatically. "I'm out of here. And maybe while I'm gone you should reconsider what's most important to you."

The twins that bound Maddie and Hunter together with happiness were tearing Aliah apart. She fled the room enraged and, as soon as she was gone, the calm returned. With Hunter not making any move to chase after her, I hurried into the hall and ran after Aliah myself. I found her jabbing at the elevator button, as though it might make the door open faster.

"What are you doing?" I asked, a little breathless.

"I'm getting the hell out of here. He doesn't want me here anyway. I'm just getting in the way of their little family."

"You're giving up? That's not you," I stated.

"And you think that's Hunter in there? Maddie's right. Everything has changed. Hunter's not the same person he was before...before that whore got knocked up."

"He still loves you," I reminded her.

"I don't doubt that he does. But I can see that Maddie's obsessed with stealing Hunter from me, and I know for a fact that Maddie told Hunter she loves him. And you know what, Abby? He didn't even tell her to back off. I overhead them when they were naming the babies. Then he tells her how beautiful her voice is. Ugh!"

"I'm sorry."

"Like I said, he's changed and I'm fine with that."

I was having a hard time believing her. "Are you really okay?"

She sighed and nearly lost it, tears welling in her eyes. "I was acting okay and I thought I was doing a damn good job of it, so don't interrupt my performance, okay?" she croaked, trying so hard to keep it together.

I reached my arms out to her and tucked her head onto my shoulder. "Stop tormenting yourself and just let it out. You don't have to be so strong all the time."

Aliah lifted her head, and I knew she was locking her emotions away in a vault. "I appreciate what you're trying to do here, and maybe if Hunter gave a damn about anyone other than Maddie it'd be worth a tear."

Just then, Hunter spoke, appearing out of nowhere. "This has nothing to do with Maddie, so let's leave her out of it. You know I love you, Ally. But these babies are my blood. They will always be my number one."

Aliah spun around, jerking out of my arms. Hunter remained a few steps away from her, retaining his emotional distance. She scowled at him, pulling her vulgar attitude back out. "And I suppose that will make Maddie always your number two. Where do I fit in?" she demanded, so loud I'm sure Maddie and Edwin heard her.

He turned his eyes to the floor and conjured up the words. "I'm sorry..."

"Stop," Aliah hollered. "Save it. That's just not gonna fly with me. I deserve better than that." Aliah was barely hanging on to her anger, with other more feminine emotions starting to weave back into her voice.

Right on cue, the elevator door opened. She stomped inside, forgetting I was even there, and instantly hit the close button. "Have a good life," she said, coldly, as the door closed between them.

Hunter stood in front of the stainless steel doors, staring straight ahead at his scattered reflection, and voiced a deep sigh. He lowered his head again and closed his eyes. When I rested my hand on his shoulder and gave it a squeeze, he looked up at me through guilty eyes.

"It was unintentional. I didn't mean for her to get hurt like this," he said, with a sigh. "Honestly though, this is the happiest day of my life and she couldn't even spit out a congratulations."

I grabbed onto Hunter's elbow and pulled him back down the hall. There was nothing I could say that would ever undo what had just happened between them. I wasn't even sure that it was worth it for them to try and put the broken pieces back together.

"I'm going to grab a coffee," Hunter said, just as we reached the room. "You want one?"

"No, thanks. I'm good."

Hunter strode off and I returned to the room to give him his space. The first thing I saw when I walked in the door was Edwin standing there. Big, powerful, Eddie. And he was holding a baby. My heart lurched at the sight of him brimming with cheer, admiring Darien only a few inches from his face. I could see the love, and sense his pride from helping Maddie with the brand new baby.

"He's so precious," I said, as Edwin enveloped the tiny baby in his arms. Seeing Edwin in that moment was a dream come true, digging at my innermost desires and displaying them before me. My heart swelled in my throat.

Suddenly Edwin's eyes grew wide and I feared that he was having a panic attack. "Uh, oh," Edwin announced, making a sour face. "I think it's your turn to hold Darien."

I gladly scooped the little guy from his arms and quickly realized why Edwin was so eager to pass him off. "I think you need your bum changed," I said, to the adorable baby boy.

I carried Darien to the bassinet and carefully laid him down on his back. Fresh diapers were stored in plain sight and I was fully prepared to change his adorable little bottom. But when Hunter stepped in and saw what I was doing, he took over territorially.

"I've got this," he said, nudging me away with one hand, his other on the baby's tummy.

"Wow, that's a good daddy," Maddie chimed.

"Daddy. That sounds good on you," I said, as I moved out of his way.

His smile was double the size of mine.

"You're in trouble now," Edwin teased. "You change this one butt and you're sealing your fate, brother."

"It's not that bad," Hunter insisted. "I already changed Melody Rae once." He quickly swaddled Darian back up and joined Maddie at the other side of her bed. He protectively glanced over his babies, with love shining in his eyes, as Melody Rae slept peacefully in her mother's arms.

They looked like a cute little family, and what a pair they made. Hunter and Maddie were both entirely exhausted, all of their arms fully occupied, and yet it didn't obscure the happiness emanating from them.

"It looks like you're going to be pretty busy from now on," I said to them.

"Nothing we can't handle together," Maddie replied, glancing up at Hunter.

There was so much love in her eyes. Hunter's answering smile showed that he was equally as smitten. Maddie had finally gotten what she wanted.

CHAPTER SEVENTEEN

The phone was ringing off the hook, but I sure as hell wasn't going to get up to grab it. "Are you going to get it? They're obviously not giving up," I said, slamming a pillow over my head to hide from the blaring phone.

After a long sleepless night, neither I nor Edwin were in a particularly good mood to take any early morning calls, but Edwin rolled out of bed anyway. Moaning he picked up the phone.

"This better be good," he moaned, then quickly changed his tune. "Really? You're kidding."

I ripped the pillow off my face and sat up, instantly taking notice as he listened carefully and stared back at me with disbelief rampant in his features.

"Let me know if there's anything we can do. I'll let Abby know. She's right here. Okay, thanks for calling." Edwin hung up the phone and returned to the bed, sitting next to me without spitting out the news.

"You'll let me know what?" I demanded, knowing it had to be serious.

"It's Samantha."

"What does she want?" I asked, not catching his drift.

"She's dead."

An overwhelming sense of shock and alarm overcame me, as he told me what he knew.

"I guess she was in the bathtub and passed out. She slipped under the water and drowned."

"No." I gasped and covered my mouth with a trembling hand, my entire body catching the jitters.

Just the other night we were partying together and I had shared more than one backstabbing comment about her. Never did I believe that karma would actually take her out like this so suddenly.

"Apparently Taylor called Sam's mother last night, since Sam didn't show up to work yesterday. Her mother went to her apartment to check on her and found her in the bathtub."

"Oh my gosh."

"You okay?" Edwin asked, petting my arm. "You're sure you want to hear this?"

I nodded, but my stomach was already roiling like a reckless tornado.

"She said it looked like there was foul play because Sam was covered in blood and had bruises on her neck, but the coroner explained to her that the injuries are always magnified in a drowning. They're saying she could have died up to twenty-four hours before they found her."

"No!" That would take us back to the night of Cameron's party.

"What's worse is her mom still believes she was strangled and intentionally drowned. The police have already tagged it as an accidental death, but are doing an investigation to appease her."

I grasped at my side, as a sharp pain wrenched my insides. "I think I'm going to be sick." I ran down the hall and flipped open the toilet seat. I couldn't handle thinking of Samantha's lifeless body, bloody and bruised in her bathroom. Even if I hadn't ever taken a liking to her, I wouldn't ever wish that on anyone.

Moments later Edwin joined me in the bathroom, finding me crouched over the toilet. He rubbed my aching shoulders. "It'll be okay." Then he helped me to my feet and wrapped me in a warm embrace.

Who, out of all the people we know, is capable of murder?

Edwin led me back to his bed. "Are you sure you're okay?"

I wasn't, but I knew what holding in my feelings did to me. "I'm shocked. Wouldn't she have choked and woken up before she drowned?" I tried to think logically while so many illogical thoughts tumbled through my head.

"If she had been startled awake, she could have suffered a heart attack from a heart condition."

"A heart attack? At her age? Not likely, unless..." My eyes grew wide with alarm from my grim discovery.

"What? What is it?"

"Jenny," I whispered.

Edwin cocked his head sideways. "Really, Abby? You have to stop with that. I get that you miss her, but your mind is obviously playing tricks on you."

"Eddie, just hear me out. There were no signs of struggle. If she had been drinking and passed out, that's believable. But what if she awoke to darkness?"

"You mean to the red-eyed monster," Edwin answered, skeptically. "You think she was scared to death." He did not sound convinced by my theory.

"I know it sounds ridiculous, but it's not impossible."

"Actually, Abby, it is. Jenny's dead." He paused, to let it sink in. "The police have listed the death as undetermined, but there's no evidence to suggest she was murdered."

"In other words, she drowned and that's good enough for them. Maybe that satisfies your curiosity."

"Abby, it's a tragic accident. Let's leave it at that. If you start telling people your two cents, they'll probably lock you up in a mental ward. You can't seriously believe your dead sister is out killing people."

"My nightmares have become pretty intense lately. I thought it was because it's getting close to our birthday."

"Maybe that's why your hallucinations have been more frequent, but that's all they are, Abby. Hallucinations. I was here the other night with you. Jennifer was not here. I think I would have noticed another woman in the room."

I narrowed my eyes at Edwin, knowing exactly how crazy I sounded. "Edwin, she was here."

The investigation for Samantha's death came and went as fast as her funeral service. The sadness was crushing, and yet I was unable to shed so much as a tear. After the church service, everyone made their way to the cemetery to say their final goodbyes.

Edwin parked his truck and waited for me to grasp his arm, before we followed the long line of mourners. The wet ground was soft and my spiked heels sunk into the mud, aerating the lawn with each step. A group of people had already begun to congregate around the raised casket in a u-shape. As we neared the shiny waxed box, we found the open grave surrounded in a carpet of flowers.

I glanced up at the patchy, grey sky. It looked like the clouds were going to open up and drop a storm on us. That's exactly how my insides felt.

The burial was terribly sad and I actually wanted to break down and cry, but I couldn't for fear that it would only fuel Jenny's unidentified motives. After the priest said his last word, the women in Samantha's family were handed a single red rose. Taylor asked for two yellow roses and handed one to me.

Wasting no time, I released Edwin's arm and approached the deep, dark hole. I stood at the foot of the casket and stared into that hole; the pit that would soon be home to Samantha's cold, dead body. An eerie breeze urged me to be quick, so I tossed the long stem rose from my fingers. I had aimed for the casket and it rested there for a moment, but then slid off the side and dropped into the hole.

I leaned forward to see where it had landed and found Jenny's lifeless body lying in its place. I covered my mouth and let out an anguished shriek. The other bystanders assumed I was grieving Samantha's death, and I was clearly upset about that too, but I was more worried that Jenny had something to do with it.

Without a single blink, I stared at Jenny's pristine body. Then I glanced over my shoulder to check if anyone else could see what I was seeing. No one seemed to notice. I turned back to the hole and all of a sudden Jenny opened her eyes. They were glowing red with resentment and I could sense an unhealthy rage seething within her.

"No!" I screamed.

Everyone stared as Edwin came to my side. He held me tight in his arms and kissed my hair. Taylor joined us too, reaching out for a hug.

"It's okay. We're all going to be okay," she said to me, between sobs. She gently rubbed my back and it seemed to soothe me.

I let them all believe I was grieving and in a way I was. I was heartbroken and traumatized that my twin sister was being so unforgiving and committing deplorable crimes for my attention.

Taylor looked into my dry, bloodshot eyes. "There's a social gathering over at Sydney's Place after this. Are you two coming?"

"We'll be there," I whispered, listlessly.

Edwin led me away, while the casket was lowered. All the women cried. All but me. I stared back with a steel gaze, unable to feel anymore.

Later, at Sydney's Place, we joined our friends. Edwin took a seat next to Maddie, who had sandwiched Hunter in between herself and Aliah. Even with a sleeping baby in her arms, Maddie managed to pull out a dramatic display of grief. I wondered how long she had practiced that one in front of the mirror this morning.

Maddie handed her baby over to Edwin, as emotions spilled from her. Hunter rubbed her back and eventually fell to her act. He handed Darien to Aliah, and consoled Maddie, who now had her face buried in her hands. The second Hunter caved, Maddie threw herself into his arms and cried on his shoulder. Aliah didn't believe it either, but it looked like she had already given up trying.

I looked away from their troubles, hoping for a change of scenery. Off in the distance I saw Cameron sitting with some of Samantha's extended family. Not the change I was looking for. At first I thought maybe he'd rather grieve alone, but I soon realized that he was actually observing us inconspicuously from afar. He was watching *me*.

Subtle or not, he couldn't fool me and I wasn't even sure that he was trying to. He delivered me pointed glances of affection, while attempting to maintain a blank expression on his face, but his adorably wrinkled forehead shared his despair with anyone willing to figure him out. It pained me to be on the receiving end of all that disappointment.

In desperate need of some fresh air, I excused myself from the table and headed for the door. A few stray eyes watched me leave, but no one followed. As I left the dining room, I noticed Owen in the corner of the lobby by himself.

"Owen?" I said, walking up behind him. "Everything alright over here?"

He cleared his throat, but refused to look at me. "I'm fine. Don't worry about me." He had clearly been crying and was embarrassed by it.

I rested my hand on his back. "You two were close. It's okay to be upset."

"This is messed up," he admitted, his eyes reaching mine. They were red and filled deeply with sadness, thickening the air between us, until it became difficult to breathe.

Upset for my own reasons, I pulled him into my arms and smoothed my hand up and down his back. He squeezed me with all he had, as he broke out in tears.

"She was so alive, Abby. I barely got the chance to know her, and now I never will." Owen released me from his arms and smeared away the tears. "I must look like a total chump. You aren't even crying and you've known her way longer than I have."

I pressed my lips together in a firm line. "I think I must have emptied my reserves."

"I was starting to wonder if you were even human," Owen said teasing, but it hit me on a guttural level and I nearly toppled over from the pain stabbing at my insides.

The room started to spin around me and I felt like I was about to fall into a bottomless pit. Tears were on the verge of spilling and, at the sight of Cameron appearing in the small lobby, they did, twisting my insides and dropping me into another man's arms.

Owen held on tight, bearing all my weight, my toes barely touching the floor. "I'm so sorry. I didn't mean to upset you. Shit."

Cameron rushed to our side and reached for me. "Come here," he ordered, and I couldn't deny him that.

Feeling dizzy, I lifted my head from Owen's shoulder and found Cameron waiting for me with open arms. My first sob escaped my mouth as I crashed into his chest. "Oh, Cameron," I cried, gripping onto him like my life depended on it.

Owen stood there, stunned, as Cameron pet my hair and dropped a kiss on my head.

"It's okay. I'm here now," he whispered, wrapping me in his warm, familiar arms.

Even more tears fell, my confusion overpowering my heart, now beating out of my chest like an African drum. Broken breaths cut off my air supply, as I lifted my head from his chest, overcome with my mistakes.

"I don't want to hurt you," I choked, pulling out of his arms, refusing to make eye contact. "I have to go." I ran off, bursting out the exit, knees still weak, cheeks still wet.

Cameron stared blankly at the door, then looked to Owen for some guidance. Owen only shook his head side to side, knowing exactly what Cameron was thinking.

"I have to," Cameron explained, then dashed outside after me.

Sadness hung over the office for weeks, and Miller couldn't bring himself to hire a new secretary. We all threw ourselves into work, hoping to make the unnerving vacancy go away. Nothing made the vacancy go away.

After five long weeks, it was time to get back to some sense of normalcy. I met Aliah at the Westmount Fit Club, ready to burn off the extra calories I had put on over the past few months.

"You and Hunter, you're good?" I asked Aliah, as I huffed and puffed on the elliptical trainer.

"I just needed time to lick my wounds," Aliah admitted, not putting in half the effort I was.

"Things are back to normal then?"

"Normal," she stated, reflecting on that single word. Aliah stopped what she was doing and turned to face me. "Honestly, I don't think our relationship will ever be *normal* again. Hunter's changed. He used to be all about me and making me happy. Now it's always Darien this or Melody Rae that. And don't even get me started on Maddie. I know the twins are adorable and he wants to spend time with them, but he's being distant. It's like he's there with me, but he's not actually there, you know?"

I nodded my head, as I forced my legs through the burn.

"Whenever it's just the two of us, it feels like he'd rather be there with Maddie and the babies. It kills me to watch him sitting there like that. If he's over us, I wish he'd just say so."

"Have you talked to Maddie lately?" I asked, carefully.

"Not because I want to, but Hunter insists. She's permanently elated. It makes me sick. Whenever Hunter's around she acts like he's hers to control and he waits on her hand and foot. It truly sucks, because I know I should leave him so he can go be happy, but that would mean that Maddie's won."

"You shouldn't stick with him out of pure jealousy." I stopped treading for a minute, to catch my breath and take a drink from my water bottle. As the room fell silent, I noticed Hunter approaching behind Aliah.

"You know what. You're right," Aliah stated.

I shook my head no and lifted a finger to stop her. "Wait..."

"I'm going to tell him what he's doing is ridiculous. It's Maddie or me. He can't have both."

My face turned ghostly white and my eyes said it all. Aliah didn't have to turn around to know that Hunter was standing there. She spun around, eager to finish him off.

"So that's it?" Hunter asked. "You're giving me an ultimatum? After all we've been through." He narrowed his tired eyes, and it was anger festering beneath them.

Aliah's expression mirrored his. "It shouldn't be that hard of a decision. If you can't just say you choose me, then it's over."

"You're jealous of Maddie?" Hunter stated, incredulously.

"You're not making me feel jealous. You're making me wonder what I ever saw in you in the first place."

Hunter waved her off as he turned to leave, then whirled back around to face her. "You're going to forget about me and move on, just like that?"

"It'll be easy," Aliah argued, her voice as sharp as a knife. "I don't have to forget you, because I already lost you months ago."

After a quiet drive into Toronto, I was in high spirits. The night grew darker as we entered the Bar and Grill where some of our friends agreed to meet to celebrate the long weekend in May. Edwin tightened his grip around my waist, just as I realized that this was our first night out since Cameron's party; the night Samantha died.

The dining area had a few stragglers taking their time with dessert. Others lounged on the stark black furniture, which stood out against the warm, brown bricks that adorned the walls. Edwin led me past the pool tables to the narrow staircase that led to the second floor.

After passing through another lounge area, we cut through the dance floor, heading straight for the rooftop patio. The weather was seasonably warm, with summer being just around the corner, which was a nice change after the long, wet spring. A waitress instantly greeted us, as we exited the open patio doors, and Edwin gave her our order.

"I guess we're the first ones here," Edwin voiced first.

Dance music flowed freely through the open patio doors and the occasional gust of cool air, drawn from the dance floor, doused the otherwise stifling heat radiating from the brick building. The lights glowed softly beneath the bamboo gazebo and dimly lit the space that was quickly coming into darkness.

I was starting to feel surprisingly relaxed when I took a seat next to Edwin. Unfortunately, that feeling wouldn't last long.

"Here comes Maddie and Hunter." Edwin stood from his chair and greeted them. "Hey, brother. Good to see you."

I stood too to give Maddie a hug. "Wow Maddie, you look great!"

"You really think I look okay? I feel so huge; my boobs especially." She started giggling. "They feel like they're going to explode."

"Who has the babies?" I asked, surprised that she left them in someone else's hands.

Hunter piped up. "Maddie's parents insisted that they be the first ones to take them."

Maddie turned to face Hunter, as though she had to defend them. "This is our first night out since we had them, you realize. I had to know that the twins were in capable hands."

Hunter rolled his eyes playfully. "Yeah, I know. You haven't stopped talking about that all the way here."

Maddie poked him in the chest. "I can't help it. Maybe it was too soon. I'm already having separation anxiety."

Hunter looped his arm around her waist and bumped her against his hip, so there would be no more jabbing fingers. "It's only for a few hours. I promise to have you back to them safely," he said, with a smirk.

"You guys aren't spending the night?" Edwin asked.

Maddie acted all flabbergasted by Edwin's insinuation. "Are you kidding? We aren't together like that. Why would we get a room?" Maddie eyed up Hunter. "Besides, I'm not ready to be away from my babies for that long. I miss them already."

"Well, at least we have one thing in common," Hunter said.

They smiled at each other and I couldn't help but notice the flame flickering vibrantly between them.

As the night went on, more friends filed onto the spacious patio, hovering around our table and a nearby lounge area. As I sipped from my drink, my eyes were drawn to a group of people lingering near the patio doors. Suddenly, I choked on my beverage, and a shot of electricity spiked through my body, my heart thrumming against my chest.

Cameron and Wesley escaped from the crowd and strolled up to the bar together. *Since when did they become buddies?* Cameron looked as sophisticated as always, his expensive jeans slung from his narrow hips, to make all the ladies swoon; myself included.

I gulped back the lump forming in my throat, but the dryness didn't subside. I downed my drink and, before Edwin could see why I was darting, I kissed him on the lips and delivered a reassuring smile. "I'll be back in a bit," I said, before scurrying for the nearest exit.

With the most casual of glances, I noticed that Cameron and Wesley were too concerned with themselves to notice me zipping through the crowd. Relief washed over me, once I realized I had managed to sneak away undetected. Finding a clearing, I blasted through the crowd and gasped for air when I finally reached the open space on the other side of the small dance floor.

Just seeing Cameron was hardly an event, but I was terribly short of breath. My chest heaved as though I had just run a marathon and a bead of sweat started to form on my brow. I tried to ignore it, but my body wouldn't lie: I was still tuned into Cameron and everything that he was about.

I observed the other patrons, staring at anything that might steal my attention away from the thoughts I was hiding from. I wasn't expecting to find Maddie working the floor. But she was, and it looked like her newfound chest was getting her the attention she had been looking for.

Turning my eyes away, so I didn't disturb Maddie's little game, I located Hunter nearby. He was methodically drinking his beer from the bottle, stalking Maddie from the bar. I made my way over to him, hoping we could help each other lighten up.

"You'd think that girl would've learned a lesson," I hollered, as I neared Hunter.

He glanced at me briefly, basically ignoring that our friendship even existed. I became uneasy when I saw the jealously raging in his eyes, and he continued to glare into the distance. I followed his eyes and found Maddie still flirting with the same cute guy. Now that Maddie had birthed his babies, he had little reason to be so overprotective of her.

"Hey! What are you doing in here all alone?" I blurted, trying to break his dark stare.

He looked at me, removing his icy, defiant eyes from the dance floor. "Just thinking," he said, as if it were the first time he noticed I was standing there.

"About what?" I imposed, not expecting much of a response.

"I was just thinking how quickly Aliah moved on. It really pisses me off."

There was no way he was thinking about Aliah. It would be too much of a coincidence that his baby momma was having a good time without him, in the direction of his glaring eyes. I checked the dance floor for Aliah, but she was nowhere to be found.

"I thought you and Aliah agreed separating was best for the both of you."

"We did. I just hate how she wasted my time. I've been blowing off Maddie, the only sure thing in my life, to keep Aliah happy all this time. Look where that got me. Now Maddie's off gallivanting and there's nothing I can do about it."

"Looks like you're wasting your own time, if you ask me."

"Excuse me." His tone was bitter.

"Everyone knows that Maddie has it bad for you. You just have to make the first move. I've never really thought of you as a benchwarmer," I said, egging him on.

Hunter's looked at me, dumbfounded. "You really think she'd give me a try? I don't want her to think I'm on the rebound."

"Then tell her that."

Hunter nodded to himself, working up the courage to do it, then guzzled the rest of his beer. He clanked his empty bottle on the bar and looked to me. "Here goes nothing."

CHAPTER EIGHTEEN

Feeling proud of myself, I waved down a bartender and had him refill my drink. I headed for the table I had been sitting at earlier and there they were: Edwin, Cameron, Wesley and Owen, all sitting together. I knew it spelled trouble, but there was nothing I could do about it.

They were all laughing, as Edwin slammed his hands down in victory and Owen left the table to sulk. When Wes slipped into the vacated seat across from Edwin, they looked like they were about to have a duel.

I rested my hand on Edwin's shoulder. "What in the world are you guys doing?"

"What does it look like? We're arm wrestling," Wes insisted.

"Seriously, Wes?" I wagered, smirking. "You don't stand a chance."

Wes' arrogance flooded me like a violent, crashing wave. "I already beat Cam."

"And I beat Owen," Edwin added. "When I win this one, I'll be the champ."

"You cheated. But, whatever," Cameron said, trying to protect his manhood. "It's only twenty bucks."

"No, it's proving that I'm the man," Edwin stated.

"There's that," Wes said, mirroring Edwin's smug expression. "But what's twenty bucks to me?" Wes' eyes slipped deviously up my body and he struck me with a naughty chew of his lip. "Now that she's here, why don't we raise the stakes?"

I don't like where he's going with this.

"I'm listening," Edwin said, waiting for the proposal. And I could tell he was intrigued, knowing his fierce, competitive nature.

"If I beat you, I take Abby to the dance floor and she's all mine for thirty minutes." He waggled his eyebrows at me and repeated himself, as if I could have missed his vulgar comment the first time. "All mine."

"Make that twenty minutes and you've got yourself a deal," Edwin answered.

My mouth fell open in horror. *What do I look like?*

"Deal," Wes responded, irrefutably.

"Excuse me?" I squealed, utterly appalled. "Do I look like a trophy to you?"

"Relax, baby," Edwin said. "I could have beat Owen with a hand tied behind my back. I'm sure beating Wes will be a breeze."

That was a far cry from reassuring and it actually fueled the ball of anxiety in my stomach that had quickly grew in size. As I turned away, I caught the fact that Cameron looked even less impressed. That made my heart skidder again, adding another layer of stress to the situation.

Focusing on Edwin, to show that I was not impressed, I huffed at him. "You're really going to play games like this? What if you lose?"

"I'm not going to lose."

A mischievous grin formed on Wes' lips. "See? Even your little lady thinks I've got the upper hand on you." He waggled his eyebrows at me again and it only egged Edwin on more.

"Let's do this," he said, looking Wes in the eye.

Wes clasped his hand and matched his glare, getting ready for the battle.

"I'm not watching this. It's totally absurd!" I turned toward the loungers, but it only made me catch Cameron staring at me.

"I would have to agree with Abby," Cameron said, his eyes protectively scanning over me. "This is pretty ridiculous."

"You're just jealous you didn't think of it first," Wes teased, as they started the competition.

I couldn't manage to keep my eyes away, giving in and watching the entire episode as it unfolded before me. Edwin and Wes showed feverish determination in their faces, but their hands were not moving at all. They stayed neutral for such a long time that I was ready to take off, until suddenly the tables turned.

When Edwin started to lean into Wes' danger zone, I got a little excited. He was overpowering Wes and looked resistant to Wes' efforts.

"Yes," I cheered, catching Edwin off guard.

Wes took advantage of that millisecond, while Edwin readjusted, and forced his hand forward. Both of their arms were shaking and slowly but surely Wesley began to lower Edwin's hand closer and closer, inch by inch, until the back of Edwin's hand skimmed the table top.

With one final grunt, Wes flattened Edwin's hand to the table. "Ah, hah!" he chanted.

"No!" I screeched.

Wes stood from the table with both hands in the air. "And that's how it's done," he announced, his tone balancing between cocky and proud.

"This isn't happening," I said, covering my eyes with a hand.

Edwin looked up to me. "I can't believe I lost."

Wes was chuckling now. "I won fair and square. Time to pay up, brother."

Edwin hesitantly lifted his eyebrows at me. "You know I'm a man of my word. I'm no cheat."

"And you think I am?"

"I have to deliver," Edwin insisted, taking my hand and tugging me onto his lap. He tucked my hair behind my ear and whispered into it. "I love you, Abs. And I know how much you love me. It's only a dance. You can stand to lighten up a bit. You're stressing out way too much these days."

Anger made its appearance on my face, as I stole a glance at Cameron storming off the patio with another drink. I couldn't untangle my thoughts with Edwin staring me down.

"What's the worst that can happen?" Edwin said, softly interrupting my thoughts. "So he might grab your ass. Big deal. It'll only remind you of how lucky you are to have me." He was so damn confident that it irked me. But it was true.

"I can't believe you're encouraging this."

Wes stepped in and grabbed onto my wrist. "A deal's a deal."

I turned my face to Edwin, who was trying to hide his amusement, and scowled at him. "I'm going to need a stiff drink first."

"Done," Wes answered.

Edwin laughed as Wes pulled me toward the bar. I downed a shot and it burned as it slid down my throat, but it didn't make that horrid feeling go away. I motioned for another.

"Wow, you mean business. Hey, bartender, can I get another one of those please?" Wes hollered.

The next shot went down a lot smoother than the first, but it still didn't fix my problems. "Oh my god. What was that?" I asked Wes, surprised by how tasty it was.

"Let's just say that the entire office will know on Tuesday that I gave you two screaming orgasms tonight," he said, smirking.

I rolled my eyes, not even caring anymore, ready to finish what he and Edwin had started. "Let's get this over with."

I hoped to make Edwin jealous from his own stupidity, when I let Wes hold my hand, but when I looked back at him, he was still smirking. *Asshole.*

After passing through the patio doors, Wes immediately locked his arms around my waist and pulled me up against his warm, lean body. It was incredibly awkward for me, with him gyrating to the beat, but he seemed to be enjoying himself profusely. And damn if he didn't know how to dance.

Wes, noticing my discomfort, brought his mouth to my ear. "This doesn't have to be so painful," he drawled, then looked me in the eye and tucked my hair behind my ear, just like Edwin had moments earlier.

"Edwin doesn't deserve you." He flashed me a slanted smile. "Then there's Cameron over there, about to have a bird. And he's my ride."

"Oh." I tilted my head slightly and caught a glimpse of Cameron's crazed glare. "I'm sorry. I can't even believe I agreed to this."

"I'm glad you did," he said, with an honest smile touching his lips.

I shook my head no. "You'd think Edwin was my pimp."

Now Wes was the one shaking his head. "All the money in the world couldn't buy a prostitute as hot as you," he said, his eyes greedily scanning over me. He brushed my cheek again and I shuddered from the intimacy of it, backing away on a sharp intake of breath.

"Please don't."

"There are boundaries. I can handle that."

Quickly moving on, he took my hand and raised it up, showing me off. Then he attempted to pull me close again. This time I made an obvious effort to back away.

"Edwin thinks you should loosen up for me, remember?"

"Will you stop with the clowning? This is awkward enough as it is."

"I'm sorry. I thought it might make it easier for you."

"Well it's not," I snapped.

"What's wrong?" he asked, honestly flabbergasted by my reaction.

"I think things have gotten a little out of hand here. It was supposed to be a dance and you're...you're..."

"I know what I'm doing." Now he looked disappointed, like I had snapped his heart in two.

"I think I've already completed my end of the bargain," I said, fluttering my eyelashes.

He teased me by licking his plump lower lip. "You're sure you don't want to have a little taste?"

And even though his lips were looking as delicious as Cameron's, I refused to budge an inch. "I'm sure."

To my surprise Wesley didn't press the issue. Instead, he followed me back out onto the patio where we instantly noticed a commotion.

"Let's go," Wes said, brushing me aside and hustling toward Edwin and Cameron.

I hoped to intervene, but it was already too late.

"I don't have a short temper," Edwin hollered. "I just have a quick reaction to bull shit!" He jumped up from his chair, bumping the table and spilling half of the drinks.

"Oh, you wanna go?" Cam yelled back, stepping closer. He tugged off his shirt and paced closer, until my fingers rested on his warm, buff chest.

"This isn't the place for this," I ordered, trying to break his heated glare from Edwin's.

It only angered Edwin to see me showing care. "Stay out of this Abby!"

"Please," I demanded, pushing Cameron away.

"Don't push me off like that," he cautioned, only flashing me an irritated scowl.

I was stunned by his forcefulness, but his anger was clearly fueled by heartache.

"Don't touch her," Edwin warned, rolling up his tight sleeves.

It was obvious that neither of them was going to listen to reason and there was no turning back time. Before I could think of something useful to say, two big guys grabbed onto them and ushered them away. A slimmer guy approached us and apologized, but insisted that we had to leave too. Choked up on emotion, I rushed down the stairs after them.

Edwin stomped through the main dining area, and Cameron hardly kept a safe distance behind him, before they reached the street. I hightailed it outside to intercede. I thought to take Edwin's arm and pull him to his truck, but before I could Cameron was already piping up again.

"I wasn't finished with you," he hollered out, provoking Edwin.

Edwin shook me off his arm and I fell back onto the pavement.   After retrieving myself from the ground, I searched for some backup and only found the bystanders snickering and pointing at Wes. I wondered myself why the hell Wes' shirt was off. He wasn't even involved in the fight, but none of the ladies were complaining.

Drawing my eyes back to the real plague, I rushed in between them again, knowing it wasn't the smartest place to put myself, but also knowing I was probably the only one who could keep them apart. Their eyes could have burned holes right through me. At that very moment, I felt invisible.

"Face it," Cameron said. "Abby was happier with me and you can't handle it."

Oh shit!

"You wouldn't know happiness if it slapped you in the face," Edwin retorted.

"If you didn't want the truth, then you shouldn't have asked for it," Cameron went on, unfolding the story.

"What do you know?" Edwin said, patronizing him. "Abby's mine."

Cameron's mouth quirked up into a dangerous smile, his chest muscles flexing at the challenge. "I know that no one in their right mind would send that beautiful woman into another man's arms."

"We've all had too much to drink. You don't want to do this," I pressed, trying to get through to one of them.

"Get her out of here," Edwin called to Wes.

Wes took me by my shoulders and pulled me back, as though I were a weak, delicate damsel. "Trust me, darlin'. You don't want to get blood on those pretty little shoes, do you?"

Cameron's face seemed apologetic for a moment, then it quickly turned to a darkness that I had never before witnessed in him.

"No!" I hollered, as Cameron threw the first punch.

He hit Edwin right in the jaw and though Edwin was forced sideways and backwards from the blow, he straightened himself immediately and hissed angrily at him.

Edwin spit out a mouthful of blood and a dark, demented rumble came from his throat. "She doesn't want you anymore. Don't you get that?"

Cameron was ready for Edwin's first swing and so he missed him. At first glance, I thought Cameron might stand a chance, but Edwin was younger and stronger and very determined. Both were drunk, but they exchanged blow for blow until they were both bloody messes. It was no use trying to intervene now. It was personal.

Edwin threw the game changing fist that sent Cameron to the ground out cold. I shrieked in voiceless agony, my body turning boneless. I collapsed in Wes's arms, horrified from the gore.

"Looks like you lose again, tuff guy," Edwin announced quietly, standing over Cameron who was now crumpled on the pavement.

Edwin spit out another mouthful of blood and greedily yanked me away from Wes.

"Help him," I breathed to Wes, as Edwin pulled me up the street.

Wes immediately ran to Cameron and shoved the others out of the way to see if he was okay. Cameron was already coming to before the bystanders again closed around him.

The night was dark and the adrenaline gleamed in Edwin's eyes, as he quickly walked us toward our getaway vehicle. I could hear sirens heading in our direction. I glanced over my shoulder, concerned for Cameron, and found him on his feet and staring at me with hurt and frustration in his eyes. Wes and Owen were there with him. *He'd be okay.*

The others swiftly fleeted the streets as a police cruiser pulled up to the curb with its lights flashing. I looked at Edwin without saying anything, torn between anger and other emotions. His sinful smile confirmed that it was an incredibly satisfying victory for him.

When we reached the truck, Edwin pulled his bloody shirt off and handed it to me. He lifted me into the driver's seat and followed me inside. I crawled into the passenger seat, without a fuss, knowing that Edwin's adrenaline had burned off any buzz he might have had.

Checking out the damage, my heart shuddered. Blood marred Edwin's handsome features. I grabbed the water bottle from the cup holder, to keep myself from bursting into tears. I dampened Edwin's ruined shirt and shifted closer to him, gently dabbing his bloodied face.

An unspoken tension simmered between us as we drove off. I was thankful that our hotel was only a few blocks away and decided it'd be smart to reserve my anger and disappointment for another time, when Edwin's face was less broken.

Edwin led the way to our room. Neither of us spoke. He opened the door and walked in ahead of me. I followed him to the foot of the bed, where I sat to remove my high heels. He stood there, motionless, staring at me.

"I'm sorry," he said, with a sigh. He could read my eyes, no matter how hard I tried to disguise my emotions. "You shouldn't have had to witness that."

I tossed my shoes near the wall and turned my gaze to the floor, emotions still running high. "I wish I hadn't."

"Are you mad at me?" he asked, his soft tone showing his concern. He sat next to me on the bed.

"Hmmm. Let me think about that," I answered, as I turned toward him. I got onto my knees and playfully wrapped my fingers around his neck to choke him.

Edwin laughed. "I suppose this means you're slightly upset."

Not giving up on the lightened mood, Edwin tickled me, forcing me to release the chokehold I had on him. He flattened me on the bed, letting up the torture, but the dried blood on his face was a harsh reminder of exactly what had happened.

"Was it arrogant of me to send you off with Wes tonight?"

I propped myself up on my elbows. "I certainly wouldn't recommend you do anything that stupid ever again."

"My trust goes a long way," Edwin insisted.

I cupped his face and brushed my finger over his swollen lip. "I'm just glad you're okay."

"Why wouldn't I be?" he asked, sliding over me.

"Well, Cameron..."

"Forget about Cameron. Some people are best left in your past, along with your other mistakes and regrets."

"And you?" I asked, gazing into his humourless eyes.

"That's easy. I'm your future."

Edwin's kiss was soft, slow and sensual. Tasting. Teasing. It was a miracle he could channel his adrenaline at all. I rested my hands on his hard chest and could feel his heart beating wild with anticipation. He trailed kisses across my neck, dipping lower, his tongue tasting my skin. Edwin carefully lifted my shirt over my head, exposing plump breasts, bursting from my lacy lingerie.

He marvelled in my flesh, his hands smoothing over my curves, as he kissed the tops of my lifted breasts. He closed his lips around the dark peaks, through the soft, thin fabric of my bra. When his tongue stroked me, wetting the soft lace, the warming sensation zapped me right between the thighs.

"You're so beautiful," Edwin said, devouring my body with sensual eyes. "And all mine."

"Yes," I gasped, as he pressed himself against me.

His breaths turned heavy, a wolfish smile on his lips, sending a cool tingle across my chest that made my nipples turn razor sharp. He unhooked my bra and flipped it up to consume a mouthful of my breast, his tongue paying special attention to my hardened nipples.

When he hauled his chest across mine, it made me shiver, the complete opposite of what I felt when I grabbed the rigid length filling his jeans. I urgently fingered the button on his pants and he laughed, pulling away from me. He stood from the bed and, seconds later, his boxers hit the floor. Then he jerked my bottoms and panties off, dropping them next to his.

I shuffled toward the headboard, holding my breath to stave off the want. Edwin lurched onto the bed and crawled toward me like a powerful animal. He drew himself between my spread legs and pressed them wider, as his lips met my soft, inner thighs. When Edwin's thumb brushed over me, a delicious shiver rocked my entire body.

"Edwin."

He chuckled again, his voice rumbling intimately against me. "You like that," he stated, his voice incredibly low and dark. "You're so wet."

Then his tongue traced where I needed him to be and he sucked on me like a vampire hungry for blood. I weaved my fingers into his hair and clenched onto him, holding him in place as volts of pleasure passed through me.

"Oh, god," I cried out.

"Mmm," he growled, those pleasant vibrations sensitizing me even more.

I clamped my legs around his head and when his tongue dipped inside, a violent orgasm gripped me. "Oh, Edwin. Oh, yes!"

My body throbbed with a want so strong, then exploded, releasing the tightly wound tension in waves of pleasure. On a deep sigh of exhilaration, my boneless body sunk deeper into the plush bed. Edwin dove for a condom, ripped the packet open and slid himself between my lazy legs, before the aftershock had even worn off.

Holding himself over me, he brushed his head against my sex, tempting me back to life. He was evidently very aroused, all of his blood rushing to please me again. A fresh arousal stirred within me, despite the sated feeling that pinned me to the bed beneath him.

"Mmm," I said, my response making him pulse harder. With eyes pressed closed, I nibbled on my bottom lip and waited expectantly for Edwin to take me.

Without warning, Edwin sunk into me and started pumping his hips at an inhumane pace.

"Wait," I cried, but it was so good.

He stopped, pressed deep inside me; his muscles held tight. *Oh, he was suffering.*

"Don't stop," I gasped, my hands bunching up the blankets at my sides. My excitement only fueled his violence and he slammed into me again. He was so hard, and I was so tight, but I wanted more. Needed more.

"Harder," I begged.

His mouth crashed into mine and passion circled me, as he filled me to the hilt. He tore his lips away from mine, baring his teeth, as his hips thrust forward. He slammed into me, again and again, dangerously answering to my needs. It felt like he was ripping me open, but my body screamed for more of him. More movement. Just more.

My climax crashed around me and Edwin's mouth muffled my scream, as he groaned, riding the crest of the wave. Tears sprang from my eyes, as he dropped his heavy, sweat-soaked body on top of me. Once his rapid breaths slowed, he lifted himself up, a warm gaze assessing me. I felt my body protest as he pulled himself from me.

He licked his swollen lips, then dropped a slow, soft kiss on my parted mouth, with a growl. "You're mine."

CHAPTER NINETEEN

It was the Festival of Lights tonight and, though I was feeling more than a little anxious about going, Edwin insisted. I didn't dare remind him why I might be a little hesitant to go back to that place. Was it wrong that I didn't want to jinx our relationship after what had happened there last year? I still got shivers when I remembered that icy ride home, in the dead of summer. Our relationship never survived it.

Edwin could sense I was fretting about it and had been acting kind of funny himself today. He had begged and pleaded with me to take the water taxi, but I had outright refused, feeling like it would be a tragic mistake. I had enjoyed our dinner, but still had to take a deep breath to settle the rapid patter of my heart as we strolled down the street hand in hand.

As the sky grew dark, we wandered to the riverside park and found an open spot in the grass, where everyone had gathered to watch the fireworks.

Edwin spread out a thick blanket, took a seat and finally stared me into submission. "What's wrong?"

"I'd be lying if I didn't say I'm pretty nervous about tonight." I patted the pleats out of the blanket and crouched next to him.

"I don't know what you're so worried about. We were in love one year ago and we're in love now. If that's not something worth celebrating, then I don't know what is."

I nodded and blew out a breath to steady my nerves. Then a smile broke out on Edwin's face that he couldn't wipe off. Now kneeling next to him, his natural smile squeezed my heart ever so slightly. "Now what are you smiling at?"

"You." He caught me in his arms and pulled me onto his lap. "Can't a guy smile when he's happy?" Edwin asked rhetorically, as he secured his lips to mine.

The music was fairly loud and there was enough commotion around us that we could get away with it, so I melted into him and let him kiss away my worries. After making out for a few minutes, like young, passionate lovers, Edwin eased back.

"I don't know about you," he said, with his smile still firmly in place, "but I'm feeling a lot better now."

I crawled off of him, only to find myself under the scrutiny of a few gawking men and their controlling wives. Still, Edwin still couldn't stop with the smiles. When the music stopped, Edwin pulled away from me, and when I saw the red glow over the water, I thought it was Jenny. Then the fireworks began and I realized it was only the lighters.

A coolness tingled down my exposed back, causing me to turn around to see where Edwin had gone.

"There's something I wanted to tell you," Edwin said, in an instant. "I was going to do it on the water taxi. But since you nixed that idea, I figure now is as good as ever." A slanted smile crossed his lips replacing that serious look.

Was he breaking up with me? My chest fell sharply as I pressed out a huge breath, relieving the tightness from my lungs. That would be the ultimate revenge.

"You can take that look off your face. I know what you're thinking and you're wrong," Edwin stated.

I tried to obey him, but that worry was stuck in my gut, as Edwin hovered over me in limbo. The fireworks grew increasingly spectacular, but I was too anxious to look away from Edwin, whose eyes had turned incredibly dark and serious. My heart beat erratically out of my chest, while my eyes trained on Edwin standing over me.

"I'm ready," he stated, as if I should know what that meant.

I stood up next to him, trying to understand.

Edwin took a gulp and wet his lips, appearing very nervous. "We all have that one person we would take back in a second, no matter how much they hurt us in the past. You're it. If there's one thing I've learned over the past year, it's that you should never let go of your dream until you're ready to wake up and make it happen. That's exactly what I'm going to do here tonight."

Mesmerized by his warm gaze, I couldn't even bring myself to glance at the reds and purples exploding in the dark sky above us. Then Edwin pulled a ring from behind his back and lowered down to one knee, and it was as though my dream was playing out in reality.

"Oh!" My hand sprang to my mouth and I inhaled my last breath.

Edwin took my other hand and kissed it, then reached the ring up to me. "I love you, Abs. You're my best friend, but I know now that it'll never be enough. Please say you'll marry me." He stared up at me expectantly, waiting for my response.

I gulped, wanting to say yes, but too many worries flooded my mind. One stood out more than the others. *Did he think I was pregnant?* "If you're only doing this because you think it's the right thing to do…"

He shook his head. "The only thing I want to do is to make you my wife." Edwin presented the ring again. "Abigail Jenkins, will you please marry me?"

I blinked twice, then noticed that others were waiting for my answer as anxiously as Edwin was. I was too breathless for words. Edwin gently squeezed my hand and my eyes landed on his. In that moment, happiness fluttered through my chest like a butterfly and I knew that he knew my answer. I nodded yes eagerly, with a smile plastered on my face. He took no time wiggling the ring onto my finger.

Edwin stood up and looped his arms around my waist. "Yeah?" he asked, making sure he had understood me correctly.

I flung my arms around his neck. "Yes!"

Edwin lifted me in the air and twirled me around. When he put me back down, I didn't want him to ever let go. "She said yes!" he hollered, ecstatic about it.

Now the centre of attention, I began to blush. "What do you say we get out of here."

Without the need to answer, Edwin picked up our blanket, waved at the gawkers and pulled me away into the darkness, fireworks still popping behind us.

"Where are we going?" I asked, my body pressed against his side.

"Here, there, anywhere. I don't care, as long as I'm with you. I'm ready to start our life together, Abs. I want to make a family with you."

My lashes fluttered down, when I realized that I would finally get what I had always dreamed of.

"You want a baby? I'll give you a baby," he said, totally serious. "No more waiting."

The air fell silent and all I could hear was my rapid breaths, suddenly terrified by the thought of having to wear a maternity dress to my own wedding. "You know I want my baby born in wedlock."

Edwin smirked. "That's easy. We'll be married in the next nine months for sure. Problem solved."

I smiled at his enthusiasm, but this was my dream. "I don't want people to think you're only marrying me because you got me knocked up. Besides, I don't want to look like a cow in my wedding gown."

Edwin smirked again. "Not everyone gets pregnant in one try, you realize. It could take some time. I thought we could go practice." He waggled his eyebrows, and I was so tempted to throw my well thought out plans into the fire.

"I could practice," I said, with a provocative smile.

"Now?" he stated, very excited with the notion of sex in public.

I started laughing instantly. "Not right now!"

"You're right," Edwin admitted. "We should probably wait until we get home."

I laughed at his acceptance. Little did he know, had he pressed a little harder, a little longer, we would have been making babies already.

CHAPTER TWENTY

I hung up the phone with the flower shop - *my* flower shop – not the one his mother insisted that I use. "Edwin!" I wailed. "I've had it up to here with your mother. I can't take it anymore!"

After tormenting Edwin with months of wedding planning, he finally gave up all involvement. Aside from monitoring the budget and nixing a couple of my crazy *money wasting* ideas, he had left all of the planning to me. Or so I had thought.

His mother was so kind as to slip her foot in the door and step into his place, as though her say was as good as his. I believe she said, *it is in the best interest of the Santora family that I be involved.*

I understood how having a houseful of unwed boys would make Vera very interested in getting involved, but she was starting to give off the impression that this was *her* special day. While I was grateful to Vera for paying for a good portion of the expenses, I was tired of being pushed around.

"You can handle it," Edwin insisted. "We have one week to go. Suck it up."

"I really don't think I can," I warned dramatically, like it was a life or death situation.

"What is it now?"

"She's ignoring what I want and changing things without my approval. Fine, she upgraded the transportation, I'm not going to complain about that. But changing my bouquet? *My* bouquet. She didn't even have to nerve to tell me. If the flower shop hadn't called to confirm the order, I would have been forced to walk down the aisle with a bunch of lilies. You know how much I hate lilies!"

Edwin's lips quirked at the edges, until I scowled at him. He had better not smile. "She means well, Abs. Give her a break."

I leapt from the couch and matched his stance, my hands thrust on my curvy hips. "Excuse me? Tell me you're not siding with her."

Edwin reached for my shoulder, but I stepped away, not allowing him to touch me. Then he smirked.

"Is this funny to you?" I screeched.

"Don't be upset. She's really excited about it and only wants everything to be perfect for you."

"For me? Really? I think not. If it was about me, she'd butt out."

He smiled and scooped me into his arms, before I had time to react. "I hate to tell you this, babe, but it's only going to get worse with age. You realize you're marrying into the Santora family."

I tried to pry myself from his grip, but he wouldn't let me free. I finally stopped squirming and huffed at him.

Edwin's lips hovered over mine, then slowly dropped down, to soften the blow. He backed up to look at me, then pressed another delicious kiss to my mouth.

I forced myself out of Edwin's arms, refusing to let him change the subject. Edwin cupped my chin, silently pleading for me to drop it. His thumb stroked my bottom lip, then he kissed me again; and again, sinking his soft wet tongue into my mouth. Was he trying to seduce me into cooperation? I hated to admit that it was working.

I had to hand it to her. Vera knew what she was doing. My bachelorette party went off without a hitch and I even managed to suffer through her pleasant enthusiasm without too much aggravation. I may have even had a lot of fun. With Edwin's bachelor party set for tonight, the night before our big day, I was sure to have a nervous breakdown.

It was already past five, but I had a lot of work to do before I could enjoy my honeymoon, guilt-free. Moments after I kissed Edwin off, him and twenty-one of his closest friends took off in a glorified limo bus. Owen and Wes went along, leaving me by myself in our corner of the office. I struggled to keep my eyes open, still tired from my wild night on the town with my ladies.

I worked away for the next hour or so, trying not to think about what Edwin was doing, until I decided it was time to head home. I wished I could catch up on my beauty sleep, but I knew I wouldn't be able to sleep a wink. As I locked the front door of the office, I noticed my phone was flashing. I was mentally exhausted, but I listened to the voicemail message anyway.

"Abigail, it's me. Cameron." He hesitated on a sigh, and it crunched my heart. "Can you meet me for coffee? I'll be at our favourite place. Please? It's important."

It sounded important. Urgent even. I wondered if it had to do with Pheobe. Without thinking twice, I punched his number into my cell and turned it onto speaker as I hurried to my car. His phone seemed to ring off the hook, then it finally went to voicemail. Maybe I was too late.

"Shit!" I tossed my phone on the seat next to me, then stepped on the gas. My anxiety strangled me as I slipped out of my car and headed for the front door of the diner.

Meeting Cameron - my ex - on the night before my wedding, was probably not the smartest thing I'd ever agreed to do. Was I trying to jinx myself? If anything though, I had to close off my relationship with him once and for all, before I started the rest of my life with Edwin. Things had been weird between us lately, and I didn't want for us to end like that.

The Thorncliffe café hadn't changed in the eight months that Cameron and I had been apart. Neither had my aching heart when I thought about poor Pheobe and how she took the news about our separation. As I entered the long, narrow room, I glanced around until I found Cameron sitting alone at the table farthest from the door. He looked good – casual – very put together.

Why did he have to look like that?

As I approached him, he stood from his seat and stared me down, a light smile touching his mouth. His dark blonde hair was cut super short and he wore it wild and spiky. I forced a smile, hoping it would hide my anxiety. Unfortunately, the closer I got to him, the stronger the sensation became.

I had hoped I wouldn't feel this way. I had hoped it would be a cinch. But our attraction had never faded. It still ran hot. Cameron had gone away, out of sight, but *it* was still there. Unsure how to greet him, I avoided an awkward hug or handshake and took the seat across from him. He smirked and sat down without making me feel uncomfortable about it.

"What's so important?" I asked, skipping to the point.

"Don't you at least want to get a drink first? You must be hungry."

I couldn't imagine sitting at the table for a whole meal with his desirous cologne flooding my nostrils. But when the waitress rounded the counter with my favourites, how could I say no?

"I took the liberty of ordering for you. I hope you don't mind." He wrinkled that adorable forehead and it took me a second to regain my cool.

"You didn't have to do that."

"I wanted to."

Suddenly, my stomach was feeling very full; full of regret and full of an alarming sadness. I nibbled on the food, but I couldn't swallow a single bite. I dropped my fork onto the plate and stared up at him. "Are you going to tell me what this is about? I don't have a whole lot of time."

Cameron held his eyes on me and it shook me like a rumble of thunder to my core. "Don't do it."

I choked on the air, seemingly empty of oxygen, and struggled with my drink to clear my throat. "I'm sorry?"

"I don't know how I'm supposed to live without you, Abby. Don't marry Edwin."

Cameron glanced at the floor, appearing very vulnerable. Then he looked up at me, and it felt like he was calling the shots again. "You have to give us another chance."

In an instant, the wound that I had so carefully stitched up after we had called it quits, was gaping wide open. I pushed away my plate, and took a deep breath to steady my jitters.

"You know I gave us a chance, Cam. It didn't work out the way I planned either. We both need to move on already."

"No."

I was stunned by his convictions. "It's not healthy, hanging on like this."

Cameron slid his hand on top of mine and toyed with the ring he found there. "What's not healthy is this thing you're calling a wedding. If you don't want me, fine. But don't settle with Edwin."

I wanted to get angry, but all I could feel was sadness. For him. "I'm in love Edwin."

"Really? How much do you love him? Enough to give up your dream? I saw the feathery gown you ripped from a wedding magazine, Abby. It didn't look anything like the one I saw Edwin's mother carrying out of the bridal shop. This boring, traditional wedding sounds nothing like the one I imagined for us."

Outwardly, I scowled at that statement. "The flowers I want don't grow naturally in the fall. The place I picked for the ceremony wasn't available on such short notice and it'd be too cold outside for the guests anyway. Not everyone's dreams come true. I'm being realistic."

Silence enveloped us, as I stared blankly at him, unsure what else I could say to him. I could have sliced the atmosphere with a knife.

"All I'm saying is, why rush it? What's the rush?" Compassion dripped from his every plea.

I closed my eyes and squeezed them shut. "Cameron, you're so not doing this right now."

"Actually, I am. Were you hoping that we could go on ignoring each other and forget that anything every happened between us? I can't pretend that you don't exist,

Abigail. I tried it. It's not working for me. We were so happy together."

"You said it," I whispered. "Were. Past tense." Sadness rushed my throat and tears rushed my eyes, but I refused to let them escape. "You expect me to believe anything's changed? I still want children of my own. My mind will never change on that subject."

"But mine has," he stated, profoundly.

I froze with panic-filled eyes. "Oh, and you just came up with this crazy idea now? The day before my wedding." I was too upset to notice that the other patrons of the café were growing restless and most were starting to stare.

Cameron leaned forward and whispered privately to me, hinting for me to quiet down. "I've done a lot of thinking since I left the firm. Yes, I want to give you children, and yes Pheobe has been asking for you. I miss you, Abby. We both do."

A single tear dripped down my cheek. "You're too late," I whispered. "I'm marrying Edwin tomorrow."

He shook his head no. "Maybe Edwin loves you. Maybe you think you love him too. But know I never stopped loving you." His voice became softer, but it was getting so much more demanding. "I haven't given up. I will never give up on us."

"You'll have to," I said, sadly.

"No. Don't do it, Abby."

Another tear snuck down my face and I tried to wipe it before he noticed, but his eyes pierced me with desperation. I snatched up my purse, hoping to take off before he realized that it was over for good.

"I'm sorry. Please tell Pheobe I said hello." I rushed from my seat and flicked away a tear, but it was useless. I raced to my car, to escape from my feelings, but they beat me there. I crashed into my seat on a whirl of emotions and didn't look back to see if Cameron had followed me, mostly afraid to see that he had.

Without turning back, I had hurried home, pulled on my favourite pj's and slipped into bed for some much needed rest. As my eyes slipped shut, the nightmares resumed. It was late, and I was alone, lost in my head full of dreams and darkness.

CHAPTER TWENTY ONE

Opening my eyes was the first mistake of the day. I blinked them closed again but, despite my terrible mental hangover, I decided that I was still in control of my own destiny. Today was *my* day.

When I tried to move to check my alarm clock, a heavy arm pinned me down and I recognized the warmth of a body behind me. Edwin must have skipped the hotel to come home. *What a sweetheart.*

I wriggled to get closer to him and he nestled his nose in my hair. His breath was warm on my skin and his lips were soft on my neck. Still mostly sleeping, eyes mostly shut, I rolled over for an early morning kiss.

Edwin's lips were just as soft and sweet as I had imagined they would be.

"Mmm," he growled, as he woke from his peaceful slumber. He was supposed to spend the night at the hotel, so he didn't see the bride on his wedding day. The fact that he was here only made me love him that much more.

I felt like a puzzle, colourful and complete. No more would I be left to my own mind where I talked to dead people and believed that my destiny wasn't in my own hands. It turned out that a twist of fate was exactly what was needed to get me and my heart to this place, where the love of my life stood to give me everything I had ever dreamed of.

Aubrey yanked on her sister's arm. "Come on! No one's supposed to see you." She didn't believe in all that hocus pocus, but Abby never was one for luck.

"You don't seriously believe that bull, do you?" Abigail asked, smirking. "Besides, there was only like five cars in the entire church parking lot."

Again, she didn't believe that anything would happen. But, yes, there were five cars. She had counted. Because she could've sworn that one looked a lot like Cameron's. A shimmer of anxiety warmed her cheeks, as she dragged Abigail into the church.

As they made their way through the back halls, Aubrey heard a commotion echoing in the main service room. Realizing that Abigail hadn't yet heard anything, she shuffled toward the dressing room and raised her voice.

"Why don't we find out where they're putting you. We can go check out the flowers in a few," Aubrey insisted dramatically, hoping to distract her.

"Okay," Abigail answered, curious as to why her sister was acting so weird and clueless as to what was unfolding on the other side of that arched doorway.

Abigail remained oblivious, as Hunter entered the hallway. "Abby. I didn't realize you were here already." He checked over his shoulder, to be sure he didn't have company behind him. "Aliah was looking for you. Why don't you go see her? She's down there," Hunter said, pointing in the opposite direction from where Cameron had just walked off.

The second Abigail disappeared down the hall, Aubrey whispered to Hunter. "Cameron?"

Hunter's eyes looked cold and determined. "Yeah. He asked to see her, but I turned him away. I was probably a bit too hard on him, but I had to get the point across. Abigail's marrying Edwin today."

Aubrey covered her mouth with her hand. *Poor Cameron.* "What did you say?"

Hunter checked over his shoulder again, but no one was there. When he turned back to Aubrey, she could see the remorse in his expression. "I told him if Abigail wanted *him*, he'd be the one in the tux."

Calyfa Jenkins slowly approached the massive, whimsical church.   It was mounted on a lush, grassy hillside, overlooking the nearby city. While the hillside was covered with a pristine, green lawn, the city was swallowed in dry, autumn leaves that buried any sign of growth and clarity. The skies were blue, but the wind was brisk and wisped around the arriving guests, daring the ladies to leave their skirts unattended.

Cally adjusted the skirt of her short, gold party dress and headed toward the long flight of stairs. More and more guests arrived around her, crossing through the well-retained gardens, passing the fanciful fountains and filing into the picturesque church that looked like a castle from a little girl's dream. She always knew one day Edwin would sweep Abby off her feet and put a ring on it. It had certainly taken him long enough.

Once inside the church, Cally gaped at the romantic flower arrangements that were beautifully arranged on a series of white, custom-made columns. As she approached the gathering of family and friends, she felt less than welcomed by their reception. The majority of women in Edwin's family were glaring at her with envy, as every man in the vicinity stared with fascination. She was used to that and, as usual, held her head high as she moved toward the handsome, young usher.

He charmed her by extending his arm and flashed her a confident smile. When she grasped onto his elbow, he whispered in her ear. "I don't have to ask. With beauty like yours, you must be here for the bride."

Cally was all smiles. "Aren't you a sweetheart. I'm Cally, Abby's cousin. And what do they call you?"

"I'm Caleb, a friend of Edwin's. Pleased to meet you."

"Very pleased to meet you," she said, flashing him a flirtatious smile.

Caleb continued to grin, as he led her down the long, main isle, passing row upon row of dark-cherry pews. Without another word, Cally released his arm and sashayed to the next pew. She slipped past a few relatives and took a seat, flashing a look back at Caleb, to catch a look at his fine ass as he walked away.

Maddie stared around the room that was quickly filling with guests.

"What's Caleb's problem? He's drooling all over himself," Maddie said to Taylor.

Taylor glanced across the aisle at the beautiful blonde that had just taken a seat across from them and smirked. "Can you blame him? That girl is gorgeous. I only wish I could be that young and blonde."

"I'll never look like that ever again," Maddie whined. "Trust me. Having kids ruins you. Enjoy your bod while you still have one."

Taylor broke out laughing. "Thanks for the compliment, but my body's been hanging south for years. A baby isn't the only thing that ruins you. Age can do a number on you too."

Maddie casually glanced behind her, where a couple of handsome men in expensive suits conversed in the aisle.

Taylor had noticed them too. "I knew this place would be swarming with gorgeous men." She couldn't even hide the wide grin on her face, as she took another peek at the handsome fellows. She caught the attention of the one with the shaggy brown hair. He smiled at her and she instantly craned her neck back to its resting place, wide-eyed and speechless.

Maddie slapped her leg, and bent forward, with a voiceless, open-mouthed laugh. Taylor's reaction to seeing Edwin's brothers was entertaining to say the least. Yes, the men were fascinating. The majority of the men on the Santora side were. But Maddie only had eyes for Hunter.

Just then, Maddie saw TJ and Hunter enter through a spectacular arched doorway. Hunter walked to the front of the room, with his hands casually stuffed in his pants pockets.

"That's my man," she whispered, staring straight ahead at him.

Edwin's brother, Payton, walked up the centre aisle and lined up next to Hunter. Maddie watched Hunter stare down the line at his fellow groomsmen. All three of them were suited in matching black tuxedos, with golden silk vests and ties. Maddie was thrilled when Edwin had asked Hunter to be his best man.

Vera Santora's smile could have been seen from a mile away. She had been battling with Abigail for months about every little detail and it looked like it had paid off.

Edwin's oldest brother, Anthony, and youngest, Keelan, stood on either side of Vera in the first pew. Though they weren't groomsmen, they looked just as stunning in their designer tuxedos.

"I must say, the groomsmen are looking pretty sharp," Maddie said to Taylor.

"They really are, but it's the ladies who I can't wait to see."

"Shhh, it looks like it's time." Maddie nodded her head toward Edwin, who had now joined Hunter at the head of the main aisle.

Edwin appeared to be suffering from pre-wedding jitters. His face was red and sweat poured from his forehead, as his eyes swept over the crowd. The churchgoers started to grow quiet, as the clock ticked down the minutes before the ladies would grace them with their presence. Then Maddie caught Edwin covering his mouth to whisper to Hunter.

The groomsmen stirred, their answering stance being anything but casual. Something was seriously wrong.

Ashley yanked on her date's arm, demanding that he keep up. "I will not be late for this wedding because of you," she growled.

As they ran up the stairs, with only a minute to afford, Ashley noted that no expense had been spared for Abigail's wedding. Victorian chandeliers were draped from the ceiling, setting the stage for a romantic affair. The stunning architecture of the church and gothic style canopy only added to the fantasy. Even on such short notice, this wedding was the most elaborate event she had attended all year, and that really pissed her off.

Ashley pulled her handsome date through the old, wooden doors. "You're sure you want to witness this?" she asked, snobbishly.

"I've come this far, haven't I?"

Natural light flooded through grand arches and when they stepped onto the dark, carpeted aisle, the large cathedral seemed to shrink instantly. All eyes zoomed in on them. On Cameron.

Ashley kept her smile pasted on her face, knowing that she looked hot in her black rouched dress. *Maybe it wasn't such a bad idea to bring him after all.*

"Whose wedding is this anyways?" Ashley whispered, insinuating that it was worthy of royalty.

Cameron shrugged his shoulders, knowing that no answer would satisfy her.

"Lighten up," she snapped, as they shuffled into the last pew. "I don't even know why you came. Why would anyone intentionally put themselves through this?"

Cameron turned his somber blue eyes on her. "It's supposed to be me. She has to know that she's making a mistake. I can't just let Abby walk off into the sunset with Edwin."

Ashley's eyes grew wide, displaying her anger. "Don't even think about it!" Her voice echoed through the room, her lips left in a sour pucker. And again, all eyes were on them.

Cameron took his turn, pasting on a fake smile. He nodded his head, apologetically, hoping the guests would forget about them. After the looks dissipated, Ashley turned to Cameron to force her disapproval on him.

"We did not come here to mess with the ceremony. Don't be stupid." Ashley's anxiety was causing her to ramble. "I mean, look at Edwin. What woman wouldn't want to marry that? Oh, and *you've* got a boatload of baggage. It's no wonder Abby didn't want you," she stated, hoping to break his spirit.

But Ashley's words didn't stop Cameron from quietly voicing his opinion. "The right path isn't always the easiest, Ash. But have you ever known me to take the easy road?"

"Haven't you ever heard that sometimes it's better to leave it broken, rather than hurt yourself putting the pieces back together? Your relationship is one of those things. Get it through your thick skull. She chose him."

When Cameron shook his head in disagreement, she knew her words went in one ear and out the other. Ashley puckered her mouth out of annoyance, and turned away to inspect the bridesmaids who were now congregating at the base of the aisle. She couldn't deny that they looked hot in their champagne-coloured dresses that were cinched above the waist with a black sash.

Crystals glittered on the strapless tops and light glimmered off the shiny, champagne skirts. They all wore strappy, black sandals, but each wore a different variation of the lacy black flower adorned on them. She leaned forward to get the first look at the bride's dress.

Abigail looked stunning. *Big surprise there.* But the real shocker was seeing her wearing the beautiful dress of feathers. Aubrey had said it was on back order, but there Abigail was, working that strapless heap of silk and feathers like she was royalty. A belt, encrusted with crystals, wrapped around her waist in a soft v that dipped just below her hips. The flowing snowy silk, and soft flawless feathers, fell delicately down the skirt like they belonged there.

When Cameron caught a glimpse of the bride, he felt like he was drowning in a living nightmare. Stunning didn't even begin to describe how she looked. Abigail took his breath away. And she looked so happy. But he had been so determined to prove to her that he deserved another chance.

He tried to stick to his guns, telling himself that she had to agree with him. She had to change her mind. But he knew in his heart that she had already chosen.

Suddenly feeling enlightened, Cameron lost his nerve. The last thing he wanted to do was ruin her special day.

CHAPTER TWENTY TWO

Thirty minutes earlier.

The dressing room was cool, but Abigail still couldn't catch her breath. She gasped for air as she anxiously prepared for her big day. Aubrey and Aliah had agreed to check on the flowers and give her a minute to herself.

Her mother and Vera were questioning the wedding planner about the reception hall, while she slipped into the long, silky gown and stood before the free-standing mirror, tilting it up to take a look at herself. The dress was perfect. Vera had secretly ordered it months earlier, having it handmade and flown in from overseas, after having seen the scrapbooking she had done as a child.

That had to be the most amazing gift that anyone had ever given her. To say that Abigail was surprised would have been a nonsensical understatement.

Everything had turned out so beautiful and sophisticated, just like she had always imagined. This was the day she had waited her entire life for and everything was exceeding her expectations. Then there was a light knock at the door.

Her stomach twitched, just slightly, as she bunched her gown into her hand to avoid tripping over the length of the phenomenal train. She paced to the door and opened it a crack to see who it was. Edwin stood there, staring at the floor, clearly panicked.

"You realize if you're mother sees you with me she's going to have a fit," Abigail said, without letting him in the door.

"Abs, seriously? This is ridiculous. I need to talk to you."

She huffed for a second, knowing that she was being childish, then gave in to his adorable pleas. "Can you do me up first?" She opened the door and Edwin quickly slipped inside the room, closing the door behind him.

Abigail turned away and Edwin's eyes skimmed over her soft, bare skin. He swallowed a gulp of air and slowly zipped the dress all the way up. He brushed aside the soft veil of fabric sprouting from her hair and kissed her neck. "You look amazing," he whispered.

Tears pooled in her eyes. Happy tears. "Thank you."

"Come." Edwin clasped her free hand and pulled her to an elaborate, antiquated chair.

She took a seat, as Edwin pulled up another chair for himself, careful not to disrupt her gown. He leaned forward and took both of her hands in his.

"How're we doing?" he asked, gulping back another breath.

"Honestly?" she said, letting her nerves start to show. "I'm terrified."

Edwin delivered a teasing smile. "And here I thought you might be a little more encouraging."

Abigail cupped Edwin's cheek and tilted her head to express her love. "Eddie, I can't imagine my life without you in it."

Even with his beautiful bride-to-be near tears, he couldn't help but tease her. "You realize once you say I do, there's no turning back."

"I do," she answered.

A genuine smile kicked up on Edwin's mouth, as he leaned forward to give his beautiful bride a kiss. With a tender press of his lips, Edwin massaged away her tension, and charmed her back under his spell.

"I love you," he said, then brushed a kiss on her chin.

Abigail hooked her arms around his neck and stole another kiss. "I love you so much."

Edwin brushed his lips against hers one last time, before pulling her to her bare feet. "Before I go, I just wanted to give you this." He pulled out a beautiful, white gold locket from inside his jacket and dangled it out to her. "I know it might not go with your gown and I understand if you don't want to wear it today, but I wanted you to remember that this is the day I gave you the other piece of my heart."

He dropped the locket into Abigail's hand and handed her a small scrap of paper folded into a small square. "Read this after I go," he said, smiling. "I'd better get back out there anyway, before they come looking for me."

Abigail nodded, doing her best to keep it together, then pressed a firm kiss to Edwin's lips. "I love you," she whispered, unable to quit saying it. She was so happy.

Her hand brushed off of his silky chest as Edwin hurried for the door. "I'll see you at the altar," he said, waggling his eyebrows and taking off before he could catch her resulting smile.

Abigail smoothed her fingers over the dainty heart-shaped pendant, feeling an engraving on the back. Holding it between her finger and thumb, she squinted to read the inscription. "*Just Friends* Forever."

She pressed her lips together, to hold back the tears, certain that she was going to drop some when she opened it up. Taking her time, she opened one half of the pendant. Inside, she found her favourite engagement photo. When she slowly opened the other side, she was shocked to find that it was empty.

After carefully unfolding the little note, Abigail broke out in a tearful laugh.

"This piece of my heart may appear empty,
But you know that's not a fact,
After our vows our said, I'm taking you to my bed,
And our baby will fill that gap."

It was a sad attempt at a rhyme, but it had Abigail clutching at her heart. She closed the trinket and wrapped the dainty chain around her wrist a couple of times, holding Edwin's heart in the palm of her hand.

Abigail disappeared into the private bathroom and dusted a fresh powder over her face. She was surprised how flawless her skin looked, considering how poorly she had slept last night. The nightmares she had endured had been enough to put her in a mental hospital. Tears started to well in her eyes as she remembered the threats, but she refused to mess up her face again.

As she reached for the door handle to bolt from the small, windowless room, darkness splashed over her. The air grew thin and cool, and a chill skipped up her spine. Abby tore her eyes from the blackened door and straightened herself to face the large wall of mirror, knowing exactly what was happening. Jenny was going to make good on her threats.

Red glowing eyes stared back at her in the reflection. Abigail slid her hand up the wall, without blinking, her fingers inching toward the light switch. She managed to get the lights to flicker back on, but she never took her eyes from her sister. Jenny sat cross-legged on the bathroom counter and her eyes flickered a magnificent shade of purple.

"But...but..." Abigail stuttered.

"But...but," Jenny repeated, mocking her.

"I thought you could only come out at night."

"I prefer the shadows," Jenny said, with an evil grin set on her face. "And it adds to the mystery, wouldn't you agree?"

"What do you want?" Abigail snapped, the words bursting from her lips.

"Ooh, feisty. You know exactly why I'm here." Jenny gave Abby a pointed glare, her violet eyes seeing right through her. "I warned you."

Abigail nodded her head, trying to convince herself of a blatant lie. "I've been distracted from reality lately. That's why I'm dreaming you up right now," she told herself.

"Oh, trust me. This is no dream. I think it's time for you to cash out while you still can. There's the door." Jenny pointed toward the closed door. "Start walking and don't look back. Vera can take it from here. She doesn't want you to marry Edwin anyway."

Though Abigail knew that Vera never really approved of her, it hurt to hear Jenny say it out loud. "How do you get off making my life a living hell? What did I ever do to you?"

"You. You. You," Jenny chanted. "It's always about you. Do you think my life is so peachy? I'm dead, Abigail. You lived. You think life isn't fair? Try death on for size."

"No," Abigail shouted, more angry than sad.

Jenny's legs were draped over the vanity, and she kicked them up and down, like a carefree child. "Cameron still grapples with himself over Pheobe's loss of her mother, you know. He still blames himself for Tessa's death. I can just imagine what kind of effect it's going to have on him to know that he could have saved you. Then there's Edwin."

"You would never." With teeth clenched, Abigail had officially lost her cool.

"Oh, I would and I will. It's too bad that your luck will cause yet another tragic accident. And on your wedding day. What a shame."

"Stop it!" Abigail screamed, unable to take much more.

"I know what you're feeling about Cameron right now. It's okay, Abby." Jenny crossed her leg and rested her hands on her knee. "It's hard to pretend not to love someone, when every time you look at him all you see is everything you ever wanted."

If what Jenny said was true, Abigail was sure to die a mysterious death and join her in eternal misery by weekend. But Jenny was wrong. And Abigail had already reached her daily limit for craziness. "That's enough!" she shouted.

"You marry Edwin and you're signing his death certificate," Jenny stated, then disappeared on a black flame sparking from the vanity light.

Aubrey forced the door open and rushed inside the bathroom to hold Abigail in her arms. "What's going on?" she asked, rocking Abigail into submission.

"I don't know," Abigail whispered, relieved that Aubrey had come alone.

"You don't have to do this if you don't want to," Aubrey insisted, surprised that Abigail was having second thoughts.

"It's not that... it's Jenny."   Abigail took a tissue from Aubrey's hand and dabbed it under her eyes to prevent her mascara from running.

"Jenny?"

"She's coming to me again, Aubrey.   I know how ridiculous it sounds, but she is.   And now she says she's going to kill Edwin if I marry him."

"And you really think she's capable of it?" Aubrey said, not doubting her for one second.

"I wish I could say I'm not willing to risk it, but marrying Edwin is the one thing I'm not willing to leave up to fate."

"It's time!" Vera chimed, floating into the room.

Abigail's best girls, with help from her mother, had put her back together, and not a minute too soon. Vera thrust the bouquet of flowers into Abigail's hand and urged the bridesmaids to get a move on, pushing Abigail along after them.

Abigail's father met up with her in the hall and reached for her arm to help her along. "Hi, Dad," she said, softly, still clutching Edwin's heart in her palm.

He smiled at her, his eyes lighting up.   "You look beautiful, honey."

Abigail started to get choked up, when the music flooded the church. "Thanks, Dad." She had been waiting for this day for what seemed like an eternity. No one – not even Jenny – would stop her now.

The wedding planner handed out the bundles of soft ivory flowers to the bridesmaids. After adjusting the dark ribbon on them, she insisted that Aliah go.   On cue, moments later, Aubrey gracefully stepped onto the aisle. She instantly discovered the uninvited guest. She smiled and nodded at Cameron, despite the terrifying squeeze in her stomach when she saw him sitting there.

Hiding from the rising crowd, Abigail anxiously squeezed her father's hand. The wedding planner was calling for her, but her feet wouldn't move. Tears glistened in her eyes. This was the happiest moment of her life.

"Are you ready for this?" her father asked, with a whisper.

The wedding planner stomped her heel to grab their attention and shot daggers from her eyes.

"I've been ready for this since the day I was born," she said, showering her father with a soft smile. Though her voice was smooth and she looked entirely put together, her knees were knocking under her silky dress of feathers.

Her father kissed her on the cheek and pulled the wispy veil over her face, before towing her to the main stage. The organ sounded, deep from the choir's canopy, and Abby appeared in the archway at the foot of the aisle. She clutched her bouquet of warm-hued roses and prepared to take her first step.

Abigail clutched onto her father's arm and he led her proudly down the length of the aisle. Her spectacular train spread out behind her and whispered across the floor, making a glorious trail of silk and lace and feathers. The thin transparent material covering her face only amplified her sense of serenity, as she fixed her eyes on her handsome target.

Everyone stared as Abigail breezed toward her groom. Then her father lifted the veil, kissed each of her cheeks and whispered in her ear. "Jenny is here today, watching over you," he insisted, as if that were a good relief to hear.

Abigail heard a soft cackle coming from the canopy and she knew that Jenny was surely listening. *If he only knew.* She drew out her best poker face, handed her flowers to Aubrey and turned whole-heartedly to her groom.

"You look absolutely radiant," Edwin whispered.

Abigail blushed and glanced at the floor as she accepted both of his big, warm hands. A sense of comfort and familiarity washed over her, but a tedious ache lurked in her side. Abigail's mother dabbed the tears from her eyes as the priest proceeded with the prayers.

As the ceremony advanced closer to the exchange of vows, Abigail's hands grew warm. She wondered how long she had before Jenny unleashed her wrath on the wedding party. Edwin too was perspiring heavily, though the room was cool and breezy. A pew near the back of the room continued to creak and groan and Edwin knew it was only a matter of time before shit hit the fan.

Cameron shifted uncontrollably in his seat. Ashley glared at him and pressed her hand firmly on his leg to steal his attention.

"Don't wreck this for her," she warned, scowling at him.

At that very moment, the priest announced the unnerving words that every young couple dreaded after watching one too many chick flicks. "If anyone has an objection as to why these two shalt not be joined in this holy union, then speak now or forever hold your peace."

An unnerving silence washed over the crowd for that breath-holding moment, as Ashley clutched onto her brothers leg with a crushing grip of death. Then the moment passed, the vows were shared, and Abigail was pronounced Edwin's wife.

The priest stood at the head of the couple, his small eyes widening behind his small reading glasses, when the couple's ceremonial lip lock continued a little longer and a little more heated than he preferred.

The company cheered and rose out of respect, focusing on the bride and groom, as the happy couple hustled down the aisle and out of the church.

Ashley squeezed her brother's leg, remaining seated with him. "You did the right thing."

He slumped in his seat, knowing that he had. She had chosen Edwin. He had always known they would find a way to be together in the end.

Jenny's eyes sparkled red as she gazed over the canopy waiting for the news. But the news never came. Abigail was supposed to terminate the deal. She was supposed to tell Edwin it wasn't going to work. Cameron was supposed to put an end to this madness. But no one stepped up to the plate.

"No!" Jenny cried out, as the jovial couple made their exit.

Unfortunately, for Jenny, it was too late. She had her chance, and that chance had been blown. Abigail won. With that knowledge, Jenny's eyes slowly stewed until they turned a soft green, much like her sisters. Then her skin tingled and grew warmer, until she vanished in a cloud of misty, black smoke.

A couple of the choir members had heard the beautiful woman in the balcony, who looked strikingly similar to the bride, and were looking around to see where she had gone. They both looked at each other recognizing that the woman had just disappeared. Poof. Gone.

And that was the last Edwin and Abigail Santora would ever see of Jenny Jenkins.

EPILOGUE

Two years later.

After a long day at work, I peeled off my shoes and hobbled through the house. "Honey, I'm home!" I shouted. *Where was everyone?*

I figured Maya must have been asleep but, as I approached the couch, I heard lots of sweet, girly giggles. *Maya was definitely not sleeping.*

"Where's your dad?" I asked her, wondering why he would leave a toddler unattended. Then I peered over the sofa. There was Maya, sitting on her father's perfectly firm abs and pointing at his sleeping face, wearing the biggest and happiest of smiles.

I gasped and covered my mouth, unable to hide my smirk. "Oh, Maya. What did you do?"

Edwin began to stir when he heard his baby girl's fresh round of giggles.

"Edwin, honey," I said, in an attempt to wake him. "Long day?"

His dark lashes fluttered open, confusion marring his handsome features. "I must have fallen asleep." His lips were covered in a beautiful coat of red lipstick and his eyelids were stained a dark shade of blue.

"You think?" I said, snickering now.

"Hey. What are you girls laughing at?" he asked, tickling his baby doll's belly.

I scooped her into my arms and kissed her cheek repeatedly. I had only been gone for a few hours, but I had missed her so very much. Her pudgy cheeks were so soft and edible. "Maybe we should go get your father a mirror to show him how beautiful he looks," I said to Maya, smirking with her.

Edwin combed his fingers through his hair, his hand getting caught on a handful of clips that Maya had not-so-carefully arranged there. "Girls!" he growled, as if somehow I was involved in his beautification. "Uh, oh," he said.

"What?" I asked, crouching down to put my squirming toddler on the floor.

He started to growl and Maya squealed. "You're in trouble now." Edwin let her have a head start and then chased after her. He lifted her into his arms, growling like a beast, and then kissed her repeatedly, until the lipstick was smeared all over her face.

Edwin lowered a giggling Maya to the floor and she came running right to me. Edwin followed her and casually laced his fingers in mine. "That'll teach me to fall asleep on the job," he admitted, with a generous smile.

Maya cupped her tiny hand on her father's face. "Uh oh," she said, her adorable lips puckered into a beautiful o shape, as she stared at the red stains that had spread across his mouth.

Edwin kissed his beautiful baby on the cheek and then shared a gentle kiss with me, all while rubbing his hand over my full, rounded tummy. "*You* have made me the happiest man alive," he said, his eyes warm and dreamy.

Hiking our little bundle of sweetness higher on my hip, I drew his attention to Maya. "I think I may have had some help."

A smile tugged at Edwin's lips, as they closed over mine again. Then he withdrew from our kiss to share his promise with me and our growing family. "I will love you and my girls for the rest of my days."

THE END.

SUPPORT THIS AUTHOR!
LEAVE A REVIEW!

www.goodreads.com/christasimpson
http://amazon.com/author/christasimpson

ABOUT THE AUTHOR

Christa Simpson is a Romance Author who enjoys entertaining her readers with sexy alpha males and sassy heroines. She writes sexy new adult and steamy adult romances loaded with passion, suspense and sarcasm. In her "free time", she loves reading, writing, music, movies and dancing. She likes her men muscled, her music loud and her kids happy.

She's a small town girl, living in Southwestern Ontario with her husband and two beautiful daughters. She's a legal assistant by day, wielding a sexy imagination by night. She's a dreamer and has always believed that you can do anything you set your mind to.

Please visit her website:
http://christasimpson.com

Author of...
THE TWISTED TRILOGY
Book 1: Twisted
Book 2: Twist & Turn
Book 3: A Twist of Fate
Book 4: Twisted Desire

THE DESTINY SERIES
Book 1: Finding Destiny

www.twitter.com/_christasimpson
www.pinterest.com/christamsimpson
http://plus.google.com/+christasimpson
www.facebook.com/authorchristasimpson

TWISTED DESIRE

Find the girl. Trick the girl. Collect the reward.
His plan was foolproof.

Strong, seductive and sexy as hell. Harley Gates is all those things. He's a renowned PI who rides above the law, because he's worth more to the cops on the front line than in a jail cell. When a new client puts him on the task of tracking down her boyfriend's so-called mistress, the size of the pay check says he's going to do it. The plan is foolproof. Find the girl. Trick the girl. Collect the reward.

Miss Aliah Brooklin is no fool. She's as feisty as they come, provoking him with every lick of her lips. But Aliah isn't ready to turn in her glass slippers just yet. Being once burned, twice shy, she's careful to guard her heart. No man means no problems. She knows this. But this motorcycle man who calls himself Harley has her swooning like a fairy tale princess. She knows something's not quite right with him, but their chemistry alone has her surrendering to his wiles.

Is Aliah doomed to a life without love? That's what she keeps telling herself. But tattooed sexy sure throws a kink in her plans. When the investigation flips to a new mystery, a vicious twist will change everything.

BLACK WIDOW
Publishing

AVAILABLE NOW!

http://christasimpson.com